ABOUT THE AUTHOR

STEVE BERRY is the *New York Times* bestselling author of *The Paris Vendetta, The Charlemagne Pursuit, The Venetian Betrayal, The Alexandria Link, The Templar Legacy, The Third Secret, The Romanov Prophecy, The Amber Room,* and the short story "The Balkan Escape." His books have been translated into thirty-seven languages and sold in fifty countries. He lives in the historic city of St. Augustine, Florida, and is at work on his next novel. He and his wife, Elizabeth, have founded History Matters, a nonprofit organization dedicated to preserving our heritage. To learn more about Steve Berry and the foundation, visit www.steveberry.org.

THE EMPEROR'S TOMB

STEVE BERRY

The Emperor's Tomb

HODDER &
STOUGHTON

First published in Great Britain in 2011 by Hodder & Stoughton
An Hachette UK company

2

Copyright © Steve Berry 2010
Map copyright © David Lindroth, Inc. 2010

Published by arrangement with Ballantine Books, an imprint of
Random House Publishing Group, a division of Random House, Inc.

A CIP catalogue record for this title is available from the British Library.

Hardback ISBN 978 1 444 70935 3
Trade Paperback ISBN 978 1 444 70936 0

Printed and bound by Griffin Press

Hodder & Stoughton policy is to use papers that are natural, renewable
and recyclable products and made from wood grown in sustainable forests.
The logging and manufacturing processes are expected to conform
to the environmental regulations of the country of origin.

Hodder & Stoughton Ltd
338 Euston Road
London NW1 3BH

www.hodder.co.uk

For Fran Downing, Frank Green, Lenore Hart,
David Poyer, Nancy Pridgen,
Clyde Rogers, and Daiva Woodworth

Teachers extraordinaire

ACKNOWLEDGMENTS

To the folks at Random House: Gina Centrello, Libby McGuire, Cindy Murray, Kim Hovey, Katie O'Callaghan, Beck Stvan, Carole Lowenstein, Rachel Kind, and all those in promotions and sales. Once again, thanks.

To Mark Tavani, thanks for being a persistent editor.

To Pam Ahearn I offer a ninth bow of gratitude and my continued appreciation.

To Simon Lipskar, I deeply appreciate your wisdom and guidance.

A few special mentions: Charlie Smith, who performed some much-appreciated reconnoitering in China; Grant Blackwood, a superb thriller writer who saved me from falling in Denver; Els Wouters, who provided, on short notice, vital on-site research in Antwerp; Esther Levine for opening doors at the terra-cotta warrior exhibit; Bob and Jane Stine, who stimulated my imagination over lunch and connected me with "Julia" Xiaohui Zhu; James Rollins for once again helping save the day; Michele and Joe Finder, who offered some sage advice; Meryl Moss and her wonderful staff; Melisse Shapiro, who is more helpful than she could ever realize; and Esther Garver and Jessica Johns who keep History Matters and Steve Berry Enterprises running.

I also want to say thank you to every one of my readers around the world. I appreciate your loyal support, insightful comments, infectious enthusiasm, and, yes, even your criticisms. You are what keeps me writing every day.

And there's Elizabeth—critic, cheerleader, editor, wife, muse. The whole package.

Finally, this book is dedicated to Fran Downing, Frank Green, Lenore Hart, David Poyer, Nancy Pridgen, Clyde Rogers, and Daiva Woodworth. Together, they showed me how to teach myself to be a writer.

Whether I succeeded is still a matter of debate.

One thing, though, is clear.

Without their influence, nothing ever would have been printed.

Study the past if you would define the future.

—CONFUCIUS

History is a maiden, and you can dress her however you wish.

—CHINESE PROVERB

All countries large and small suffer one defect in common:
the surrounding of the ruler with unworthy personnel.
Those who would control rulers, first discover their secret fears
    and wishes.

—HAN FEI TZU, *3rd century* BCE

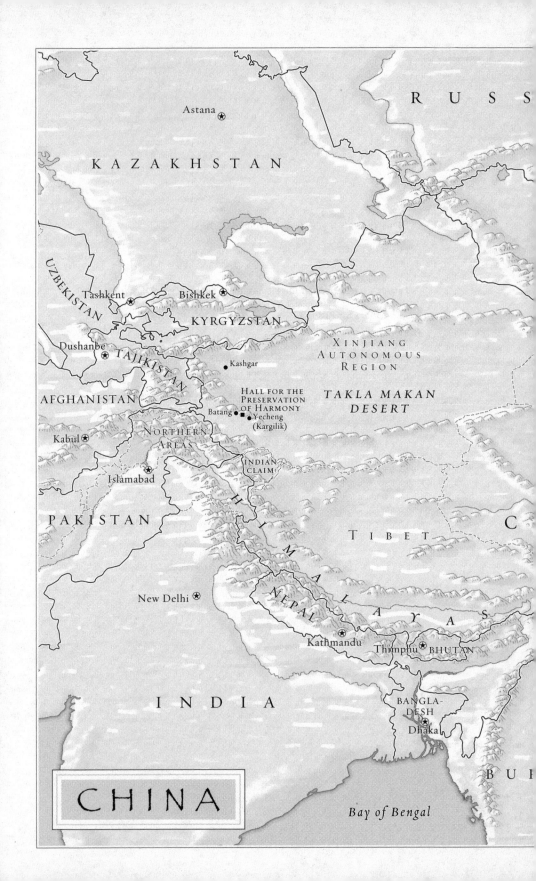

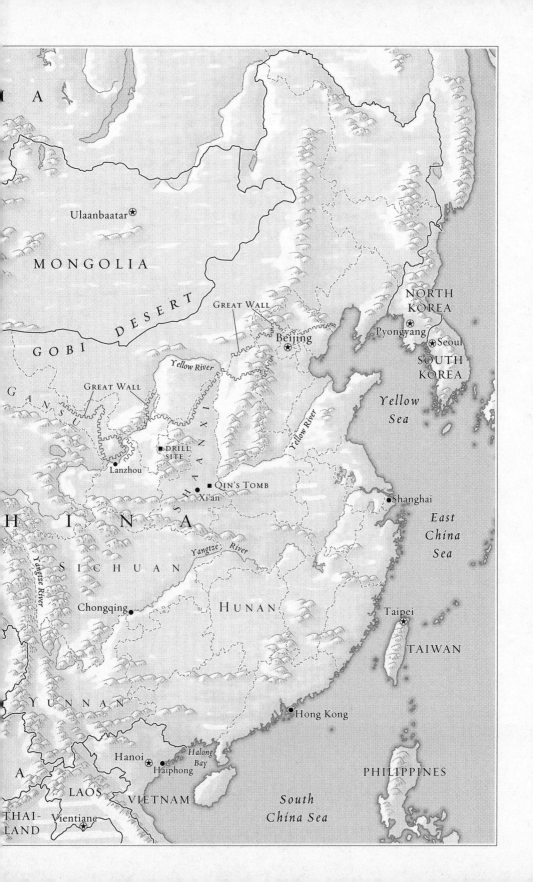

TIMELINE OF RELEVANT
EVENTS OF CHINESE HISTORY

1765–1027 BCE	Shang Dynasty (earliest known)
770–481 BCE	Spring and Autumn Period
551–479 BCE	Confucius lives
535 BCE	Origin of the eunuch system
481–221 BCE	Warring States Period and emergence of Legalism
200 BCE	Chinese first drill for oil
221 BCE	Qin Shi unifies the warring states into China and becomes First Emperor
210 BCE	Qin Shi dies; terra-cotta army is completed and interred with First Emperor in Imperial tomb mound
146 BCE–67 CE	Eunuch system expands into a political force
89 BCE	Sima Qian completes *Records of the Historian (Shiji)*
202 CE–1912 CE	Dynastic rule of China flourishes
1912 CE	Last emperor is forced from throne; dynastic rule ends; eunuch system is abolished; Republic of China is formed
1949 CE	Communist Revolution; People's Republic of China is formed
1974 CE	Terra-cotta army is rediscovered
1976 CE	Mao Zedong dies

THE EMPEROR'S TOMB

PROLOGUE

A BULLET ZIPPED PAST COTTON MALONE. HE DOVE TO THE rocky ground and sought what cover the sparse poplars offered. Cassiopeia Vitt did the same and they belly-crawled across sharp gravel, finding a boulder large enough to provide the two of them protection.

More shots came their way.

"This is getting serious," Cassiopeia said.

"You think?"

Their trek had, so far, been uneventful. The greatest congregation of towering peaks on the planet surrounded them. The roof of the world, two thousand miles from Beijing, in the extreme southwestern corner of China's Xinjiang Autonomous Region—or the Northern Areas of Pakistan, depending on whom you asked—smack up against a hotly disputed border.

Which explained the soldiers.

"They're not Chinese," she said. "I caught a glimpse. Definitely Pakistanis."

Jagged, snowy summits as high as twenty thousand feet shielded glaciers, patches of green-black forest, and lush valleys. The Himalaya, Karakoum, Hindu Kush, and Pamir ranges all merged here. This was the land of black wolves and blue poppies, ibex and snow leopards.

Where fairies congregated, Malone recalled one ancient observer noting. Possibly even the inspiration behind James Hilton's *Shangri-la.* A paradise for trekkers, climbers, rafters, and skiers. Unfortunately, India and Pakistan both claimed sovereignty, China retained possession, and all three governments had fought over the desolate region for decades.

"They seem to know where we're headed," she said.

"That thought occurred to me, too." So he had to add, "I told you he was trouble."

They were dressed in leather jackets, jeans, and boots. Though they were more than eight thousand feet above sea level, the air was surprisingly mild. Maybe sixty degrees, he estimated. Luckily, both of them carried Chinese semi-automatic weapons and a few spare magazines.

"We have to go that way." He pointed behind them. "And those soldiers are close enough to do some damage."

He searched his eidetic brain for what they needed. Yesterday, he'd studied the local geography and noted that this slice of earth, which wasn't much larger than New Jersey, was once called Hunza, a princely state for over nine hundred years, whose independence finally evaporated in the 1970s. The fair-skinned and light-eyed locals claimed to be descendants of soldiers in Alexander the Great's army, from when Greeks invaded two millennia ago. Who knew? The land had remained isolated for centuries, until the 1980s, when the Karakoram Highway passed through and connected China to Pakistan.

"We have to trust that he'll handle it," she finally said.

"That was your call, not mine. You go first. I'll cover."

He gripped the Chinese double-action pistol. Not a bad weapon. Fifteen rounds, fairly accurate. Cassiopeia prepared herself, too. He liked that about her—ready for any situation. They made a good team, and this striking Spanish Arab definitely intrigued him.

She scampered off toward a stand of junipers.

He aimed the pistol across the boulder and readied himself to react at the slightest movement. To his right, in the tomb-like illumination that filtered through the spring foliage, he caught the glimmer of a rifle barrel being aimed around a tree trunk.

He fired.

The barrel disappeared.

He decided to use the moment and followed Cassiopeia, keeping the boulder between himself and their pursuers.

He reached her and they both raced forward, using more trees as cover.

Sharp bursts of rifle fire echoed. Bullets pinged around them.

The trail twisted out of the trees and rose in a steep but climbable slope, held to a rocky bluff by retaining walls of loose boulders. Not much cover here, but they had no choice. Beyond the trail, he spied canyons so deep and sheer that light could enter only at high noon. A gorge dropped away to their right, and they ran along its edge. Bright sun blazed on the far side, dulled by black mountain slate. A hundred feet below water rushed and tumbled, gray with sand, tossing foamy spray high into the air.

They clambered up the steep embankment.

He spotted the bridge.

Exactly where they'd been told.

Not much of a span, just shaky poles wedged upright between boulders on each end, horizontal timbers fastened on top, connected by thick hemp. A footwalk of boards dangled over the river.

Cassiopeia reached the top of the trail. "We have to cross."

He didn't like that prospect, but she was right. Their destination was on the far side.

Gunfire echoed in the distance and he glanced behind them.

No soldiers.

Which bothered him.

"Maybe he's leading them away," she said.

His distrust made him defensive, but there was no time to analyze the situation. He stuffed the gun into his pocket. Cassiopeia did the same, then stepped onto the bridge.

He followed.

The boards vibrated from the rush of water below. He estimated less than a hundred feet to the other side, but they'd be suspended in open air with zero cover, moving from shadows to sunlight. Another trail could be seen on the far side, leading across loose gravel into more trees. He spotted a figure, maybe fifteen feet high, carved in the rock face beyond the trail—a Buddhist image, just as they'd been told.

Cassiopeia turned back toward him, Eastern eyes peering from her Western face. "This bridge has seen better days."

"I hope it has at least one more left."

She gripped the twisted ropes that held the span aloft.

He tightened his fingers around the coarse strands, too, then decided, "I'll go first."

"And the reason for that?"

"I'm heavier. If they hold me, they'll hold you."

"Since I can't argue with that logic"—she stepped aside—"be my guest."

He assumed the lead, his feet attuned to the steady vibrations.

No sign of any pursuers.

He decided a brisk pace would be better, not giving the boards time to react. Cassiopeia followed.

A new sound rose over the rushing water.

Deep bass tones. Far off, but growing louder.

Thump. Thump. Thump.

He whipped his head to the right and caught the first glimpse of a shadow on a rock wall, maybe a mile away, where the gorge they were negotiating met another running perpendicular.

At the halfway point it seemed the bridge was holding, though the moldy boards gave like a sponge. His palms loosely gripped the rough hemp, ready to apply a death lock if the bottom fell out beneath him.

The distant shadow grew in size, then was replaced with the distinct shape of an AH-1 Cobra attack helicopter.

American-made, but this was no salvation.

Pakistan operated them, too, provided by Washington to help a supposed ally with the war on terrorism.

The Cobra powered straight toward them. Twin-bladed, dual-engined, it carried 20mm guns, anti-tank missiles, and aerial rockets. Fast as a bumblebee, and equally maneuverable.

"That's not here to help," he heard Cassiopeia say.

He agreed, but there was no need to voice that he'd been right all along. They'd been herded to this spot, for this precise purpose.

Damn that son of a bitch—

The Cobra started firing.

A steady procession of pops sent 20mm rounds their way.

He dove belly-first to the bridge boards and rolled, staring past his feet as Cassiopeia did the same. The Cobra roared toward them, its turboshafts sucking through the dry, limpid air. Rounds found the bridge, ripping wood and rope with a savage fury.

Another burst arrived.

Concentrated on the ten feet between him and Cassiopeia.

He spied fury in her eyes and watched as she found her gun, came to her knees and fired at the copter's canopy. But he knew that armor plating and an aircraft moving at more than 170 miles an hour reduced the chances of causing damage to zero.

"Get the hell down," he yelled.

Another burst of cannon fire annihilated the bridge between him and Cassiopeia. One moment the wood-and-rope construction existed, the next it was gone in a cloud of debris.

He sprang to his feet and realized the entire span was about to collapse. He could not go back, so he ran ahead, the final twenty feet, clinging to the ropes as the bridge dropped away.

The Cobra flew past, toward the opposite end of the gorge.

He held tight to the ropes and, as the bridge divided, each half swinging back toward opposite sides of the gorge, he flew through the air.

He slammed into rock, rebounded, then settled.

He did not give himself time to be terrified. Slowly, he pulled himself upward, scaling the remaining few feet to the top. Rushing water and the thump of chopper blades filled his ears. He focused across the gorge, searching for Cassiopeia, hoping she'd managed to make it up to the other side.

His heart sank when he saw her clinging with both hands to the other half of the bridge as it dangled against the sheer cliff face. He wanted to help her, but there was nothing he could do. She was a hundred feet away. Only air between them.

The Cobra executed a tight turn within the gorge, arching upward, then began another run their way.

"Can you climb?" he screamed over the noise.

Her head shook.

"Do it," he yelled.

She craned her neck his way. "Get out of here."

"Not without you."

The Cobra was less than a mile away. Its cannon would start firing any second.

"Climb," he screamed.

One hand reached up.

Then she fell fifty feet into the rushing river.

How deep it flowed he did not know, but the boulders that protruded along its path did not offer him any solace.

She disappeared into the churning water, which had to be nearly freezing, considering its source was mountain snow.

He waited for her to surface. Somewhere.

But she never did.

He stared down at the roaring gray gush, which carried silt and rock along with a swish of foam in a formidable current. He wanted to leap after her, but realized that was impossible. He wouldn't survive the fall, either.

He stood and watched, disbelieving.

After all they'd been through the past three days.

Cassiopeia Vitt was gone.

PART ONE

Three Days Earlier

ONE

COTTON MALONE TYPED THE WEB ADDRESS WITH TREMBLING fingers. Like a phone that rings in the middle of the night, nothing about an anonymous message was ever good.

The note had arrived two hours ago, while he'd been out of his bookshop on an errand, but the employee who'd accepted the unmarked envelope forgot to give it to him until a few minutes ago.

"The woman didn't say it was urgent," she said in her defense.

"What woman?"

"Chinese lady, dressed in a gorgeous Burberry skirt. She said to give it only to you."

"She used my name?"

"Twice."

Inside had been a folded sheet of gray vellum upon which was printed a Web address with a dot-org suffix. He'd immediately climbed the four flights of stairs to his apartment above the bookshop and found his laptop.

He finished typing and waited while the screen blackened, then a new image appeared. A video display console indicated that a live feed was about to engage.

The communications link established.

A body appeared, lying on its back, arms above the head, ankles and wrists bound tight to what looked like a sheet of plywood. The person was angled so that the head was slightly beneath the feet. A towel wrapped the face, but it was clear the bound form was a woman.

"Mr. Malone." The voice was electronically altered, disguising every attribute of pitch and tone. "We've been waiting. Not in much of a hurry, are you? I have something for you to see."

A hooded figure appeared on the screen, holding a plastic bucket. He watched as water was poured onto the towel that wrapped the bound woman's face. Her body writhed as she struggled with her restraints.

He knew what was happening.

The liquid penetrated the towel and flowed unrestricted into her mouth and nose. At first a few gulps of air could be stolen—the throat constricted, inhaling little of the water—but that could be maintained only for a few seconds. Then the body's natural gag reflex would kick in and all control would be lost. The head was angled downward so gravity could prolong the agony. It was like drowning without ever being submerged.

The man stopped pouring.

The woman continued to struggle with her restraints.

The technique dated back to the Inquisition. Highly favored since it left no marks, its main drawback was harshness—so intense that the victim would immediately admit to anything. Malone had actually experienced it once, years ago, while training to become a Magellan Billet agent. All recruits had to take their turn as part of survival school. His agony had been amplified by his dislike of confinement. The bondage, combined with the soaked towel, had created an unbearable claustrophobia. He recalled the public debate a few years ago as to whether waterboarding was torture.

Damn right it was.

"Here's the purpose of my contact," the voice said.

The camera zoomed tight on the towel wrapping the woman's face. A hand entered the frame and wrenched the soaked cloth away, revealing Cassiopeia Vitt.

"Oh, no," Malone muttered.

Darts of fear pierced his skin. A light-headedness overtook him.

This can't be happening.

No.

She blinked water from her eyes, spit more from her mouth, and gained her breath. "Don't give them a damn thing, Cotton. Nothing."

The soaked towel was slapped back across her face.

"That would not be smart," the computerized voice said. "Certainly not for her."

"Can you hear me?" he said into the laptop's microphone.

"Of course."

"Is this necessary?"

"For you? I believe so. You're a man to be respected. Former Justice Department agent. Highly trained."

"I'm a bookseller."

The voice chuckled. "Don't insult my intelligence, or risk her life any further. I want you to clearly understand what's at stake."

"And you need to understand that I can kill you."

"By then, Ms. Vitt will be dead. So let's stop with the bravado. I want what she gave you."

He saw Cassiopeia renew her struggle against the restraints, her head whipping from side to side beneath the towel.

"Give him nothing, Cotton. I mean it. I gave that to you for safe-keeping. Don't give it up."

More water was poured. Her protests stopped as she fought to breathe.

"Bring the item to Tivoli Gardens, at two PM, just outside the Chinese pagoda. You'll be contacted. If you don't show—" The voice paused. "—I think you can imagine the consequences."

The connection was severed.

He sat back in the chair.

He hadn't seen Cassiopeia in more than a month. Hadn't spoken to her for two weeks. She'd said that she was headed out on a trip but, characteristically, offered no details. Their *relationship* was hardly one at all. Just an attraction that they both tacitly acknowledged. Strangely, Henrik Thorvaldsen's death had drawn them closer, and they'd spent a lot of time together in the weeks after their friend's funeral.

She was tough, smart, and gutsy.

But waterboarding?

He doubted if she'd ever experienced anything like that.

Seeing her on the screen tore at his gut. He suddenly realized that if anything happened to this woman his life would never be the same.

He had to find her.

But there was a problem.

She'd obviously been forced to do whatever was necessary in order to survive. This time, however, she may have bitten off more than she could ever chew.

She'd left nothing with him for safekeeping.

He had no clue what she, or her captor, was talking about.

TWO

KARL TANG ASSUMED AN EXPRESSION THAT CONVEYED NOT the slightest hint of what he was thinking. After nearly three decades of practice, he'd mastered the art.

"And why have you come this time?" the doctor asked him. She was an iron-faced, stiff-bodied woman with straight black hair, cut short in a proletarian style.

"Your anger toward me has not waned?"

"I have no hostility, Minister. You made it quite clear during your last visit that you are in charge, regardless of the fact that this is my facility."

He ignored her insulting tone. "And how is our patient?"

The First Infectious Disease Hospital, located just outside Chongqing, cared for nearly two thousand people afflicted with either tuberculosis or hepatitis. It was one of eight facilities scattered throughout the country, each a forbidding complex of gray brick surrounded by green fences, places where the contagious could be safely quarantined. But the security these hospitals enjoyed also made them ideal for the housing of any sick prisoners from the Chinese penal system.

Like Jin Zhao, who'd suffered a brain hemorrhage ten months ago.

"He's lying in his bed, as he's done since the first day he was brought here," the doctor said. "He clings to life. The damage is enormous. But—again, per your order—no treatment has been administered."

He knew she hated his usurpation of her authority. Gone were Mao's obedient "barefoot doctors," who, according to the official myth, had willingly lived among the masses and dutifully cared for the sick. And though she was the hospital's chief administrator, Tang was the national minister of science and technology, a member of the Central Committee, first vice premier of the Chinese Communist Party, and first vice president of the People's Republic of China—second in power only to the president and premier himself.

"As I made clear last time, Doctor," he said, "that was not my order, but the directive of the Central Committee, to which I, and you, owe absolute allegiance."

He voiced the words for the benefit of not only the foolish woman but also the three members of his staff and two captains from the People's Liberation Army who stood behind him. Each military man wore a crisp green uniform with the red star of the motherland emblazoned on his cap. One of them was surely an informant—reporting most likely to more than one benefactor—so he wanted any account to speak glowingly of him.

"Take us to the patient," he calmly commanded.

They walked down halls lined with lettuce-green plaster, cracked and lumpy, lighted by weak fluorescent fixtures. The floor was clean but yellowed from endless moppings. Nurses, their faces hidden by surgical masks, tended to patients clad in striped blue-and-white pajamas, some wearing brown robes, looking much like prisoners.

They entered another ward through a set of swinging metal doors. The room beyond was spacious, enough for a dozen or more patients, yet only one lay in a single bed beneath dingy white sheets.

The air stank.

"I see you left the linen alone," he said.

"You did order me to do so."

Another mark in his favor for the informant to report. Jin Zhao had been arrested ten months ago, but had suffered a hemorrhage during questioning. He was subsequently charged with treason and espionage, tried in a Beijing court, and convicted, all in absentia since he'd remained here, in a coma.

"He is just as you left him," the doctor said.

Beijing lay nearly a thousand kilometers to the east and he supposed that distance bolstered this woman's nerve. *You may rob the Three Armies of their commander in chief, but you cannot deprive the humblest peasant of his opinion.* More of Confucius' nonsense. Actually the government could, and this insolent bitch should heed that fact.

He motioned and one of the uniforms led her across the room.

He approached the bed.

The man lying prostrate was in his mid-sixties, his dirty hair long and unkempt, his emaciated frame and sunken cheeks reminiscent of those of a corpse. Bruises splotched his face and chest, while intravenous lines snaked from both arms. A ventilator fed air in and out of his lungs.

"Jin Zhao, you have been found guilty of treason against the People's Republic of China. You were afforded a trial, from which you lodged an appeal. I regret to inform you that the Supreme People's Court has approved your execution and denied your appeal."

"He can't hear a word you're saying," the doctor said from across the room.

He kept his eyes down on the bed. "Perhaps not, but the words must be spoken." He turned and faced her. "It is the law, and he is entitled to proper process."

"You tried him without him even being there," she blurted out. "You never heard a word he had to say."

"His representative was afforded the opportunity to present evidence."

The doctor shook her head in disgust, her face pale with hate. "Do you hear yourself? The representative never had the opportunity to even speak with Zhao. What evidence could possibly have been presented?"

He couldn't decide if the informant's eyes and ears belonged to one of his staff or one of the army captains. Hard to know anything for sure anymore. All he knew was that his report to the Central Committee would not be the only retelling, so he decided to make clear, "Are you sure? Not once has Zhao communicated anything?"

"He was beaten senseless. His brain is destroyed. He will never awaken from the coma. We keep him alive simply because you—no, excuse me, the Central Committee—ordered it."

He caught the disgust in the woman's eyes, something else he'd seen more and more of lately. Especially from women. Nearly the entire hospital staff—doctors and nurses—were women. They'd made great strides since Mao's Revolution, yet Tang still adhered to the adage his father had taught him. *A man does not talk about affairs inside the home, and a woman does not talk about affairs outside.*

This insignificant doctor, employed at a minor state-run hospital, was incapable of understanding the enormity of his challenge. Beijing ruled a land that stretched five thousand kilometers east to west and more than three thousand north to south. Much was uninhabitable mountains and desert, some of the most desolate regions in the world, only 10% of the country arable. Nearly one and a half billion people—more than America, Russia, and Europe combined. But only 60,000,000 were members of the Chinese Communist Party—less than 3% of the total. The doctor was a Party member, and had been for more than a decade. He'd checked. No way she could have risen to such a high managerial position otherwise. Only Party-membered, Han Chinese achieved such status. Hans were a huge majority of the population, the remaining small percentage spread across fifty-six minorities. The doctor's father was a prominent official in the local provincial government, a loyal Party member who'd participated in the 1949 Revolution and personally known both Mao and Deng Xiaoping.

Still, Tang needed to make clear, "Jin Zhao owed his loyalty to the People's government. He decided to aid our enemies—"

"What could a sixty-three-year-old geochemist have done to harm the People's government? Tell me, Minister. I want to know. What could he possibly do to us now?"

He checked his watch. A helicopter was waiting to fly him north.

"He was no spy," she said. "No traitor. What did he really do, Minister? What justifies beating a man until his brain bleeds?"

He had not the time to debate what had already been decided. The informant would seal this woman's fate. In a month she'd receive a transfer—despite her father's privileges—most likely sent thousands of kilometers west to the outer reaches, where problems were hidden away.

He turned toward the other uniform and motioned.

The captain removed his holstered sidearm, approached the bed, and fired one shot through Jin Zhao's forehead.

The body lurched, then went still.

The respirator continued to force air into dead lungs.

"Sentence has been carried out," Tang declared. "Duly witnessed by representatives of the People's government, the military . . . and this facility's chief administrator."

He indicated that it was time to leave. The mess would be the doctor's to clean up.

He walked toward the doors.

"You just shot a helpless man," the doctor screamed. "Is this what our government has become?"

"You should be grateful," he said.

"For what?"

"That the government does not debit this facility's operating budget for the cost of the bullet."

And he left.

THREE

MALONE LEFT HIS BOOKSHOP AND STEPPED OUT INTO HØJBRO Plads. The afternoon sky was cloudless, the Danish air comfortable. The Strøget—a chain of traffic-free streets, most lined with shops, cafés, restaurants, and museums—surged with commerce.

He'd solved the problem of what to bring by simply grabbing the first book off one of the shelves and stuffing it into an envelope. Cassiopeia had apparently opted to buy herself time by involving him. Not a bad play, except the ruse could only be stretched so far. He wished he knew what she was doing. Since last Christmas, between them, there'd been visits, a few meals here and there, phone calls, and e-mails. Most dealing with Thorvaldsen's death, which seemed to have hurt them both. He still couldn't believe his best friend was gone. Every day he expected the cagey old Dane to walk into the bookstore, ready for some lively conversation. He still harbored a deep regret that his friend had died thinking he'd been betrayed.

"You did what you had to in Paris," Cassiopeia told him. "I would have done the same."

"Henrik didn't see it that way."

"He wasn't perfect, Cotton. He sent himself into a spiral. He wasn't thinking and wouldn't listen. There was more at stake there than just his revenge. You had no choice."

"I let him down."

She reached across the table and squeezed his hand. "Tell you what. If I'm ever in big trouble, let me down the same way."

He kept walking, hearing her words in his head.

Now it was happening again.

He left the Strøget and crossed a boulevard clogged with the gleaming metal of cars, buses, and bicycles. He hustled through the Rådhuspladsen, another of Copenhagen's many public squares, this one stretching out before the city's town hall. He spotted the bronze trumpeters atop, soundlessly blowing their ancient *lurs*. Above them stood the copper statue of Bishop Absalon who, in 1167, expanded a tiny fishing village into a walled fortress.

On the plaza's far side, beyond another traffic-choked boulevard, he spotted Tivoli.

He gripped the envelope in one hand, his Magellan Billet–issued Beretta tucked beneath a jacket. He'd retrieved the weapon from under his bed, where it stayed inside a knapsack with other reminders of his former life.

"I think you're a little nervous," Cassiopeia said to him.

They stood outside his bookshop in chilly March weather. She was right. He was nervous. "I'm not much of a romantic."

"Really? I wouldn't have known. Lucky for you, I am."

She looked great. Tall, lean, skin the color of pale mahogany. Thick auburn hair brushed her shoulders, framing a striking face highlighted by thin brows and firm cheeks.

"Don't beat yourself up, Cotton."

Interesting that she'd known he was actually thinking about Thorvaldsen.

"You're a good man. Henrik knew that."

"I was two minutes too late."

"And there's not a damn thing you can do about it."

She was right.

But he still could not shake the feeling.

He'd seen Cassiopeia both at her best and when circumstances had stripped her of all confidence—when she was vulnerable, prone to mistakes, emotional. Luckily, he'd been there to compensate, as she'd been for him when the roles reversed. She was an amazing blend of femininity and strength, but everyone, even she, occasionally stepped too far.

A vision of Cassiopeia tied to plywood, a towel over her face, flashed through his mind.

Why her?

Why not him?

KARL TANG STEPPED ONTO THE HELICOPTER AND SETTLED HIM-self in the rear compartment. His business in Chongqing was at an end.

He hated the place.

Thirty million people consumed every square meter of the hills surrounding the confluence of the Jialing and Yangtze rivers. Under Mongol, Han, and Manchu rule it had been the empire's center. A hundred years ago it became a wartime capital during the Japanese invasion. Now it was a mix of old and new—mosques, Daoist temples, Christian churches, communist landmarks—a hot, humid, wretched place where skyscrapers broke the horizon.

The chopper rose into a carbon-laced fog and vectored toward the northwest.

He'd dismissed his aides and the captains.

No spies would come on this part of the journey.

This he must do himself.

MALONE PAID HIS ADMISSION AND ENTERED TIVOLI. PART amusement park, part cultural icon, the treed and flowered wonder-land had entertained Danes since 1843. A national treasure, where old-style Ferris wheels, pantomime theaters, and a pirate ship blended with more modern gravity-defying rides. Even the Germans had spared it during World War II. Malone liked visiting—easy to see how it inspired both Walt Disney and Hans Christian Andersen.

He fled the main entrance and followed a flora-bordered central avenue. Bulb gardens, roses, lilacs, as well as hundreds of lime, chestnut, cherry, and evergreen trees grew in an ingenious plan that, to him, always seemed bigger than a mere twenty-one acres. Scents of popcorn and cotton candy wafted in the air, along with the sounds of a Vienna waltz and big-band tunes. He knew that Tivoli's creator had justified the excess by advising Denmark's Christian VIII that *when the people are amusing themselves, they do not think about politics.*

He was familiar with the Chinese pagoda. Within a leafy bower it stood four stories tall and faced a lake. More than a hundred years old, its Asiatic image adorned nearly every brochure that advertised Tivoli.

A cadre of young boys, smartly dressed in red jackets, bandoliers, and bushy bearskin hats marched down an adjacent lane. The Garden Guard, Tivoli's marching band. People lined the route and watched the parade. All of the attractions were unusually crowded, given it was a Tuesday in May, the summer season beginning only last week.

He caught sight of the pagoda, three vertical repetitions of its base in diminishing proportions, each story with a projecting roofline and upturned eaves. People streamed in and out of the pagoda's ground-floor restaurant. More revelers occupied benches beneath the trees.

Just before 2 PM.

He was on time.

Wandering ducks from the lake mingled with the crowd, showing little fear. He could not say the same about himself. His nerves were alert, his mind thinking like the Justice Department agent he'd been for twelve risky years. The idea had been to retire early and flee the danger, becoming a Danish bookseller, but the past two years had been anything but quiet.

Think. Pay attention.

The computerized voice had said that once he was here he'd be contacted. Apparently, Cassiopeia's captors knew exactly what he looked like.

"Mr. Malone."

He turned.

A woman, her thin face more long than round, stood beside him. Her black hair hung straight, and long-lashed brown eyes added a mysterious quality. Truth be known, he had a weakness for Oriental beauty. She was smartly dressed in clothes cut to flatter her contours, which included a Burberry skirt wrapping her tiny waist.

"I came for the package," she said.

He motioned with the envelope he held. "This?"

She nodded.

She was in her late twenties, casual in her movements, seemingly unconcerned about the situation. His suspicions were rapidly being confirmed.

"Care to stay and have a late lunch?" he asked.

She smiled. "Another time."

"Sounds promising. How would I find you?"

"I know where your bookshop is."

He grinned. "How stupid of me."

She pointed at the envelope. "I need to be leaving."

He handed her the package.

"Maybe I'll drop by your shop again," she said, adding a smile.

"You do that."

He watched as she sauntered off, merging with the crowd, walking leisurely, not a care in the world.

TANG CLOSED HIS EYES AND ALLOWED THE DRONE OF THE HELI-copter's turbine to calm his nerves.

He checked his watch.

9:05 PM here meant 2:05 PM in Antwerp.

So much was happening. His entire future was being determined by a collision of circumstances, all of which had to be tightly controlled.

At least the problem of Jin Zhao had been resolved.

All was finally assuming its assigned place. Thirty years of dedication about to be rewarded. Every threat had either been eliminated or contained.

Only Ni Yong remained.

FOUR

NI YONG SETTLED INTO THE BLACK LACQUERED CHAIR, A QING-period reproduction. He was familiar with the elegant lines and beautiful curves, this one an excellent example of pre–18th century Chinese craftsmanship, the quality and accuracy of its joinery so precise that nails and glue were unnecessary.

His austere-looking host rested in a cane armchair, his face longer than most Chinese, eyes rounder, forehead high, the sparse hair slightly curled. Pau Wen wore a jade-colored silk jacket and white trousers.

"Your home is elegant," Ni said in their native language.

Pau nodded at the compliment, accepting the praise with the humility expected of a man nearing seventy. Too young to have been with Mao in 1949 when the People's Revolution swept Chiang Kai-shek and his Nationalists onto Taiwan, Ni knew that Pau's role grew during the 1960s and remained important even after Mao died in 1976.

Then, ten years later, Pau left China.

Ending up here, in Belgium of all places.

"I wanted my residence," Pau said, "to remind me of home."

The house, located a few kilometers outside Antwerp, appeared on the exterior to be a simple structure of high gray walls, with multi-tiered roofs, flaring eaves, and two towers that incorporated all the fundamental elements—enclosure, symmetry, hierarchy—of traditional

Chinese architecture. The inside was bright, airy, and reflected the colors and styles of classic décor, though all the modern conveniences—air-conditioning, central heat, a security system, satellite television—were present.

Ni was familiar with the design.

A *siheyuan*.

The ultimate symbol of Chinese wealth—a multifamily residence with a central courtyard enclosed by four buildings, usually embellished with a garden and deck. Once the homes of nobles, now they were affordable only to Chinese military, Party hierarchy, or the abominable new rich.

"This," Ni said, "reminds me of a residence I visited recently in the northeast, owned by a local mayor. We found two hundred and fifty gold bars hidden inside. Quite a feat for a man who barely made a few thousand yuan a year. Of course, being the mayor, he controlled the local economy, which the area's business owners, and foreign investors, apparently recognized. I arrested him."

"Then you executed him. Quickly, I'm sure."

He realized Pau would be familiar with the Chinese judicial system.

"Tell me, Minister, what brings you to Europe, and to me?"

Ni headed the Central Commission for Discipline Inspection of the Communist Party of China. Directly under the National Congress, on the same level as the all-powerful Central Committee, he was charged with rooting out corruption and malfeasance.

"You are not an official I would want as an enemy," Pau said. "I have been told that you are the most feared man in China."

He'd heard that label, too.

"Others say you may also be the most honest man in China."

He'd heard that description, as well. "And you, Pau Wen, are still one of our citizens. You never relinquished those rights."

"I am proud of my Chinese heritage."

"I've come to reclaim some of that heritage."

They sat in a drawing room that opened toward an inner courtyard dotted with flowering trees. Bees flitted from one fragrant bloom to another, their buzzes and the fountain's gurgle the only disturbances. Glass doors and silk curtains separated them from an adjacent study.

"Apparently," Ni said, "when you left the homeland, you decided that some of our artifacts would come with you."

Pau laughed. "Do you have any idea what it was like when Mao was alive? Tell me, Minister, in your exalted position, as keeper of the Party's conscience, do you have any conception of our history?"

"At the moment, only your thievery concerns me."

"I have been gone from China nearly three decades. Why is my *thievery* only now becoming important?"

He'd been warned about Pau Wen, a trained historian, skillful orator, and master at turning adversity into advantage. Both Mao and Deng Xiaoping had made use of his talents.

"Your crime has only recently come to my attention."

"An anonymous informant?"

He nodded. "We are fortunate to have them."

"And you make it so easy. You even have a website. All they do is forward an e-mail, with no name or address, loaded with accusations. Tell me, are there any repercussions for filing a false report?"

He wasn't going to fall into that trap. "On the walk in from the front gate I noticed a pottery horse from the Han dynasty. A bronze chime bell from the Zhou period. A Tang dynasty figurine. All originals, stolen by you."

"How would you know that?"

"You were the overseer of a number of museums and collections, an easy matter for you to appropriate whatever you may have desired."

Pau rose. "Might I show you something, Minister?"

Why not? He wanted to see more of the house.

He followed the older man out into the courtyard, which triggered memories of his own family's ancestral home in Sichuan, a province of jade-green hills and well-tended fields. For 700 years Nis had lived there, within a copse of bamboo that outlined fertile rice paddies. There'd been a courtyard in that house, too. One difference, though. It wasn't bricks, but pounded earth that had paved that space.

"Do you live here alone?" Ni asked.

So large a house would demand constant care, and everything appeared immaculate. Yet he'd seen or heard no one.

"More of that investigator in you. Asking questions?"

"It seems a simple inquiry."

Pau smiled. "My life is one of self-imposed solitude."

Not really an answer, but he'd not expected one.

They wove a path around potted shrubs and dwarf yews and approached a tall black door, with a red disk, at the courtyard's opposite side. Beyond lay a spacious hall, supported by massive pillars that stood beneath green-colored fretwork. One wall displayed bookshelves, another hung scrolls of Chinese script. Soft light permeated window papers. He noticed the careful woodwork, the silk hangings, curio cabinets, hardwood tables, the objects displayed as if in a museum.

"My collection," Pau said.

Ni stared at the trove.

"It is true, Minister. You saw valuable objects of art when you entered my home. Those are precious. But this is the real treasure." Pau motioned and they walked farther into the room. "Here, for example. A glazed pottery model. Han dynasty, 210 BCE."

He studied the sculpture, fashioned out of a lime-colored stone. The figure of a man turned a crank handle for what looked like a rotary mill.

"It shows something quite remarkable," Pau said. "Grain was poured into an open receptacle on top and the mill winnowed what was inside, separating the husks and stalk. This type of machine was not known in Europe until nearly two thousand years later, when Dutch sailors imported it from China."

Another pedestal displayed a ceramic figure on horseback, with a stirrup lying beside. Pau caught his interest.

"That's a Tang dynasty piece. 6th to 7th century CE. Notice the warrior on the horse. His feet are in stirrups. China developed the stirrup centuries ago, though it did not make it to Europe until their Middle Ages. The concept of a medieval knight, on horseback, armed with lance and shield, would not have been possible but for the Chinese stirrup."

He gazed around at the artifacts, maybe a hundred or more.

"I collected these from village to village," Pau said, "grave to grave. Many came from imperial tombs located in the 1970s. And you're right, I did have my choice from museums and private collections."

Pau pointed to a water clock that he said was from 113 BCE. A sundial, gun barrels, porcelain, astronomical etchings, each invention evidence of Chinese ingenuity. One curious item caught Ni's attention— a small ladle balanced on a smooth bronze plate upon which he noticed engravings.

"The compass," Pau said. "Conceived by the Chinese 2,500 years ago. The ladle is carved from magnetic lodestone and always comes to rest facing south. While Western man was barely capable of existing, the Chinese learned how to navigate with this device."

"All of this belongs to the People's Republic," Ni said.

"To the contrary. I saved this from the People's Republic."

He was tiring of the game. "Say what you mean, old man."

"During our glorious Cultural Revolution I once watched as a 2,000-year-old corpse, discovered in perfect condition at Changsha, was tossed by soldiers into the sun to rot, while peasants threw stones at it. That was the fate of millions of *our* cultural objects. Imagine the scientific and historical information lost from such foolishness."

He cautioned himself not to listen too closely to Pau's talk. As he'd taught his subordinates, good investigators never allowed themselves to be swayed by an interrogee.

His host motioned to a wooden and brass abacus. "That is 1,500 years old, used in a bank or an office as a calculator. The West had no idea of such a device until many centuries later. The decimal system, the zero, negative numbers, fractions, the value of pi. These concepts— everything in this room—all were first conceived by the Chinese."

"How do you know this?" Ni asked.

"It's our history. Unfortunately, our glorious emperors and Mao's People's Revolution rewrote the past to suit *their* needs. We Chinese have little idea from where we came, or what we accomplished."

"And you know?"

"Look over there, Minister."

He saw what looked like a printer's plate, characters ready to be inked on paper.

"Movable type was invented in China in 1045 CE, long before Gutenberg duplicated the feat in Germany. We also developed paper before the West. The seismograph, the parachute, the rudder, masts and sailing, all of these first came from China." Pau swept his arms out, encompassing the room. "This is our heritage."

Ni clung to the truth. "You are still a thief."

Pau shook his head. "Minister, my thievery is not what brings you here. I've been honest with you. So tell me, why have you come?"

Abruptness was another known Pau trait, used to command a conversation by controlling its direction. Since Ni was tired of the banter, he glanced around, hoping to spot the artifact. As described, it stood about three centimeters tall and five centimeters long, combining a dragon's head on a tiger's body with the wings of a phoenix. Crafted of bronze, it had been found in a 3rd century BCE tomb.

"Where is the dragon lamp?"

A curious look spread across Pau's wrinkled face. "She asked the same thing."

Not the answer he expected. "She?"

"A woman. Spanish, with a touch of Moroccan, I believe. Quite the beauty. But impatient, like you."

"Who?"

"Cassiopeia Vitt."

Now he wanted to know, "And what did you tell her?"

"I showed her the lamp." Pau pointed at a table toward the far end of the hall. "It sat right there. Quite precious. I found it in a tomb, from the time of the First Emperor. Discovered in . . . 1978, I believe. I brought the lamp, and all these items, with me when I left China in 1987."

"Where is the lamp now?"

"Miss Vitt wanted to purchase it. She offered an impressive price, and I was tempted, but said no."

He waited for an answer.

"She produced a gun and stole it from me. I had no choice. I am but an old man, living here alone."

That he doubted. "A *wealthy* old man."

Pau smiled. "Life has been kind to me. Has it to you, Minister?"

"When was she here?" he asked.

"Two days past."

He needed to find this woman. "Did she say anything about herself?"

Pau shook his head. "Just pointed her gun, took the lamp, and left."

A disturbing and unexpected development. But not insurmountable. She could be found.

"You came all this way for that lamp?" Pau asked. "Tell me, does it relate to your coming political war with Minister Karl Tang?"

The question threw him. Pau had been gone from China a long time. What was happening internally was no state secret, but neither was it common knowledge—not yet, anyway. So he asked, "What do you know of that?"

"I am not ignorant," Pau said in nearly a whisper. "You came because you knew Tang wanted that lamp."

Outside of his office, that fact was unknown. Concern now rifled through him. This old man was far better informed than he'd ever assumed. But something else occurred to him. "The woman stole the lamp for Tang?"

Pau shook his head. "She wanted it for herself."

"So you allowed her to take it?"

"I thought it better than Minister Tang acquiring it. I have anticipated that he might come and, actually, was at a loss as to what to do. This woman solved the problem."

His mind reeled, assessing the changed situation. Pau Wen stared at him with eyes that had surely borne witness to many things. Ni had come thinking a surprise visit to an elderly, ex-Chinese national would provide an easy opportunity. Obviously, the surprise was not Pau's.

"You and Minister Tang are the two leading contenders for the presidency and premiership," Pau said. "The current holder of that office is old, his time draws to a close. Tang or Ni. Everyone will have to choose their side."

He wanted to know, "Which side are you on?"

"The only one that matters, Minister. China's."

FIVE

MALONE FOLLOWED THE CHINESE COURIER, HIS SUSPICIONS confirmed. She knew nothing about what she was sent to retrieve, only to take what he offered. Hell, she'd even flirted with him. He wondered how much she was being paid for this dangerous errand, and was also concerned about how much Cassiopeia's captor knew. The voice on the laptop had made a point to taunt him about his government experience—yet they'd sent an uninformed amateur.

He kept the courier in sight as she eased her way through the crowd. The route she was taking would lead them out a secondary gate in Tivoli's northern boundary. He watched as she passed through the exit, crossed the boulevard beyond, and reentered the Strøget.

He stayed a block behind her as she continued her stroll.

They passed several secondhand-book stores, the owners all competitors and friends, and countless outdoor tables for the many eateries, ending at Højbro Plads. She veered right at the Café Norden, which anchored the square's east edge, and headed toward the steeple of Nikolaj, an old church that now served as a public exhibition hall. She turned along a side street that led away from Nikolaj, toward Magasin du Nord, Scandinavia's most exclusive department store.

People paraded in the streets, enjoying a collective joviality.

Fifty yards away, cars and buses whizzed back and forth where the Strøget ended.

She turned again.

Away from the department store and the traffic, back toward the canal and the charred ruins of the Museum of Greco-Roman Culture, which still had not been rebuilt from a fire that had destroyed it last year. Cassiopeia Vitt had appeared that night and saved his hide.

Now it was his turn to return the favor.

Fewer people loitered here.

Many of the 18th- and 19th-century structures, their façades long restored, had once been brothels frequented by Copenhagen's sailors. Apartments, favored by artists and young professionals, dominated today.

The woman disappeared around another corner.

He trotted to where she'd turned, but a trash receptacle blocked the way. He peered around the plastic container and spied a narrow alley closed in by walls of crumbling bricks.

The woman approached a man. He was short, thin, and anxious. She stopped and handed over the envelope. The man ripped it open, then yelled something in Chinese. Malone did not have to hear what was said to understand. Clearly, he knew what was expected, and it damn well wasn't a book.

He slapped her face.

She was thrown back and struggled to regain both her balance and composure. A hand went to her wounded cheek.

The man reached beneath his jacket.

A gun appeared.

Malone was way ahead of him, already finding his Beretta and calling out, "Hey."

The man whirled, saw both Malone and the gun and immediately grabbed the woman, jamming the barrel of his weapon into her neck.

"Toss the gun in that trash bucket," the man yelled in English.

He was deciding whether to risk it, but the terrified look on the woman's face told him to comply.

He dropped the gun over the container's edge, which thumped around, signaling that little else lay inside.

"Stay put," the man said as he backed down the street with his hostage.

He could not allow the trail to end here. This was his only route to Cassiopeia. The man and his captive kept easing toward where the alley connected to another busy street. A constant stirring of people passed back and forth at the intersection.

He stood, fifty feet away, and watched.

Then the man released his grip on the woman and, together, they ran away.

NI ASSESSED PAU WEN, REALIZING THAT HE'D FALLEN DIRECTLY into the trap this clever man had set.

"And what *is* best for China?"

"Do you know the tale of the crafty fox caught by a hungry tiger?" Pau asked.

He decided to indulge Pau and shook his head.

"The fox protested, saying, 'You dare not eat me because I am superior to all other animals, and if you eat me you will anger the gods. If you don't believe me, just follow and see what happens.' The tiger followed the fox into the woods and all the animals ran away at the first sight of them. The awed tiger, not realizing that he was the cause of their alarm, let the fox go." Pau went silent for a moment. "Which are you, Minister, the crafty fox or the unwitting tiger?"

"Seems one is a fool, the other a manipulator."

"Unfortunately, there are no other contenders for control of China," Pau said. "You and Minister Tang have done a masterful job of eliminating all challengers."

"So do you say I am the fool or the manipulator?"

"That is not for me to decide."

"I assure you," Ni said, "I am no fool. There is corruption throughout our People's Republic. My duty is to rid us of that disease."

Which was no small task in a nation where 1% of the population owned 40% of the wealth, much of it built from corruption. City mayors, provincial officials, high-ranking Party members—he'd arrested them all. Bribery, embezzlement, misappropriation, moral decadence, privilege seeking, smuggling, squandering, and outright theft were rampant.

Pau nodded. "The system Mao created was littered with corruption from its inception. How could it not be? When a government is accountable only from the top down, dishonesty becomes insidious."

"Is that why you fled?"

"No, Minister, I left because I came to detest all that had been done. So many people slaughtered. So much oppression and suffering. China, then and today, is a failure. There is no other way to view it. We are home to sixteen of the world's twenty most polluted cities, the world leader in sulfur dioxide emissions. Acid rain is destroying our land. We pollute the water with no regard for consequences. We destroy culture, history, our self-respect, with no regard. Local officials are rewarded only for more economic output, not public initiatives. The system itself assures its own destruction."

Ni cautioned himself that those observations could all be a deception. So he decided to utilize some misdirection of his own. "Why did you allow that woman to steal the lamp?"

Pau appraised him with a glare that made him uncomfortable, akin to his own father's gaze that he'd once respected.

"That is a question to which you should already know the answer."

MALONE TIPPED THE TRASH BIN OVER, FOUND HIS GUN, THEN bolted down the alley.

He should have known.

The courier was no victim. Just an accomplice who'd messed up. He came to the alley's end and rounded the corner.

His two adversaries were a hundred feet ahead, running toward bustling Holmens Kanal, its lanes jammed with speeding vehicles navigating toward Copenhagen's busiest square.

He saw the two dart left, vanishing around a corner.

He stuffed the gun away and mixed force with polite phrases to bump his way past the crowd.

He came to a traffic-lighted intersection. The Danish Royal Theater stood across the street. To his right, he caught sight of Nyhavn, busy with people enjoying themselves at colorful cafés that stretched the new harbor's length. His two targets were making their way down a crowded sidewalk, paralleling traffic and a busy bicycle lane, heading toward the Hotel d'Angleterre.

A Volvo eased to the curb just before the hotel's entrance.

The man and woman crossed the bicycle lane and headed straight for the car's open rear door.

Two pops, like balloons bursting, and the man was thrown back, his body dropping to the pavement.

Another pop and the woman fell beside him.

Crimson rivulets poured from each body.

Fear spread, a ripple that sent a panic through the afternoon crowd. Three people on bicycles collided with one another, trying to avoid the bodies.

The car sped away.

Tinted windows shielded the occupants as it roared past, then whipped left in a sharp turn. He tried to spot the license plate, but the Volvo disappeared around Kongens Nytorv.

He rushed forward, knelt down, and checked pulses.

Both were dead.

The bicyclists appeared injured.

He stood and yelled in Danish, "Somebody call the police."

He ran a hand through his hair and heaved a sigh.

The trail to Cassiopeia had just vanished.

He eased himself away from the throng of gawkers, close to the outside tables and windows for the Hotel d'Angleterre's restaurant. People with shocked faces stood and stared. Dead bodies on the sidewalk were not commonplace in Denmark.

Distant sirens signaled that help was coming.

Which meant he needed to go.

"Mr. Malone," a voice said, close to his left ear.

He started to turn.

"No. Face ahead."

The distinctive feel of a gun barrel nestled close to his spine told him to take the man's advice.

"I need you to walk with me."

"And if I don't?" he asked.

"You do not find Cassiopeia Vitt."

SIX

KARL TANG STARED OUT ACROSS THE VAST ENCLOSED SPACE. The helicopter ride north, from Chongqing, across the Qin Mountains, had taken nearly two hours. He'd flown from Beijing not only to personally supervise the execution of Jin Zhao but also to deal with two other matters, both of equal importance, the first one here in Shaanxi, China's cultural cradle. An archaeologist in the Ministry of Science had once told him that if you sank a shovel anywhere in this region, something of China's 6,000-year-old history would be unearthed.

Before him was the perfect example.

In 1974 peasants digging a well uncovered a vast complex of underground vaults that, he'd been told, would eventually yield 8,000 life-sized terra-cotta soldiers, 130 chariots, and 670 horses, all arrayed in a tightly knit battle formation—a silent army, facing east, each figure forged and erected more than 2,200 years ago. They guarded a complex of underground palaces, designed specifically for the dead, all centered on the imperial tomb of Qin Shi, the man who ended five centuries of disunity and strife, eventually taking for himself the exalted title *Shi Huang*.

First Emperor.

Where that initial well had been dug now stood the Museum of Qin Dynasty Terra-cotta Warriors and Horses, its centerpiece the exhibition hall spanning more than two hundred meters before him, topped by an impressive glass-paneled arch. Earthen balks divided the excavated scene into eleven latitudinal rows, each paved with ancient bricks. Wooden roofs, once supported by stout timbers and cross-beams, had long ago disappeared. But to bar moisture and preserve the warrior figures beneath, the builders had wisely sheathed the area with woven matting and a layer of clay.

Qin Shi's eternal army had survived.

Tang stared at the sea of warriors.

Each wore a coarse tunic, belt, puttees, and thonged, square-toed sandals. Eight basic faces had been identified, but no two were exactly alike. Some had tightly closed lips and forward-staring eyes, revealing a character of steadiness and fortitude. Others displayed vigor and confidence. Still others evoked a sense of thoughtfulness, suggesting the wisdom of a veteran. Amazingly, the still poses, repeated innumerable times in a given number of defined postures, actually generated a sense of motion.

Tang had visited before and walked among the archers, soldiers, and horse-drawn chariots, smelling the rich Shaanxi earth, imagining the rhythmic beat of marching feet.

He felt empowered here.

Qin Shi himself had walked this hallowed ground. For 250 years, ending in 221 BCE, seven ruling kingdoms—Qi, Chi, Yar, Zhao, Han, Wei, and Qin—had fought for dominance. Qin Shi ended that conflict, conquering his neighbors and establishing an empire with all authority centered in himself. Eventually, the land itself acquired his name. A perversion of the way *Qin* would come to be pronounced by foreigners.

Chin.

China.

Tang found it hard not to be impressed by such grand accomplishments, and though Qin Shi had lived long ago, the man's impact still resonated. He was the first to divide the land into prefectures, each composed of smaller units he named counties. He abolished the feudal system and eliminated aristocratic warlords. Weights, measures, and currencies became standardized. A uniform code of laws was enacted. He built roads, a wall to protect the northern border, and cities. Even more critical, the various and confusing local scripts were replaced with one written alphabet.

But the First Emperor was not perfect.

He enforced severe laws, imposed heavy taxes, and requisitioned people by the thousands for both military and construction services. Millions died under his reign. *To begin an enterprise is not easy, but to keep hold of success is even more difficult.* Qin Shi's descendants failed to heed the First Emperor's lesson, allowing peasant revolts to ferment into widespread rebellion. Within three years of the founder's death, the empire crumbled.

A new dynasty succeeded.

The Han.

Whose descendants continued to dominate even today.

Tang was a Han, from Hunan province, another hot, humid place in the south, home to revolutionary thinkers, Mao Zedong its most prominent. He'd attended Hunan's Institute of Technology, then transferred to Beijing's School of Geology. After graduating, he'd worked as a technician and political instructor on the Geomechanics Survey Team, then served as head engineer and chief of the political section for the Central Geological Bureau. That's when the Party had first noticed him and he was assigned positions in Gansu province and the Tibet Autonomous Region, gaining a reputation as both a scientist and administrator. Eventually, he returned to Beijing and rose from assistant to director of the general office of the Central Committee. Three years later he was elevated to the Central Committee itself. Now he was first vice premier of the Party, first vice president of the republic, one step away from the tip of the political triangle.

"Minister Tang."

He turned at the sound of his name.

The museum's curator approached. He could tell from the man's clipped stride and polite expression that something was amiss.

Tang stood on the railed walk that encircled Pit 1, fifteen meters above the terra-cotta figures. The 16,000-square-meter exhibit hall was closed for the night, but the overhead lighting in the hangar-like space had been left on, per his earlier instruction.

"I was told you had arrived," the curator said. Eyeglasses dangled like a pendant from a chain around the man's neck.

"Before going to Pit 3, I wanted a few moments here," Tang said. "The sight of these warriors never disappoints me."

Outside, six more halls stood in the darkness, along with a theater, book counters, and a menagerie of shops and stalls that tomorrow would hawk souvenirs to just a few of the two million who flocked here every year to see what many called the eighth wonder of the world.

He spat at such a designation.

As far as he was concerned, this was the only wonder of the world.

"We must speak, Minister."

The curator was a conservative intellectual, part of a Zhuang minority, which meant he would never rise any higher. The entire Qin Shi site came under Tang's Ministry of Science, so the curator clearly understood where his allegiance lay.

"I'm having trouble containing things," the curator told him.

He waited for more explanation.

"The discovery was made two days ago. I called you immediately. I ordered no one to speak of it, but I'm afraid that instruction was not taken seriously. There is . . . talk among the archaeologists. Several know that we broke through to another chamber."

He did not want to hear that.

"I realize you wanted the discovery kept secret. But it's proven difficult."

This was not the place, so he laid a reassuring hand on the man's shoulder and said, "Take me to Pit 3."

They left the building and walked across a darkened plaza toward another broad structure lit from the inside.

Pit 3 had been discovered 20 meters north of Pit 1 and 120 meters east of Pit 2. The smallest of the three excavations, U-shaped, and barely five hundred square meters made up its space. Only sixty-eight terra-cotta figures and one chariot drawn by four horses had been found there, none in battle formation.

Then they'd realized.

The dress, gestures, and formation of the warriors suggested Pit 3 to be the underground army's command center, reserved for generals and other senior officials. The warriors here had been found arrayed with their backs to the wall, wielding bronze poles with no blades, a unique weapon utilized only by imperial guards of honor. In addition, its location, in the far northwest corner, ensured that it was well protected by the armies of the other two pits. In life Qin Shi had led a million armored soldiers, a thousand chariots, and ten thousand horses to conquer and "gloat over the world." In death, he'd clearly intended something similar.

Tang descended the earthen ramp to the bottom of Pit 3.

Bright overhead lights illuminated the surreal scene. A stable and a chariot filled the first recess. Two short corridors, one on the left and one on the right of the stable, connected with two deeper chambers.

He waited until they were both below ground level before addressing the problem with the administrator.

"I counted on you," he said, "to make sure the discovery was contained. If you can't handle the matter, perhaps we need someone else in charge."

"I assure you, Minister, it is now contained. I just wanted you to know that its existence has leaked beyond the three who broke through."

"Tell me again what was found."

"We noticed a weakness." The director pointed to his right. "There. We thought that was where the pit ended, but we were wrong."

He saw a gaping hole in the earthen wall, dirt piled to the side.

"We have not had time to clear the debris," the director said. "After the initial inspection, I halted excavations and called you."

A jungle of flat cables sprouted from metal boxes and a transformer resting on the ground nearby. He stared at the opening, the bright lights burning on the other side.

"It's a new chamber, Minister," the curator said. "Not known before."

"And the anomaly?"

"It's inside, waiting for you."

A shadow danced along the interior walls.

"He's been there all day," the director said. "Per your order. Working."

"Undisturbed?"

"As you requested."

SEVEN

NI STUDIED PAU WEN, IRRITATED WITH HIMSELF FOR HAVING underestimated this cagey man.

"Look around," Pau said. "Here is evidence of Chinese greatness dating back 6,000 years. While Western civilization had barely begun, China was casting iron, fighting wars with crossbows, and mapping its land."

His patience had drained. "What is the point of this discussion?"

"Do you realize that China was more advanced agriculturally in the 4th century BCE than Europe was in the 18th century? Our ancestors understood row cultivation, why hoeing of weeds was necessary, the seed drill, the iron plow, and the efficient use of the harness centuries before any other culture on the planet. We were so far ahead that no comparison can even be made. Tell me, Minister. What happened? Why are we not still in that superior position?"

The answer was obvious—which Pau obviously realized—but Ni would not speak seditious words, wondering if the room, or his host, could be wired.

"A British scholar studied this phenomenon decades ago," Pau said, "and concluded that more than half of the basic inventions and discoveries upon which the modern world is based came from China. But who knew this? The Chinese themselves are ignorant. There's a story, recorded in history, that when the Chinese were first shown a mechanical clock by Jesuit missionaries in the 17th century they were awestruck, not knowing that it was their own ancestors who had invented it a thousand years before."

"All of this is irrelevant," he made clear, playing to any audience that might be listening.

Pau pointed to a redwood desk against a far wall. Items needed for calligraphy—ink, stone, brushes, and paper—were neatly arranged around a laptop computer.

They walked over.

Pau tapped the keyboard and the screen sprang to life.

The man stood straight. He appeared to be in his thirties, his features more Mongolian than Chinese, black hair wrapped in a loose coiffure. He wore a broad-sleeved white jacket trimmed at the collar with pale green. Three other men, dressed in black trousers and long gray garments under short indigo jackets, surrounded him.

The man shed his robe.

He was naked, his pale body muscular. Two of the attendants began to tightly wrap his abdomen and upper thighs with white bandages. With their binding complete, the man stood as a third attendant washed his exposed penis and scrotum.

The cleansing was repeated three times.

The man sat in a semi-reclining position on a chair, his legs spread wide and held firmly in place by the two attendants. The third participant stepped to a lacquered table and lifted from a tray a curved knife with a cracked bone handle.

He approached the man on the chair and asked in a clear, commanding voice, "Hou huei pu hou huei?"

The man remained poised as he considered the question—will you regret it or not?—and shook his head no, without the slightest show of fear or uncertainty.

The attendant nodded. Then, with two quick swipes of the knife, he removed the man's scrotum and penis, cutting close to the body, leaving nothing exposed.

Not a sound was made.

The two attendants held the man's shaking legs steady.

Blood poured out, but the third man worked the wound, causing obvi-

ous pain to the seated man. Still not a sound was uttered. Agony gripped the face, but the recipient seemed to gain control and steadied himself.

Something that appeared to be paper soaked in water was slapped across the wound, several layers thick, until no more blood oozed through.

The man was helped from the couch, visibly trembling, his face half excited, half afraid.

"He was walked around the room for the next two hours, before being allowed to lie down," Pau said.

"What . . . what *was* that?" Ni asked, making no effort to disguise the shock in his voice at the video.

"A ceremony that has occurred in our history hundreds of thousands of times." Pau hesitated. "The creation of a eunuch."

Ni knew about eunuchs and the intricate role they played in China for 2,500 years. Emperors were deemed recipients of a mystical "mandate of Heaven," a concept that officially sanctified their right to rule. To preserve an aura of sacredness, the personal life of the imperial family was shielded, lest anyone be in a position to observe their human failings. Only effeminate eunuchs, dependent on the emperor for their lives, were deemed humble enough to bear such witness. The system was so successful that it became ingrained, but such frequent and intimate association allowed eunuchs an easy opportunity. Childless, they should not have coveted political power to pass on to sons, nor should they have had any need for riches.

But that proved not to be the case.

Emperors eventually became playthings for these pariahs and they became more powerful than any government minister. Many emperors never even met with government administrators. Instead, decisions were shuttled in and out of the palace by eunuchs, no one knowing who actually received or issued the decrees. Only the most diligent and conscientious rulers avoided their influence, but they were few and far between. Finally, during the early 20th century, as the last emperor was forced from the imperial palace, the system was abolished.

"Eunuchs don't exist anymore," he declared.

"Why would you think that?"

Thoughts of being recorded faded. "Who are you?"

"I am a person who appreciates our ancestry. A man who witnessed the wholesale destruction of all that we have held sacred for thousands of years. I am Chinese."

He knew Pau had been born in the northern province of Liaoning, educated in France at a time when young Chinese had been allowed to attend universities abroad. Well read, a published author of six historical treatises, he'd managed to survive all of Mao's purges, which, Ni assumed, had been no easy feat. Eventually, Pau had been allowed to leave the country—rare beyond rare—taking with him personal wealth. Still—

"You speak of treason," he made clear.

"I speak the truth, Minister. And I think you suspect the same."

Ni shrugged. "Then you would be wrong."

"Why are you still standing here? Why do you continue to listen to me?"

"Why did you show me that video?"

"Faced with death, he who is ready to die will survive while he who is determined to live will die. That thought has been expressed another way. *Shang wu chou ti.*"

He'd heard the phrase before.

Pull down the ladder after the ascent.

"The most common interpretation instructs us to lure the enemy into a trap, then cut off his escape," Pau said. "Different adversaries are lured in different ways. The greedy are enticed with the promise of gain. The arrogant with a sign of weakness. The inflexible by a ruse. Which are you, Minister?"

"Who is luring me?"

"Karl Tang."

"Actually, it seems more like you are doing the luring. You haven't answered my question. Why did you show me that video?"

"To prove that you know little of what's happening around you. Your self-righteous commission spends its time investigating corrupt officials and dishonest Party members. You chase ghosts, while a real threat stalks you. Even within your sacrosanct world, which prides itself on being the Party's conscience, you are surrounded. Eunuchs still exist, Minister."

"How do you know any of this?"

"Because I am one of their number."

EIGHT

CASSIOPEIA VITT WAS SHOVED BACK INTO THE ROOM THAT had been her prison for the past two days. Her shirt was soaked, her lungs aching from trying to breathe.

The door slammed shut.

Only then was she allowed to remove the blindfold from her face.

Her cell was perhaps four by two meters, under a staircase, she assumed, as the ceiling sloped sharply. The room was windowless, light coming from a low-wattage bulb that was never extinguished. No furniture, just a thin mattress lying on a plank floor. She'd tried to learn what she could during the limited times she'd been removed. It appeared she was inside a house, the distance from here to the torture room only a few steps and in between them a bathroom that she'd visited twice.

But where was she?

Two days ago she had been in Antwerp.

She bent forward, hands on her knees. Her legs were limp, her heart pounding, and she shuddered.

Twice she'd been strapped to the board, the towel slapped across her face. She'd thought herself capable of withstanding anything, but the sensation of drowning, while her arms and feet were restrained, her head lower than her legs, was proving too much. She'd read once that mental violence needed no punches.

She believed it.

She doubted she could take another session.

Near the end of the first one, she'd involved Malone, which seemed like a smart play. In the few hours between leaving Pau Wen's residence and her capture, she easily could have handed the artifact off.

And they'd apparently believed her.

Cotton was all she had.

And she could not give these people what they wanted. Would they kill her? Not likely, at least until they made contact in Copenhagen.

After that?

She didn't want to think about the possibilities.

She was proud that she hadn't begged, whined, or compromised herself.

But she had compromised Cotton.

Then again, he'd told her many times that, if she ever needed anything, she shouldn't hesitate. This situation seemed to qualify.

Over the past two days she'd played mental games, remembering dates in history, forcing her thoughts away. She'd multiplied numbers to the tens of thousands.

But thoughts of Malone had also kept her grounded.

He was tall and handsome, with burnished-blond hair and lively green eyes. Once she'd thought him cold, emotionless, but over the past year she'd learned that this was not the case. They'd been through a lot together.

She trusted him.

Her breathing settled. Her heart slowed.

Nerves calmed.

She stood upright and rubbed her sore wrists.

Pushing forty years old and in another mess. But usually it beat the heck out of anything else she could imagine doing. Actually, her project to reconstruct a 14th-century French castle, using only tools and materials available 700 years ago, was progressing. Her on-site superintendent had reported a few weeks ago that they were at the 10% point in construction. She'd intended to devote herself more to that endeavor, but a call from China had changed that.

"They took him, Cassiopeia. He's gone."

Lev Sokolov was not a man prone to panic. In fact, he was a smart, clever, concise individual. Born and raised in the old Soviet Union, he'd managed to flee, escaping to China, of all places.

"My son was playing at his grandmother's vegetable stall," Sokolov said in Russian, voice cracking. "One of his grandmother's neighbors passed by and offered to bring him back home on his way, so she allowed him. That was eight weeks ago."

"What about that neighbor?"

"We went straight to his door. He said that after giving him money for sweets, he left him at our apartment block. He is a lying bastard. He sold him, Cassiopeia. I know he did. There is no other explanation."

"What did the police do?"

"The government does not want to talk about child stealing. To them it's isolated and under control. It's not. Two hundred children disappear here every day."

"That can't be right."

"It is. Now my boy is one of them."

She hadn't known what to say.

"Our options are limited," Sokolov said, his voice wretched with despair. "The media is too close to the government to do anything. The police will not speak to us. Even parents' support groups that exist for others like us have to meet in secret. We plastered the province with posters, but the police threatened to arrest us if we kept on. No one wants reminders of a problem that officially doesn't exist." He paused. "My wife has fallen apart. She is barely coherent. I have nowhere else to turn. I need your help."

That was a request she could not refuse.

Five years ago Lev Sokolov had saved her life, and she owed him.

So she'd obtained a thirty-day tourist visa, bought a ticket to Beijing, and flown to China.

She lay down on the mattress, belly-first, and stared at a wall of unfinished gypsum. She knew every crack and crevice. A spider occupied one corner, and yesterday she'd watched it snare a fly.

She sympathized with that fly.

No telling how long until the next time she'd be summoned. That all depended on Cotton.

She was tired of being caged, but a four-year-old boy was depending on her. Lev Sokolov was depending on her.

And she'd messed up.

Footsteps outside the door signaled someone was coming. Unusual.

She'd been visited only five times. Twice for torture, a third to leave some rice and boiled cabbage, two more to take her blindfolded to a bathroom a few feet down the hallway.

Had they discovered Cotton to be a dead end?

She extended her arms above her head, palms flat on the wood floor, which pulsated with each approaching step.

Time to do something, even if it's wrong.

She knew the drill. The lock would release, the door would open on squeaky hinges, a blindfold then tossed inside. Not until its elastic was firmly around her head would anyone enter. She assumed her captor was armed and he was clearly not alone, as at least two had always been with her. Both times a man had questioned her, the same man who'd spoken to Malone via computer in a clipped voice with no accent.

A key was inserted in the lock.

She closed her eyes as the door eased open. No blindfold was tossed inside. She cracked her lids and saw a shoe appear. Then another. Perhaps it was feeding time? The last time food had been left, she'd been asleep, dozing from pure exhaustion. Maybe her jailers thought she was too spent from the ordeal to be a threat?

She was indeed tired, her muscles aching, limbs sore.

But an opportunity was an opportunity.

The man entered the room.

Pressing her hands onto the floor, she pivoted up and clipped the legs out from under him.

A tray with bread and cheese clattered away.

She sprang to her feet and slammed the sole of her boot into the man's face. Something snapped, probably his nose. She pounded her heel into his face one more time. The back of his head popped against the floorboards and he lay still.

Another kick into the ribs made her feel better.

But the attack had generated noise. And there was at least one more threat lurking nearby. She searched the man's clothes and spotted a gun in a shoulder holster. She freed the weapon and checked the magazine.

Fully loaded.

Time to leave.

NINE

COPENHAGEN

MALONE STARED AT HIS KIDNAPPER. THEY'D ABANDONED THE
street just as the police arrived, rounding a corner and plunging back
into the Strøget.

"You have a name?" he asked.

"Call me Ivan."

The English laced with a Russian accent made the label appropriate, as did the man's appearance—short, heavy-chested, with grayish
black hair. A splotchy, reddened skink of a face was dominated by a
broad Slavic nose and shadowed by a day-old beard that shone with
perspiration. He wore an ill-fitting suit. The gun had been tucked away
and they now stood in a small plaza, within the shadow of the Round
Tower, a 17th-century structure that offered commanding views from
its hundred-foot summit. The dull roar of traffic was not audible this
deep into the Strøget, only the clack of heels to cobbles and the laughter of children. They stood beneath a covered walk that faced the tower,
a brick wall to their backs.

"Your people kill those two back there?" Malone asked.

"They think we come to whisk them away."

"Care to tell me how you know about Cassiopeia Vitt?"

"Quite the woman. If I am younger, a hundred pounds lighter."
Ivan paused. "But you do not want to hear this. Vitt is into something

she does not understand. I hope you, ex-American-agent, appreciate the problem better."

"It's the only reason I'm standing here."

His unspoken message seemed to be received.

Get to the damn point.

"You can overpower me," Ivan said, nodding. "I am fat, out-of-shape Russian. Stupid, too. All of us, right?"

He caught the sarcasm. "I can take you. But the man standing near the tree, across the way, in the blue jacket, and the other one, near the Round Tower's entrance? I doubt I'd evade them. They're not fat and out of shape."

Ivan chuckled. "I am told you are smart. Two years off job have not changed this."

"I seem to be busier in retirement than I was working for the government."

"This bad thing?"

"You need to talk fast, or I may take my chances with your friends."

"No need to be hero. Vitt is helping man named Lev Sokolov. Ex-Russian, lives in China. Five years ago, Sokolov marries Chinese national and leaves against wishes of Russian government. He slips away and, once in China, little can be done."

"Sounds like old news," Malone said.

"We think him dead. Not true."

"So what else changed?"

"Sokolov has four-year-old son who is recently stolen. He calls Vitt, who comes to find boy."

"And this worries you? What about the police?"

Ivan shook his head. "Thousands of children go in China every year. It is about having the son. In China this is necessity. Son carries family name. He is child who helps parents in old age. Forget daughters. Son is what matters. Makes no sense to me."

He kept listening.

"China's one-child policy is nightmare," Ivan said. "Parents must have the birth permit. If not, there is fine that is more than Chinese man makes in the year. How can he be sure to get son in one try?" The Russian snapped his pudgy fingers. "Buy one."

Malone had read about the problem. Female fetuses were either aborted or abandoned, and decades of the one-child policy had caused a national shortage of women.

"Problem for Sokolov," Ivan said, "is that he fights criminal network." He gestured with his short arms. "Is worse than Russia."

"That's hard to imagine."

"Is illegal to abandon, steal, or sell child in China, but is legal to buy one. Young boy costs 900 dollar, U.S. Lot of money when worker earns in year 1,700 dollar, U.S. Sokolov has no chance."

"So Cassiopeia went to help. So what. Why are you concerned?"

"Four days ago she travels to Antwerp," Ivan said.

"To find the kid there?"

"No. To find boy she must find something else first."

Now he understood. "Something you obviously want?"

Ivan shrugged.

Malone's mind envisioned the torture video. "Who has Cassiopeia?"

"Bad people."

He didn't like the sound of that.

"Ever deal with eunuchs?"

Ni did not know whether to be amazed or repelled by what Pau Wen had revealed about himself. "You are a eunuch?"

"I was subjected to the same ceremony you just witnessed, nearly forty years ago."

"Why would you do such a thing?"

"It was what I wanted to do with my life."

Ni had flown to Belgium thinking Pau Wen might have the answers he sought. But a whole host of new, disturbing questions had been raised.

Pau motioned for them to leave the exhibit hall and retreat to the courtyard. The midday air had warmed, the sun bright in a cloudless sky. More bees seemed to have joined in the assault on the spring blossoms. The two men stopped beside a glass jar, maybe a meter wide, containing bright-hued goldfish.

"Minister," Pau said, "in my time, China was in total upheaval. Before and after Mao died, the government was visionless, stumbling from one failed program to another. No one dared challenge anything. Instead a precious few made reckless decisions that affected millions. When Deng Xiaoping finally opened the country to the world, that was a daring move. I thought perhaps we might have a chance at success. But change was not to be. The sight of that lone student confronting a tank in Tiananmen Square has been etched into the world's consciousness. One of the defining images of the 20th century. Which you well know."

Yes, he did.

He was there that day—June 4, 1989—when the government's tolerance ran out.

"And what did Deng do after?" Pau asked. "He pretended like it never happened, moving ahead with more foolishness."

He had to say, "Strange talk from a man who helped forge some of those policies."

"I forged nothing," Pau said, anger creeping, for the first time, into his voice. "I spent my time in the provinces."

"Stealing."

"Preserving."

He was still bothered by the video. "Why was that man emasculated?"

"He joined a brotherhood. That initiation occurred three months ago. He is now healed, working with his brothers. He would not have been permitted to drink anything for three days after surgery. You saw how the attendant plugged the man's urethra before wrapping the wound with wet paper. On the fourth day, after the plug was removed, when urine flowed the operation was considered a success. If not, the initiate would have died an agonizing death."

He could not believe anyone would willingly submit to such an atrocity. But he knew Pau was right. Hundreds of thousands throughout Chinese history had done just that. When the Ming dynasty fell in the mid-17th century, more than 100,000 eunuchs had been forced from the capital. The decline of Han, Tang, and Ming rule were all attributed to eunuchs. The Chinese Communist Party had long used them as examples of unrestrained greed.

"Interestingly," Pau said, "of the hundreds of thousands who have been castrated, only a tiny percentage died. Another of our Chinese innovations. We are quite good at creating eunuchs."

"What brotherhood?" he wanted to know, irritation in his voice.

"They are called the *Ba.*"

He'd never heard of such a group. Should he have? His job was to safeguard the government, and the people, from all forms of corruption. In order to accomplish that goal he enjoyed an autonomy no other public official was extended, reporting directly to the Central Committee and the premier himself. Not even Karl Tang, as first vice premier, could interfere, though he'd tried. Ni had created the elite investigative unit himself, on orders from the Central Committee, and had spent the last decade building a reputation of honesty.

But never had there been any *Ba.*

"What is that?" he asked.

"With all the resources at your command you can surely learn more about them. Now that you know where to look."

He resented the condescending tone. "Where?"

"All around you."

He shook his head. "You are not only a thief, but a liar."

"I'm simply an old man who knows more than you do—on a great many subjects. What I lack is time. You, though, are a person with an abundance of that commodity."

"You know nothing of me."

"On the contrary. I know a great deal. You rose from squad leader to platoon captain to commander of the Beijing military area—a great honor bestowed only on those in whom the government has much trust. You were a member of the esteemed Central Military Commission when the premier himself chose you to head the Central Commission for Discipline Inspection."

"Am I to be impressed that you know my official history? It's posted on the Internet for the world to see."

Pau shrugged. "I know much more, Minister. You are a subject that has interested me for some time. The premier made a difficult decision, but I do have to say he chose well in you."

He knew about the opposition that had existed at the time of his appointment. Many did not want a military man in the position to investigate anyone at will. They worried that it might lead to the military gaining more power.

But he'd proven the pundits wrong.

"How would you know about any difficult decision?"

"Because the premier and I have spoken at length about you."

TEN

TANG TOLD THE DIRECTOR TO REMAIN WITHIN THE PIT 3 building and stand guard at ground level, ensuring that he was not disturbed. Not that he would expect to be. He was the second most powerful man in China—though, irritatingly, others had begun elevating Ni Yong to that same plateau.

He'd been against Ni's appointment, but the premier had nixed all objections, saying Ni Yong was a man of character, a person who could temper power with reason, and from all reports, that was precisely what Ni had done.

But Ni was a Confucian.

Of that there was no doubt.

Tang was a Legalist.

Those two labels had defined Chinese politics for nearly 3,000 years. Every emperor had been labeled one or the other. Mao had claimed to eliminate the dichotomy, insisting that the People's Revolution was not about labels, yet nothing really changed. The Party, like emperors before it, preached Confucian humanity while wielding the unrelenting power of a Legalist.

Labels.

They were problematic.

But they could also prove useful.

He hoped the next few minutes might help decide which end of that spectrum would factor into his coming battle with Ni Yong.

He stepped through the makeshift portal.

The dank room beyond had been dug from the earth and sealed centuries ago with clay and stone. Artificial lights had been brought in to illuminate the roughly five-meter-square chamber. The silence, decrepitude, and layers of soot made him feel like an interloper trespassing in a grave of things long dead.

"It is remarkable," the man inside said to him.

Tang required a proper assessment and this wiry and short-jawed academician could be trusted to provide just that.

Three stone tables dusted with thick layers of dirt supported what looked like brittle, brown leaves stacked on top of one another.

He knew what they were.

A treasure trove of silk sheets, each bearing barely discernible characters and drawings.

In other piles lay strips of bamboo, bound together, columns of letters lining each one. Paper had not existed when these thoughts had been memorialized—and China never used papyrus, only silk and wood, which proved fortuitous since both lasted for centuries.

"Is it Qin Shi's lost library?" Tang asked.

The other man nodded. "I would say so. There are hundreds of manuscripts. They deal with everything. Philosophy, politics, medicine, astronomy, engineering, military strategy, mathematics, cartography, music, even archery and horsemanship. This could well be the greatest concentration of firsthand knowledge ever found on the First Emperor's time."

He knew what that claim meant. In 1975 more than a thousand Qin dynasty bamboo strips had been discovered. Historians had proclaimed those the greatest find, but later examinations had cast doubt on their authenticity. Eventually, it was determined that most of them came from a time after Qin Shi, when later dynasties refashioned reality. This cache, though, had lain for centuries within a kilometer of the First Emperor's tomb, part of his grand mausoleum, guarded by his eternal army.

"The amazing thing is I can read them," his expert said.

Tang knew the importance of that ability. The fall of a ruling dynasty was always regarded as a withdrawal of Heaven's mandate. To avoid any curse, each new dynasty became critical of the one before. So complete was the subsequent purge that the system of writing would even be altered, making any later deciphering of what came before that much more difficult. Only in the past few decades had scholars, like the expert with him tonight, learned to read those lost scripts.

"Are they here?" Tang asked.

"Let me show you what I found."

The expert lifted one of the fragile silks.

Wisps of dust swirled in the air like angry ghosts.

Qin Shi himself had assured that none of the writings from his time would survive his reign when he ordered all manuscripts, except those dealing with medicine, agriculture, or divination be burned. The idea was to "make the people ignorant," and prevent the "use of the past to discredit the present." Only the emperor would be trusted to have a library, and knowledge would be an imperial monopoly. Scholars who challenged that decree were executed. Particularly, any- and everything written by Confucius was subject to immediate destruction, since those teachings directly contradicted the First Emperor's philosophy.

"Listen to this," his expert said. *"Long ago Confucius died and the subtle words were lost. His seventy disciples perished and the great truth was perverted. Therefore the* Annals *split into five versions, the* Odes *into four, and the* Changes *was transmitted in variant traditions. Diplomats and persuaders argued over what was true and false, and the words of the master became a jumbled chaos. This disturbed the emperor so he burned the writings in order to make idiots of the common people. He retained, though, the master's original thoughts, stored in the palace and they accompanied him in death."*

That meant all six of the great Confucian manuscripts should be here.

The *Book of Changes,* a manual on divination. The *Book of History,* concerned with the speeches and deeds of the legendary sage-kings of antiquity. The *Book of Poetry,* containing more than three hundred verses laced with hidden meanings. The *Spring and Autumn Annals,* a complete history of Confucius' home state. The *Book of Ritual,* which explained the proper behavior of everyone from peasant to ruler. And finally, the *Book of Music,* its content unknown, as no copy existed.

Tang knew that the Hans, who had succeeded the First Emperor with a 425-year dynasty of their own, tried to repair the damage Qin Shi inflected by reassembling many of the Confucian texts. But no one knew if those later editions accurately reflected the originals. Finding a complete set of texts, untouched, could be monumental.

"How many manuscripts are actually here?" Tang quietly asked.

"I've counted over two hundred separate texts." The expert paused. "But none is by Confucius."

His fears were growing.

Confucius was the Roman label given by 17th-century Jesuits to a sage whom disciples knew in the 5th century BCE as Kong Fu-Zi. His ideas had survived in the form of sayings, and his central belief seemed to be that man should seek to live in a good way, always behaving with humanity and courtesy, working diligently, honoring family and government. He emphasized "the way of the former kings," encouraging the present to draw strength and wisdom from the past. He championed a highly ordered society, but the means of accomplishing that order was not by force, rather through compassion and respect.

Qin Shi was no Confucian.

Instead, the First Emperor embraced Legalism.

That counter-philosophy believed naked force and raw terror were the only legitimate bases for power. Absolute monarchy, centralized bureaucracy, state domination over society, law as a penal tool, surveillance, informers, dissident persecution, and political coercion were its fundamental tools.

Both philosophies desired a unified state, a powerful sovereign, and a population in absolute submission, but while Legalists knocked heads, Confucians taught respect—the willing obedience of the people. When the Legalist First Empire fell in the 3rd century BCE, Confucianism became its replacement, and remained so, in one form or another, until the 20th century, when the communists brought a return of Legalism.

Confucian thought, though, was once again popular. The people identified with its peaceful tenets, especially after sixty years of harsh oppression. Even more disturbing was the rise of democracy, a philosophy more troubling than Confucianism.

"There is some good news," the expert said. "I found some further confirmation on the other matter."

He followed the man to another of the stone tables.

"These bamboo scrolls are like annual reports of the First Empire."

Tang knew that the ancient Chinese maintained detailed records of almost everything, especially natural phenomena. Within his specialty, geology, they classified rocks into ore, nonmetals, and clays. They noted hardness, color, and luster, as well as shape. They even isolated which substances were formed deep within the earth and determined how they could be found reliably.

"There are accounts here of drilling exploration," the expert said. "Quite specific."

He'd already spotted other silks. Maps. "Is our site noted?"

The man nodded. "The general area is shown. But without geographic reference points it's impossible to know for sure."

Though the ancients developed the compass and cartography, they lacked latitude and longitude, one of the few revolutionary concepts the Chinese did not first develop.

"Remove and preserve the maps, and anything else that directly relates to our search."

His expert nodded.

"The rest are unimportant. Now, to the other problem. Show me."

The man reached into his coat pocket and handed him a silver object, shiny in the light.

A watch.

Industrial looking, with a face and digits that glowed in the dark. A winding screw protruded from one side, and the word SHANGHAI indicated its place of manufacture.

"This is decades old," he said.

"It was found inside when they broke through. This, even more than the manuscripts, is what the museum's archaeologists became excited about."

He now understood the gravity of the director's containment problem. "Somebody has been in here before?"

The expert nodded. "Clearly. There were no watches in Qin Shi's day. Turn it over."

Engraved on the back were a series of Chinese characters. He stepped closer to the light and read the script.

SERVE THE PEOPLE.
1968

He'd seen a watch with the same inscription before. They were given to select Party members on the occasion of Mao Zedong's seventy-fifth birthday. Nothing pretentious or expensive, just a simple remembrance of a grand occasion.

December 26, 1968.

Precious few of those first-generation leaders remained alive. Though they held a special status in the communist pantheon, many fell victim to Mao's purges. Others died from old age. One, though, remained active in the government.

The premier, who'd occasionally displayed his gift from the former Chairman.

Tang needed to know for sure. "There are no Confucian texts here? You are sure?"

The expert shook his head. "This room has been purged of every one of them. They should be here, but they are gone."

Challenges to his plans seemed to come from all fronts. Jin Zhao. Lev Sokolov. Ni Yong.

Now this.

He stared at what he held.

And knew exactly who the watch had once belonged to.

ELEVEN

CASSIOPEIA STEPPED AWAY FROM THE MAN LYING STILL ON THE floor and approached the doorway. Finally, she was on the offensive, and she'd shoot anyone who came between herself and freedom.

Carefully, she peered into the narrow hall. Two meters away the door for the bathroom hung half open. Another door, a meter or so past on the other side, was closed. The corridor ended in what looked like a brightly lit entrance hall.

She stepped out.

The walls were a dingy rose, the plaster ceiling in need of painting. Definitely a house. Some rental. Surely out of the way, with a convenient windowless room beneath a staircase.

She wore the same jeans and shirt from two days ago. Her jacket had been taken the first day. Interestingly, she still carried her wallet and passport. Everything smelled of sweat and she could use a hot shower, though the thought of more water flowing across her face made her stomach uneasy.

She was careful with her steps, each one pressed lightly, the gun at her side, finger on the trigger.

At the hall's end she moved toward the front door, but the sound of a murmured voice halted her exit.

She stopped and listened.

Somebody was talking. Then silence. More speaking. As if on a telephone. She kept listening and confirmed only one voice. She decided that she owed that SOB, too. She'd already vented her anger on the man lying back in her cell, so why not finish things.

She identified the location down another short corridor that ended at a partially shut door. Before venturing that way she eased over to one of the windows and glanced out, spotting nothing but trees and pasture. They were somewhere in the countryside. She'd been transported here tied in the trunk of a car, blindfolded. She'd estimated about half an hour's driving time, which given Antwerp's location could place her anywhere in Belgium, Holland, or France.

A dark-colored Toyota was parked out front. She wondered if the keys were in the ignition or with one of her captors.

The muffled voice continued to speak on the telephone.

Might as well take advantage of the privacy they'd so conveniently arranged. She needed to find out who these people worked for. They could help lead her to Lev Sokolov's missing son. Finding him was her only concern. Thank goodness she'd thought ahead and done what she did, involving Cotton.

Otherwise, she'd be dead and the boy lost forever.

She stopped outside the door, keeping her gaze locked on the vertical strip of bright light escaping from the room on the other side.

Something about the voice tugged at her memory.

She had no idea how many people were waiting in the next room, but she didn't give a damn. Her nerves were frayed. Her patience exhausted.

She was tired, dirty, hungry, and pissed off.

She gripped the gun, planted her left foot on the floor, and slammed her right heel into the wood.

The door swung inward, smashing into the wall.

She lunged forward and immediately spotted only one man, talking on a cell phone.

He showed not the slightest surprise at her entrance.

Instead, he merely closed the phone and said, "About time."

She stared at the face, as if she'd seen a ghost.

And in some ways, she had.

MALONE HAD NEVER ACTUALLY HEARD THE WORD *EUNUCH* USED in a conversation before.

"As in castrated male?" he asked.

"There is other kind?" Ivan said. "These are nasty people." He spread out his short arms. "They lay down, open legs wide, snip, snip, everything gone." He raised one finger. "And do not make sound. Not peep from the lips."

"And the reason they do that?" he asked.

"Honor. They beg for this. You know what they do with the parts cut off? They call them *pao,* treasure, place them in jars on the high shelf. The *kao sheng.* High position. Symbolic of attaining high position. Whole thing is madness."

He agreed.

"But they do it, all the time. Now eunuchs are prepared to take China."

"Come again?"

"This southern slang? I understand you from American South. This where name Cotton comes from."

"Get to the damn point."

Ivan seemed to like for his audience to think him stupid, but this burly Russian was anything but.

"The *Ba.* Secret Chinese organization. Goes back two thousand years. The modern version is no better than original. They intend the play for power. Not good for my country or yours. These are bad people."

"What does that have to do with Cassiopeia?"

"I do not know exactly. But there is the connection."

Now he knew the man was lying. "You're full of crap."

Ivan chuckled. "I like you, Malone. But you do not like me. Lots of negativity."

"Those two back on the street aren't feeling much positivity."

"No worry about them. Killing rids world of two problems."

"Lucky for all of us you were here, on the job."

"Malone, this problem we have is serious."

He lunged forward, grabbed Ivan by his lapels and slammed him into the bricks behind them. He brought his face inches away. "I'd say that was true. Where the hell is Cassiopeia?"

He knew the backups were most likely reacting. He was prepared to whirl around and deal with them both. Of course, that was assuming they didn't decide to shoot first.

"We need this anger," Ivan quietly said, his breath stale.

"Who is *we*?"

"Me, Cotton."

The words came from his right. A new voice. Female. Familiar.

He should have known.

He released his grip and turned.

Ten feet away stood Stephanie Nelle.

CASSIOPEIA COCKED THE GUN'S HAMMER AND AIMED THE weapon straight at Viktor Tomas. "You sorry, no-good mother—"

"Don't say things you'll regret."

The room seemed some sort of gathering place, as there was one chair that held Viktor, three empty chairs, and a few tables and lamps. Windows opened to the front of the house through which she saw the Toyota.

"You tortured me."

He shrugged. "Would you rather it not have been me? I made sure the experience was at least bearable."

She fired into the base of the upholstered chair, aiming for a point between his legs. "Is that what you call it? Bearable?"

He never flinched, his eyes owlish and inexpressive. "Got that out of your system?"

The last time she'd seen this man was a year ago. He'd been serving a Central Asian dictator. Apparently, he'd found new employment.

"Who are you working for?"

He stood from the chair. "Chinese first vice premier Karl Tang."

A renewed burst of anger surged through her. "Give me one good reason why I shouldn't shoot you dead."

"How about that I know where Lev Sokolov's son is being held."

TWELVE

Ni was astonished. "You and the premier have spoken about me?"

Pau nodded. "Many times. We also talk of the nation."

"And why would he talk to you about that?"

"A long time ago, he and I shared much together. He is not the impotent imbecile many think him to be."

Ni knew that most of the Central Committee no longer cared what the premier thought. He was nearing eighty, sickly, and held the position simply because no one had, as yet, emerged with enough support to seize control.

Pau was right.

A division existed within the Chinese Communist Party. Similar to when Mao lay dying in 1976, and Mao's wife and three others formed the infamous Gang of Four. The then-premier and Deng Xiaoping allied to oppose the gang, ultimately winning political control in another ideological battle—Legalism versus Confucianism—the conflict settled outside the public eye, within the Party hierarchy, just as the current conflict would be.

"What is it the premier is working for?"

"Trying to determine what is best for China."

That told him nothing.

"Minister, you may think you enjoy widespread political support, and perhaps you do. But that support would evaporate in an instant if the *Ba* were to seize control. They have always been Legalists. Their every act geared to oppressive, single-minded domination. They would have no tolerance for you."

"What could I have to fear from a group of eunuchs?"

Pau motioned at the open doorway across the courtyard that led back into the exhibit hall. "I have many great manuscripts from our past stored there. Fascinating texts, but there is no Magna Carta. No great forums or halls of independence. Minister, despotism is our inheritance. Chinese history is dominated by warlords, emperors, and communists. Legalists, one and all."

"As if I do not know that. You worked for them once."

"Tell me, what makes you think your future will be any different? What would you have for China? If given the premiership, what would you do?"

Privately, he'd considered that question many times. The nation teetered literally on the brink of collapse. The current national system was simply incapable of generating enough wealth and technology to both compete with the world and effectively contain a billion and a half people. Following Mao's beliefs, concentrating all economic resources in the hands of the state, had failed. But so had Deng's subsequent policies of encouraging unregulated foreign investment.

That had led to exploitation.

Governing China seemed like flying a kite on a windless day. You could adjust the tail, change the design, run faster, but without a breeze to sweep the thing skyward nothing would happen. For decades Chinese leaders had ignored that there was simply no breeze. Instead they tinkered and tinkered, trying to force the kite upward, always failing.

"I want to change everything," he quietly said, surprised he'd voiced the words.

But Pau had finally coaxed them from him.

How did this old man know so much about him?

"Minister, there once was a time when the superiority of Chinese life, with its advanced agriculture, written language, and highly developed arts, was so attractive that those we conquered, or those who conquered us, willingly sought assimilation. They came to admire us, and wanted to be part of *our* society. That desire was complemented by an application of humane Confucian ritual—which stressed harmony, hierarchy, and discipline. There are countless ancient texts that reference peoples who, centuries ago, ceased to exist as separate ethnic groups, so complete was their assimilation. What happened? What changed us into something to be avoided?"

"We destroyed ourselves," he said.

China had indeed gone through successive cycles of unification and fragmentation—and each time something was lost. Something irretrievable. A part of the collective conscience. A part of China.

"Now you understand why I left," Pau quietly said.

No, he actually still didn't.

"Our dynasties have fallen with an almost eerie predictability," Pau said. "Often early leaders are masterful, while later ones are feeble, unmotivated, or mere puppets. Inevitably, corruption combines power and money, without the benefit of the law to prevent abuse. An absence of clear rules on political succession generates chaos. Rebellions eventually ferment, as the military weakens. The government then isolates itself and weakens. The end is never in doubt." Pau went silent a moment. "That has been the fate of every Chinese dynasty for 6,000 years. Now it's the communists' turn."

He could not argue with that conclusion. He recalled a trip to the south a few months ago during another investigation. A local official, an old friend, had driven him from the airport. Along the way they'd passed billboards advertising new apartments with swimming pools, gardens, and modern kitchens.

"The people are tired of Cultural Revolutions and wars," his friend had said. "They like material things."

"And you?" he'd asked.

"I like them, too. I want a comfortable life."

That comment had stuck with him. It spoke volumes about China's current state, where the government merely mended or patched problems, making do. Mao had preached a pride in poverty. Trouble was, nobody believed that anymore.

Pau bent down and, in the garden sand, sketched two characters.

Ni knew what they meant. "Revolution."

Pau stood. "More accurately, 'withdrawal of the mandate.' Every Chinese dynasty justified its rise with that phrase. When the Qing dynasty fell in 1912, and the last emperor was forcibly removed, this was how we referred to that historic event. In 1949 Mao stole Chiang Kai-shek's mandate to build a post-Qing republic. It is time for another withdrawal of the mandate. The question is who will lead that effort."

He stared at the older man, his head spinning with suspicions. The investigator within him had retreated. Now he was thinking like the politician—the leader—he wanted to be.

"Communism has outlived its historical role," Pau said. "Unchecked economic growth and raw nationalism can no longer support it. There simply is nothing connecting the current Chinese form of government to its people. The demise of the Soviets proved that flaw clearly. Now it's happening again. Unemployment within China is out of control. Hundreds of millions are affected. Beijing's condescension, like Moscow's decades ago, is inexcusable. Minister, you must realize that the same nationalism that comforts the Party today could well hurl China into fascism tomorrow."

"Why do you think I am fighting for power?" he spit out. "Do you think I want that? Do you think the people who support me want that?"

"But you have discovered a problem, haven't you?"

How did this sage, whom he'd met only today, know all that troubled him?

"Moscow's collapse frightens you," Pau said. "How could it not? But we are different. We are better suited to living with contradictions. Our rulers have long proclaimed themselves Confucians, then ruled as Legalists, yet no one ever questioned that dichotomy. And unlike Russians, most Chinese do not lack for the necessities of life, or a few gadgets in their home. Our Party is not ignorant. Even with all of our flaws, we will not commit political suicide. So your dilemma is clear. How do you persuade a billion and a half people to discard the norm and follow you to the unknown?"

He waited for the answer to that question.

"Pride, Minister. Such a simple thing. But appealing to that could well be your answer."

THIRTEEN

MALONE SAT AT THE TABLE IN THE CAFÉ NORDEN, NESTLED close to an open second-story window. Outside, Højbro Plads vibrated with people. Stephanie Nelle and Ivan had also found chairs. Ivan's two minders were downstairs, at one of the exterior tables.

"The tomato bisque soup is great here," he told them both.

Ivan rubbed his belly. "Tomatoes give me the gas."

"Then by all means, let's avoid that," Stephanie said.

Malone had known Stephanie a long time, having worked as one of her original twelve agents at the Magellan Billet. She'd created the Justice Department unit, personally recruiting twelve men and women, each bringing to the table a special skill. Malone's had been a career in the navy, where he rose to commander, capable of flying planes and handling himself in dangerous situations. His law degree from Georgetown, and ability in a courtroom, only added to his résumé. Stephanie's presence here, on this beautiful day in Denmark, signaled nothing but trouble. Her association with Ivan compounded the situation. He knew her attitude on working with the Russians.

Only when necessary.

And he agreed.

The café tables were crowded, people drifting up and down from a corner staircase, many toting shopping bags. He wondered why they were talking in public, but figured Stephanie knew what she was doing.

"What's going on here?" he asked his former boss.

"I learned of Cassiopeia's involvement with Lev Sokolov a few days ago. I learned about the Russian's interest, too."

He was still pissed about the two murders. "You killed those two I was after so we'd have no choice but to deal with you," he said to Ivan. "Couldn't let me learn anything from them, right?"

"They are bad people. Bad, bad people. They deserve what they get."

"I didn't know that would happen," Stephanie said to him. "But I shouldn't be surprised."

"You two acquainted?" he asked her.

"Ivan and I have dealt with each other before."

"I not ask you to help," Ivan said. "This not involve America."

But he realized Stephanie had interjected herself into their business practicing the old adage *Keep your friends close and your enemies closer.*

"Cotton," she said. "Cassiopeia has involved herself in something that is much bigger than she suspects. China is in the midst of an internal power struggle. Karl Tang, the first vice premier, and Ni Yong, the head of the Communist Party's anti-corruption department, are about to square off for control. We've been watching this battle, which is rapidly escalating into a war. Like I said, I became aware of Cassiopeia's entrance a few days ago. When we dug further, we found Ivan was also interested—"

"So you hopped on a plane and flew to Denmark."

"That's my job, Cotton."

"This isn't my job. Not anymore."

"None of us," Ivan said, "wants Tang to win. He is Mao again, only worse."

He pointed at Ivan. "You told me about a missing child and man named Lev Sokolov."

"Comrade Sokolov is the geologist," Ivan said. "He is Russian, but works for Chinese. Let us say he knows information that would be better he not know."

"Which is why it was better when he was dead," he pointed out.

Ivan nodded.

"What is it he knows?"

Ivan shook his head. "It is better you not know."

He faced Stephanie. "I hope you know."

She said nothing.

His anger rose. "What has Cassiopeia stumbled into that's so damn important somebody would waterboard her?"

Stephanie again did not answer him, though it was clear she knew the answer. Instead, she leveled her gaze at Ivan. "Tell him."

The Russian seemed to consider the request, and Malone suddenly realized that Ivan was no field agent. He was a decision maker.

Like Stephanie.

"Vitt," Ivan said, "is after the artifact. A lamp Karl Tang wants. When Sokolov does not cooperate, Tang steals Sokolov's son. Then Sokolov does two things Tang does not expect. He calls Vitt and disappears. No one sees Sokolov for two weeks now." He snapped his fingers again. "Gone."

"So Karl Tang grabbed Cassiopeia?" Malone asked.

Ivan nodded. "I say yes."

"What happened out there today, Cotton?" Stephanie asked.

He told her about the note, the waterboarding, his improvisation. "Seemed like the best play. Of course, I didn't know I had an audience."

"I assure you," she said, "we were going to pursue those two to see where they led. I was going to brief you after. Killing them was not part of my plan."

"You Americans nose into my business," Ivan said. "Then want to tell me how to do it."

"Get real," Malone said. "You killed the two leads that could point us somewhere so we're more dependent on you."

Ivan shrugged. "Bad things happen. Take what you have."

He wanted to plant a fist in the irritating SOB's face, but knew better. So he asked, "Why is that lamp so important?"

Ivan shrugged. "It comes from old tomb. Sokolov has to have it to satisfy Karl Tang."

"Where is it?" he asked.

"In Antwerp. That is why Vitt travels there four days ago. She disappears two days later."

He wondered what could possibly have rankled the Russians to the point that they mounted a full-scale intelligence operation, dispatching a mid- to high-level operative and, to thwart the Americans, brazenly shooting two people in the middle of Copenhagen. Somebody, somewhere, was screaming that *this was important.* And why was Washington interested enough to have the Magellan Billet involved? Stephanie was usually called in only when conventional intelligence channels no longer were viable. Cassiopeia had certainly stumbled into something important enough that people were willing to torture her. Was she being tortured again, right now? Those two lying dead in front of the Hotel d'Angleterre had not reported in, so whoever sent the video surely suspected that the retrieval had gone wrong.

"I should get to my computer," he said. "They may try to contact me again."

"I doubt that's going to happen," Stephanie said. "When Ivan decided to improvise, he may have sealed Cassiopeia's fate."

He didn't want to hear that, but she was right. Which made him madder. He glared at Ivan. "You don't seem concerned."

"I am hungry."

The Russian caught the attention of a server and pointed toward a plate of røget in a glass-fronted case, displaying five fingers. The woman acknowledged that she understood how many of the smoked fish to bring.

"They will give you gas," Malone said.

"But they are tasty. Danes are good at fish."

"Is this now a full-scale Billet operation?" he asked Stephanie.

She nodded. "Big time."

"What do you want me to do?" He pointed at Ivan. "Sergeant Schultz here knows nothing, sees nothing, hears nothing."

"Who says this? I never say this. I know plenty. And I love *Hogan's Heroes.*"

"You're just a dumb Russian."

The stout man grinned. "Oh, I see. You want to anger me. Aggravate, yes? Big, stupid man will lose temper and say more than he should." He waggled a stubby finger. "You watch too many *CSI* on television. Or *NCIS.* I love that show. Mark Harmon is the tough guy."

He decided to try a different tack. "What was to happen when Cassiopeia found the lamp?"

"She gives to Tang, who returns boy."

"You don't really believe that."

"Me? No. Karl Tang is not honest. That boy is gone. I know that. You know that—"

"Cassiopeia knows that," Stephanie finished.

"Exactly," Malone said. "So she hedged her bets and hid the lamp away. They grabbed her. She told them I had it, bargaining for time."

"I know little of her," Ivan said. "She is smart?"

Maybe not smart enough, considering. "Ivan here tells me that eunuchs are going to take over China. The *Ba,* he called them."

Stephanie nodded. "They're a radical faction. They have big plans, none of which is good for us, or anyone else. The State Department thought them improbable, but they were wrong. That's another reason why I'm here, Cotton."

He caught her quandary. Russians or Chinese? A headache or an upset stomach? But he sensed something else. More than she wanted to discuss at the moment.

The server brought the five fish, smelling as if they'd just been caught.

"Ah," Ivan said. "Wonderful. You are sure you do not want any?"

He and Stephanie shook their heads.

Ivan chomped down on one of the corpses. "I will say this concerns big things. Important. Things we do not want the Chinese to know."

"How about the Americans?" he asked.

"You either."

"And Sokolov told the Chinese?"

Ivan chewed his fish. "I not know. This is why we need to know about the lamp."

Malone glanced outside. His shop stood across the sunny square. People streamed in and out the front door, more swarming the busy square like bees around their honeycombs. He should be selling books. He liked what he did. He employed four locals who did a good job keeping the shelves stocked. He was proud of his business. Quite a few Danes now regularly bought their collectible editions from him. Over the past three years he'd gained a reputation as a man who could deliver what they wanted. Similar to the dozen years when he was one of Stephanie Nelle's agents.

At the moment, Cassiopeia needed him to deliver.

"I'm going to Antwerp," he said.

Ivan was devouring another fish. "And what to do when you get there? You know where to look?"

"Do you?"

Ivan stopped eating and smiled.

Bits of flesh had lodged between his brown teeth.

"I know where Vitt is."

FOURTEEN

CASSIOPEIA ASSESSED WHAT VIKTOR HAD SAID ABOUT LEV Sokolov's missing child. Again she asked, "Who do you work for?"

"When I left the Central Asian Federation, I headed east and ended up in China. I found lots of employment opportunities there."

"Especially for a lying, double-dealing SOB like you."

He shook his head. "I can't believe you feel that way. What I did in Central Asia was my job. And I did it well. The mission objectives were all met."

"And I was almost killed. Twice."

"That's the operative word. *Almost.* Again, I did my job."

She knew he was avoiding the question. "Who do you work for?"

"I'm telling the truth. Karl Tang."

"A bit of a drop for you. From the supreme president of the Central Asian Federation to China's second in command."

"He pays well, there's health and dental and three weeks' paid vacation. He's starting a retirement plan next year."

His humor did not interest her. "You sent those men after me two days ago?"

Viktor nodded. "We couldn't let you leave Belgium with that lamp."

"Why? Tang wanted it."

"He has no intention of returning Sokolov's boy. So he decided to take control of the lamp here."

"Why not just go to Pau Wen himself? Or send you? Why me?"

"I honestly don't know."

She kept the gun leveled. "*Honestly?* Now there's a word not in your vocabulary." Her gaze zeroed in. "You tortured me."

"I made sure you weren't tortured."

"Not from my perspective."

The features on his face softened. "Would you rather have been waterboarded by someone who really meant it?"

He'd changed from a year ago. Though still short and burly, his shocks of then-unkempt hair had been replaced with a neat trim above the ears. The wide nose and deep-set eyes, from some Slavic influence, remained, but the skin was swarthier than in Central Asia. He was early forties, no older, and had shed baggy clothes, which had then concealed shoulders and arms obviously accustomed to exercise, for more stylish, and snugly fitting, trousers and a designer shirt.

"Where's the boy?" she asked.

"Sokolov played the Russians. Now he's playing the Chinese. And those two you don't mess with, especially the Chinese. They kill with no repercussions, since they are the law."

"We're not in China."

"But Sokolov is. Tang is looking for him. I assume you hid him away, but it's only a matter of time before he's found. Tang has spies by the tens of thousands, every one of whom want to please the first vice premier, perhaps even the man who will be the next premier of China. You or I don't really matter in the overall scheme."

She doubted that. "What are you doing for him?"

"Tang hired me last fall. He needed a non-Chinese operative, and I was between jobs. He didn't have me working this particular assignment until I heard your name mentioned. When I explained my connection—with some necessary adjustments to the facts—Tang sent me here."

She lowered the gun, her emotions riding a thin edge. "Do you have any idea what you put me through?"

"I had no choice. Tang gives the orders. I gave you an opportunity to escape yesterday when I had food brought, but you were asleep. I sent my compatriot in there a little while ago, hoping this time you'd act." He pointed at the gun. "Which you apparently did. I was waiting here for you." He motioned at the phone lying on the table. "The call was fake."

"And what made you think I wouldn't just leave?"

"Because you're angry."

This man knew her well. "Any more helpers around?"

"Just the one in your room. You hurt him?"

"It'll leave a mark."

"Cassiopeia, Karl Tang wants that lamp. Can't you just give it to him and be done with this?"

"And lose that child? Like you say, my having that lamp is the only bargaining chip I possess. You said you know where the boy is being held. Tell me."

"It's not that easy. You'd never get near him. Let me help."

"I work alone."

"Is that why you involved Malone? And I knew you were lying on that one, but Tang made me make contact."

"What happened in Copenhagen?"

"I haven't heard from the two who were hired for the job. But with Malone, something bad surely happened to them both."

She needed to call Denmark and explain. But not here. "Where are the keys to that car outside?"

"In the ignition." He stood from the chair. "Let me go with you. I can't stay. No matter what I say, Tang will hold me responsible for your escape. My job with him is over. I have good intel on his operation that could prove valuable."

She considered the proposal. It actually made sense. No matter how she felt about Viktor Tomas, he was clearly resourceful. Last year, he'd cleverly managed to wedge amazingly close to the president of the Central Asian Federation. Now he was near Karl Tang, who held the key to reuniting Lev Sokolov with his son. No doubt she'd made a mess of things. She needed to retrieve the lamp, then broker a deal. So why not a little assistance from a man who could make direct contact with Tang?

And who knew where Sokolov's child was located.

"All right," she said. "Let's go."

She stepped aside and allowed Viktor to leave first.

He reached for the cell phone and pocketed the unit. Just as he passed, headed for the door, she raised the gun above her head and slammed the butt into the base of his neck.

A moan seeped from his mouth as a hand reached upward.

She drove the gun's hard metal into his left temple.

His eyes rolled skyward and he collapsed to the floor.

"Like I'm going to believe a word you say."

FIFTEEN

TANG WANDERED AMONG THE CLAY WARRIORS, KEEPING THEIR eternal guard. He'd left Pit 3 and returned to Pit 1. His expert was gone. The fact that the Pit 3 repository contained no Confucian texts, though all six should have been there, was telling. As was the silver watch, which he still held.

He'd suspected much had happened thirty years ago.

Now he knew.

Back then this region of Lintong County had been rural farmland. Everyone realized that the First Emperor lay beneath the hill-like mound that had stood there for the past 2,200 years. But no one had known of the underground army, and its discovery had led to a flurry of digging. For years workers toiled night and day removing layers of earth, sand, and gravel, photographing and recording the hundreds of thousands of shards. More workers then reassembled the shattered figures, one piece at a time, the fruits of their exhaustive labors now standing all around him.

The terra-cotta army had come to be regarded as a monumental expression of Chinese communal talents, symbolizing a unified state, a creative, compliant culture, a government that worked for and with its people.

A near-perfect symbolism.

One of the few times he'd agreed with using the past to justify the present.

But apparently, during all that digging, a cache of documents—Qin Shi's lost palace library—had also been found.

Yet no one was told.

And a reminder of that omission remained.

A watch.

Left on purpose?

Who knew.

But given the person who'd most likely made the discovery, Tang could not discount anything.

Pau Wen.

Special counsel to the Central Committee, adviser to both Mao Zedong and Deng Xiaoping, a learned man whose value came from his ability to deliver desired results—as nothing secured privilege better than repeated success. Neither Mao nor Deng was the most effective administrator. Both governed with broad strokes across vast canvases and left the details to men like Pau. Tang knew Pau had led many archaeological digs throughout the country and had, at one point, overseen the terra-cotta warrior excavations.

Was the watch he held Pau's?

It had to be.

He faced one of the warriors who stood at the army's vanguard. He and the others with him would have been the first to descend on an enemy, followed by waves and waves of more terrifying men.

Seemingly endless. Indestructible.

Like China itself.

But the nation had come to a crossroads. Thirty years of unprecedented modernization had produced an impatient generation, one unmoved by the pretensions of a communist regime, one that focused on family, cultural and economic life, rather than nationality. The doctor at the hospital seemed an excellent example.

China was changing.

But not a single regime in all Chinese history had relinquished power without bloodshed, and the Communist Party would not be the first.

His plan for power would take daring, but he hoped that what he was searching to prove could provide a measure of certainty, an air of legitimacy, perhaps even a source of national pride.

Movement above caught his attention.

He'd been waiting.

At the railing five meters overhead a figure sheathed in black appeared, then another. Both forms were lean and muscular, their hair cut short, their faces unemotional.

"Down here," he quietly said.

Both men disappeared.

When he'd summoned his expert from the West, he'd also ordered that two more men accompany him. They'd waited nearby until his call, which he'd made on his walk over from Pit 3.

The men appeared at the far end of the line of warriors and approached without a sound, stopping a few meters away.

"Burn it all," he ordered. "There are electrical cables and a transformer, so the lights can be blamed."

Both men bowed and left.

MALONE AND STEPHANIE CROSSED HØJBRO PLADS. THE LATE-afternoon sun had receded behind Copenhagen's jagged rooflines. Ivan was gone, back in one hour, saying there were matters that required his attention.

Malone stopped at a fountain and sat on its damp edge. "You had a purse snatched right here a couple of years ago."

"I remember. Turned into quite an adventure."

"I want to know exactly what this is all about."

She remained silent.

"You need to tell me what's at stake," he said. "All of it. And it's not a lost child or the next premier of China."

"Ivan thinks we don't know, but we do."

"Enlighten me."

"It's kind of remarkable, really. And turns on something Stalin learned from the Nazis."

Now they were getting somewhere.

"During World War II, refineries in Romania and Hungary supplied much of Germany's oil. By 1944 those refineries had been bombed to oblivion, and not so coincidentally the war ended soon after. Stalin watched as Germany literally ran out of oil. He resolved that Russia would always be self-sufficient. He saw oil dependency as a catastrophic weakness to be avoided at any cost."

Not a big shock. "Wouldn't everyone?"

"Unlike the rest of the world, including us, Stalin figured out how to do it. A professor named Nikolai Kudryavtsev supplied him the answer."

He waited.

"Kudryavtsev postulated that oil had nothing to do with fossils."

He knew the conventional wisdom. Over millions of years an ancient primeval morass of plants and animals, dinosaurs included, had been engulfed by sedimentary deposits. Millions more years of heat and pressure eventually compressed the mix into petroleum, and gave it the name *fossil fuel*.

"Instead of being biotic, from once-alive material, Kudryavtsev said oil is abiotic—simply a primordial material the earth forms and exudes on a continual basis."

He instantly grasped the implications. "It's endless?"

"That's the question that's brought me here, Cotton. The one we have to answer."

She explained about Soviet oil exploration in the 1950s that discovered massive reserves thousands of feet deep, at levels far below what would have been expected according to the fossil fuel theory.

"And it may have happened to us," she said, "in the Gulf of Mexico. A field was found in 1972 more than a mile down. Its reserves have been declining at a surprisingly slow rate. The same thing has occurred at several sites on the Alaskan North Slope. It baffles geologists."

"You're saying wells replenish themselves?"

She shook her head. "I'm told it depends on the faulting in the surrounding rock. At the Gulf site the ocean floor is cut with deep fissures. That would theoretically allow the pressurized oil to move from deep below, closer to the surface. There's one other thing, too."

He could tell that, as usual, she'd come prepared.

"The geological age of the crude coming out of those wells I mentioned, the ones seemingly replenishing, is different than it was twenty years ago."

"And that means?"

"The oil is coming from a different source."

He also caught what else it meant.

Not from dead plants or dinosaurs.

"Cotton, biotic oil is shallow. Hundreds or a few thousand feet down. Abiotic oil is much deeper. There is no scientific way for organic material to end up so deep beneath the surface, so there has to be another source for that oil. Stalin figured that the Soviet Union could obtain a massive strategic advantage if this new theory about oil's availability could be proven. He foresaw back in the early 1950s that oil would become politically important."

He now grasped the implications, but wanted to know, "Why have I never heard of this?"

"Stalin had no reason to inform his enemies of what he learned, especially us. Anything published on this was printed in Russian, and back then few outside of the Soviet Union read the language. The West became locked into the fossil fuel theory and any alternative was quickly deemed crackpot."

"So what's changed?"

"We don't think it's crackpot."

TANG LEFT THE PIT 1 MUSEUM AND STEPPED OUT INTO THE warm night. The plaza that encompassed the historical complex loomed still and quiet. Midnight was approaching.

His cell phone vibrated.

He removed the unit and noted its display. Beijing. He answered.

"Minister," he was told, "we have good news. Lev Sokolov has been found."

"Where?"

"Lanzhou."

Only a few hundred kilometers to the west.

"He's under close surveillance, and is unaware we are there."

Now he could move forward. He listened to the particulars, then ordered, "Keep him under watch. I'll be there in the morning. Early."

"There is more," his assistant said. "The supervisor at the drill site called. His message says you should hurry."

Gansu lay two hundred kilometers north. The final stop on this planned journey. His helicopter waited nearby, fueled, ready to go. "Tell him I'll be there within two hours."

"And a final matter."

His subordinates had been busy.

"Minister Ni has been inside Pau Wen's residence for three hours."

"Have you learned if Ni's trip was officially sanctioned?"

"Not that we can determine. He booked the flight two days ago himself and left abruptly."

Which only confirmed that Ni Yong possessed spies within Tang's office. How else would he have known to go to Belgium? No surprise, but the depth of Ni's intelligence network worried him. Precious few of his staff were aware of Pau Wen's significance.

"Is Ni still within the compound?" he asked.

"As of ten minutes ago."

"Have both Ni and Pau eliminated."

SIXTEEN

NI FOCUSED ON THE INTERESTING WORD PAU WEN HAD USED. Pride.

"We were once the greatest nation on earth," the older man said. "Possessed of a proven superiority. During the Tang dynasty, if a foreign resident took a Chinese wife he was not allowed to leave China. It was deemed unthinkable to take a woman out of the bounds of civilization, to a lesser realm."

"So what? None of that matters any longer." He was frustrated and it showed. "You sit here, safe in Belgium, while we fight in China. You talk of the past as if it is easily repeated. My task is far more difficult than you imagine."

"Minister, your task is no different from the tasks of many who have come before you. In my time there was no refuge from Mao. No public building was without a statue or bust of him. Framed pictures hung everywhere—on matchboxes, calendars, taxis, buses, planes. Fire engines and locomotives displayed giant photos fixed to the front, banked by red flags. Yet, as now, it was all a lie. Mao's unblemished face rosy with health? That image bore no resemblance to the man. He was old and sick, his teeth blackened. He was ugly, weak looking." Pau motioned at the bowl with fish swimming inside. "Then, and now, China is like fish in trees. Totally lost. Out of place. No hope to survive."

Ni's thoughts were in chaos. His moves after he returned home seemed no longer viable. He'd planned on initiating his quest for the premiership. Many were ready to assist him. They would start the process, recruiting more to their cause. But a new threat had arisen, one that might foretell failure.

He stared around at the courtyard, reminded of what his grandfather had taught him about feng shui.

Where one chose to live had great importance. How one orientated one's house could be even more important. *Face it south. Choose right and the hills are fair, the waters fine, the sun handsome.*

His grandfather had been wise.

Amid confusion, there is peace. Amid peace, one's eyes are opened.

He tried to take heed of that lesson and gather his thoughts back into order, telling himself to stay in control.

"Karl Tang recognizes China's confusion," Pau said. "He also understands the value of national pride. That is most important, Minister. Even as change occurs, no one can lose face, least of all the Party."

"And this lamp is part of that plan?"

Pau nodded. "Tang is many steps ahead of you."

"Why are you telling me this?"

"That explanation would take far too much time, just accept that what I am saying is sincere." Pau's callused hand reached out and touched Ni on the arm. "Minister, you must adjust your thinking. It is good that you learned of Tang's interest and traveled here, but the threat to China is greater than you realize."

"What would you have me do?"

He hated himself for even asking guidance of this thief.

"You are a man to be respected. A man trusted. Use that."

He was not impressed by Pau's flattery.

Truth would be better.

"A few hours after she left this house, Cassiopeia Vitt was taken prisoner by Tang. She managed to hide the lamp before being captured, and I know where. I planned to retake it myself, but the task should now belong to you."

The extent of Pau's deceit became clear. He'd played Ni from the start. And Ni did not like it. But since he had no choice, he asked, "Why is that lamp so important?"

"The fact that you do not know the answer to that question is proof of how far behind Karl Tang you truly are."

He couldn't argue with that. "How do I gain ground?"

"Retrieve the lamp, return to China, then locate a man named Lev Sokolov. He works for the Ministry of Geological Development, in Lanzhou, but he is presently in hiding. Tang abducted his son and is using the boy as leverage to obtain Sokolov's cooperation. I am told Sokolov is the person who can explain the lamp's significance."

"Cooperation for what?"

"That is for you to discover."

Though he sensed Pau Wen well knew. "My information network is extensive, especially regarding Tang. When I learned of his interest in the lamp, I came here personally. Yet not a hint of anything you have said has ever come to my attention."

"Which should make you question your staff. Perhaps there is a spy among them? You will have the lamp soon enough. Return home and find Sokolov."

"And what of those eunuchs who surround me? The ones you say I should fear."

"They will show themselves."

"Is Tang also in danger from them?"

"Obviously not."

"How do I know who *they* are?"

Pau grinned. "Once, we would have a change of voice, an unpleasant falsetto. Beardless, we became soft and fat with little strength. As we aged, that weight shed and deep wrinkles appeared in our faces. The lack of testosterone also manifested itself in odd emotions—we were quick to anger and tears. None of that is true today. Modern supplements mask all side effects, especially if the man is not castrated until adulthood, which is generally the case. Know that it will be nearly impossible, without a visual inspection, for you to know."

"Is Tang after Sokolov?"

Pau nodded. "With all the resources he can muster."

Ni would have to verify everything he'd learned before becoming a convert. "Where is the lamp hidden?"

"Inside the Dries Van Egmond Museum, in Antwerp. It holds a private collection of art and furniture from the 17th and 18th centuries. Cassiopeia Vitt hid the lamp in a boudoir, on the third level, decorated in the Chinese style, that includes some unremarkable Ming porcelain. I have visited there myself. Perhaps she thought it would go unnoticed, at least for a few days. Or if it was noticed, the museum staff would safeguard it. Not a bad decision, considering she had so few options."

Pau telling him the location seemed some verification that the older man was finally being truthful.

"I should go."

"Before you leave," Pau said, "I have one more thing to show you."

He accompanied his host back into the house, following a long corridor to a black lacquered door. On the other side, a wooden staircase wound upward inside a rectangular tower. An open doorway appeared at the top of the stairs. Beyond shone the afternoon light, its warmth allowed in through bare window frames that wrapped all four walls.

"Stay here," Pau said. "Just inside the doorway. That way we won't be visible from outside."

He wondered about the subterfuge.

"If you will glance around the corner," Pau said, "there will be an excellent view of the front drive. Past that, at the highway, you will see a vehicle parked in the woodlands, perhaps half a kilometer away from the main entrance."

He did as instructed, squinting in the bright sunlight and spotting a car, barely visible in the thick trees.

"Careless people," Pau said, behind him. "They work for Tang. They watch this house. Not always. They come and go. But they have been here often the past two days."

"Is that how you suspected Tang would come for the lamp?"

"It seemed logical."

In the distant shadows he saw the front grille of another car brake beside the parked one. Two men exited each car, assault rifles being shouldered.

Fear pricked his spine.

The men advanced toward the gray walls, walking toward the open front gate.

"That's somewhat unexpected," Pau calmly said.

Men with guns were approaching, and all this man could say was *unexpected*.

He was concerned.

Greatly.

SEVENTEEN

MALONE ASSESSED THE STARTLING INFORMATION STEPHANIE was providing.

"The Western mind-set," she said, "is that oil is a fossil fuel. Remember, back in the 1960s, when all the Sinclair gas stations displayed a dinosaur as a trademark? There were TV commercials that showed dinosaurs dying, decaying, and turning into oil. Ask ten people where oil comes from and they all would say dead dinosaurs."

He recalled the ads she was referring to, and he had to admit that he, too, had been indoctrinated. Oil was a fossil fuel, a finite resource.

"Imagine, Cotton, if oil is infinite. The earth produces it continually, as a *renewable* resource. The Russians have long believed this."

"Stephanie, what does any of this have to do with Cassiopeia?"

A chill had crept into the late-afternoon air. Ivan would return shortly, and they would all leave for Antwerp. He must understand the problem before then.

"Ever heard of the Dniepr-Donetsk basin in eastern Ukraine?"

He shook his head.

"In the 1950s the area was abandoned as a prospective place to drill. *No potential for oil production* was the conclusion of the survey team. We know this because an American well driller, a man named J. F. Kenney, was part of the team that studied the site with the Russians. No source rock for fossil fuels was located there." She paused. "Today, that basin contains more than 400 million barrels of proven reserves, found deep underground. The man who determined that to be the case is Lev Sokolov. He was a Russian expert on the abiotic theory of oil."

"How do we know that the survey team in the 1950s wasn't just wrong, and there was oil there all the time?"

"It happened again. On the Kola Peninsula, in northern Russia. Another place that had no prospect of production—under the fossil fuel theory. Yet the Russians drilled down seven miles and hit methane gas. No one ever believed that methane would be found that deep in granite rock. The fossil fuel theory would never support the finding, but the gas was right where Sokolov predicted."

"And now Washington is finally interested in all this."

"With a vengeance. This could change the world balance of power, which explains why Karl Tang is interested. Ivan's right. Tang's a threat to us all. If he assumes control of China, the destabilization across the region, across the globe, will be enormous. Especially if he has unlimited oil at his disposal."

"President Daniels wants Tang stopped?"

"Actually, Cotton, we want him dead."

He understood the enormity of the statement. America did not *officially* assassinate people.

But it happened.

"And you're hoping the Russians do the deed?"

She shrugged. "Enough that I forced myself into their business. Ivan wasn't happy to see me. Bad enough that Sokolov was alive, he sure did not want us involved."

"How did he know about me?"

"From those two couriers, is my guess. When the one brought that note to your shop, his men were watching."

She'd left something out. "And where were you?"

"Watching too. He informed me about your meeting at Tivoli only after you were already on your way there."

"So you already knew some of what Ivan told you back in the café?"

She nodded. "I did. I figured we'd have a talk."

"What did you know about Cassiopeia?"

"I had no idea she was being tortured."

He believed her on that one.

"We've done the math, Cotton. If Tang becomes premier, he will undo fifty years of hard-fought diplomacy. He thinks China has been mistreated by everyone and he wants retribution. He'll reassert Chinese dominance any way and every way he can. Right now, we keep China in line thanks to its foreign energy dependence. We maintain a sixty-day oil reserve, and Japan keeps a hundred. China has barely ten days' worth. A naval blockade could easily choke the country into submission. Eighty percent of China's imported oil passes through the Strait of Hormuz or the Strait of Malacca. Those are a long way from China, and we control both."

"So they behave themselves, knowing what we could do?"

"Something like that, though the threat is never voiced. Bad form, when dealing with the Chinese. They don't like reminders of weakness."

He was glad not to be a diplomat.

"If Tang has unlimited oil available to him," she said, "we'll lose what little leverage we have. China practically controls the world currency markets now, and they are the number one lender to us. Though *we* don't like to admit it, we need China. If Chinese oil wells flow forever, they'll be able to expand their economy at will, force whatever policies they want, unconcerned about what anyone cares or thinks."

"Which makes Russia nervous."

"Enough that they just might take Karl Tang out."

Okay, he was convinced. This was serious.

"I know you may think me foolish. But believe me, I've hedged my bets. I'm not relying on Ivan 100 percent. Still—"

"You need a little more help."

"Something like that."

"I assume that means we have to find Sokolov before Ivan does. And Cassiopeia seems the fastest route in."

She nodded. "Let's play the Russian's game and find her. If Ivan can stop Tang along the way, then that's good for us. If not, I need your help getting Sokolov away from them."

He knew the score. Even if Tang prevailed and seized control of China, if the West had Sokolov, one bargaining chip would be replaced by another.

"I just hope Cassiopeia can hold out until we get there."

TANG GLANCED OUT THE HELICOPTER WINDOW AS THE CHOPper rose into the night air. He caught sight of flickering bursts of light from the Pit 3 building and realized the remaining cache of Qin Shi manuscripts was burning. Only a few moments would be required to vaporize every silk and turn brittle bamboo into ash. By the time any alarm was sounded, nothing would remain. The cause? Electrical short. Faulty wiring. Bad transformer. Whatever. Nothing would point to arson. Another problem solved. More of the past eradicated.

What was happening in Belgium now concerned him.

The copilot caught his attention and motioned to a nearby headset. Tang snapped it over his ears.

"There is a call for you, Minister."

He waited, then a familiar voice said, "Everything went well."

Viktor Tomas, calling from Belgium. About time.

"Is Vitt on her way?" Tang asked.

"She escaped, exactly as I predicted. However, she managed to knock me out cold before she left. My head aches."

"Can you track her?"

"As long as she keeps that gun with her. So far the signal from the pinger inside is working."

"Excellent forward thinking. Was she glad to see you?"

"Not particularly."

"You need to know that Pau Wen is receiving a visit, as we speak. I ordered a strike."

"I thought I was in charge here."

"Whatever gave you that impression?"

"I can't ensure success if you override me. I'm here, you're not."

"I ordered a strike. End of discussion."

A moment of silence passed, then Viktor said, "I'm headed out to track Vitt. I'll report when there's a development."

"Once you have the lamp—"

"Not to worry," Viktor said. "I know. Vitt will not be left alive. But I do it my way. Is that acceptable?"

"As you say, you're there, I'm here. Handle it *your* way."

PART
TWO

EIGHTEEN

CASSIOPEIA SLAMMED THE GEARSHIFT INTO FIRST, RELEASED the clutch, and charged the Toyota down the highway. Another two clicks and she was in third. She was unsure where she was headed, only that it was away from Viktor Tomas.

Did he really think she'd take him along?

She glanced in the rearview mirror. No cars in sight. A treeless landscape stretched out on each side of the road, and the only bumps breaking the green monotony were grazing cattle and the slender steeples of distant churches. She'd already determined that she was somewhere in north-central Belgium, since the country's wooded valleys and high plateaus were confined to its southern portions. Near the German border she knew were bogs and swamps, none of which was visible here. Neither was the ocean, which bordered the extreme north.

She shifted into fourth, kept cruising, and glanced at the digital clock: 5:20 PM. The gas gauge read three-quarters full.

Awfully convenient.

Viktor sent the guard into her cell knowing that she'd overpower him, then waited, faking a call, for her to confront him.

She thought of Central Asia the last time Viktor was supposedly on her side.

"No way," she said.

She locked the brakes.

The Toyota slewed side-to-side, clutching its way to a stop. Viktor had then played a role, flipping sides by the hour—with the Asians, then the Americans, then back. True, he'd ultimately ended on her side and helped, but still—what about today?

Viktor wanted her to take the car.

Okay, she'd take it, but not where he assumed. The Dries Van Egmond Museum in Antwerp was surely closed for the day. She'd have to wait until dark before retrieving the lamp.

And she could not lead Viktor there.

She shifted into first and drove on. Two kilometers later she came to an intersection. A sign informed her that Antwerp lay twenty kilometers west.

She sped in that direction.

NI DESCENDED FROM THE STAIRCASE AND FOLLOWED A SUR-prisingly spry Pau Wen back into the courtyard, where his host clapped his hands three times. A door slid open and four young Chinese appeared, each wearing a gray jumpsuit and black sneakers.

One of the men he immediately recognized.

From the video.

"Yes, Minister," Pau said. "He serves me."

The compatriots moved with the firm steps of athletes, stopping before Pau in an attentive line, their eyes flat and hard, faces immobile.

"Four armed men are approaching through the front gate. You know what to do."

They nodded in unison and fled the courtyard.

"I thought you lived alone," Ni said.

"I never actually said that."

He grabbed Pau's arm. "I'm tired of your lies. I am not someone to play with."

Pau clearly did not appreciate the assault. "I'm sure you are not. But while you are demonstrating your importance, armed men are approaching this house. Have you considered the possibility that you may be their target?"

He released his grip.

No, he hadn't.

Pau motioned and they reentered the house, finding a small ante-room, bare except for a red oval rug and two black laquered cabinets. Pau removed a key from his pocket and unlocked one of the cabinets. Inside, hanging on silver pegs, were assorted handguns.

"Choose, Minister," Pau said.

He reached for a Glock.

"The magazine is fully loaded," Pau said. "Spares are in the drawer."

He checked his weapon to be sure, then retrieved three magazines.

A gun in hand felt good.

Pau gripped his shoulder. "Let us send a message to Karl Tang that the coming fight will not be easy."

CASSIOPEIA ENTERED THE OUTSKIRTS OF ANTWERP. SHE KNEW the city, having visited many times. The Scheldt River flanked one side, the other three protected by a series of boulevards whose names re-called Allied powers that fought for Flanders' freedom in the First World War. Its historic center fanned out around a slim-spired cathe-dral, a Renaissance town hall, and a brooding castle. Not a tourist-thronged medieval theme park but a working, thriving city loaded with reminders from when it was one of the Continent's most influential places.

She found the central railway station, an early 20th-century riot of marble, glass, and wrought iron, and parked a block away in a clearly marked illegal zone. If Viktor was tracking her by the car, the trail would end here. She hoped the local police would tow the thing quickly.

She stuffed the gun at her waist and allowed her open shirttail to conceal the bulge. Her mind and body were at the breaking point. She needed sleep. But she also had to rid herself of Karl Tang, at least until she was ready to negotiate.

She crossed the street and passed beneath a flurry of blooming trees, toward Antwerp's zoo. Between the train station and the city's natural history museum stretched a park overgrown with foliage. A quiet locale, particularly now as the zoo had closed for the day. She found an empty bench that afforded her a view of the parked car a couple of hundred meters away, with the added benefit of a tree trunk behind her.

She lay on the bench, the gun atop her navel beneath her shirt.

Darkness was at least three hours away.

She'd rest till then.

And watch.

NINETEEN

TANG STEPPED FROM THE CAR AND STUDIED THE WELL-LIT SITE. The portable rig supported a red-and-white derrick that towered forty meters. When he'd requisitioned the equipment from the oil ministry, he'd known that at least a 600hp mechanically driven plant, equipped with an inner circulation and water-cooling system, rated to at least 3,000 meters of drilling, would be required. Quietly, he'd dispatched the proper rig overland to Gansu, where he'd once served in the provincial government. According to legend, this region had been the birthplace of Fú Xi, the mythical patriarch of all Chinese, and some recent excavations had confirmed that people had in fact lived here as far back as 10,000 years ago.

He'd slept during the ninety-minute flight, preparing himself for what lay ahead. The next forty-eight hours would be critical. Every move had to be made with no miscalculations, every opportunity maximized with no mistakes.

He listened to the grind of diesel turbines, electrical generators, and circulation pumps. Gansu was a treasure trove of natural resources, brimming with coal, iron, copper, and phosphorous. His ancestors had known that, too. Their records, some of which survived, some of which he'd stumbled onto in the newly opened chamber at Pit 3, noted extensive inventories of precious metals and minerals. He'd ordered this particular exploration in search of one of those resources—oil.

The ground upon which he stood had once supported one of China's main sources. Unfortunately, Gansu's wells had run dry more than 200 years ago.

The site superintendent approached, a man with a thin face, a high forehead, and strands of stringy black hair swept back. He worked directly for the Ministry of Science, sent here by Tang, along with a trusted crew. Gansu's governor had questioned the unauthorized activity but was told simply that the ministry was exploring, and if all went well the results might prove economically beneficial.

Which was the truth.

Just more so for him than the governor.

"I'm glad you were nearby," the superintendent yelled over the noise. "I don't think I could have contained it much longer." A smile came to the man's thin lips. "We've done it."

He realized what that declaration meant.

This site had been specifically selected eleven months ago, not by geologists but by historians. An area had been cleared and leveled, then an access road cut through the nearby forest. A 2,200-year-old map, discovered in northwest Gansu, had been the source. The map, drawn on four identical pine plates, depicted the administrative division, geography, and economics of this region during the time of Qin Shi. Eighty-two locales were denoted by name, along with rivers, mountains, and forests. One of those rivers still flowed five hundred meters away. Even the distances of the imperial roadways were clearly specified. Lacking longitude and latitude coordinates, transposing those locales to reality had proven difficult, but it had been done.

By Jin Zhao.

Before he was arrested, before his hemorrhage, before his trial, conviction, and execution, Zhao had found this site.

"We hit the depth three days ago," his superintendent reported. "I waited to call you until I was sure." He saw the smile on the man's face. "You were right."

"Show me."

He was led to the drilling platform, where workers were busy. He'd intentionally kept this crew to a minimum.

"We hit oil sand five days ago," the superintendent told him above the intense noise.

He knew what that meant. When cuttings from the mud being drawn up revealed oily sand, oil was not much farther.

"We lowered sensors into the hole. Checked the pressures and extracted core samples. It all looked good. So we started to seal off."

Tang knew what had been done next. Small explosive charges would have been lowered down to blast holes in the newly installed plug. Then tubing would have been snaked through the holes and any leaks sealed. At the top of the tubing, multivalves would have been cemented into place. Oil gushing from a well, in a massive blowout, was the last thing anyone wanted. "Taming the crude" with a measured flow, was far better.

"We've been pumping acid," the superintendent said, "since yesterday. I stopped a few hours ago to wait for your arrival."

Acid was used to dissolve the last remaining centimeters of limestone between the capped well and the oil. Once that was gone, the pressurized oil would flow upward, controlled by the valves.

"Unfortunately, I stopped the acid a little too late. An hour ago this happened."

He watched as the superintendent twisted a valve and black crude drained out into a barrel.

He immediately noticed the pressure. "That's strong."

The man nodded. "There's a lot of oil down there. Especially for a field that went dry two hundred years ago."

He stepped back from the drill hole, remaining beneath the red-and-white derrick. He started thinking more like a scientist and less like a politician, considering the implications.

Incredible.

Jin Zhao had been right.

TWENTY

BELGIUM

NI GRIPPED THE GLOCK AND ADVANCED TOWARD THE FRONT of the house. He entered the vestibule, its walls gray brick with what he assumed was artificial bamboo fronting one section. Steps led down to the main entrance, where a stone fountain gurgled. A clear view of the oak doors was blocked by a green silk screen. He'd not seen Pau's four minions since they had disappeared from the courtyard. Pau had told him to cover the main entrance, then vanished, too.

Four *rat-tat-tats* could be heard outside.

Gunfire.

He wasn't interested in joining the melee, but Pau's words rang in his ears. *Have you considered the possibility that you are their target?*

More shots. Closer this time.

His gaze locked on the doors.

Bullets thudded against the thick wood from the outside, then tore through, pinging off the walls and floor. He dove for cover behind a polished timber that held the roof aloft.

The front doors smashed open.

Two men burst inside with automatic rifles.

He crouched in a defensive posture, aimed, and sent a round their way.

The men scattered.

He was a couple of meters above them, but they carried heavy-duty assault rifles and he wielded only a pistol.

Where was Pau? And his men?

A spurt of automatic fire splintered the timber shielding him. He decided that a retreat was in order, so he rushed deeper into the house.

He passed a tall wooden cabinet, which offered momentary protection.

A slug whistled past his ear.

Sunlight from a sky well illuminated the hall, but there was no way to reach the opening, at least ten meters high. To his right, past swinging lattice door panels, several of which hung open, he spied movement in a courtyard. Another man wielding an automatic rifle and not wearing a gray jumpsuit.

His options were rapidly diminishing. It did seem as if these four were after him, not Pau. He glimpsed the squatting form in the courtyard and spotted a glint of metal as the gunman took aim through the lattice doors. He flattened himself on the floor, scrambling across the varnished wood, as bullets exploded through the wooden slats and cut a path barely a meter above him.

His mind throbbed.

Though a career military man, he'd never actually been under fire. Plenty of training, but the utter confusion of this situation smashed any practiced response he might have offered.

This was insane.

He rolled twice toward a heavy wooden armchair and overturned it so that its thickest portions would offer cover.

He saw a shadow play across the room. The man in the courtyard was advancing.

He came to his knees and sent three rounds through the latticework.

Flesh and bones thudded to stone.

Bullets instantly came in response.

The two from the front door had arrived.

He fired twice in their direction then bolted for the exterior lattice doors, crashing through, his arms forcing splintered wood away as his eyes searched for more danger.

The courtyard was empty.

The man with the automatic rifle lay on the pavement, downed not by two bullet holes, but by an arrow that protruded from his spine.

Ni heard movement behind him and knew what was coming so he sought cover behind a stone planter. Another chattering of gunfire sent a burst of bullets zipping through the courtyard, a few finding the huge glass jar—which shattered, sending a cascade of water and goldfish to the pavement.

He knew little about the remainder of the house, except the exhibit hall, whose door loomed ten meters away. If he could make it there, perhaps he could flee through one of its windows.

But any hope of salvation was dashed when a man appeared, pointing a rifle straight at him.

With two in the house and one dead a few meters away, all four assailants were now accounted for.

"Stand," the man ordered in Chinese. "Leave the gun on the ground."

The two remaining assailants emerged from the house.

He laid the pistol down and rose.

Goldfish slapped their way across the wet stones in desperation. He understood their horror. His breathing was labored, too.

He assessed the three. All Chinese, wiry and strong. Hired help. He employed several thousand just like them, throughout China.

"Have you already killed Pau?" he asked.

"You first," the one man said, shaking his head.

Two swishes preceded the thud of arrows sucking into flesh. Two of the men began to realize that a shaft with feathered ends had pierced their chests. Before they could draw another breath, their bodies shrank to the ground, their guns falling away.

Three men in gray jumpsuits materialized from the sides of the courtyard, each holding a stretched bowstring, an arrow threaded, ready to fire, aimed at the final attacker.

"You may be able to shoot one, two, or maybe all three," Pau's disembodied voice said. "But you will not stop us all."

The man seemed to consider his options, decided he did not want to die, and lowered his rifle.

Pau and the fourth man stepped from the exhibition hall. Two of Pau's men assumed control of the last intruder, leading him away at arrow-point.

"Were you planning on letting them kill me?" Ni yelled at Pau.

"Every trap needs bait, Minister."

He was furious and raised his weapon, but Pau simply ignored him and motioned. The two other men laid aside their bows and quickly gathered the fish from the pavement, disappearing back into the house.

"I raised those goldfish since birth," Pau said. "I hope the shock will not kill them."

He could not care less. "Do you realize what just happened? Those men came to kill me."

"Which was the possibility I mentioned before they arrived. Tang apparently sent them to eliminate us both."

He tasted the acrid flavor of adrenaline in his mouth. His heart pounded. "I must return home."

"What of the lamp?" Pau asked. "I thought you wanted it."

"It's not as important as what awaits there."

"Don't be so sure. I think the answers you seek are here, and I know exactly how to obtain them."

TWENTY-ONE

TANG SAT ALONE. HIS HELICOPTER HAD LEFT TO REFUEL AT AN airport fifty kilometers to the south. He'd need full tanks, ready to fly, in four hours. That's when he'd deal with Lev Sokolov.

The portable buildings used by the drilling crew as sleeping quarters were located a quarter of a kilometer from the derrick, and the superintendent had offered his trailer. The room was neat, the hot plate and refrigerator clean, a few plastic dishes stacked beside a microwave oven. Not his usual accommodations, but perfect for the next few hours. He wasn't sleepy, as the short nap on the flight from the museum had been adequate. He welcomed the solitude, and pondered the fact that everything around him had once been a thriving part of Qin Shi's First Empire.

Incredible what they had achieved so long ago.

His ancestors had invented the umbrella, the seismograph, the spinning wheel, porcelain, the steam engine, kites, playing cards, fishing reels, even whiskey.

But salt.

That was the most amazing leap of all.

Five thousand years ago coastal dwellers boiled seawater to produce salt. But as they settled farther and farther inland, salt, critical as a food supplement and preservative, essential to their survival, became hard to find, and transporting it hundreds or thousands of kilometers proved daunting. Another source would have to be found, and the discovery of brine aquifers—places where groundwater seeped from below, loaded with salinity—solved the problem.

The first recorded discovery came during the time of the First Emperor, not far from where Tang now sat. At first wells were shallow, dug by hand, but deeper exploration led to the invention of drilling.

The first bits were forged of heavy iron, the pipe and rig from bamboo. One or more men would stand on a wooden plank, designed like a seesaw, which lifted the bit a meter or so off the ground. Once dropped, it pulverized the ground rock. Centimeter by centimeter, that process would be repeated. Historians later theorized that the idea had come from the practice of pounding rice into flour.

The technique eventually became highly sophisticated, and working solutions to many of the problems still common to drilling—cave-ins, lost tools, deviated wells, the removal of debris—were perfected. Wells to 100 meters became common in Qin Shi's time. No comparable technology existed anywhere else in the world until more than 2,000 years later. By 1100 CE, wells to 400 meters were routine, and while American drillers barely managed 500 meters in the 19th century, Chinese drillers explored below 1,000 meters.

Those first innovators, who sank wells searching for salt brine, also discovered something else.

An odorless emission, highly combustible.

Natural gas.

They learned that it could be burned, producing a clean, hot energy source that dissolved the brine and revealed the salt.

And they also found oil.

A sludgy material—*fatty and sticky, like the juice of meat,* one observer noted—that bubbled up from deeper wells. At first the greenish black ooze was a mystery, but they soon learned that it, too, could be burned, producing a long-lasting, bright flame. It also could make the axles of their wagons turn faster. Oil became the substance of emperors, powering the lamps of their palaces and illuminating their tombs—even providing a fiery weapon used to devastate an enemy.

Tang marveled at the accomplishments.

In the process of inventing the mechanics of drilling, he knew they also had discovered the best places to bore, creating the science of geology. They became skilled at spotting salt frostings on surface rocks and detecting the pungent smell of hidden brine. They learned that yellow sandstone would yield brine high in ferric chloride, while black sandstone led to wells loaded with hydrogen sulfide. Of course, they were ignorant as to the chemical compositions, but they determined how to effectively recognize and use those compounds.

His ministry had studied in detail the history of Chinese brine drilling. There was even a museum in Zigong that told the story to the masses. Incredibly, over the past two millennia, nearly 130,000 wells had been drilled, a few hundred of those during the time of the First Emperor.

One in particular had been sunk about a quarter kilometer away.

"How do you know this?" he demanded of Jin Zhao.

The irritating geochemist had refused to cooperate, so he'd finally ordered Zhao's arrest.

"Minister, I know nothing. It's all theory."

He'd heard that explanation before. "It's more than theory. Tell me."

But his prisoner refused.

He motioned and the soldier standing a few feet away advanced on Zhao, yanking him from the chair and pounding him twice in the stomach. He heard the breath leave the older man. Zhao dropped to his knees, arms wrapping his gut.

A slight nod from him signaled that two blows were enough.

Zhao struggled to breathe.

"It will only get worse," he said. "Tell me."

Zhao calmed himself. "Don't hit me anymore. Please. No more."

"Tell me what I want to know."

He'd thoroughly investigated Jin Zhao and knew that he was not a Party member, not associated with any Party activities, and often spoke disparagingly about the government. His name appeared regularly on a local watch list, and he'd been warned several times to cease dissident activities. Tang had acted as protector on more than one occasion, blocking an arrest, but that had been conditioned on cooperation.

Zhao pushed himself up from the floor. "I will not tell you a thing."

The soldier slammed a fist into Zhao's jaw. Another found the chest. A third blow crashed down on the man's skull.

Zhao collapsed.

Blood seeped from his half-opened mouth.

Two teeth were spit out.

A kick to the stomach and Zhao retreated into the fetal position, arms and legs brought tight to his body.

A few minutes later Jin Zhao lapsed into an unconsciousness from which he never awoke. A cerebral hemorrhage protected all that he knew, but a search of his house and office revealed enough documents for Tang to learn that right here, 2,200 years ago, men had drilled for brine and found oil. And while Jin Zhao lay on the floor, begging for help, screaming that his head exploded with pain—

"Tell me this," Tang said. "One simple thing and I will call the doctor. You can receive care. No more beatings."

He saw the hope of truth in the older man's eyes.

"Has Lev Sokolov found the marker?"

Zhao's head nodded yes.

At first slowly, then quickly.

TWENTY-TWO

CASSIOPEIA HUSTLED DOWN THE STREET SEARCHING FOR A *place to hide. Three men had been following her since she'd left the hotel. Her left arm cradled the dragon lamp. She carried it carefully, nestled within a plastic bag, surrounded by balled paper.*

Redbrick buildings and whitewashed houses surrounded her, all guarding a maze of empty cobbled streets. She rushed past a quiet square, the three men fifty meters behind. No one else could be seen. She could not allow them to take the lamp. Losing it meant losing Sokolov's son.

"Over here," she heard a voice say.

Across the street stood Cotton Malone.

"I got your message," Cotton said. "I'm here."

He was waving her toward him.

She ran, but when she made it to the corner he was gone.

The three men kept pace.

"Here."

She stared down a narrow lane. Cotton was fifty meters away, still waving her forward.

"Cassiopeia, you're making a mistake."

She turned.

Henrik Thorvaldsen appeared.

"You can't help him," he said.

"I have the lamp."

"Don't trust him," he said, and then the Dane was gone. Her eyes searched the street and buildings. The three men had not advanced closer and Cotton was still waving for her to come.

She ran.

Cassiopeia awoke.

She was lying on the park bench. Daylight had waned, the sky now the color of faded ink. She'd been asleep awhile. She glanced back, past the tree trunk. The Toyota remained parked and there were no police or loiterers in sight. She shook the grogginess from her brain. She'd been more tired than she realized. The gun lay beneath her shirt. The dream lingered in her mind.

Don't trust him, Thorvaldsen had said.

Cotton?

He was the only other person there.

She was a good thirty-minute walk away from the Dries Van Egmond Museum. The jaunt would allow her to make sure no one was following. She tried to force her emotions to subside, her mind to stop questioning, but she couldn't. Viktor Tomas' appearance had unnerved her.

Was that who Henrik was referring to?

She spotted a water fountain, walked over, and savored a few long gulps.

She wiped her mouth and steadied herself.

Time to get this over with.

MALONE STEPPED OFF THE NATO CHOPPER AT A SMALL AIR-field north of Antwerp. Ivan followed Stephanie onto the tarmac. Stephanie had arranged the quick flight from Copenhagen. When they were clear of the blades, the helicopter departed back into the night sky.

Two cars awaited with drivers.

"Secret Service," she told them. "Out of Brussels."

Ivan had said little on the trip, just small talk about television and movies. The Russian seemed obsessed with American entertainment.

"All right," Malone said. "We're here. Where's Cassiopeia?"

A third car approached from the far side of the terminal, passing rows of expensive private planes.

"My people," Ivan said. "I must talk to them."

The pudgy Russian waddled toward the car, which stopped. Two men emerged.

He stepped close to Stephanie and asked, "He has people here?"

"Apparently so."

"Do we have *any* independent intelligence on this?" he quietly asked.

She shook her head. "Not enough time. It'll be tomorrow, at the earliest, before I have anything."

"So we're bare-ass-to-the-wind, flying blind."

"We've been there before."

Yes, they had.

Ivan stepped back toward them, saying as he walked, "We have problem."

"Why does that not surprise me?" Malone muttered.

"Vitt is on the move."

"How's that a problem?" Stephanie asked.

"She escapes her captors."

Malone was suspicious. "How do you know that?"

Ivan pointed at the two standing beside the car. "They watch and see."

"Why didn't they help her?" But he knew the answer. "You want her to lead you to the lamp."

"This is intelligence operation," Ivan said. "I have job to do."

"Where is she?"

"Nearby. Headed for a museum. Dries Van Egmond."

His anger grew. "How the hell do you know that?"

"We go."

"No, we don't," Malone said.

Ivan's face stiffened.

"I'm going," Malone made clear. "Alone."

Ivan's haggard face cracked a smile. "I am warned of you. They say you are Lone Ranger."

"Then you know to stay out of my way. I'll find Cassiopeia."

Ivan faced Stephanie. "You take over now? You think I allow that."

"Look," Malone said, answering for her. "If I go alone, I have a better chance of finding out what you want. You show up with the goon squad and you're going to get zero. Cassiopeia is a pro. She'll go to ground."

At least he hoped so.

Ivan jabbed a forefinger at Malone's chest. "Why do I trust you?"

"I've been asking myself the same thing about you."

The Russian removed a pack of cigarettes from his pocket and clamped one between his lips. He found matches and lit the smoke. "I not like this."

"Like I care what you like. You want the job done. I'll get it done."

"Okay," Ivan said as he exhaled. "Find her. Get what we want." He pointed toward the car. "Has navigation that can lead the way."

"Cotton," Stephanie said. "I'll arrange a little privacy. The Antwerp police are aware of what's happening. They just don't know where. I have to assure them there will be no property destruction, besides maybe a broken window or door. Just get her and get out."

"Shouldn't be a problem."

"I realize it shouldn't be a problem, but you have a reputation."

"This isn't a World Heritage Site, is it? I seem to destroy only those."

"Just in and out, okay?"

He turned to Ivan. "Once I make contact, I'll call Stephanie. But I'm going to have to gauge Cassiopeia. She may not want partners."

Ivan raised a finger and pointed. "She might not want, but she gets partners. This matter is bigger than one four-year-old boy."

"That's exactly why you're staying here. First time those words are uttered and she's gone."

He did not plan to make the same mistake he'd made in Paris with Thorvaldsen. Cassiopeia needed his help and he was going to give it to her. Unconditionally and with full disclosure.

And Ivan could go to hell.

TWENTY-THREE

NI, STILL SHAKEN FROM THE ATTACK, WATCHED IN DISGUST. The fourth man, captured by Pau Wen, had been led from the house, beyond the gray walls, to a barn fifty meters behind the compound, among thick woods. Pau's four acolytes had stripped off the man's clothes, bound his body with heavy rope, then lifted him into the air, suspended from an L-shaped wooden crane.

"I have horses and goats," Pau said to him. "We use the hoist to store hay in the top of the barn."

The crane rose ten meters to a set of double doors in the gable. One of Pau's men, the one from the video, stood in the upper doorway. The remaining three men—each wearing a green, sleeveless gown—fanned the flames of a steady blaze below, using dried logs and hay as fuel. Even from ten meters away, the heat was intense.

"It has to be hot," Pau said. "Otherwise, the effort could prove fruitless."

Night had come, black and bleak. The bound man hung suspended near the top of the hoist, his mouth sealed with tape, but in the flickering light Ni saw the horror on the man's face.

"The purpose of this?" he asked Pau.

"We need to learn information. He was asked politely, but refused."

"You plan to roast him?"

"Not at all. That would be barbaric."

He was trying to remain calm, telling himself that Karl Tang had ordered his death. Plots, purges, arrests, torture, trials, incarcerations, even executions were common in China.

But open political murder?

Perhaps Tang thought that since the assassination would occur in Belgium, it could be explained away. The sudden demise of Lin Biao, Mao's chosen successor, in 1971 had never been fully documented. Biao supposedly died in a Mongolian plane crash while trying to escape China, after being accused of plotting to overthrow Mao. But only the government's version as to what happened had ever been released. No one knew where or how or when Lin Biao had died only that he was gone.

And he kept telling himself that the man dangling from the hoist had come to kill him.

One of the men motioned that the fire was ready.

Pau craned his neck and signaled.

His man in the barn rotated the hoist so that it was now no longer parallel but perpendicular to the building. That caused the bound man's bare feet to hang about three meters above the flames.

"Never allow the fire to touch the flesh," Pau quietly said. "Too intense. Too quick. Counterproductive."

He wondered about the lesson in torture. This old man apparently was a connoisseur. But from all Ni knew about Mao, the entire regime had been masters of the art. Pau stood motionless, dressed in a long gown of white gauze, watching as the bound man struggled against the ropes.

"Will you," Pau called out, "answer my questions?"

The man did not signal any reply. Instead he kept struggling.

"You see, Minister," Pau said, "the heat alone is excruciating, but there is something worse."

A flick of Pau's wrist and one of the men hurled the contents of a pail into the flames. A loud hiss, followed by a rush of heat, spewed the powder upward as it vaporized, engulfing the prisoner in a scorching cloud.

The man's thrashings increased wildly, his agony obvious.

Ni caught a scent in the night air.

"Chili powder," Pau said. "The hot plume itself causes incredible agony, but the lingering chemical vapor increases the heat's intensity on the skin. If he failed to close his eyes, he would be blind for several hours. The fumes irritate the pupils."

Pau motioned and another batch of chili powder was tossed.

Ni imagined what the prisoner must be enduring.

"Don't sympathize with him," Pau said. "This man is an associate of Karl Tang. Your enemy. I simply want him to tell us all that he knows."

So did Ni, actually.

The fire continued to rage, the flames surely beginning to scorch the man's feet.

The prisoner's head started to nod, signaling surrender.

"That didn't take long." Pau motioned, and the man in the barn rotated the body away from the flames. The tape was ripped from the man's mouth. An agonizing scream pierced the night.

"There's no one to hear," Pau called out. "The nearest neighbors are kilometers away. Tell me what we want to know, or back you go."

The man stole a few breaths and seemed to steady himself.

"Tang . . . wants you dead. Minister Ni, too."

"Tell me more," Pau called out.

"He's going . . . after the . . . lamp. As we . . . speak."

"And Cassiopeia Vitt?"

"She's going after . . . it . . . too. She was . . . allowed to . . . escape. Men are . . . following."

"You see, Minister," Pau quietly whispered. "This is why torture has endured. It works. You learn a great many vital things."

The sickening feeling in his stomach grew. Were there no rules, no boundaries, to his morality? What had happened to his conscience?

Pau motioned again, and the prisoner was lowered to the ground. One of the robed men immediately produced a gun and shot the bound man in the head.

Ni stood silent, then finally asked, "Was that necessary?"

"What would you have me do? Release him?"

He did not answer.

"Minister, how will you lead China if you have not the stomach to defend yourself?"

He did not appreciate the reprimand. "I believe in courts, laws, justice."

"You are about to embark on a battle that only one of you will survive. No courts, law, or justice will decide that conflict."

"I was unaware that this would be a fight to the death."

"Has not Karl Tang just made that clear?"

Ni supposed he had.

"Tang is ruthless. He sent men to end the battle before it even began. What will be your response, Minister?"

The past few hours, in this no-nonsense place, had made him feel strangely vulnerable, challenging all that he thought he knew about himself. He'd never directly ordered the death of anyone—though he'd arrested many who'd eventually been executed. For the first time the enormity of what he was about to do weighed down on him. Perhaps Pau was right. Ruling China required strength. But he wondered. Could he kill with the same cool detachment Pau Wen displayed?

Probably not.

"We must go," Pau said. "It's only a short drive."

He knew where.

To the Dries Van Egmond Museum.

Before it was too late.

TWENTY-FOUR

GANSU PROVINCE, CHINA

TANG OPENED THE TRAILER'S DOOR AND STEPPED OUT TO A moonless night, the stars blocked by clouds. The air here, hundreds of kilometers from the nearest city, was refreshingly clear. He flexed his legs. Old emotions boiled within him. He was close—so close—and knew it.

He thought of his father, his mother, naïve souls who knew nothing of the world beyond their simple village. They'd lived surrounded by trees and terraced vegetable plots, tucked away on the slopes of a mountain. His only brother had died in Tibet, keeping rebels at bay. No one ever explained what had happened there. His parents never would have asked, and no records existed.

But it didn't matter.

Fight self. That's what Mao had preached. Believe in the Party, trust the state. The individual meant nothing.

His family had worshiped Mao. Yet his father had also held a great affection for Confucius, as had his father before him.

Only after Tang had left the village, specially chosen to attend secondary and higher education, had he come to realize the dramatic contradiction. His philosophy teacher at university had opened his eyes.

"Let me tell you about a man who lived in the state of Song and dutifully tilled his field. His efforts provided ample food for his family and his village. In the middle of the

field stood the stump of a tree. One day a hare, running at full speed, bumped into the stump, broke his neck, and died. This was quite fortuitous, since the meat was greatly enjoyed by all. Thereupon the man left his plow and kept watch at the stump, hoping to obtain another hare in the same manner. But he never did, and both his family and the village suffered from his neglect. That is the flaw of Confucianism. Those who try to rule the present with the conduct of the past commit the same foolishness."

He listened to the distant rumblings of the derrick's generators. Dawn was not far away. He thought again of that teacher at Hunan's university, the one who asked him—

"What will you do upon graduating?"

"I intend to study in Beijing and obtain a higher degree in geology."

"The earth interests you?"

"It always has."

"You have spirit and promise. I've seen that these past three years. Would you perhaps consider something in addition to your studies, something that might answer those questions you constantly pose to me?"

In the days after, he'd listened as his teacher explained about the distant Shang dynasty, the earliest for which there was any documentary evidence, existing nearly 4,000 years ago. A highly developed state with a tax collection system, a penal code, and a standing army, it was ruled by an autocrat who styled himself *I the single one man.*

"That was significant," his teacher said. "The first time we know of one man assuming total power over many."

The Zhou dynasty succeeded the Shang and carried forward that autocratic ideal, expanding the ruler's authority.

"It was said that all the land under Heaven belonged to the king and all people on the shores were his subjects."

But governing such a large kingdom from one locale proved difficult, so the Zhou kings created feudalism—kinsmen who were bestowed limited sovereignty over portions of the domain, along with titles such as *duke, marquis, earl,* and *baron.*

"A system Western civilization would not envision for another thousand years."

Loyalty to the king was bound by blood rather than oath but, over time, the local lords began to establish their own fiefdoms. Eventually, these vassals revolted and eliminated the king of Zhou, demoting him to their equal.

"This led to the Spring and Autumn period, a chaotic war of all against all. Within two and a half centuries, 500 wars were fought among the feudal states. Eventually, everyone believed the state of Cu, which occupied the middle reaches of the Yangtze River, would emerge victorious. This fear led the smaller states to turn to the state of Qi for protection. With a strong military, sound economy, and able ruler, Qi was in a position to help. A mutual defense league was established and the duke of Qi was appointed Hegemon, or Ba of the league, charged with preserving the peace. And this he did."

He'd thought that apt since *Ba* meant "father, protector."

But it was how the protection had been accomplished that so interested him.

The entire population had been organized along military lines. Marketplaces were regulated, a monopoly established on coinage, salt and iron production placed under state control. The results were a strong army and a sound economy, which not only offered protection from enemies but also strengthened the power of the Hegemon.

"These were the first Legalists," his teacher said. *"A school of statecraft dedicated to exalting the ruler and maximizing authority. Their philosophy was simple. The sovereign is the creator of law, the officials are the followers of law, the people are subjects of the law. The wise sovereign holds six powers. The ability to grant life, to kill, to enrich, to impoverish, to promote, and to demote."*

And the concept spread among the other states.

At the end of the Spring and Autumn period, after 300 years of constant turmoil, around 481 BCE, twenty-two states survived. The rest had been absorbed by their neighbors.

"The struggle became worse in the Warring States period, which followed," his teacher had said. *"Eventually, after another two hundred years of conflict, seven states emerged, each led by a Hegemon. Their councilors were all brothers of the Ba, Legalists who taught that he who has the greatest force will be paid tribute to by others, while he who has less force will pay tribute to others. The Ba consolidated their influence over the kings, advocating an end to the feudal system. Inherited posts were replaced with appointed bureaucrats, whom the ruler could discharge or even execute at will. Inherited fiefdoms were redrawn into administrative units called counties. Cleverly, by appointing officials who were mere extensions of himself, the Hegemon gathered all power into himself."*

By the end of the Warring States period, the *Ba* had assumed virtual control over the monarchs. Though other technological feats were better known—the discovery of gunpowder, the cultivation of silkworms—Tang believed that the Chinese invention of totalitarianism may have had the greatest impact on the world.

"It was a revolution from above," his teacher had explained. "The people gave little resistance. Five centuries of incessant warfare had left them prostrate, and no one could argue with the order the Legalists provided. And though all that occurred over 2,500 years ago, to this day all Chinese have an irrational fear of chaos and disorder."

A decade later the kingdom of Qin conquered the seven surviving states, transforming a backward dukedom and six warring neighbors into the First Empire.

"Qin Shi embedded Legalism in our culture, and it remains part of our culture today, though the concept has changed over the centuries. Those changes are why you and I must talk further."

And they had, many times.

"Study Mao," his teacher had advised. "He was a modern Legalist. He understood how the Chinese mind fears chaos—and that, more than anything else, explains both his success and his failure."

Tang had studied.

Nationally, Mao had wanted to make China united, strong, and secure, just as Qin Shi had done. *Socially,* he had wanted China to evolve into an egalitarian society in the Marxist tradition. *Personally,* he wanted to transcend his own mortality and ensure that his Revolution became irreversible.

On the first goal he succeeded. The second was an utter failure.

And the third?

That was the unanswered question.

Amazing how like Qin Shi Mao had become. Both established new regimes, bringing unity after long periods of bloody turmoil, crushing all local fiefdoms. They were standardizers, social engineers, insisting on one language, currency, orthodoxy, and loyalty. Grandiose building projects became common. They both loathed merchants and silenced intellectuals. They encouraged worship of themselves and invented new titles to match their egos. Qin had chosen *First Emperor,* while Mao had preferred *Chairman.* In death, they were lavishly entombed and harshly criticized, but the framework of their regimes had endured.

"That was no accident," his teacher told him during one of their final conversations. "Mao understood the First Emperor. You should, too."

And he did.

No 20th-century Chinese leader had captured the people's devotion like Mao. He became emperor-like, and not a single pact that Beijing later made with the people could compare to the "destiny of Heaven" that emperors like Mao enjoyed.

But Mao's day was over.

Give allegiance to political solutions proposed centuries ago by long-dead scholars. That's what Confucius had advised as the way to understanding. That seemed impossible.

A second hare would not die at the same stump.

He wholeheartedly agreed with Mao's Cultural Revolution. In deference to it, that was when he'd stopped using the traditional form of his name—Tang Karl, his family name first. Instead he chose the modern incarnation Karl Tang. He recalled when the Red Guards rampaged across the country, shutting down schools, imprisoning intellectuals, restricting publications, disbanding monasteries and temples. Every physical reminder of China's feudal and capitalistic past had been destroyed—old customs, old habits, old culture, and old thinking were all eliminated.

Millions had died, millions more had been affected.

Yet Mao emerged more loved than ever, the state stronger than ever.

He checked his watch, then sucked more breaths of the clean air.

A smile formed on his lips.

Let it begin.

TWENTY-FIVE

CASSIOPEIA APPROACHED THE MUSEUM, HEADING FOR THE same rear entrance she'd scouted two days ago. She'd stumbled across the Dries Van Egmond in a hotel brochure while trying to decide where best to hide the lamp. Its rooms held a collection of Dutch, French, and Flemish objets d'art. But its Chinese boudoir, on the third level, was what really caught her attention.

She hoped the lamp had gone unnoticed.

She'd passed couples homeward-bound and walkers self-absorbed, but no one dodging into a doorway or dogging her footsteps. Advertisements plastered on plate-glass windows shouted from closed shops. But she'd ignored all distractions. She needed to retrieve the lamp, then make contact with Sokolov, that connection facilitated through a couple who shared Sokolov's agony of losing a child—who'd agreed to forward any coded e-mail messages sent from Belgium.

She wondered what had happened with Malone. Viktor had told her that he hadn't heard anything from Copenhagen, but that meant nothing coming from him. Perhaps she'd head for Denmark once this errand was completed. Cotton could help her decide what to do next.

A train would be best.

No security checks.

And she could sleep.

MALONE SPOTTED THE MUSEUM, SQUEEZED INTO A ROW OF buildings that alternated old and new. Its façade revealed details that suggested an Italian motif. Little traffic filled Antwerp's streets, only lights over empty sidewalks, the city dozing off for the night. He studied the building's sculpted window frames, stacked one atop the other in varying squares, circles, and rectangles. None glowed with life.

He'd parked two blocks away and approached with slow steps. He wasn't sure what was about to happen. How was Cassiopeia planning on entering? Breaking in? Certainly not from here. The main entrance was protected by a locked iron gate, the windows barred. Stephanie had called and said that she'd arranged for the alarm system to be disabled, as Europol and the police were working with her. Local cooperation usually meant folks many pay grades higher than Stephanie were calling the shots. Which only reemphasized that this involved far more than a missing four-year-old boy.

He hugged the side of a building and kept to the shadows, avoiding the burst of a nearby streetlight. He peered around the corner, hoping he might spot Cassiopeia.

But all he saw were three men emerging from a parked car.

No light came on when the doors opened, which caught his interest.

They were beyond the museum entrance, a good fifty yards away from where he stood, hidden by the night.

The tight cluster of dark figures stepped onto the sidewalk, walked without a sound to the museum entrance, and tested the iron gate.

"Around back," he heard one of them say in English. "She's definitely here. Get the stuff, just in case."

Two of the men retreated to the car, where each removed an oversized canister. Together the three headed to the nearest corner and turned right. Malone figured there must be another way into the building—from the rear, the next block over. So he crossed the street and decided to approach from the opposite direction.

NI STOOD IN THE DARKNESS, BEYOND THE GARDEN OF THE DRIES Van Egmond Museum, Pau Wen beside him. They'd made the journey from the countryside to Antwerp, parking several blocks away and assessing the building from the rear. Pau had brought one of his men, who'd just reconnoitered the darkness.

The man reappeared and whispered his report. "A woman is near the building, about to break inside. Three men are approaching from the far end of the street."

Pau considered the information, then mouthed, *Watch the men.*

The shadow hustled off.

Their position was adjacent to a drive that ran behind the museum, between the buildings on the next block over. A small graveled parking lot stretched the length of a row of tall hedges that separated the garden from the drive. An open gateway, framed by ivy, led into a courtyard, surrounded on three sides by the museum. Ni tried to focus, but other images floated through his mind. None good. Men speared with arrows. The bound man being shot in the head. He told himself that, at least for the moment, he was again on the offensive. Pau appeared to be helping, though Ni remained highly suspicious.

Three forms appeared, two of them carrying containers. They disappeared through the portal into the rear yard.

"Vitt has returned for the lamp," Pau whispered. "But Tang has come, too."

"How do you know that?"

"There is no other explanation. Those men work for him."

Another form appeared, this from the opposite direction. A solitary man. Tall, broad-shouldered, hands empty. He entered the garden, too. Ni wished for more light, but the moon was gone and all that stretched before them was a dense band of darkness.

"And who is that?" he asked Pau.

"An excellent question."

MALONE HAD ADDED UP HIS SUSPICIONS AND NOW HE KNEW. The three men were tracking Cassiopeia. Two of them wore ski masks over their heads and black clothing, tight over lean bodies, gloves and dark shoes on their hands and feet. The third man was dressed in dark clothing as well, but a jacket and trousers. He was shorter, a bit stouter, and seemed in charge. He carried a small device in one hand, which he kept at his waist, following its lead.

Cassiopeia had been electronically tagged.

He wondered if she knew.

The leader motioned and they picked their way through the dark, hurrying toward a set of glass doors that opened onto a terrace. Ivy veined the building's rear façade. Malone imagined that when this was once a residence, the terrace had been a gathering spot to enjoy the garden. Interestingly, unlike the front entrance, these rear doors were not barred. Perhaps that was more of Stephanie's intervention. Amazing what a few Russians coming around could do.

The leader reached through a shattered pane in the door and opened the latch from the inside, apparently just as Cassiopeia had done.

The three disappeared inside.

Malone walked between the soft fragrances and muted colors of the flower beds, toward the doors.

He found his Beretta.

TWENTY-SIX

TANG TAPPED THE KEYBOARD, ENTERING A PASSWORD THAT completed the video connection. He preferred cyber-communication to face-to-face meetings. If performed with the right encoding, security was nearly foolproof. Unless one of the parties to the conversation allowed a violation.

But that wasn't a worry here.

All of the participants were sworn by oath, bound by the brotherhood, each a loyal and dedicated member of the *Ba*.

He stroked the touch pad, and the laptop's screen divided into ten panes. A man's face appeared in each, bearing features of the Han Chinese, all of them in their fifties like himself. They served in diverse areas. One was a judge on the Supreme People's Court. Several were respected department heads. Two were generals in the military. Three were members of the all-powerful Central Committee. They'd risen in rank, just like Tang—steadily, unnoticed—and served as *Ba* division leaders. Men who supervised other brothers, scattered throughout the national and local governments and the military. Their total numbers were limited, little more than two thousand, but enough to accomplish their goal.

"Good day," he said into the laptop's microphone.

China, though 5,000 kilometers across and spread over five international time zones, stayed on Beijing time. He'd never understood the logic since it led to annoying differences in work hours, but it explained the varied dress of the men on the screen.

"I wanted to report that the premier's health is rapidly deteriorating," he said. "I have learned that he has less than a year left. Of course, that fact will be kept secret. But it is imperative we maintain a constant readiness."

He saw heads nod.

"The Central Committee is prepared," he said. "We have a solid majority to achieve the premiership."

One hundred and ninety-eight people served on the all-powerful Central Committee. He'd cultivated well over a hundred, men not of the *Ba,* who believed as he did that China must head in a direction more reminiscent of Mao than Deng Xiaoping.

"And what of Ni Yong?" one of the men asked. "He has growing support."

"That matter is being handled. A state funeral in his honor will greatly rally the people to our cause."

"Is that necessary?"

"The simplest way to eliminate the problem is to eliminate the candidate. This was discussed and approved."

"Conditionally," one of the others quickly added. "As a last resort. Ni's death could have implications, depending on the manner of his demise. We don't want a martyr."

"That will not happen. His death will be attributed to one of his many investigations, one that went terribly wrong. It will happen outside the country."

He saw that several agreed, but a few did not.

"Ni has strong support in the military," one of the generals said. "His death will not be ignored."

"Nor should it be. But in the larger view, he will be quickly forgotten as events play out. The premier's demise will be unexpected. That will inevitably lead to uncertainty, and the people will not allow that condition to exist for long. They will crave security, and we will provide it."

"How fast will we move?"

"As fast as the constitution allows. I've arranged for the provinces to call for an immediate vote. Of course, until that happens, I will be in temporary charge, as first vice president. We should have control in a matter of weeks."

Then the real work would begin, starting with a swift, hasty retreat from democratization, which should stay the Party's demise. And there would no longer be a need for the Central Discipline Inspection Commission. Instead corruption would be dealt with privately. Likewise, all dissension would be quelled with appropriate punishments. Many world observers had predicted either the Westernization of China or the end of the Communist Party, and staying the present course would almost certainly have accomplished both. His goal was to alter that course 180 degrees.

Qin Shi, the emperors after him, and Mao had all done it.

Now he would do it.

All Chinese have an irrational fear of chaos and disorder.

"We will offer the nation exactly what it craves," he said. "Stability. Order. Once those are established, the people will grant us many liberties."

"We are but a few," another of the men said. "Keeping that order could prove difficult."

"Which is why we must control the premiership. That office grants us unrestricted power. From there, we can easily reshape the nation."

He was careful when speaking with the brothers to always use the first-person plural *we*. Theirs was, in theory, a collective effort, and he realized that he could not accomplish his goal without everyone's help.

"We must be ready to act with short notice," he said to the others. "For my part, I am presently working on a tactic that could greatly enhance our position, perhaps even grant us a dominant hand in world politics. The West will not be dictating how China lives, moralizing on what is right and wrong, deciding our future."

"You sound confident."

"Their missionaries and educators tried to modernize and Christianize us. The Japanese wanted to conquer us. The Americans attempted to democratize us. The Soviets tried to insinuate control. They all failed. Even worse, we experimented with ourselves and failed, too. We are a great civilization." He paused. "We shall once again be what we were."

He saw that the men on the other end of the connection agreed with him.

"And what of the master?" one of the men finally asked. "We hear nothing from him."

"Rest assured," he made clear. "He is with us."

TWENTY-SEVEN

CASSIOPEIA PASSED THROUGH ANOTHER OF THE MUSEUM'S many parlors, recalling its layout from her first visit. The ground-floor rooms were arranged around a central hall from which a marble staircase rose in broad flights. She passed the same English long clock and two Chinese-style cases that held expensive curios. A porcelain gallery opened to her right, the 18th-century tables littered with ivories, enamels, and some 19th-century Adelgade Glasvaerker collectibles. Through a main hall, divided by four Ionic columns, she found a rear staircase, most likely once used by the household staff.

She started to climb.

Her entry had been easy. She knew that many of these old places were not alarmed. Instead, interior motion sensors were the security of choice, but on her first visit she hadn't noticed any. Perhaps it was thought that there was nothing here thieves would waste time stealing, or maybe it was a matter of cost.

She kept her steps light, her senses alert, the gun at her side. She stopped at the first landing and glanced down to the ground floor, her ears attuned to every sound. But she heard nothing.

She shook away her apprehension.

Just get the lamp and get out.

MALONE HAD NO IDEA WHERE HE WAS HEADED, BUT THE THREE men ahead of him did not suffer the same problem. They moved through the rooms in a deliberate path, following the tracker, which the one man still held. He stayed back and used furniture for cover, careful with his rubber soles on the marble floor. He was inside a gallery, probably light and airy during the day thanks to bay windows that opened to the rear garden.

He peered into the gloomy cavern and saw ceilings of enamel and carved wood. To his left opened a wainscoted room lined with walls that appeared to be leather. He could still smell the roses, lilacs, and hawthorn outside the terrace doors. He was crouched behind a high-backed upholstered chair, waiting for the three to head farther inside.

To his left, movement drew his attention.

Three more men entered through the terrace door.

He stayed low and used the darkness to his advantage.

Two of the newcomers stood tall. One moved with the slowness of age, and in the tiny bursts of light that came from outside, he caught the face. Definitely an older man.

One of the men toted a bow and a quiver of arrows slung across his shoulder.

Don't see that every day.

All three crept in silence, then stopped, the older man directing the one with the bow, who quickly disappeared into the mansion. The remaining two hesitated, then advanced.

Malone fled the room through a second portal, away from where the others had gone, and headed toward the front, finding the main entrance.

Behind a small writing desk, which seemed to act as the admission table, opened a gift shop. He stepped inside, careful to keep his attention on what might be happening behind him, but he heard nothing.

He spotted a booklet that described the mansion in several languages, one of which was English. He grabbed it and stepped to a window. On the inside rear cover was a map of the four floors. He noted three staircases and many rooms. On the third level was a space labeled CHINESE BOUDOIR. No other room carried a similar designation.

Was that where Cassiopeia had hidden the lamp?

He grabbed his bearings and decided to use one of the secondary staircases.

CASSIOPEIA CAME TO THE TOP OF THE STAIRS AND QUICKLY made her way toward the Chinese boudoir. Gilt-edged mirrors lined the walls and a rich parquet sheathed the floor. Oriental porcelain sat atop carved chests. It had been one of those, a red lacquered cabinet with a refined finish, that had solved her problem. Surely, she'd reasoned, the cabinets weren't inspected on a regular basis. From all she'd been able to learn this was a minor museum, of little consequence, something that merely preserved the formality and taste of a once-wealthy owner, which at least for a few days could provide a convenient hiding place.

Quickly she reentered the boudoir, stepped to the cabinet and opened the doors. The lamp lay exactly where she'd placed it. She had nothing to carry it in. She'd find a bag later, she figured, and taking a train directly to Copenhagen was beginning to sound like a good idea. Once there, she could decide on her next move.

She lifted out the lamp.

A dragon's head, on a tiger's body, with wings. She'd noticed at Pau Wen's residence that the lamp contained some sort of liquid, its mouth sealed with wax.

A noise rose from behind.

She whirled.

Everything in the darkness seemed frozen.

Three meters away two forms appeared in the archway that led out to the hall. A third form materialized and blocked the other exit to her right.

Silhouettes of guns materialized, pointed her way.

"Lay the lamp down," one of the two men said in English.

She considered shooting her way out, then decided that was foolishness.

She could not evade all three.

"The gun, too," the voice said.

TWENTY-EIGHT

MALONE HEARD A VOICE JUST AS HE FOUND THE TOP OF THE stairs—a man talking about a lamp and a gun. Apparently, some of the six individuals who were inside had found Cassiopeia. He recalled from the map that the Chinese boudoir lay to his left, through a portrait gallery with a collection of miniatures, then one door down the hall.

He passed through the gallery, threading his way around dark shapes, careful not to bump anything. At a doorway leading out, a quick look confirmed that two men stood in the hall, facing into another room.

Both held weapons.

Elaborate paintings inside thick frames dotted the wide corridor. He noticed that the flooring was parquetry, which meant, unlike the marble he'd traversed so far, it would announce his presence. Since he needed to do something and there was no time for subtlety, he decided the direct approach would be best.

"Excuse me," he said.

Both men whirled.

One of the men raised his gun and fired.

NI STOOD DOWNSTAIRS WITH PAU WEN. HE DID NOT LIKE ANY-thing about this situation. He was a high-ranking official in the Chinese government—a man beyond reproach, whose reputation meant everything—yet here he was inside a Belgian museum that had just been burglarized.

He heard a voice from up the main staircase.

Then another.

And a shot.

Pau said something to the third man—who'd returned a moment ago—then, with a flick of his wrist, dismissed him.

The acolyte darted up the staircase.

"This could escalate," Pau said. "I confess that I thought no one would be here. Apparently, I was wrong. We must leave."

More shots rang out.

"There's quite a fight happening up there," Ni said.

Pau grabbed his arm and they started for the terrace door. "All the more reason for us to leave. We can retreat to our previous position, away from the garden, and observe. My associate will do what he can to secure the lamp. He's—"

"Expendable?"

"I was thinking *capable*. But he is certainly both."

CASSIOPEIA HEARD A VOICE SAY "EXCUSE ME," SAW THE TWO MEN react, and decided to use their moment of distraction to deal with the man to her right. She'd laid the lamp on the floor, but instead of relinquishing her gun, as ordered, she swung around and fired at the third man.

But the doorway was empty.

She scooped up the lamp just as the two men in the archway opened fire. If she didn't know better she'd swear the voice had been Cotton's. But that would be too fortuitous even to wish for.

More shots erupted, but they were directed away from her.

She decided that since the two were occupied, the third man presented the greater threat. So she darted to the doorway, peered into the next room, and caught no sight of movement. The room was loaded with dark silhouettes—furniture and wall hangings. Another exit opened ten meters away, with many places to hide in between.

All problems.

But she had no choice.

MALONE WAS STUCK IN A FIRESTORM. HE CARRIED A FULLY loaded Beretta but only one spare magazine, so he resisted the impulse to retaliate.

Luckily, he'd anticipated their attack and slipped into the next room, just as he'd diverted their attention from Cassiopeia. At least they were now focused on him.

Glass shattered as bullets found hard targets and wood splintered. To his left a vase added its coarse fragments to the ruin of porcelain on the floor.

Stephanie was going to kill him, but this wasn't his fault. No one warned him that this could be a Shootout at the OK Corral reenactment.

He decided *Enough* and sent three shots in reply. At least now they knew he was armed. Movement confirmed they were shifting position. He fired two more rounds and fled his hiding spot, rushing down the hall, toward where the two men had first stood.

But they were gone, surely retreating toward the main staircase.

Time to find an ally.

"Cassiopeia," he called out. "It's Cotton."

CASSIOPEIA HEARD MALONE CALL HER NAME, BUT SHE COULD not reply. The third man was close. She could feel his presence, within a few meters, hidden within the maze of furniture that stretched out before her. She'd utilized the gunfire's chatter to steadily ease toward the archway that led out.

But her nemesis was probably doing the same thing.

She crouched behind a high-backed chair for cover and made it to the doorway, advancing with the lamp in one hand, the gun in the other. Coming around the way she was headed, she could catch the two men in a crossfire, Cotton on one side of the hallway, her on the other.

MALONE DARTED FROM ONE ROOM TO THE NEXT, CROSSING the hallway. The two men were ahead of him, or at least he thought so, and the gunfire had stopped.

Which was a problem.

Something popped, like metal bending.

A smell filled his nostrils.

He recalled the two containers that the first set of men had hauled inside. He'd wondered what they held. What had the lead man said?

Just in case.

He spotted a glistening ooze, reflected off the weak light from outside, seeping down the wooden floor toward him.

He caught a sweet odor.

Gasoline.

He realized what was coming and managed to drop back just as a *woosh* of air rushed his way, followed by the blinding light and intense heat of an erupting blaze.

TWENTY-NINE

NI AND PAU WEN FLED THE MUSEUM GARDEN, CROSSED THE rear drive and the graveled parking lot, and sought refuge in the shadows of the buildings of the next block over. The gunfire had stopped and Ni expected to hear sirens approaching. Surely someone had called the police.

"Should we not leave?" he asked Pau.

"We must see what happens."

He stared back at the museum and caught a bright flash from the third-floor windows.

"It's on fire," he said.

Beams of light split the blackness as the museum's third floor erupted into flames.

"This could be a problem, on a multitude of layers," Pau said, his eyes locked on the destruction.

Ni didn't want to hear that. "Care to explain?"

"Let us hope my brother can succeed. And quickly."

CASSIOPEIA'S BONES AND MUSCLES TIGHTENED AS SHE REELED from the unexpected blast of heat. Her eyes burned from the burst of

light the flames had generated. Spots dotted her vision and she struggled to see what lay before and behind her.

The corridor was burning.

Malone was somewhere at its far end, beyond the Chinese room.
No sense being subtle now.

"Cotton," she called out.

No reply, and his silence was as intolerable as the heat.

To her left dropped the main staircase, fronted by a narrow landing.
The corridor's wood flooring, oak from centuries ago, burned with
vigor, and the wall plaster was about to join the party.

She needed to leave.

But not without Cotton.

She knew there was another way down, the staircase she'd used to
climb, but flames blocked any path in that direction. She still held the
lamp and the gun and decided to see if perhaps Cotton had made his way
forward, through the connected rooms on the hallway's opposite side.

No sign of the three men.

She turned and spotted the source of the problem. Two metal can-
isters overturned on the floor, both aflame.

She came to the end of the hall, where a marble balustrade opened
to the main staircase that right-angled downward toward the second
floor. No more corridor extended past where the stairs began, and she
confronted a stone wall. Carefully she peered out and saw no movement in the fire's glow. Something cracked behind her, then crashed
and she saw the hall's ceiling give way, the old house quickly surrender-
ing. Perhaps the three men had fled? No need to hang around, except
that they would want the lamp. But they could wait outside and confront her there.

The stairway began five meters away.

She dashed forward.

As she reached the end of the balustrade and started to turn for the
stairs, something slammed shoulder-first into the back of her knees.
Arms wrapped her legs. She fell forward, smashing into the marble wall.

A man had tackled her.

She thrashed her legs, twisting her body, banging the gun into his
head. He was wiry and strong, but she managed to fling him away, sending herself sliding.

The lamp and gun flew from her grasp.

A kick sent her weapon flying toward the balustrade, where it disappeared between thick spindles over the side.

She sprang to her feet.

Her attacker was dressed in black, his face hooded by a wool mask. He was maybe thirty pounds heavier. She lunged, jamming her shoulder into his chest, ramming him back into the wall.

MALONE HEARD CASSIOPEIA CALL HIS NAME BUT CHOSE NOT TO reply. He'd spotted three forms rushing through the darkness, all headed toward the main staircase. He'd managed to creep closer, through rooms that opened one into another, careful with his approach among the warm mass of dark shapes. Smoke gathered, which made both breathing and seeing difficult.

He heard fighting and saw something slide across the burning floor, into the flames. He raced to the doorway and spotted the object. Small. A foot long and half that tall.

A dragon's head on a tiger's body with wings.

The lamp?

He reached down to retrieve it but his fingers reeled back. Its bronze exterior was hot. He used his shoe and slid it away from the burning floorboards into the room where he stood, three walls of which had now joined the blaze.

He needed to leave.

He glanced out into the corridor, toward the top of the staircase, and saw Cassiopeia and a man clad in black.

Fighting.

NI WATCHED THE DRIES VAN EGMOND MUSEUM BURN. THE top two floors were now on fire, flames roaring through the roof, licking the night. Windows shattered from heat and pressure, spewing glass into the garden.

"The Chinese were much better glass producers," Pau said. "Much higher quality than anything Europe produced."

Ni wondered about the history lesson, considering what they were witnessing.

"Did you know that at the terra-cotta warrior pit, we discovered that the weapons the figures carried—their swords and knives, which emerged from the ground sharp, shiny, and untarnished—were made of materials that actually prevented rust. We ultimately discovered that it was a copper–tin alloy combined with eleven other metals such as cobalt, nickel, chrome, and magnesium. Can you imagine? Over two millennia ago and our ancestors understood how to protect metal."

"And we slaughtered ourselves," Ni said, "with that technology."

Pau's gaze stayed on the fire. "You're not much for violence, are you?"

"It never achieves long-range goals."

"An effective state employs seven punishments to three rewards. A weak state employs five punishments to five rewards. That is a proven fact."

"If a person's life has no value, then the society that shapes that life has no value. How could anyone believe otherwise?"

"Empires, by nature, are repressive."

"Aren't you concerned that people may be dying in that fire? Your man one of them."

"He must protect himself, that is his duty."

"And you bear no responsibility?"

"Of course. I bear the burden of his failure."

He could not, and would not, ever allow himself to have so little regard for other people's lives. Ordering men to their deaths should never be taken lightly. Though he did not know the man inside, he cared about his safety.

All leaders should feel that way.

Shouldn't they?

"You are an odd man," he said to Pau Wen.

"That I am. But isn't it fortuitous that you met me."

THIRTY

CASSIOPEIA SHOVED HERSELF AWAY FROM HER ASSAILANT AND rose to her knees. The heat from the fire, raging only a few meters away, had grown in intensity, flames edging their way toward the landing. Luckily, the walls and floor here were marble. Smoke was building, making each breath a challenge. She needed to find the lamp, but there was the matter of the black-clad man who deftly came to his feet, ready for more. Her heart pounded, a heavy throbbing that rattled her ribs. Her muscles were watery with fatigue. Two days of torture and no food had taken a toll.

The man lunged.

She dodged, grabbed his arm and forced it back, twisting his body, trying to take him down. His wild kicking threatened her grasp and he managed to reverse the hold and drive her forward into the balustrade. Over the thick railing, she caught a view of a ten-meter drop below.

She was rolled so that her spine faced downward.

The back of the man's hand slapped her face. He then tried to force her over the side. She tasted the acrid tang of blood. Adrenaline rushed through her as she swung her right leg up and planted the heel of her boot into his groin.

He doubled forward, both hands reaching for the pain.

She jammed her knee into his face and sent him staggering back.

Advancing, she balled her fist.

MALONE USED HIS SHIRTTAIL TO CRADLE THE LAMP, ITS EXTErior still warm from the roasting. It seemed solid, the only opening at the dragon's head. In the flickering light he spotted bits of melted wax that had sealed the mouth clinging to the bronze. He caught a familiar smell and brought the lamp close.

Oil.

He jostled the vessel. It seemed about half full.

He spotted Chinese characters carved into the exterior and surmised that maybe the writing could be what made the thing so important. He'd seen that before—messages from the past, still relevant today. But whatever it was, he needed to get the hell out of this burning inferno while the getting was good.

He turned.

One of the men stood a few feet away, blocking the only exit. He held a gun waist-high, aimed straight ahead.

"Got to be hot in that wool mask," Malone said.

"Give me the lamp."

He motioned with the artifact. "This? I just found it in the fire. Nothing special."

"Give me the lamp."

He detected an Asian accent in the English. Fire burned all around where they stood, not raging, but spreading, using the furniture as fuel. Fresh, hot fingers ignited along the wood floor between him and the other man.

He stepped closer.

The gun was lifted higher. "The lamp. Toss it to me."

"I don't think that would be—"

"Toss it."

Malone stared down at the dragon head and the bits of wax that dripped from the mouth. He could still smell the oil and decided that if the man wanted the lamp, then that's what he was going to get.

He arced the vessel into the air but, as he released his grasp, a flick of his wrist twisted the lamp. He was careful to provide only enough velocity so that it would fall short and his assailant would have to step forward to catch his prize.

He watched as the dragon's head angled downward and spotted the first glimpse of liquid spilling from the mouth. The droplets met the heat below with a hiss and a flash, as the fire enjoyed what was surely a satisfying meal.

Oil spewed out as the armed man stepped forward and caught the lamp between its wings, upside down, the head pointed toward the floor.

Fresh flames ignited on the floor as the oil vaporized.

The fire searched upward for more.

When it found the lamp, a ball of heat and light erupted in the man's hands.

A scream pierced the boiling air as the man's clothes caught fire. He dropped the lamp and the gun, his arms flailing as his clothes disintegrated.

Malone found his Beretta on the floor and fired two shots into the man's chest.

The burning body dropped to the floor.

He stepped close and planted one last shot in the head.

"More than you would have done for me," he muttered.

CASSIOPEIA SLUGGED HER ATTACKER IN THE FACE. HE WAS weakened by her blow to his groin, stunned from the pain, all the breath smashed from him. He started coughing, gasping for bits of air among the smoke.

Another punch and he collapsed, not moving.

The fire had now consumed the hallway to her left—floor, walls, and ceiling—and smoke was spreading by the second. She, too, coughed out a lungful of carbon.

Two gunshots echoed from down the corridor.

"Cotton," she called out.

Another gunshot.

"Cotton. For God's sake answer me."

"I'm here," he yelled.

"Can you get to the stairs?"

"No. I'm going out one of the windows."

She should go to him and help. He'd come for her.

"Can you get out?" he called out over the flames.

"It's clear here."

She kept her gaze down the third-floor corridor, now completely engulfed by fire. Her knuckles throbbed and her lungs ached. The heat was stifling. She realized there was no choice. She had to leave. But—

"I need the lamp," she yelled.

"I have it."

"I'm going," she called out.

"See you outside."

She turned and headed for the stairs, but something below caught her attention. On the landing stood a man, his face gaunt, his black eyes locked on her. In his grasp was a bow, an arrow threaded onto the string, pulled tight.

Her gun was gone. There was nowhere to run.

The man kept his aim, his intentions clear.

He'd come to kill her.

THIRTY-ONE

Ni heard another of the third-floor windows shatter, followed by something flying out into the night. He watched as a chair crashed into the garden, then saw shadowy movement in the open window. Something else was tossed down. Smaller but heavy, it fell quickly, landing in one of the graveled paths.

"That could be what we seek," Pau said.

A man maneuvered his way out, grabbing hold of the vines that veined the museum's rear façade. He was not the right size or build to be Pau's minion.

"He is the one who entered after the three," Pau said.

Ni agreed.

Sirens were approaching. Soon the area would be crowded with emergency personnel.

"We must see if that was the lamp before he reaches the ground," Pau said.

He agreed. "I'll go."

"Hurry."

Ni fled their hiding place and crossed the darkness back to the garden. He kept one eye on the man, noting that he was skillfully using the vines to descend. Ni chose an oblique approach, advancing not along the graveled paths, cut with precision through the odorous flora, but down the edge, using the soft soil and a row of tall cypresses to mask his approach.

He spotted the chair broken into pieces, then looked where he'd seen the smaller object land, catching sight of a dark form in the middle of one of the paths.

He glanced up and saw the man struggling with the vines, slowly making his descent. Head and eyes seemed intent on finding hand-holds, so Ni took advantage of the moment and crept to the object.

He lifted it and found it warm.

A dragon's head on a tiger's body with the wings of a phoenix.

The lamp.

MALONE GRIPPED THE STALKS AND EASED HIS BODY DOWNWARD. He'd managed to re-retrieve the lamp from the fire, then tossed it down to the garden. He'd noticed on his initial approach that the gravel below was fine, like ball bearings, so it should have provided a cushioned landing.

He wasn't sorry the man inside was dead. No doubt once he'd turned over the lamp he would have been shot himself.

He kept his attention on the vines, grateful that they'd apparently flourished a long time, their meaty stalks firmly attached to the exterior. The second level had yet to catch fire, and the smoke from the top two floors spewed upward, away from him. Definitely cooler and easier to breathe here.

He glanced down to see how far remained and spotted a shadow creeping past the destroyed chair. He watched as the form quickly scooped up the lamp.

"That's not yours," he called out.

The form hesitated an instant, looked up, then bolted away, rushing for the garden's far exit.

His attention on the thief caused him to ignore the vines. Blindly, he reached for his next handhold and the plant gave way with a crack.

He fell backward.

And kept falling.

NI RAN FROM THE GARDEN BUT GLANCED BACK AT THE SOUND of something snapping. He watched as the man fell ten meters. No way to know if the fall would cause an injury or if the climber would come to his feet and pursue.

But he wasn't going to stay and find out.

He rushed through the gate, crossed the drive, and found Pau Wen.

"We must leave," Pau said.

Ni could not argue with that move. Enough risks had been taken. He could not be discovered here.

"I realize," Pau said, "you are concerned about the people inside the museum. But we will return home and await my brother. Then we will know the situation."

CASSIOPEIA REALIZED THERE WAS NO WAY TO FLEE. THE ARCHER would have a clear shot across the balustrade until she reached a blazing hallway, which offered no escape. She'd also never make it anywhere near the bowman, since the arrow would find her far quicker than she could move.

Game over.

She hoped Cotton had escaped. She'd miss him, though only at this moment, facing death, had she considered how much. Why had she never expressed herself? Never said a word. Why the dance they both seemed to enjoy where neither one of them wanted to commit, yet they both always turned to the other in time of need.

She regretted not being able to help Lev Sokolov. She wondered what would happen to his son. Most likely he'd never be seen again. She'd tried. Done everything she could.

But it had not been good enough.

Strange, a person's thoughts in the face of death. Perhaps there was an instinct that brought to the surface every regret. Was this what Henrik Thorvaldsen had experienced in Paris? If so, maybe Cotton was right and their friend did die thinking he'd been betrayed. How awful. Especially when it wasn't true. She now understood Cotton's anguish, his regrets at not making things right, and she wished for one more opportunity herself.

"*Tou qie zhu ren de zei bi si wu yi,*" the archer said.

She could not speak Chinese, so his words meant nothing.

"Get it over with," she called out, waiting for the slap of the bow-string, then the arrow piercing her flesh.

Would it hurt?

Not for long.

Two bangs startled her.

The archer staggered and she realized that the man had been shot. She dove to the right just as he lost his grip on the bowstring. But because he was collapsing as the arrow released, its metal tip found only marble.

She pushed herself up from the floor and stared past the thick spindles.

A man walked up from the floor below, stopping at the landing where the archer's body lay twitching in violent spasms.

Another shot and all movement stopped.

Viktor Tomas turned toward her.

She did not like the look in his eyes. He was surely angry from her attack on him back at the house. Yet he was here, holding her gun, the one that had fallen away, now aiming the weapon straight toward her, steadying his grip with both hands.

She faced the same dilemma with him that she had with the archer.

Nowhere to run.

He fired.

THIRTY-TWO

MALONE ROLLED OUT OF THE SHRUBBERY. GOD BLESS THE groundskeeper who'd groomed these hedges thick, trimming them into a perfect wall that stood six feet high. Their many branches had broken his fall, though one annoying stalk had bruised his hip.

He rose to his feet.

At forty-eight he was a little old for this, but thoughts of Cassiopeia rushed through his brain. He needed to find her. He recalled noticing on the climb down that the first two levels had yet to burn, but this might no longer be the case. Sirens were approaching, so he assumed the privacy Stephanie had arranged was gone, as were the lamp and its thief.

All in all, a total bust for the evening.

He turned toward the terrace and the doors through which they'd all first entered.

Three firemen burst out.

They seemed startled by his appearance, and one of them shouted something. Flemish was not a language he knew. But no translation was required. Two policemen appeared and drew their guns.

He knew what they wanted.

So he raised his hands.

CASSIOPEIA WAITED FOR THE BULLET, BUT ALL SHE FELT WAS A slap of air as the round zoomed past her right ear.

She heard metal sucking into flesh and whirled.

The man she'd beaten had risen to his feet, advancing toward her with a knife. Viktor's shot had caught him in the chest. The body dropped to the marble, trembled as if racked by fever, then went still.

"I told you I wasn't the enemy," Viktor said.

She caught her breath, then hustled down the stairs to the landing. "If you work for Tang, who do these men work for?"

Viktor pointed back to the top of the stairs. "He was mine. But this one." He shrugged. "I have no idea."

"You shot your own man?"

"He's actually Tang's. And would you have preferred to be stabbed?"

She pointed. "He said something before you shot him. In Chinese. I don't speak it."

"I do."

Her ears perked.

"He said, 'Death to the thief who steals from the master.'"

MALONE DECIDED TO TRY WHAT HE COULD. "THERE'S A WOMAN inside. On the third level. She needs help."

He wasn't sure if his English was being understood, as the two policemen were intent only on taking him into custody. They didn't seem to care about anybody else.

His arms were twisted behind his back and a nylon strap pulled tight at his wrists.

Too tight, but there was little he could say.

CASSIOPEIA FOLLOWED VIKTOR DOWN THE MAIN STAIRCASE, away from the fire and a black ceiling of ash above them. Streams of soot-stained sweat stung her eyes. Breathing was easier, as the smoke seemed confined to the top two stories. She heard sirens and spotted flashing emergency lights through the windows. They needed to leave. Far too many questions would be asked, and she had no satisfactory answers.

"I hope you have an exit plan," she said.

"There's a way out through the basement. I checked."

"How did you find me?"

Wood splintered below and something crashed. Voices were raised in urgency. Firemen, most likely, breaking through the main entrance.

She and Viktor stopped at the first-level landing.

Let them pass, he mouthed.

She agreed.

They abandoned the stairway and retreated into one of the first-floor rooms. No fire was here as yet. She hoped the emergency personnel would be concentrating on the upper stories.

A large billiard table provided cover, its green baize decorated with ivory accessories.

"You didn't answer my question," she whispered. "How did you find me?"

He motioned with the gun he still held. "If you hadn't pounded me on the head, I would have told you that it had a pinger inside. Tang's idea. Chinese intelligence issue. We would have left the gun. As it was, we tracked you straight here."

And she already knew who'd sent the archer. Pau Wen. *Death to the thief who steals from the master.* She'd sensed more to that old man, but had been in too much of a hurry to care.

Footfalls rang out. Firemen rushed up the staircase and kept ascending, carrying axes and hoses.

It's too risky, Viktor mouthed. *Let's find another way down.*

"There's a back staircase that way." She pointed to their left. "I used it to go up."

"Lead the way. When they find those bodies, this place is going to be heavy with police."

They scampered through a series of dim rooms to the stairs and crept down to the basement, careful their soles did not slap the risers. A black hallway led into the mansion's center, passing several doors clamped tight with hasp locks. Storage rooms, most likely. A high-pitched moan from overhead pipes suggested elevated pressure and temperature. They entered a room stuffed with gardening supplies—but it had an exit door.

"That has to lead up to ground level," Viktor said.

"More likely the side of the building," she noted. "We could be okay there."

The door unlocked from the inside. Viktor eased the metal door inward and peered out. Emergency lights brought the darkness to life in a rhythmic beat. But she heard no sounds from where a short set of stone steps ended up at ground level.

"After you," Viktor said.

She slipped out and savored the cool air. They crouched and climbed, using the stairway for cover.

At the top they darted to the right, where the street that ran before the museum stretched. She realized that they needed to emerge, unnoticed, from the narrow alley that separated the museum from the building next door.

Two meters from the end the path was suddenly blocked.

A woman stood in the way.

Stephanie Nelle.

MALONE WAS BROUGHT TO THE FRONT OF THE MUSEUM BY WAY of a police car that waited just beyond the garden, in the rear drive. A bruise on his right hip emitted a steady ache that caused him to limp.

He was pulled from the car and saw three fire trucks occupying the street that had been deserted when he first arrived. Hoses spit water into the air from ladders that extended upward off two trucks. As close as everything stood, on both sides of the block, confining the fire to one building could prove challenging. Luckily, the weather was calm.

One of the uniformed officers led him through the maze of trucks where cars were parked, maybe a hundred feet from the inferno.

He spotted Stephanie.

She didn't look happy.

"They found three bodies in there," she said as he was brought close. "All shot."

"What about Cassiopeia?"

Stephanie pointed to her right. Cassiopeia appeared from behind one of the police vans, her face blackened with smoke, wet with sweat, eyes bloodshot, but otherwise she appeared okay.

"I found her slipping out of the building."

Behind her walked a man. At first, Malone was so pleased to see Cassiopeia that he did not notice. But now, as his fears alleviated and calm returned, he focused on the face.

Viktor Tomas.

"What the hell is he doing here?" Malone asked.

"Long time, no see, Malone," Viktor said. "I love the handcuffs. They suit you." Viktor pointed a finger. "I haven't forgotten that I still owe you one."

He knew what that meant. From the last time they were together. In Asia.

"And here we are," Viktor said. "Together again."

Malone faced Stephanie. "Cut these cuffs off."

"Are you going to behave?"

Cassiopeia stepped close and said to him, "Thanks for coming."

He saw that she appeared unscathed. "I had little choice."

"That I doubt. But thanks."

He motioned with his head toward Viktor. "You and him working together?"

"He saved my life in there. Twice."

He glanced over at Viktor and asked, "What's your involvement this time?"

"I answer that, Malone," Ivan said, waddling out from behind another of the parked vehicles.

The Russian pointed at Viktor.

"He works for me."

THIRTY-THREE

HE LAY ON THE CUSHIONED BENCH AND STEADIED HIMSELF. HIS LEGS spread, his genitals exposed. Centuries ago there was a place, a ch'ang tzu, located outside the palace gates, where specialists performed the service for a modest six taels. They also taught apprentices the technique, thus transforming a profession into a tradition. The specialist he now faced was as skilled as those artisans, though he worked only for the brothers.

The final cleaning ended.

The hot water laced with pepper stung.

He'd remained rigid as the two attendants tightly wrapped his abdomen and thighs with white bandages. He could hardly breathe, but he understood their purpose.

Would it hurt?

He forced the thought from his brain.

Pain did not matter. Only his oath mattered. The bond. The brothers. They meant everything to him. His teacher had introduced him to the Ba and now, after several years of study, he would become a part. What would his mother and father say? They'd be mortified. But they were visionless nothings. Tools to be used as a shovel or a rake, discarded when either broken or no longer needed. He did not want to be one of those.

He wanted to command.

The specialist nodded and he adjusted his posture on the chair, spreading his legs wider. Two brothers clamped both limbs in place. To speak, to acknowledge the coming pain, would be a show of weakness, and no brother could be weak.

Only the strong were allowed.

He saw the knife, small and curved.

"Hou huei pu hou huei?" he was asked.

He slowly shook his head. He would never regret it.

It happened fast. Two swipes, and his severed scrotum and penis were displayed.

He waited for the pain. He felt blood seeping from the wound, the skin burning, his legs shaking. But no pain.

He watched as the organs were laid on a silver tray, blood encircling the flesh like some presentation at a restaurant.

Then the pain arrived. Sharp. Bitter. Excruciating.

His brain exploded in agony. His body trembled.

The two men maintained strong grips. He kept his mouth closed. Tears welled in his eyes but he bit his tongue to steady his control.

Silence was the only acceptable response.

One day he would lead the brothers, and he wanted them to say that he'd accepted his initiation with courage.

Tang thought back to that day thirty-six years ago. He'd lain still while the wound had been wrapped in wet paper, layer upon layer, until the bleeding stopped. He'd fought the shock that swept through his nerves, keeping a loose hold on reality. The three days that followed tested him further with agony from thirst and the inability to urinate. He recalled hoping that liquid would flow on the fourth day.

And it had.

He stood in the quiet trailer, remembering, readying himself to leave the drill site. He seldom thought of that day anymore, but tonight was special.

His satellite phone rang.

He found the unit and noted the number displayed. Overseas. A Belgian country code. He knew the number well.

Pau Wen's residence.

"I did exactly as you instructed," he said as he answered. "I ordered the strike on Ni Yong, while he was there at your residence."

"And I thwarted that strike, just as planned. Minister Ni was most grateful and now believes me to be his ally."

"Where is Ni?"

"He will shortly be on his way back to China. With the lamp."

"The lamp was to be mine."

"It matters not anymore," Pau said. "The oil is gone. Burned away."

"You assured me the lamp would be safeguarded." His voice had risen. "You told me that it would be turned over to me, intact, once Ni left Belgium."

"And you were not to disturb Cassiopeia Vitt," Pau said. "She was to bring the lamp to you."

"She couldn't be trusted."

"So you stole her away and hoped to win your prize by force?"

"I did what I thought best."

"And you were only to attack Ni Yong," Pau calmly said. "Not kill me."

He steadied himself.

"We killed three of the men you sent," Pau said. "And captured the fourth. I questioned him. He was most uncooperative, but finally told me that he and the others were ordered to kill Minister Ni and myself. No one was to be left alive at my residence. He said your orders on that were clear. Of course, he was not a brother. Only paid to do a job, which he failed to do."

The moment had come.

"You are the one no longer needed," he told Pau.

"From that comment, I assume you have taken charge of the brotherhood? The *Ba* now answers to you?"

"As they have for the past decade. I am the only master they know."

"But I am Hegemon. Their duly elected leader."

"Who abandoned us, and this country, years ago. We no longer require your involvement."

"So you ordered my death?"

"Why not? It seemed the right course."

"I conceived this endeavor. From the beginning. You were but a young initiate, fresh to the *Ba*."

"Is that when you found the Confucian texts at the terra-cotta warrior site?"

"What do you know of that?"

"The repository was rediscovered a few days ago. Your watch was found inside."

"So I did lose it there," Pau said. "I long suspected. But of course I intended on returning and examining that chamber further. Unfortunately, I never had the opportunity."

"Why did you remove only the Confucian texts?"

"To preserve them. If Mao's research fellows and archaeologists had discovered them, they would never have survived. Mao despised Confucius."

"The library is gone. Burned."

"You are no better than they were."

He resented the insolent tone. "I am not a young initiate any longer. I am first vice premier of the People's Republic of China. Poised to be the next premier and president."

"All because of me."

He chuckled. "Hardly. You have been gone for a long time. We have implemented your plan without your assistance. So stay in your refuge, safe in Belgium. China has no use for you."

"Your nemesis, though," Pau said, "is returning home far wiser. Minister Ni now knows of the *Ba*. He may well prevent you from succeeding."

"Ni is no match for me."

"But I am."

"There is no legal way for you to reenter China. No visa will be issued. On that, I have absolute control. The few brothers you have at your disposal there will be barred from returning, too."

"Not everyone supports you," Pau made clear.

He knew that could well prove true, but he was counting on success to win over any doubters.

"I have enough. Live short, Pau."

He ended the call.

There was nothing more to say.

A lesson he'd been taught long ago, during his training to become a brother, came to mind.

Never signal your intentions.

He smiled.

Not necessarily.

THIRTY-FOUR

NI STROLLED THROUGH PAU WEN'S EXHIBIT HALL, WAITING for his host to return. When they'd arrived back at the compound, Pau had excused himself. On the drive from Antwerp, Ni had called Beijing and spoken with his chief assistant, telling him he wanted an immediate report on Karl Tang's activities. Contrary to what Pau Wen might think, Ni had been watching Tang for some time, employing spies embedded deep within the first vice premier's office. Still, never had anyone spoken of eunuchs or the *Ba*.

He already knew Tang had left the capital yesterday, ostensibly to meet with local officials in Chongqing, but the true purpose of his journey had been to oversee the death sentence of a man named Jin Zhao, whose treason conviction had recently been upheld by the Supreme People's Court. He'd instructed his chief assistant to learn more about Zhao's case, along with Tang's interest in the man's death.

The vibration of his cell phone startled him. His staff had been fast, as usual. He answered, hoping that Pau would be delayed at least a few minutes more since this conversation must be private.

"Jin Zhao was an experimental geochemist who worked under the Ministry of Geological Development," his aide reported. "He supposedly passed sensitive information about oil exploration to the Russians."

"What type of information?"

"The record is silent. State secret."

"And the Russian agent?"

"No mention."

"Was the information actually passed?"

"No. An attempt thwarted, or so the trial record notes. However, the name you provided, Lev Sokolov, was also mentioned during the proceedings."

He'd taken Pau's advice and asked his office for a dossier on and current whereabouts of Lev Sokolov.

"He's a Russian expatriate who worked with Jin Zhao at a petro-chemical research facility in Lanzhou, a lab under the direct jurisdiction of the Ministry of Geological Development."

Which meant Karl Tang controlled the facility.

"Were Zhao and Sokolov colleagues?"

"They were working on an experimental project relative to ad-vanced oil exploration. That's what the facility's budget reveals. Beyond that, we learned no details."

"Learn them," he said. He knew there were ways, especially in his department.

He listened as he was told about Tang's busy night, traveling from Chongqing to the terra-cotta warrior site. Interestingly, a portion of one of the display pits had been destroyed by a fire, preliminarily blamed on an electrical short. Tang had been gone when the destruc-tion occurred, flown to an oil exploration site in northern Gansu. Nothing out of the ordinary there, as Tang oversaw the nation's entire oil exploration program.

"He's in Gansu now," his aide reported. "We have no eyes or ears at that location, but it's not necessary. We know his next destination. Lev Sokolov has been missing for the past two weeks. Tang's emissaries found him yesterday in Lanzhou. The minister is flying there."

"We have men in Lanzhou?"

"Five. Ready."

He recalled what Pau Wen had said. *Find Sokolov. He is the person who can explain the lamp's significance.* "I want Sokolov taken before Tang gets him."

"It will be done."

"I'm on my way back." He already held a reservation on a flight leaving Brussels, which he'd confirmed on the ride from the city. "It will be fifteen hours or so before I'm there. Send whatever you learn on Sokolov and Zhao by e-mail. I'll be able to access it while en route. I want to know how they are connected and why Tang is so intent on them both."

Beyond the open doors he spotted Pau Wen strolling through the courtyard, headed his way.

"I have to go."

He ended the call and hid the phone.

The older man entered the room and asked, "Have you enjoyed another look at my wonders?"

"I'm more interested in the lamp."

Pau had given the artifact to one of his men upon their arrival. "I'm afraid it was scarred from the fire, and the liquid it contained is gone."

"I want to take it back to China."

"Of course, Minister. You may have it. I only ask that you keep it from Karl Tang. I also have some disturbing news."

He waited.

"Tang conducted a virtual meeting with members of the *Ba* a few hours ago. Quite a gathering, I'm told. They are preparing for their final assault."

He decided he'd had enough of accepting what this man said on blind faith. "Where is Tang?"

Pau appraised him with a curious glare. "A test, Minister? To see if I speak with authority?" The older man paused. "All right. I understand your skepticism, though after what happened at the museum I had hoped we were making progress. But it is good to be cautious. It will keep you alive much longer."

"You haven't answered the question."

"He's at an oil exploration site, in northern Gansu."

Exactly what his aide had reported.

"Did I pass?"

"What assault has begun?"

Pau smiled, pleased at knowing he'd been right. "The *Ba* is again alive, after decades of self-imposed sleep."

"I'm leaving for home."

Pau nodded. "The lamp is packaged and ready."

"And you still have no idea of its significance?"

Pau shook his head. "Only that Minister Tang and Cassiopeia Vitt both wanted it. There is writing on the outside. Perhaps it's significant. Surely you have experts who can interpret it for you."

He did, but this old man was lying and he knew it. No matter. A war awaited him in China, and he was wasting time. He did need to know, "What happened at the museum?"

"Three bodies were removed. I assume one of those was my brother. Miss Vitt and two other men were brought out by the authorities."

"What will happen now?"

"For you, Minister? Nothing. For me, it means Cassiopeia Vitt will be returning here."

"How do you know that?"

"Years of experience."

He was tired of this man's pedantics, knowing now that the dull face and clever words were a mask for a callous, calculating mind. Pau was an expatriate who'd obviously interjected himself, once again, into Chinese politics. But Pau was in Belgium, a long way from the fight. A nonplayer. He was curious, though, on one point. "What will you do when Vitt returns?"

"Perhaps it's better you not know, Minister."

He agreed.

Perhaps it was.

THIRTY-FIVE

MALONE RUBBED HIS WRISTS AND ALLOWED THE CIRCULATION to return. The police had bound them too hard. Perhaps they were pissed about the museum, thinking him the culprit? But they were wrong. The culprit was standing a few feet away beside his new bene-factor.

"You told me you worked for Karl Tang and the Chinese," Cassiopeia said to Viktor.

"I do. But I'm there because of the Russians."

Malone shook his head. "Same as in Central Asia. Working for us, them, then us, then them. Hell, I don't see how you keep it straight."

"I'm a talented individual," Viktor said, adding a smile. "I've even worked for her." And he pointed at Stephanie.

Stephanie shrugged. "I used him on a couple of freelance assign-ments. Say what you want, but he does a good job."

"Last time, he almost got us killed," Malone pointed out. "I went in there blind, thinking he was on our side."

"I was," Viktor added.

"Is good agent," Ivan said. "Is close to Karl Tang, right where we want him."

Which explained how Ivan had such square-on intelligence about what was happening to Cassiopeia. But Malone had to ask, "What did you need us for?"

"Tang involved you," Viktor said. "I told him to leave you alone."

Ivan shook his head. "I not ask Stephanie to get in my business. Her idea, not mine. I hire Viktor for job. He do job well."

"Sokolov's son is the important thing," Cassiopeia said. "He's why I'm here. And I need to get going."

Stephanie grabbed Cassiopeia's arm. "Like hell. Look around you. There's a museum burning to the ground, three men are dead. And by the way, which one of you killed them?"

Malone raised his hand. "I shot one. But I was being nice."

"Meaning you shot him after you set him on fire?" Stephanie asked.

He shrugged. "Call me crazy, but it's the kind of guy I am."

"Viktor killed the other two," Cassiopeia added.

Malone heard the gratitude in her voice, which bothered him.

"What of this lamp?" Ivan asked Cassiopeia. "Do you find it?"

"I had it, but it's gone," Malone said.

He told them what happened in the garden. Ivan seemed agitated—things apparently weren't going according to plan.

"Must have the lamp," the Russian declared. "We need to know who is the man in garden."

"It's not hard," Cassiopeia said. "The archer, that thief in the garden, they were Pau Wen's men. He has the lamp. Again."

"How do you know that?" Stephanie asked.

Cassiopeia repeated what the archer had said.

Ivan faced Malone. "When it falls does lamp stay together?"

"The thing was made of bronze. It was fine. But I used the oil inside to take care of the man I killed."

Ivan's brow creased. "Oil is gone?"

He nodded. "Burned up."

"Then we are all in trouble. Karl Tang not want the lamp. He want oil inside."

TANG WATCHED DAWN BREAK TO THE EAST, THE FIRST SHAFTS of sunlight brightening the sky from violet, to salmon, to blue. His helicopter was rising into the early-morning air, their destination

Lanzhou, four hundred kilometers to the west, but still inside Gansu province.

He felt invigorated.

The conversation with Pau Wen had gone well. Another element completed. Now it was time to deal with Lev Sokolov.

What that man knew could well determine all of their futures.

"IT'S YOUR OWN FAULT," MALONE SAID TO IVAN. "IF YOU'D TOLD us the truth, that wouldn't have happened."

"Why is that particular oil so critical?" Stephanie asked, and Malone heard the interest in her voice.

Ivan shook his head. "Is important. To Tang. To Sokolov. To us."

"Why?"

A broad smile creased the Russian's pudgy cheeks. "Oil is from long ago. Direct sample from the earth. It stays in tomb for over two thousand years. Then it stays in lamp till tonight."

"How do you know that?" Malone asked.

"We only know," Viktor said, "what Karl Tang said. He told me the lamp was removed from an excavation by Pau Wen back in the 1970s and has stayed in Pau's possession ever since. The dragon's mouth was sealed with beeswax."

Malone nodded. "Until the fire. Which your men started."

"Against my wishes," Viktor said.

"That's not what you told them when you arrived. You said to get the gasoline, *just in case.*"

"Ever heard of playing a part?" Viktor asked. "Tang ordered us to retrieve the lamp and mask any evidence we were there. If we got in and out cleanly, then there would have been no need. Of course, I had no idea that we were going to have this wonderful reunion."

Malone saw the defeat on Cassiopeia's face.

"Sokolov's son is gone," she said to him. "No oil. No lamp."

"But none of this makes sense," he said.

"We need to pay Pau a visit."

He nodded. "I agree. But we also need some rest. You look like you're about to drop. I'm tired, too."

"That little boy is depending on me."

He saw resolve re-form in Cassiopeia's eyes.

"I will make contact with Pau," Ivan said.

Malone shook his head. "Really bad idea. What do you think you can learn? Cassiopeia's been there. She owes him. We have a reason to show up."

"I do not like that plan. Look what happen last time I listen to you."

"He probably is thinking himself clever at the moment," Cassiopeia said. "One of those people down the street watching this spectacle is surely working for Pau. So he knows I'm alive."

He caught what she hadn't voiced.

And one of his men isn't.

"I want to know all about Pau Wen," Malone said to Stephanie. "Before we go. You think you can get us some quick background?"

She nodded.

He stared at Ivan. "We'll find out what we need to know."

The burly Russian nodded. "Okay. Give try."

"I have to leave," Viktor said.

Malone motioned with his arms. "Don't let the door hit you in the ass on the way out."

Cassiopeia blocked Viktor's path. "Not before you tell me where Sokolov's child is. You told me you knew."

"I lied, so you'd take me with you."

"Where is the child?" she asked, the plea in her voice clear.

But Viktor seemed unmoved. "I really don't know." He faced Ivan. "Tang will want to hear from me. Of course, his men are dead and I don't have the lamp. That's not going to make him happy."

"Get back to him," Ivan said. "Do what you do best."

"Lie." Malone couldn't resist.

"I can handle Tang," Viktor said. "But there's something you people should know."

Malone was listening.

"Tang ordered a strike on Pau Wen. He may not even be alive."

"And you're just now mentioning this?" Malone asked.

"You know, Malone, I've only been around you a few minutes, but I've already had enough."

"You're welcome to take your best shot."

"Settle this later," Stephanie said. "Right now, I'm concerned about this Pau Wen. Cotton, you and Cassiopeia check him out. I'll get what you need, and Ivan and I will wait to hear from you. Viktor, go do what you have to do."

"Who die and make you in charge?" Ivan asked.

"We don't have time to argue."

And he saw that Ivan agreed.

Malone watched as Viktor hustled off among the parked cars.

"You could have been a little easier on him," Cassiopeia said. "He's in a tough spot."

Malone could not care less. "He didn't save *my* life. Twice."

THIRTY-SIX

TANG DISLIKED LANZHOU NEARLY AS MUCH AS HE DID CHONG-qing. The town hugged the banks of the Yellow River, crammed into a narrow valley and hemmed by steep mountains. Hundreds of brickyards and smoking kilns dotted its outskirts, everything cast in the same shade of clay as the landscape. Once it had served as the gateway to China, the last place to change horses and buy provisions before heading west into the harsh desert. Now it was the capital of Gansu province—skyscrapers, shopping centers, and a convergence of railway lines stimulating commerce. No trees, but plenty of chimneys, minarets, and power lines, its overall impression one of bleakness.

He stepped from the car that had driven him from the airport. He'd been informed that Lev Sokolov was now in custody, his men having entered the house where Sokolov had hidden.

He approached the apartment building, passing a fountain that contained nothing but dirt and dead mice. An overhead mist thinned with the rising sun, revealing a sky tinted the color of ash. The odor of fresh cement mixed with the smoggy exhaust of cars and buses. A labyrinth of alleys and lanes radiated in all directions, bisecting blocks of more ramshackle housing. A mad tangle of pushcarts, peddlers, bicycles, and farmers selling produce engulfed him. The faces mainly Arab and Tibetan. Everyone wore variations of gray, the only bright colors coming from displays in some of the shops. He'd changed clothes, discarding his tailored suit for trousers, an untucked shirt, running shoes, and hat.

He stopped before the granite-faced building, a flight of wooden steps leading to the upper floors. He'd been told it contained housing for midlevel managers at the nearby petrochemical refinery. He climbed, the stairway musty and dim, the landings piled with boxes, baskets, and more bicycles. On the second floor he found the pocked wooden door, a man waiting outside.

"There were men watching us," the man reported.

He stopped at the door and waited.

"They work for Minister Ni."

"How many?"

"Five. We dealt with them."

"Quietly?"

The man nodded.

He acknowledged his praise with a smile and a slight nod of the head. The leak within his office was worse than he believed. Ni Yong had sent men straight here. That would have to be corrected.

But first.

He stepped inside.

The single room held a few chairs and a low table, the kitchenette along one wall littered with filthy utensils, food wrappers, plates, and rotting food. On a Naugahyde sofa sat Lev Sokolov, his hands and feet bound, a strip of black tape across his mouth, his shirt soaked with sweat. The Russian's eyes went wide when he spotted Tang.

He nodded and pointed. "You should be afraid. You've put me through a great deal of trouble."

He spoke in Chinese, knowing that Sokolov understood every word.

Tang removed his hat. Two more of his men flanked the sofa at each end. He gestured for them to wait outside, and they left.

He glanced around at walls painted beige, low-wattage bulbs doing little to brighten the gloom. Green fungus sprouted near the ceiling.

"Not much of a hiding place. Unfortunately for you, we assumed you never left Lanzhou, so we concentrated our efforts here."

Sokolov watched him with eyes alight with fear.

A cacophony of grinders, power drills, and air jacks, along with the chatter of people, could be heard out a window no bigger than a baking sheet.

Sokolov was tall, broad-shouldered, with a narrow waist and thin hips. A short, straight nose with a slight bump protruded above the tape sealing his mouth, while a dark mop of black hair, long and uncut, dropped to his ears. The beginnings of a beard dusted his cheeks and neck. Tang knew this foreigner was brilliant. Perhaps one of the world's greatest theorists on oil geology. Together he and Jin Zhao may well have proven a theory that could forever change the planet.

"I have you," Tang said. "And I have your son. I offered you a way to have your son back, but you chose another path. Know that Cassiopeia Vitt failed. She is most likely dead by now. She did not obtain the lamp. In fact, its oil is gone."

Terror filled Sokolov's eyes.

"That's right," he said. "What use are you any longer? And what of your son? What will happen to him? Wouldn't it be fitting that he be reunited with his mother? At least he'll have one parent."

Sokolov shook his head in a furious attempt to block out the harsh reality.

"That's right, Comrade Sokolov. You will die. Just as Zhao died."

The head shaking stopped, the eyes bright with a question.

"His appeal was denied. We executed him yesterday."

Sokolov stared in horror, his body trembling.

Tang reminded himself that he needed Sokolov alive, but he also wanted this man to know terror. Months ago, he'd ordered a complete profile. From that he'd learned of the Russian's devotion to his son. That was not always the case. Tang knew many men who cared little for their children. Money, advancement, even mistresses were more important. Not so with Sokolov. Which was, in a way, admirable. Not that he could sympathize.

Something else from the profile came to mind.

A small item that only last night had become important.

He stepped to the door, opened it, and motioned for one of the men to draw close.

"In the car below there are a few items," he said in a low voice. "Retrieve them. Then," he paused, "find me a few rats."

MALONE DROVE WHILE CASSIOPEIA SAT SILENT IN THE PASSENger seat. His hip still hurt, but his pride was more deeply wounded. He should have kept his cool with Viktor. But he had neither the time nor the patience to deal with any distractions, and that man bore constant watching. Perhaps, though, he was more bothered by Cassiopeia's defense of Viktor.

"I meant it," she said. "I appreciate you coming."

"What else would I have done?"

"Sell books."

He smiled. "I don't get to do that as much as I thought I would. Video links from friends getting waterboarded keep getting in the way."

"I had to do this, Cotton."

He wanted to understand.

"Five years ago, I was involved with something in Bulgaria that went bad. I met Sokolov there. He worked for the Russians. When trouble hit, Sokolov got me out of there. He took a big chance."

"Why?"

"He hated Moscow and loved his new wife. A Chinese. Who was pregnant at the time."

Now he understood. The same child now at risk.

"What were you doing in the Balkans? That's a tough place to roam around."

"I was after some Thracian gold. A favor to Henrik that turned ugly."

Things with Henrik Thorvaldsen could go that way. "You find it?"

She nodded her head. "Sure did. But, I barely made it out. With no gold. Cotton, Sokolov didn't have to do what he did, but I would never have made it out of there, but for him. After, he found me on the Internet. We'd communicate from time to time. He's an interesting man."

"So you owe him."

She nodded. "And I've screwed the whole thing up."

"I think I had a little to do with that, too."

She motioned to the intersection approaching in the headlights and told him to turn east.

"You had no idea about the oil in the lamp," she said. "You were flying blind." She paused. "Sokolov's wife is destroyed. That boy was her world. I met her last week. I don't think she can survive knowing he's gone forever."

"We're not done yet," he said.

She turned her head and looked at him. He glanced across the darkness and caught sight of her face. She looked tired, frustrated, angry.

And beautiful.

"How's your hip?" she asked.

Not exactly what he wanted her to ask, but he knew she was as skittish as he was about emotions.

"I'll live."

She reached across and laid a hand on his arm. He recalled another time they'd touched, just after Henrik's funeral, on the walk back from the grave, through trees bare to winter, across ground dusted with snow, holding hands in silence. No need to speak. The touch had said it all.

Like now.

A phone rang. His. Lying on the console between them.

She withdrew her hand and answered. "It's Stephanie. She has the info on Pau Wen."

"Put it on speaker."

CASSIOPEIA DIGESTED THE INFORMATION STEPHANIE RELATED on Pau Wen. Her mind drifted back to a few hours ago when she thought she was about to die. She'd regretted things, lamented on how she would miss Cotton. She'd caught his irritation when she'd defended Viktor, though it really wasn't a defense since she still believed that Viktor knew far more about Sokolov's son than he was willing to admit.

Viktor was obviously playing another dangerous game. The Russians against the Chinese, the Americans against them both.

Not an easy thing.

Stephanie continued with her information.

Cotton was listening, his eidetic memory surely filing away every detail. What a blessing that could be, but also a curse. There was so much she'd prefer not to recall.

One thing, though, she clearly remembered.

In the face of death, staring at the archer, his arrow aimed straight at her, then again when Viktor's gun had pointed her way, she'd desperately wished for one more opportunity with Cotton.

And received it.

THIRTY-SEVEN

BELGIUM

MALONE STARED AT THE MAN. THOUGH IT WAS AFTER MID-night, black as soot outside, and the entrance bore evidence of gunfire, the older man who'd opened the doors—short-legged, thin-chested, with red-rimmed eyes, bleary but alert—seemed unfazed.

A faint smile came to his lips. Malone recognized the face.

From the museum, with two others, one of whom had carried a bow and arrows.

Cassiopeia was right. Pau Wen did indeed have the lamp.

Cassiopeia did not give Pau time to react. She withdrew her gun, the same one Viktor had used to track her, and jammed the barrel into the man's neck. She shoved Pau from the doorway and slammed him against a stone wall, pinning a few artificial stalks of bamboo between his silk robe and the wall.

"You sent that bowman to kill me," she said.

Two younger Chinese appeared at the top of a short flight of wide stairs that led up into the house. Malone withdrew his Beretta and aimed it their way, shaking his head, telling them not to interfere. The two halted their advance, as if they knew Cassiopeia would not pull the trigger.

Glad they thought so. He wasn't so sure.

"You came into my home," Pau said. "Stole my lamp at gunpoint. Did I not have the right to retrieve my property?"

She cocked the gun's hammer. The two standing above them reacted to the increased threat, but Malone kept them in place with his weapon.

"You didn't send that man to kill me because of the lamp," she said. "You *wanted* me to take the damn thing."

"It was Minister Tang, not I, who changed this situation."

"Perhaps we ought to let him speak," Malone said. "And he might feel more inclined to do that if you took that gun away from his throat."

"And men came to kill me today, as well," Pau said. "Sent by Tang. You see evidence of that in the doors. Sadly, for them, they died trying."

"And no police?" Malone asked.

Pau smiled.

Cassiopeia lowered the gun.

Pau smoothed his sleeveless gown and dismissed the other two men with a wave of his hand.

"You knew we'd come," Malone said.

He'd seen that certainty in the man's eyes.

"Not you. But her. I realized she would be here before the sun rose."

NI WAS WAITING TO BOARD HIS FLIGHT FROM BRUSSELS TO BEIjing. He'd used his diplomatic passport to have the lamp stored on board, to be waiting for him in the terminal when he deplaned in China. He'd already telephoned his office, and a car would be at the airport to drive him straight to his office. Hopefully, by then, he would know more about the *Ba* and Karl Tang's connection to it. Seemingly nothing had gone right over the past few hours, but he was far more informed and that was a plus. Pau Wen had proven helpful, perhaps too helpful, but Ni was now more concerned about Tang.

An announcement came that the first-class cabin could now board.

He'd booked that luxury for two reasons—because he needed to rest and because the airline offered in-flight Internet connection to its first-class passengers. He had to stay in touch.

He stood.

His phone vibrated in his pocket, and he answered.

"We don't have Sokolov," his assistant informed him. "Our men have disappeared. No contact for two hours."

"Is Tang in Lanzhou?"

"He's with Sokolov now."

He thought quickly. They'd lost the element of surprise.

"Do you want more men sent?" came the question.

The course seemed clear. Retreat, reassess, then decide.

"No. Lay low. Stand down."

"And Sokolov? That could prove fatal for him."

"We're just going to have to hope that it doesn't."

CASSIOPEIA FOLLOWED MALONE AND PAU WEN INTO ONE OF the gathering rooms. She noticed again the woodwork, the paneling and lattice, as well as the olden silk hangings, couplets, and lanterns. She watched as Malone absorbed the surroundings, too, surely concluding as she had during her first visit that this place expressed wealth and taste. Soft incandescent lighting cast a warm glow of candles, which calmed her nerves.

A map had caught Malone's attention, and she noticed it, too. Maybe two meters long by a meter high, painted on silk—fine, stiff, and textured. A series of Chinese symbols wrapped its four sides, forming a border. She admired the colors—crimson, sapphire blue, yellow, and green, each hue appearing faded from a brownish yellow glaze.

"That's impressive," Malone said.

"It's a reproduction of something I once saw. An ancient representation of China." Pau pointed. "The Gansu and Qinghai desert plateaus to the west. South to Guangdong and Guangxi. The sea on the east and, to the north, the Ten Thousand Mile Long Wall."

Malone smiled at the phrase.

"Chinese do not call it the Great Wall," Pau said.

The map was quite detailed, showing lakes and rivers and what appeared to be roads that connected towns, all delineated by pictographs.

Pau pointed to some of the locations. "That's Ling-ling at the bottom, the southernmost city. Chiu-yuan, beside the long wall, protected the north. Ch'i-fu and Wu guarded the Yellow Sea. The rivers shown are the Wei, Yellow, and Yangtze."

"Is it accurate?" Malone asked.

"The Chinese were excellent cartographers. They actually developed the technique. So yes, quite accurate."

Malone pointed to the extreme southwestern portion and what appeared to be a representation of mountains. Three symbols denoted a location.

阿 房 宫

"That's a lonely outpost."

Pau nodded. "The Hall for the Preservation of Harmony. An ancient site that actually still exists. One of thousands of temples in China."

Their host motioned to two rattan couches, and they sat. Pau faced them from a Cantonese easy chair. Malone, apparently remembering Stephanie's briefing on the phone, kept the facts to a minimum and made no mention of the Russians. But he did say, "We understand the lamp is not important. It was the oil inside that Karl Tang wanted. You don't happen to know why?"

Pau's eyes stayed flat and hard.

She'd been oblivious to the man's manipulations on her first visit, thinking herself in charge. Now she knew better.

"Only that Tang required a sample of ancient oil for some purpose."

"You're a liar," she declared.

Pau frowned. "And what if I am? What do you have to offer for the information you seek?"

"What do you want?" Malone asked. Then he motioned at the room. "Obviously, you don't need money."

"True, I am a man of means. But I do have a need. Let me inquire of Ms. Vitt. Do you intend to return to China?"

"You know about Sokolov, the boy, Tang. You know about everything, don't you?"

"And the answer to my question?"

"I wasn't. But I am now."

"I assume your reentry will be without the Chinese government's knowledge?"

"That would probably be best," Malone said.

"I want to accompany you."

"Why would we even consider doing such a thing?" she asked.

"I know where there is another sample of oil from 2,200 years ago."

TANG HELD A METAL PAIL THAT HAD BEEN BROUGHT FROM THE car. He'd obtained it at the drill site, along with a few other items, before leaving. His man had returned with two rats, one of fairly good size, found in the alley behind the building. He knew it would not be hard. Buildings like this were infested.

He heard the pests scurrying inside a cardboard box that had been hastily utilized as a cage. He realized it would not take them long to discover that they could burrow through. His background investigation on Sokolov had revealed a terrible phobia of rats, which made the Russian's choice of refuge even more strange. But under the circumstances, he'd probably not had many options. Hiding among the million and a half inhabitants of Lanzhou probably had seemed a safe bet.

He walked back to where Sokolov had been secured to a chair with heavy tape, his hands and feet still bound. He'd ordered the man's shirt removed, his bare chest exposed. Some rope, which he'd brought, a couple of lengths about two meters long, lay on the floor behind the chair.

Sokolov had yet to see the rats, though he surely heard their chatter.

Tang motioned and the chair was tipped back. Sokolov was now facing the ceiling, his spine to the floor, feet in the air. The cardboard box was opened and Tang scooped the rats into the pail. Its slick metal prevented their claws any traction, though they tried in vain to climb.

He approached Sokolov.

"It's time for you to understand just how serious I am."

THIRTY-EIGHT

BELGIUM

MALONE HAD BEEN TOLD ENOUGH ON THE PHONE BY STEPHANIE to know that Pau Wen had maneuvered Cassiopeia a few days ago and was now trying to do it again.

"Why do you want to go to China?" he asked Pau. "I'm told you fled the country decades ago."

"And what is your involvement here?"

"I'm your travel agent. The one who can book your ticket, depending on how I feel about you."

Pau grinned. "There is about to be a revolution. Perhaps even a bloody one. In China, changes in power have always involved death and destruction. Karl Tang intends to assume control of the government—one way or another."

"Why does he need a sample of oil from centuries ago?" Cassiopeia asked.

"Do you know about the First Emperor, Qin Shi?" Pau asked them.

Malone knew some. Lived two hundred years before Christ, a hundred years after Alexander the Great, and united seven warring states into an empire, forming what would later be called China, named after him. The first to do that, starting a succession of dynasties that ruled until the 20th century. Autocratic, cruel, but also visionary.

"Might I read you something?" Pau asked.

Neither he nor Cassiopeia objected. Malone actually wanted to hear what this man had to say, and he was glad Cassiopeia seemed to agree.

Pau clapped twice and one of the younger men who'd watched the encounter at the front door appeared with a tray, upon which lay a stack of brittle silk sheets. He laid the tray in Pau's lap, then withdrew.

"This is a copy of *Records of the Historian* or *Shiji*, as it has come to be called. It was written to cover the whole of human history, from a Chinese perspective, up to the time of its author's death in 90 BCE. It is China's first work of recorded history."

"And you just happen to have an original?" Malone asked. "Ready to show us."

"As I said, I knew she would come."

He smiled. This man was good.

"*Shiji*'s creator was the grand historian of the Han dynasty, Sima Qian. He supposedly consulted imperial records and traveled widely, learning from private documents, libraries, and personal recollections. Unfortunately, Qian eventually lost his emperor's favor. He was castrated and imprisoned, but upon his release he again became the palace secretary and completed this work."

"He was a eunuch?" Malone asked.

Pau nodded. "Quite an influential one, too. This manuscript still enjoys immense prestige and universal admiration. It remains the single best source that exists on the First Emperor. Two of its one hundred and thirty chapters specifically address Qin Shi."

"Written over a hundred years after he died," Malone said.

"You know your history."

Malone tapped his skull. "Got a mind for details."

"You are correct. It was written a long time after the First Emperor died. But it is all we have." Pau motioned to the top silk, brown and stained as if tea had been spilled upon it. Faded characters, written in columns, were visible.

"May I read you something?" Pau asked.

And the First Emperor was buried at Mount Li.
From the time he came to the throne, Qin Shi had begun the excava-

tion and building at Mount Li, and when gathered into his hands the whole empire, more than 700,000 workers were sent to the site to toil.

Through three underground springs they dug, and they poured molten bronze to make the outer coffin and to make the models of the palaces, pavilions, and government offices with which the tomb was filled.

And there were marvelous tools and precious jewels and rare objects brought from afar. Artisans were ordered to fashion crossbows as traps so that any grave robbers would meet sudden death.

Using quicksilver, they made the hundred rivers of the land, the Yellow and Yangtse, and the wide sea, and machines kept the waters in motion. The constellations of the heavens were reproduced above and the regions of the earth below.

Torches were made of oil to burn for a long time. Concubines without sons were ordered to follow the emperor in death, and of the artisans and workers not one was allowed to emerge alive.

Vegetation was planted so that it appeared to be a mountain.

"No ruler before, or since," Pau said, "has created a memorial of this magnitude. There were gardens, enclosures, gates, corner towers, and immense palaces. Even a terra-cotta army, thousands of figures who stood guard, in battle formation, ready to defend the First Emperor. The tomb complex's total circumference is over twelve kilometers."

"And the point?" Cassiopeia asked, impatience in her voice. "I caught the reference to torches made of oil that burned for a long time."

"That mound still exists, just a kilometer away from the terra-cotta warrior museum. It's now only fifty meters high—half has eroded away—but inside remains the tomb of Qin Shi."

"Which the Chinese government will not allow to be excavated," Malone said. "I've read news accounts. The site is filled with mercury. Quicksilver, as you said. They used it to simulate the rivers and oceans on the tomb floor. Ground testing a few years ago confirmed high amounts of mercury in the soil."

"You are correct, there is mercury there. And I was the one, decades ago, who wrote the report that led to the no-excavation rule."

Pau stood and walked across the room to another hanging silk image, this one of a portly man in long robes.

"This is the only representation of Qin Shi that has lasted. Unfortunately, it was created centuries after his death, so its accuracy is doubtful. What has survived is how one of Qin's closest advisers described him. *He has the proboscis of a hornet and large, all-seeing eyes. His chest is like that of a bird of prey and his voice like that of a jackal. He is merciless, with the heart of a tiger or a wolf.*"

"How does any of this help us?" Malone asked.

A satisfied look came to Pau Wen's aged face. "I have been inside the tomb of Qin Shi."

THIRTY-NINE

TANG SHOWED LEV SOKOLOV WHAT WAS SCURRYING AROUND inside the bucket. The Russian's eyes went wild.

"Active ones," Tang said.

Sokolov still lay on the floor, strapped to the chair, his legs folded above his head, eyes to the ceiling, like an astronaut in his capsule. His head began to shake back and forth, pleading for everything to stop. Sweat beaded on the Russian's forehead.

"You have lied to me for the last time," Tang said. "And I protected you. Officials here in Gansu wanted you arrested. I prevented that. They wanted to banish you from the province. I said no. They called you a dissident, and I defended you. You have been nothing but a problem. Even worse, you've caused me personal embarrassment. And that I cannot allow to go unanswered."

His three men stood beside the chair, two at the legs, one at the head. He motioned and they gripped Sokolov so his body would stay in position. Tang quickly approached and righted the metal pail, pressing down hard, holding the bucket in place, the rats trapped underneath, now scurrying around on Sokolov's bare chest. The Russian's head whipped left and right, held tight by Tang's man, the eyes closed in agony.

Tang pressed his own chest against the bucket's end to secure it in place and brought the ropes lying on the floor up, securing the pail to Sokolov's body.

Tang allowed a moment for things to calm, but Sokolov continued to struggle.

"I would suggest lying still," Tang said. "You'll agitate them less."

The Russian seemed to gain some measure of control and stopped thrashing, though the three men retained a firm hold.

Tang stepped to the table and retrieved one of the last two items he'd brought with him from the oil platform. A small, handheld instant-ignition torch fueled with acetylene. The kind of tool utilized for quick fixes on the rigs. He opened its brass valve. Gas hissed from the tip. He stood the torch upright on the table, gripped the final item, a striker, and sparked the end to life.

He adjusted the flame to blue hot.

He crouched down and allowed the heat to lick the bucket's bottom, then painted the sides of the pail with the flame. "As it warms, the rats instinctively shun the metal. They'll quickly sense a desperate need to leave their prison. But there's no way out. Everything is resistant to their claws, except your flesh."

He heard the rats popping against the inside of the bucket, squealing at their predicament.

Sokolov screamed behind the tape, but only a murmur could be heard. The Russian's restrained body was knotted in tension and wet with perspiration. Tang kept heating the bucket, careful not to make it too hot, just enough to entice the rats to attack the flesh.

Sokolov's face squeezed with anguish. Tears welled in the Russian's eyes and rained from the edges.

"The rats will claw down to your stomach," he said. "They will burrow through your flesh, trying to escape the heat." He kept stroking the metal with the flame. "They can't be blamed. Any creature would do the same."

Sokolov screamed again—a long, deep murmur muted by the tape. Tang imagined what was happening. The rats scratching furiously, aided by their teeth, softening the flesh that might allow them to escape faster.

The trick, as Tang had been taught, was knowing when to stop. Too long and the victim would receive severe, perhaps even fatal wounds from the infections the rats left behind. Too short and the point would not be made, and repeating the process was problematic, unless it didn't matter if the subject survived.

Here, it did.

He withdrew the torch.

"Of course," he said, keeping his eyes as gentle as his voice, "there is an alternative to this, if you're willing to listen."

FORTY

MALONE CAUGHT THE SIGNIFICANCE OF WHAT PAU WEN HAD said. "How is that possible?"

"When the terra-cotta army was discovered in 1974, I was dispatched by Chairman Mao to investigate and determine the extent of the find. I immediately realized that what had been discovered could prove immensely important. No one had any idea that the underground army existed." He pointed at the silks before him. "*Shiji* is silent on the matter. No written record mentions its existence. It seems to have been conceived, produced, buried, then forgotten."

Malone recalled reading about the find. Pau was right—it had proven significant for China. Millions flocked to the site every year. No visiting head of state left without a peek. Even the pope came during an unprecedented visit to China last year.

"While at the site," Pau said, "on a fortuitous day, I happened onto something even more remarkable."

The digging had been ongoing night and day for three months. Already, several hundred clay warriors had been unearthed, most in pieces, piled one atop the other like trees fallen in the forest. Luckily, the pieces were all near one another, so Pau ordered that a restoration workshop be constructed and the figures reassembled. His archaeologists and engineers had assured him that it could be done. In fact, they were confident that the entire army could be resurrected and stood up again, one warrior at a time. There could be thousands of them, he'd been told. Along with chariots and horses.

What a site that would be.

And he agreed.

But the nearby mound interested him more. It stood a kilometer away, south of the Wei River, beside the slopes of Black Horse Mountain. A vast, shallow-sided, earth pyramid with a wide base, veiled in fir trees towering over the grassy plain, seemingly part of the landscape.

But that had been the whole idea.

Men of Qin Shi's day believed that the dead lived on, only in a different world, and they should be treated as the living. So the First Emperor fashioned for himself a massive imperial necropolis, a subterranean empire, to continue his rule in the netherworld. Once created, everything had been hidden with dirt, creating a mound that once rose more than a hundred meters.

Had it ever been breached?

Literary references penned hundreds of years after Qin's time reported that the tomb had twice been entered. First by rebels in search of weapons three years after the First Emperor's death, then 700 years later for plunder. Scattered ashes, fired earth, and the broken warriors themselves suggested that the first violation may well have occurred. Few of the weapons the warriors once carried had so far been found. But the mound itself was not part of that first violation, and no one knew for sure if the second invasion ever occurred. He'd read Shiji and knew that there well could be rivers and oceans of mercury inside, part of an elaborate representation of Qin's empire, and this could pose a problem. Though thought of as medicine in ancient times, mercury was anything but and most likely contributed to the First Emperor's death. The fool would ingest an elixir each day of quicksilver, thinking that it would grant him immortality. Then again, looking at the mound that had stood for over two thousand years, Pau thought that perhaps Qin had been right after all.

Here was his immortality.

Mao himself had taken a keen interest in what was happening here. The Cultural Revolution was seven years past. Gangs waving their little *red books of Mao's thoughts were long gone, thank goodness. Schools and universities had reopened. The army was stable. Commerce had returned. China was again engaging the world. Warriors from the First Emperor's time—a massive, silent, heretofore unknown underground army—might be helpful in steering Mao's master blueprint for nation building. So the government had assumed control of the site, sealed off by the military, and workers were searched on both arriving and leaving. Some looting had occurred, mostly brass arrowheads sold for scrap. Several had been arrested and examples would have to be made, for nothing could jeopardize the area's potential. The Chairman had told him to do whatever was necessary to preserve the find.*

Mao trusted him and he could not disappoint.

So he'd ordered more exploratory digs.

Shiji made clear that there were countless aspects to the tomb complex. Already the digs had proven fruitful. Areas of interest had been identified. In one, horses and a chariot were discovered. Not representations, but the bones of horses and an actual chariot. What else lay in the earth around him? He could only imagine. It would take years to discover it all.

"Minister."

He turned to face one of several supervisors he'd entrusted with the local workers, men he could depend on to keep order.

"We have something."

He followed a group across the main excavation site—what they had started calling Pit 1—to an area twenty-five meters northwest.

A ladder protruded from a black yaw dug into the reddish earth.

"I found Qin Shi's imperial library below that ground," Pau said. "Several hundred manuscripts. Each one precious beyond measure."

"I've never heard of any such find," Malone said.

"That's because I resealed the repository. Mao was not interested in manuscripts. The past was unimportant to him, except as it could be used to further his Revolution. Mao was a Legalist, not a Confucian—if you understand the difference."

"Benevolence versus oppression," Cassiopeia said.

Pau nodded. "It is a debate China has engaged in for a long time."

"And which are you?" Malone asked.

"I have served many a Legalist."

"That doesn't answer the question."

"I am for what is best for China. That has always been my concern."

Still not an answer, so he tried, "Why did you reseal the library?"

"To prevent Mao from destroying what was inside."

"And what was that?"

"Thoughts that contradicted Mao's."

"You're good at not answering questions."

Pau smiled. "I intended to return and explore the repository further, but circumstances changed and I was never able. What's important is what else I found in that repository."

Malone waited.

"A path into Qin Shi's tomb."

TANG WATCHED AS LEV SOKOLOV CONSIDERED WHAT HE'D JUST said. The Russian remained bound to the chair, but the bucket had been removed. The rodents had viciously clawed his skin and blood oozed from nasty-looking wounds.

"You will do as I say?" he asked Sokolov.

Tape remained across the scientist's mouth, so all he could do was nod.

He pointed to the chest. "You're going to need antibiotics, and quickly. No way to tell how many diseases you have been exposed to. I suggest you not disappoint me."

A furious nod of the head signaled that would not happen.

His satellite phone vibrated in his pocket. Any interruption had to be vital, so he checked the display.

Viktor Tomas.

He fled to the hallway outside and answered.

"I have some things to tell you," Viktor said.

He listened to what was happening in Belgium, then said, "You were right about Cotton Malone. I should have listened."

"He's uncontrollable."

"You don't like him much, do you?"

"He's trouble."

"Are Malone and Vitt with Pau right now?"

"They are."

This was not part of the plan. "I must know what comes of that meeting. Can you learn that?"

"I'm waiting for the information right now."

MALONE SAW THAT CASSIOPEIA'S PATIENCE HAD EVAPORATED. He realized that her concern was Sokolov's son and that they currently had nothing to offer Karl Tang, so he tried asking Pau, "What did you see inside the emperor's tomb?"

"I can tell you that the reports of plunder were wrong. It was a virgin site. Untouched."

"And no one was told?" he asked. "Not even your good buddy Mao?"

"The times, Mr. Malone. Those things were not then important. Mao's Cultural Revolution caused countless amounts of Chinese history to be lost forever. The gangs broke pianists' hands, burned books and paintings, forced surgeons to clean bathrooms, teachers to wear dunce hats. Mao wanted great disorder so as to achieve a greater order, through him. It was a time when we willingly destroyed our heritage. The terra-cotta army discovery eventually helped change such foolish thinking, but that was a few years off. At the time of my discovery, I chose to keep what I saw to myself."

"But not anymore," Cassiopeia added.

"I must return to China—"

"Unnoticed," Malone said.

Pau nodded. "You have a way. I'm in need. But you have needs, too. Inside Qin's tomb are hundreds of lamps, filled with oil. I even lit one."

Their host led them back to the silk map on the opposite side of the room and pointed to its center. "That is Xianyang, Qin's capital. The First Emperor's tomb was built here, nearby. If you can get me to Xi'an, I can deliver the oil sample you seek."

Malone studied the map more closely. He wished he could read the lettering on both its surface and in the surrounding border. "Are these ancient designations?"

Pau nodded.

"If we get you there, can you get back inside Qin's tomb?" Cassiopeia asked.

"The library repository I located was refound just a few days ago, discovered adjacent to Pit 3 at the terra-cotta museum."

"Then they found the way into the tomb," Malone said.

"My reports are that those who found the chamber have been concentrating on the manuscripts. They have not found the entrance, and they will not. I concealed that passage well."

"How do you know all this?" Malone asked.

"Karl Tang told me, just a short while ago. We spoke on the phone. He mentioned the manuscripts, but nothing about the entrance passage."

That information piqued his interest.

"And why are you talking to Karl Tang?"

"We were once allies, but not any longer. I must return to China immediately. In return, I'll show you the entrance to the tomb and provide a lamp filled with oil from the time of Qin Shi."

"Where's the dragon lamp?" Cassiopeia asked.

"Minister Ni Yong has taken it back to China. He came here, after you, in search of it, too. Since it's unimportant, I let him have it."

"He doesn't know about the oil?"

Pau shook his head. "I did not tell him."

"And you're still not going to tell us why that oil is so important to Karl Tang," Cassiopeia asked.

"I will. Once I'm in China."

"Tell me this," Malone said. "And your seat on the plane is dependent on a really good answer." He paused. "How were you and Tang once allies?"

"We are both of the *Ba*. Eunuchs. Though I sense that you already suspected that."

Yes, he had.

He found his cell phone and said, "I need to make a call."

Pau motioned at the windows and the lit courtyard beyond.

Malone stepped outside and dialed Stephanie. She listened to his report and his request, spoke a moment with Ivan, who was there with her, then said, "We can make it happen. Bring him along."

"Lot of trust we're placing here."

"I know," she said. "One more thing, Cotton. Robin Hood from the museum, the one who tried to spear Cassiopeia. When they examined the body they discovered something interesting that's now even more relevant."

But he already knew. "He was a eunuch, too."

TANG STOOD IN THE HALLWAY AND QUIETLY DIGESTED THE new developments.

The Americans were involved?

Unexpected, to say the least. But not insurmountable. He was about to step back inside and conclude his time with Lev Sokolov when the phone again demanded his attention.

He answered.

"My Russian handler just informed me," Viktor said. "Malone, Vitt, and Pau are coming to China."

"Do you know how?"

"The Russians are going to assist. They are working with the Americans."

Troublesome on one count, a relief on another. He listened as Viktor explained the travel plan, then said, "That should allow us the opportunity to eliminate them all at once."

"My thoughts exactly."

"When are you returning?"

"In a few hours. I'm already booked on a flight."

"I'll need you to personally take charge, once you're here." He thought of the spies in his office. "Communicate with me only. There are few here I can trust with this information."

"I'll finalize everything while on the way," Viktor said.

"I realize that you may actually enjoy Malone's death, but I've sensed that it's a different matter with regard to Vitt. Earlier you made clear that she would not survive the night. Of course, that did not happen."

"Because of Pau's interference."

"What you really mean is *my* interference."

"I didn't say that."

"You didn't have to. I ordered the strike on Ni, which failed. Pau obviously retaliated, which caused unforeseen problems."

"You're in charge," Viktor said.

"Still, I sense you are somewhat glad I interfered, at least as it relates to her."

"I do as you say."

"I want to know." He paused. "Any reluctance on your part to Vitt dying with the others?"

The line stayed silent a moment.

He waited.

"None," Viktor said. "I'll handle it."

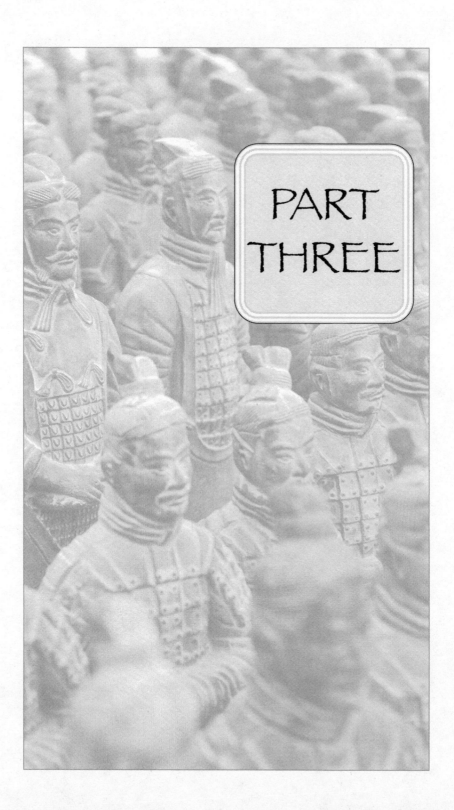

PART
THREE

FORTY-ONE

MALONE STARED AT THE MAGNIFICENT SCENE.

He knew the tale. Once, a great dragon ran toward the coast with its tail flailing, gouging valleys and crevasses along the way. As the beast plunged into the sea, water filled the low spots and left towering monoliths, like a crop of unfinished sculptures, one after the other, rising skyward. Standing on the dock, admiring Halong Bay, whose name meant "where the dragon descended into the sea," he found it easy to believe that legend. The tranquil waters stretched over six hundred square miles, eventually spilling out into the Gulf of Tonkin. Three thousand islands dotted the turquoise expanse, most uninhabited blocks of gray limestone. Verdant shrubs and trees sheathed most of them, the startling contrast of their spring color to the dull sheen only adding to the surreal scene.

Malone, Pau Wen, Cassiopeia, Stephanie, and Ivan had flown on a U.S. Air Force EC-37 from Belgium to Hanoi. The modified Gulfstream had made the trip in a little over ten hours, thanks to a free pass over Russian airspace courtesy of Ivan. They'd then taken a helicopter for a short flight east to the coast and Quang Ninh province. Russia apparently enjoyed a close relationship with the Vietnamese, as their entrance into the country had been met with unquestioned cooperation. When Malone had inquired about the lovefest, Ivan had only smiled.

"Have you ever been here before?" Cassiopeia asked him.

They stood near a cluster of houses that formed a floating village. Multidecked tour boats rested at anchor, as did many of the junks, their fan-shaped sails finding no wind. A tiny boat appeared with a fisherman standing in it, rowing with two oars crossed in an X. Malone watched as the man found his footing and tossed a net out into the water, its weights opening the mesh like a flower.

"Once," he said, "years ago. On an assignment, I came through on the way into China."

"As you will today," Ivan said. The Russian was studying the sky, looking for something. "Border is less than two hundred kilometers north. But we do not go that way."

"I get the feeling you've done this before," Stephanie said.

"Sometimes."

Pau Wen had remained quiet during the long flight, sleeping most of the way, as had they all, trying to adjust to a six-hour time difference. Pau gazed out at the calm sea with a sense that he'd been here before, too. A light fog steamed from the sea's surface, filtering a rising sun. Oyster-colored clouds dotted a blue sky.

"Tran Hung Dao, Vietnam's grand commander, faced off Kublai Khan's army here," Pau quietly said, "in 1288. He placed bamboo stakes in the rivers so that when the Chinese boats arrived at low tide, which he knew they would, the hulls would be pierced. When that occurred, his troops swooped down and slaughtered the invaders."

Malone knew the rest of that story. "But the Chinese returned, conquered, and dominated here for nearly a thousand years."

"Which explains why Vietnam and China are not friends," Ivan said. "Long memories."

On the flight, Malone had read what Stephanie had hastily amassed on Pau Wen. His background was one of academics, focusing on history, anthropology, and archaeology, but clearly he was a consummate politician. How else could someone become the confidant of both Mao Zedong and Deng Xiaoping, two utterly different personalities, and prosper under both?

"My uncle was a fisherman," Pau said. "He sailed a junk. As a boy, I would go out on the water with him."

Maybe fifty or more of the distinctive ships floated in the bay.

"The cotton sail is dipped in a liquid that comes from a plant similar to a yam," Pau said. "That's what gives the red-tan color. It also prevents rot and mildew. My task, as a boy, was to care for the sails." Pau made no effort to hide a nostalgic tone. "I loved the water. I still recall sewing the coarse cotton panels together, one seam at a time."

"What are you after?" Malone asked.

"Are you always so direct?"

"Do you ever answer a question?"

Pau smiled. "Only when I want to."

Cassiopeia grabbed three bags from the dock. Earlier, she'd volunteered to find food and drink, and Ivan had provided her with several hundred Vietnamese dong.

"Soft drinks and bread," she said. "Best I could do this early. In another hour there's a café open just beyond the end of the dock."

A small village nestled close to the shore—a cluster of low-slung pastel-colored buildings, rooftops bare and silent, a few faint curls of smoke wafting from several of the chimneys.

Malone accepted a Pepsi and asked Ivan, "Let's see if *you* can answer a question. What exactly are we going to do?"

"Time to time, we sneak into China. They have coastal radar, but rocks and mountains give shelter."

"We're going to sail a junk in?"

Ivan shook his head. "Not today."

Malone had also asked and received from Stephanie three other reports. One was on Karl Tang, China's first vice president and the Party's vice premier. Tang came from simple beginnings, trained as a geologist, rising steadily within the Communist Party until he was now one step from the top. In China's convoluted political system, the Communist Party was intimately interwoven with the national government. Every key governmental position was occupied by a Party official. Which explained why the president also served as Party premier. No one ever achieved election to any position without the Party's consent, which meant Karl Tang was a man of great power. Yet he required an oil lamp from an ancient grave so badly that he stole a four-year-old boy?

Ni Yong seemed the antithesis of Tang. Right off was his name, using the traditional form of last first. He'd grown up in Sichuan province in a village where nearly everyone was named Ni. He served two decades in the military, rising to high rank. He'd also been in Tiananmen Square in June 1989 when the tanks appeared. The West considered him a moderate, perhaps even a liberal, but they'd been fooled before by Chinese bureaucrats who said one thing then did another. Ni's administration of the central disciplinary commission was widely regarded as admirable, a refreshing change of pace from the Beijing usual. The hope was that Ni Yong could become a new breed of Eastern leader.

The final report dealt with Viktor Tomas.

Beyond their direct contact, Malone knew little about the man. Their first encounter last year, in Central Asia, had been brief. Viktor had once worked with the Croatian security forces and, not wanting to be tried for war crimes, he'd switched sides and helped American intelligence as a random asset. Last year, when it was learned that Viktor had managed to position himself close to the head of the Central Asian Federation, pressure had been applied on him to exact his cooperation. On the plane, earlier, while the others slept, he'd asked Stephanie, "Is he Bosnian?"

She'd shook her head. "His father was American. He was raised partly in Bosnia, some in California."

Which explained the lack of any European accent and his proficient use of slang.

"He's helpful, Cotton."

"He's a random asset. Nothing but a whore. Where is he now?"

"Back with Tang. In China."

"So what is it? Is he with the Russians? The Chinese? What's his mission?"

She said nothing.

"We're placing our asses right back in his hands," he said. "And I don't like it."

Stephanie had still not commented—which spoke volumes.

But he meant what he'd said about random assets. No loyalty, usually reckless as hell. He knew that not only from Viktor, but from others he'd once encountered as a Magellan Billet agent. The mission may or may not be critical to them. Results didn't matter. Surviving and getting paid, that's what counted.

Malone watched as Ivan continued to study Halong Bay. The sun, the temperature, and the morning mist had all quickly risen.

"It's a UNESCO World Heritage Site," Stephanie said.

He caught the twinkle in her eye. "How much damage could I do to this bay?"

"I'm sure you could find a way."

"There," Ivan said. "Finally."

He saw what had grabbed the Russian's attention. A plane, dropping from the sky, out over open water, making its way toward them.

FORTY-TWO

NI ENTERED THE TOMB OF MAO ZEDONG.

The granite edifice stood on the southern side of Tiananmen Square, a squat building, lined with columns, erected in a little more than a year after the Chairman died. Seven hundred thousand workers had supposedly participated in its construction, a symbol of the love that the Chinese harbored for their Great Helmsman. But that had all been propaganda. Those "workers" had been bused into the capital every day—ordinary people, each forced to carry a brick to the site. The next day, another busload would remove the same bricks.

Foolishness, but nothing unusual for China.

For the past year the mausoleum had been closed for renovations. In the rush to erect a memorial, little care had been taken on placement. Feng shui had been ignored. Consequently, there had been many structural problems over the years, ones his grandfather easily might have prevented.

On the flight from Belgium, he'd e-mailed a request for an immediate audience with the premier. Staff had responded quickly and said he would be seen as soon as he was in the country. His reporting directly on a pending investigation was nothing unusual, since the Central Commission for Discipline Inspection answered only to the premier. Meeting at Mao's tomb, though, was different. The explanation had been that the premier was there, making a final inspection before the site reopened in a few days.

In the mausoleum's vestibule, a massive white marble armchair held a sitting statue of Mao. Behind, a mural featured the geopolitical range of the Chairman's posthumous rule. Security men ringed the polished floor. He knew the drill. Two of the suited officers approached and he raised his arms, ready for a search.

"No need," he heard a voice, cracking with age, say.

The premier entered the vestibule, a short, stumpy man with bushy eyebrows that swept up toward his temples. He wore his characteristic dark suit and dark tie and walked while leaning on a red lacquered stick.

"Minister Ni has my trust." The premier motioned with his cane. "Allow him to pass."

The security men withdrew, never confiscating the pistol from his shoulder harness. A weapon had been waiting for him when he stepped off the plane. He had thought it wise, under the uncertain circumstances.

"Let us walk," the premier said.

They drifted deeper inside.

Evidence of renovations was everywhere, including fresh paint and sparkling stone.

"What is so urgent?" the premier asked.

"Tell me about Pau Wen."

The old man stopped.

Though his breath was short, the voice weak and halting, the hands and fingers bony, Ni realized that there was nothing sluggish about this man's mind.

"He is a dangerous man."

"In what way?" he asked.

"He's a eunuch."

"And what does that mean?"

The premier smiled. "Now you're not being honest with me. You know precisely what that means."

Few lights burned inside and the building's air-conditioning had chilled the interior to a winter's feel.

He'd made his move. Now he awaited a response.

"A eunuch cannot be trusted," the premier said. "They are inherently dishonest. They destroyed dynasty after dynasty with their treachery."

"I don't need a history lesson."

"Perhaps you do. When the First Emperor died, his chief eunuch conspired to have the eldest son, the chosen heir, commit suicide. He then aided the next son in becoming Second Emperor, thinking that he, himself, from behind the throne, would be in actual control. But that reign lasted only four years. Everything Qin Shi fought to create—what millions died to achieve—disappeared within three years of his death. And all because of a eunuch. That pariah is still recalled by history as 'a man who could confidently describe a deer as a horse.'"

He could not care less. "I need to know about Pau Wen and your contacts with him."

The older man's eyes narrowed, but no rebuke came. "Pau Wen likewise can confidently describe a deer as a horse."

He could not argue with that observation.

They continued ahead, a steady click of the lacquered cane off the marble floor accompanied by the shuffle of leather soles.

"Decades ago," the old man said, "Pau Wen and I were friends. We did much together. We both became disenchanted with Mao."

The premier stopped, his face contorted, as if trying to assemble a long train of hitherto unconnected thoughts, some of which might be unpleasant.

"The Cultural Revolution was an awful time. The young were encouraged to attack the old, the foreign, the bourgeois. We thought all of it right, all of it necessary. But it was insanity, and it all happened for nothing. In the end, the strong dragon proved no match for the local snake."

He nodded at the ancient saying.

"China changed," the premier said. "The people changed. Unfortunately, the government didn't."

He had to ask, "Why are you telling me this?"

"Because, Minister, I fear you will not win your coming battle with Karl Tang."

FORTY-THREE

MALONE SHOOK HIS HEAD AT THE UP-WING TWIN-ENGINE amphibian, a Twin Bee, built like a tank with rivets, hefty struts, and thick walls of sheet metal painted red and white. Its hull rested in the calm water like a boat.

"Your way into China," Ivan said.

"You can't be serious," Cassiopeia said. "They'll blow us out of the sky."

The Russian shook his head. "It never happens before."

Ivan unfolded a map, laid it across the dock's wooden railing, and rested a pudgy finger with dirty nails atop Halong Bay. He then traced a line to the northwest, straight across northern Vietnam, passing the border with China, ending at the city of Kunming, in Yunnan province, 500 miles away.

"You have clear passage from here to border," Ivan said.

"Apparently you and the Vietnamese are asshole buddies."

Ivan shrugged. "They have no choice."

Malone smiled.

"Lakes everywhere, south of Kunming. Dian Chi is the best one. Forty kilometers long. Plenty of places to land unnoticed."

"And what do we do once we're there?" Malone asked.

"We can take the train north to Xi'an," Pau said. "A few hours. From there we can bus out to the terra-cotta warrior site."

Malone wasn't impressed. "This isn't some jaunt across Europe. You're talking about flying 500 miles into a closed country, with a massive air force, unannounced. Somebody could easily get the wrong idea."

"I will provide pilot," Ivan said, "who can handle controls."

"I can fly the damn thing," he said. "I just want to be alive to land."

Ivan waved off his worries. "Yunnan province is friendly."

Pau nodded. "It has always been a renegade. Remote location, harsh terrain, diverse population. One-third of all the Chinese minorities live there."

"We have friends," Ivan said, "who help us. The route will be clear. Take this chart, which I mark. I assume you navigate?"

Cassiopeia snatched the map away. "I'll handle that chore."

"Fully gassed?" Malone asked Ivan about the plane.

"Enough to get there. But understand, it is one-way trip."

NI WOULD NOT ALLOW THE NEGATIVE OBSERVATION ABOUT himself to spark a response. He knew better. So he returned to his original question. "Tell me about Pau Wen."

"I do not answer to interrogation. I am not one of your investigations."

"Perhaps you should be."

"Because of Pau Wen? You give that man far too much credit."

"In Belgium, Karl Tang sent men to kill me. Pau Wen prevented that. He also told me things about Tang and you. Spoke of conversations between you and him. He said you even spoke of me. I want to know about those talks."

They stood at the entrance to the crypt. Mao's body lay in the center, sheathed by a crystalline sarcophagus.

"I had him brought from below," the premier said. "I wanted to see him in all his glory."

Ni knew that like so many others in Beijing, Mao traveled to work each day. The body was raised and lowered from an earthquake-proof chamber deep underground, sealed inside a transparent cocoon, surrounded by pure nitrogen. Halogen lights cast the corpse in a golden glow.

"You think Pau, Tang, and I are co-conspirators?" the premier finally asked.

"I don't know what to think. I'm simply asking a question. Tell me about your conversations with Pau Wen."

"I recall when Mao died," the premier said, gesturing toward the corpse. "September 9, 1976, just after midnight. Ten days the nation mourned. Loudspeakers and radio stations broadcasting somber music. Newspapers proclaimed him *the greatest Marxist of the contemporary era* and said *he will forever illuminate the road of advance of the Chinese people.* For three minutes that day the entire country stood in silence." The old man paused, his eyes still locked on the spectacle. "But for what, Minister? Tell me, for what?"

He realized he was being ignored. "I wasn't there. You were. What did you hope to gain from canonizing him?"

The premier faced him. "Do you know what happened after he died?"

Ni shook his head.

"Publicly, Mao had written that he wanted to be cremated. He said, after people die they should not be allowed to occupy any more space. They should be cremated. He publicly proclaimed that he'd take the lead and be burned to ashes, used for fertilizer. But we all knew that was propaganda. He wanted to be worshiped. The problem came when no one knew about embalming. It's simply not our way. The doctors located a Russian text in the national library and followed its procedure, but they injected so much formaldehyde that the face swelled like a ball and the ears projected at right angles. Can you imagine what a sight that was. Mao's skin turned slimy from the chemicals that oozed out the pores. I was there. I saw it."

Ni had not heard this story before.

"They couldn't drain the excess off, so they used towels and cotton balls, hoping to massage the fluid down into the body. One of them pressed too hard and a hunk of the right cheek broke off. Eventually, they had to slit the jacket and pants just to get the body into the clothes."

He wondered why he was being told this.

"But they were not entirely foolish, Minister. Before injecting the formaldehyde, they made a wax effigy of the entire body." The fingers of the old man's left hand pointed to the sarcophagus. "And that is what you see now."

"It's not Mao?"

He shook his head. "Mao is gone, and has been for a long time. This is but an illusion."

MALONE FOLLOWED CASSIOPEIA AND PAU WEN TO THE END OF the pier, Stephanie walking beside him.

"You realize this is crazy," he said in a low voice.

"Ivan says they slip in all the time. Usually from the shoreline to the north. Only difference here is half the flight will be over Vietnam."

"And that's supposed to make me feel better?"

She smiled. "You can handle it."

He pointed at Pau. "Bringing him along is crazy, too."

"He's your guide."

"We're not part of whatever he's after. I doubt he'll be much help."

"Since you know that, be ready."

He shook his head. "I should be selling books."

"How's your hip?"

"Sore."

"I need to make contact before we leave," Cassiopeia called out, stopping at the pier's end. She'd told them that a neighbor of Lev Sokolov's had agreed to act as go-between. All she needed was a laptop, which Stephanie produced, and a satellite connection, which Ivan arranged.

Cassiopeia balanced the computer on the dock's wooden railing, and Malone held it in place. He watched as she typed in an e-mail address, then a message.

I HAVE BEEN READING THE THOUGHTS OF MAO, BUT CAN-
NOT FIND HIS WORDS REGARDING UNITY. COULD YOU
HELP ME?

"That's clever," he said.

He knew the Chinese censored the Internet, restricting access to search engines, blogs, chat rooms, any site that allowed open conversation. They also employed filters that screened all digital content in and out of the country for anything suspicious. They were in the process of creating their own *intranet*, solely for China, which would be far easier to regulate. He'd read about the venture and its skyrocketing costs and technological challenges.

"I found a copy of the *The Little Red Book* and worked out a code," she said. "The words of Mao would never arouse suspicion. The neighbors said they would check constantly for any message."

Quotations from Chairman Mao Zedong—or, as the West labeled it, *The Little Red Book*—was the most printed book in history. Nearly seven billion copies. Once, every Chinese was required to carry one, and those editions now were valuable collector's items. Malone had bought one himself a few months ago, at the monthly book auction in Roskilde, for one of his customers.

The laptop dinged with an incoming message.

IT IS THE DUTY OF THE CADRES AND THE PARTY TO SERVE THE PEOPLE. WITHOUT THE PEOPLE'S INTERESTS CONSTANTLY AT HEART, THEIR WORK IS USELESS.

She looked up at him. "That's the wrong response. Which means trouble."

"Can they clarify what's going on?" Stephanie asked.

She shook her head. "Not without compromising themselves."

"She is correct," Pau Wen said. "I, too, use a similar coding method when communicating with friends in China. The government watches cyberspace closely."

Malone handed the laptop back. "We need to go. But first I have to do something."

Ivan had been talking on the phone for the past few minutes, standing away from them. Malone walked down the dock and, as the Russian ended his call, asked, "Anything you're willing to tell us?"

"You do not like me much, do you?"

"I don't know. Try a new posture, different clothes, a diet, and a change in attitude and maybe our relationship will improve."

"I have job to do."

"So do I. But you're making it difficult."

"I give you plane and way in."

"Viktor. Where is he? I miss him."

"He is doing job, too."

"I need to know something, and for once tell me the truth."

Ivan stared back at him.

"Is Viktor there to kill Karl Tang?"

"If opportunity arise, this will be good thing."

"And Sokolov? Is he there to kill him, too?"

"Not at all. That one we want back."

"He knows too much? Maybe some things you don't know?"

Ivan only glared at him.

"I thought so. Sokolov must have been busy while in China. Tell me, if it's not possible for Viktor to retrieve Sokolov or, God forbid, we get our hands on him first, what are his orders?"

Ivan said nothing.

"Just like I thought, too. I'm going to do us all a favor and keep this to myself." He gestured to the end of the dock. "She's not going to let that happen to Sokolov."

"She may have no say. Much better when we thought Sokolov dead. Now it is Viktor's choice."

"We'll make sure he makes the right one."

He headed back toward the others where Cassiopeia was climbing into the plane's cabin, followed by Pau.

"Spry sucker," he whispered to Stephanie.

"Watch him, Cotton."

He pointed at Ivan. "And you watch him."

He climbed inside. Two leather seats rested side by side, Cassiopeia in one, a center bench behind them where Pau sat. The instrument panel did not extend to the passenger side, which provided Cassiopeia a wide view ahead through the forward windows. He strapped himself in and studied the controls, noticing the top speed to be around 200 kilometers per hour. One fuel tank in the keel, below the cabin door, held 320 liters. Another auxiliary tank in the tail carried 60 liters. He did the math. About a 1,500 kilometer range. Plenty for a one-way trip, as Ivan had said, which he hoped did not have a double meaning.

"I assume you know what you're doing?" she asked.

"As good a time as any to learn."

She gave him a quizzical look.

"What?" he asked.

"You *can* fly this, right?" Doubt clouded her tone.

He adjusted the throttle, props, and fuel mixture. He glanced down at the keel plugs and noticed that they were intact. A flick of a switch and the twin engines roared to life. He played with the fuel mixture until the props spun firm. He twisted the cranks for the elevator and rudder trims.

"No problem," he said.

Cassiopeia did not appear to share his confidence.

The plane started to drift, so he grasped the yoke and maneuvered out onto the bay. He turned toward the south so the faint breeze he'd noted on shore would be at their back.

He throttled up the engines to 180 horsepower.

The Twin Bee skimmed across the surface, the controls tightened, and he gripped the yoke.

This would be his first off-water takeoff. He'd always wanted to do it.

Less than five hundred feet was needed before the wings caught air and the plane lifted, slow and steady, as if in an elevator. They found open water beyond the bay. He banked left and adjusted course toward the northwest, heading back over shore. The controls were sluggish, but responsive. Not a P-3 Orion, he reminded himself, or even a Cessna or a Beechcraft. This tank was designed for little more than short water hopping.

"Take a look at that chart," he said to Cassiopeia.

She studied the map.

"We're going to ground-track our way there," he made clear.

"Assuming this chart is correct."

"Not to worry," Pau said at his right ear. "I know this part of Vietnam and China well. I can get us there."

NI WATCHED THE PREMIER'S FACE, TRYING TO GAUGE IF THIS man was friend or foe. He truly had no idea.

"What you see is the wax replica made before the Chairman was embalmed. The body decayed long ago and, in fulfillment of Mao's wishes, was burned to ash."

"Then why keep all this open?"

"An excellent question. One I have asked myself many times. The simplest answer is that the people expect it."

Ni had to say, "I don't think that's the case any longer."

"You may well be correct. That is the sad thing about our heritage. We have no single legacy. Just a succession of dynasties, each rising with its own agenda, opposing the one before it, welcomed by the people, then descending into the same corruption of its predecessor. Why should our future be any different?"

"You sound like Pau."

"I told you that he and I were once close. But there came a time when we deviated. He took one path, I another."

An uncomfortable feeling swept over him. Usually, he was in command of a situation, knowing the questions and the answers. Not here. Others were many steps ahead of him. So he asked what he truly wanted to know. "Why will I lose to Karl Tang?"

"Because you are unaware of the threats around you."

"That's what Pau Wen said, too."

"I want to know something. If I perceive you are lying, or telling me what I want to hear, this will be the last time we will ever speak."

He didn't particularly appreciate being spoken to like a schoolchild, but he recognized that this man had not risen to the top of the political triangle by being a fool. So he decided that he would answer the question honestly.

"What will you do with China if given my job?"

Ever since Pau Wen asked him the same question yesterday he'd thought about its answer. "First, I will separate the Communist Party from the government. That merger is the root of all our corruption. Next, the personnel system must be reformed, a reliance placed on merit, not patronage. The role of the National People's Congress, and the other lower congresses in the provinces, has to be raised. The people must be heard. Finally, the rule of law must be established, which means the judiciary has to become independent and functioning. We have enacted five constitutions since 1949 and ignored every one of them."

"You are correct," the premier said. "The Party's authority has been undermined by irrational policies, corruption, and no vision. At present, and this is the greatest fear I possess, only the military has the ability to rule if we fail. I understand you are of the military, but the nation would not last long as a puppet."

"Of that there is no doubt. Three million active troops, controlled by seven regional commanders, of which I was once one, could not govern. We must locate and promote technical competence, managerial skills, and a business ability in our people. The glacial pace to our decision making does incalculable damage."

"Do you want democracy?"

The question was asked in a whisper.

"It is inevitable. In some form. Not like the West, but elements of it cannot be avoided. A new middle class has emerged. They are smart. They listen to not only the government but also one another. They are compliant for now, but that is changing. *Guanxi* must be abolished. It is the root of all our corruption problems."

The principle of "not what you knew, but who you knew" compelled dishonesty. *Guanxi* relied on connections, forcing entrepreneurs to bond with government and Party officials who could approve their requests and grant them favors. The system, ingrained so deeply that it was literally a part of the government's fabric, allowed money and power to meld seamlessly, with no resistance from morality.

The premier nodded. "That system must be dismantled. I have no way to make that happen. But youth is gaining power. The individual is emerging. Mao's philosophy is gone." A pause. "Thank goodness."

"In an age of instant texting, Internet access, and cell phones one small incident of corruption could become a riot," Ni said. "I've seen that nearly happen several times. The people's tolerance level for corruption is dropping by the day."

"The days of blind allegiance are over. I recall once when I was young. We all wanted to show our love for Mao, so we went to the river. We were told how Mao swam across the Yangtze, so we wanted to do that as well. Thousands jumped in. So many there was no room to swim. You couldn't move your arms. The river was like a soup, our heads like dumplings." The old man paused. "Hundreds drowned that day. My wife was one of those."

He did not know what to say. He'd long noticed that many of the former generation refused to openly speak about the three decades between the 1949 Revolution and Mao's death. It was as if they were too overwhelmed by what happened to discuss its pain, the resentment, so they mentioned it casually, as they would the weather, or in a whisper, as if no one was listening.

He harbored his own share of bitter memories. Pau Wen had reminded him of Tiananmen Square—June 4, 1989—apparently knowing that Ni had been there.

He often thought about that day, when his life changed.

"Where is my son?" the woman asked.

Ni could offer her no answer. He was guarding one segment of the massive square, his division charged with making sure that Tiananmen's perimeter remained secured.

The cleanout had started yesterday, most of the protestors now gone, but the air still stank of their waste and death. Every day, since April, people had appeared until more than a million eventually occupied the pavement. Students had started the rebellion, but unemployed workers had eventually formed the bulk of the crowd, decrying double-digit inflation and public corruption. For the past week he'd been here, sent by his commander to watch the agitators, but he'd found himself doing far more listening.

"You must leave," he said to her.

"My son was here. I have to find him."

She was middle-aged, a good twenty years older than him. Her eyes cast a sadness that only a mother could know. His own mother would have risked everything for him. Both his parents had defied the one-child policy and birthed four children, which brought an enormous burden to their family. He'd been the third, something of a disappointment, hating school, performing poorly, staying in trouble. When he failed the national high school entrance exam, his future became clear.

The military.

There he had found a home and a purpose, defending Mao, serving the motherland. He'd thought his life had finally defined itself.

Until the past two days.

He'd watched as the bulk of the crowd had been peacefully dispersed by the army's 27th and 28th divisions, brought in from the outer provinces because Beijing had thought local divisions might be sympathetic. The soldiers, nearly all of them unarmed, had moved in on foot and dispersed the people with tear gas, and most of the demonstrators fled peacefully.

A core group of about 5,000 had remained.

They attacked the soldiers with rocks and bricks, using burned-out buses as barricades. Tanks were called in and the protestors attacked them, too, one of them catching fire, killing two occupants.

That's when everything changed.

Last night the army had returned with rifles, bayonets, and more tanks. The shooting raged for several hours. Soldiers and demonstrators alike died. He'd been there, on the fringes, charged with protecting the outer boundaries while more of the 27th and 28th divisions exacted revenge.

All previous orders not to shoot had been rescinded.

Rickshaws and bicyclists had darted through the melee, rescuing the wounded, trying to transport them to hospitals. People had been beaten, stabbed, and shot. Tanks crushed both bodies and vehicles.

He'd seen too many die to count.

The mothers and fathers had started arriving a few hours ago, pushing their way closer to the now empty square. All had been warned off, told to leave, and most had. But a few, like the mother he now confronted, refused.

"You must leave this area," he told her again, his voice gentle.

She studied his uniform. "Captain, my son would be about your age. He has been here since the beginning. When I heard what was happening I had to come. Surely, you understand. Let me look for him."

"The square is empty," he said. "He is not here."

"There are bodies," she said in a voice cracking with emotion.

And there were. Stacked like wood, out of sight, a mere hundred meters away. One reason his men had been ordered here was to keep everyone away from them. They would be discarded after dark, taken away and buried in a common pit so no one could count the dead.

"You must leave," he ordered again.

She thrust out an arm and shoved him aside, walking ahead, past the point that he'd ordered his men to defend. She reminded him so much of his own mother, who'd taught him how to swim, to roller-skate, to drive a truck. A loving soul who cared only that her four children grow old.

Before he could stop the woman, another soldier, a captain, like him, leveled his rifle and fired.

The bullet thudded into the mother's spine.

Her body lurched forward, then slammed face-first to the pavement.

Anger surged through him. Ni aimed his rifle at the soldier.

"You warned her not to advance. I heard you. She ignored you. I was following orders."

The captain stared down the gun, not a hint of fear in his eyes.

"We don't kill unarmed women," Ni slowly declared.

"We do what we must."

That captain had been right.

The People's Liberation Army did whatever it had to, including killing unarmed men and women. To this day no one knew how many had died in Tiananmen Square, or in the days and weeks after. Several hundred? Thousands? Tens of thousands?

All he knew for sure was that one woman had lost her life.

A mother.

"We were foolish," the premier said. "So many stupid things we did for Mao."

FORTY-FOUR

TANG WAS PLEASED THAT THE FACILITY HAD BEEN SECURED.
He'd ordered his men to take charge of the petrochemical laboratory,
sending home all non-essential personnel and otherwise restricting access. Luckily, just a dozen people worked in the building, mostly clerks
and assistants, and only one of the lab's two research scientists was still
alive.

Lev Sokolov.

The Russian expatriate had been brought from the city yesterday,
after a doctor had tended to his wounds. The rats had left their mark,
both physically and mentally. Killing Sokolov was not out of the question, but not before Tang learned what he needed to know. Jin Zhao
had been unable to reveal anything except that Lev Sokolov had found
the proof.

But what was it?

Sokolov stood with one arm wrapping his gut, guarding the bandages that Tang knew were there. Tang motioned to the stainless-steel
table and the sealed container that rested on top. "That is a sample of
oil extracted yesterday from a well in western Gansu. I had it drilled at
a spot where the ancients drilled in the time of the First Emperor." He
caught recognition in Sokolov's face. "Just as Jin Zhao instructed. I assumed you knew. Now tell me what *you* found. Zhao said you located a
marker."

Sokolov nodded. "A way to know for sure."

Excellent.

"The world has been aggressively extracting oil from the ground for a little over 200 years," Sokolov said, his voice in a low monotone. "Biotic oil, fossil fuel, waits not far beneath the surface. It's easy to get, and we have taken all of it."

"How do you know that?"

"Because I've tested a sample from every well on the planet. There is a repository in Europe where those are stored. None of those samples contains fossil fuels."

"You still haven't said how you know that to be true."

"Abiotic oil looks, smells, and acts the same as biotic oil. The only difference is that you have to drill deep to get it. But I'm not sure that even matters anymore. Where's my boy? I want him back."

"And you'll get him. When I get what I want."

"You're a liar."

He shrugged. "I'm the only path to your son. Right now, he's just one of thousands of young boys who disappear each year. Officially, the problem doesn't even exist. Do you understand? Your son doesn't even exist."

He saw the utter hopelessness in the Russian's face.

"Biotic oil is gone," Sokolov quietly continued. "It once was plentiful. Formed from decomposing organic matter, shallow in the earth, and easy to get. But as we pumped fossil fuels from the ground, the earth replenished some of those reserves with oil created deeper in the crust. Not all wells replenish. Some are biotic with no way for the deeper, abiotic oil, to filter upward. So they go dry. Others lie over fissures where oil can seep up from below."

Questions formed in his brain. 2,200 years ago, oil had first been found in Gansu. 200 years ago, that same field went dry. He'd studied the subterranean geography and knew that the fissures there ran deep—earthen channels through which pressurized oil could easily move upward. Jin Zhao had theorized that abiotic oil might have seeped up from below and restored the Gansu field. "How do we know that the site in Gansu simply did not contain more oil than was known?"

Sokolov appeared to be in pain. His breathing was labored, his attention more on the floor than on Tang.

"Your only chance to see your son again is to cooperate with me," he made clear.

The Russian shook his head. "I will tell you nothing more."

Tang reached into his pocket, found his phone, and dialed the number. When the call was answered, he asked, "Is the boy there?"

"I can get him."

"Do it."

He stared straight at Sokolov.

"He's here," the voice said in his ear.

"Put him on the phone."

He handed the unit to Sokolov, who did not accept the offer.

"Your son wants to speak with you," he said.

Defiant lines faded from the Russian's face. A hand slowly came up to grip the phone.

Tang shook his head, then pressed the SPEAKER button.

An excited voice—young, high-pitched—started talking, asking if his father was there. Clearly, Sokolov recognized the voice and opened his mouth to speak, but Tang muted the mouthpiece with another press of a button and said, "No."

He brought the unit back to his own ear and unmuted the call.

"Stay on the line," he directed the man on the other side. "If Comrade Sokolov does not tell me exactly what I want to know in the next minute, I want you to kill the boy."

"You can't," Sokolov screamed. "Why?"

"I tried persuasion, then torture, and I thought we had made progress. But you remain defiant. So I will kill your son and find out what I need to know elsewhere."

"There is no elsewhere. I'm the only one who knows the procedure."

"You've recorded it somewhere."

Sokolov shook his head. "I have it solely in my head."

"I have no more time to deal with your lack of cooperation. Other matters require my attention. Make a decision."

An iron ceiling fan slowly rotated overhead, barely stirring the lab's warm air. Defeat filled the geochemist's face as his head nodded.

"Keep the boy there," he said into the phone. "I may call back in a few moments."

He ended the call and waited for Sokolov to speak.

"If that sample on the table contains the marker," the scientist said, "then it's proof that the oil is from an abiotic source."

"What marker?"

"Diamondoids."

He'd never heard the term before.

"Smaller than the wavelength of visible light. Tiny specks of diamond that form within oil created deep in the earth's crust, where there is high temperature and high pressure. A million of them would barely fit on the head of a pin, but I found them, and I named them. Adamantanes. Greek for 'diamond.'"

He caught pride in the declaration, ignored it, and asked, "How did you find them?"

"Heating oil to 450 degrees Celsius vaporizes away the chemical compounds. Only diamondoids remain, which X-rays will reveal."

He marveled at the concept.

"They are shaped as rods, disks, even screws, and they are not present in biotic oil. Diamond can only be formed deep in the mantle. It is conclusive proof of abiotic oil."

"And how do you know that the earth actually produces the oil?"

"Right here, in this lab, I heated marble, iron oxide, and water to 1,500 degrees Celsius at 50,000 times atmospheric pressure, mimicking conditions one hundred miles beneath the earth. Every time, I produced both methane and octane."

Tang grasped the significance of that result. Methane was the main constituent of natural gas and octane the hydrocarbon molecule in petrol. If those could be produced in a lab, they could be produced naturally, along with oil itself.

"The Russians know all this, don't they?" he asked.

"I personally found over eighty fields in the Caspian Sea applying this theory. It is still doubted by some, but yes, the Russians are convinced oil is abiotic."

"But they have no proof."

Sokolov shook his head. "I left before I discovered the diamondoids. Zhao and I did that here."

"So the Russians work from an unproven theory?"

"Which is why they speak little of this publicly."

And why, Tang thought, they were so interested. Surely they wanted Sokolov back. Maybe even permanently silenced. Thank goodness Viktor Tomas had kept him apprised of exactly what the Russians were doing. But he made no mention of that intrigue and instead said, "And that's also why they maintain the myth of scarcity?"

"They watch, amused, as the rest of world pays too much for oil, knowing it is endless."

"But they are likewise cautious, since they have no proof that their concept is true."

"Which is understandable. They lack what you have. A verified sample from a place where ancients drilled for oil. Only the Chinese could have such a sample." Disgust had invaded his voice. "This was the only place on earth man drilled for oil two centuries ago."

Pride swelled within him.

Sokolov pointed to the table. "If diamondoids are in that sample, then the oil is abiotic. All you would need is another sample, from long ago, from the same field, for comparison. To prove the theory, that sample must test biotic with no diamondoids."

He appreciated the simplicity of the equation. Biotic oil first, siphoned away with drilling, replaced with abiotic oil. And Gansu might be the only place on earth where such a comparison could be made. Every surviving historical record made clear that those first explorers, more than 2,000 years ago, drilled exclusively in the vicinity of the well in Gansu. Any oil surviving from that time would have come from the ground there.

All he required was a confirmed sample of that oil.

"You told me the lamp is gone," Sokolov said. "Along with its oil. So where will the comparison sample come from?"

"Not to worry, comrade. I secured that sample and you will soon have it."

FORTY-FIVE

BEIJING

Nɪ ʀᴇᴀʟɪᴢᴇᴅ ᴛʜᴀᴛ ᴛʜᴇ ᴘʀᴇᴍɪᴇʀ ᴇxᴘʀᴇssᴇᴅ ʜɪᴍsᴇʟꜰ ɪɴ ᴀ sᴜʙᴛʟᴇ manner devised to keep his listener on edge. Before, a desk had always stood between them, his investigative reports received with only a flicker of interest and little comment. But this talk was different.

"I remember," the old man said, "when every bus window was plastered with slogans and pictures of Mao. Store windows the same. Radios only broadcast revolutionary music, Mao's thoughts, or state news. Movie houses showed only Mao greeting Red Guards. Even the opera and ballet performed only revolutionary works. We all carried our book of quotations since you never knew when you would be called upon to cite a section."

The premier's voice was quiet, rough, as if the memories were bitterly painful.

"*Serve the People.* That was Mao's message. In reality, we all simply served him. This building is proof we still do."

Ni began to understand why they were here.

"Hegemony is our weakness," the premier said. "That unwillingness within us to work with any foreign power, even when there is no threat. Hegemony is a natural expression of our totalitarianism, just as peaceful relations are to democracy. We have always believed ourselves to be the geographic and geopolitical center of the world. For centuries, and especially since 1949, the sole goal of our foreign policy has been to dominate our neighbors and then, eventually, the remainder of the world."

"That is totally beyond our grasp."

"You and I know that, but does the remainder of the world know? I recall when Kissinger came in 1971, on a secret mission to lay the groundwork for renewed contact between the United States and China. The use of the word *hegemony* baffled the American translators. They could not adequately convey its meaning. The concept was literally unknown to them." The premier pointed to the crypt. "Mao said then, *China has stood up.* He was telling the world that no outsiders would ever control us again. I'm afraid, though, no one was listening."

"We have always been ignored," he said. "Thought of as backward, unmodernized. Even worse, repressive and dictatorial."

"Which is our own fault. We never have done much to counter that perception. We seem to actually revel in a negative light."

Ni was puzzled. "Why are you so cynical?"

"I'm simply speaking the truth—which, I suspect, you well know. Democracy is the nemesis of hegemony. Dispersing power among elected officials, instead of concentrating it in the hands of the ruler, empowering rather than subjugating the people—those concepts are beyond our comprehension."

"But they cannot remain so any longer."

"I recall the 1950s, when Mao was at the height of his power. Maps were drawn showing our borders extending far to the north, south, and west, into lands we did not then control. These were distributed to officials solely to motivate them to think in such grandiose terms. And it worked. We eventually intervened in Korea, invaded Tibet, bombarded Quemoy, attacked India, and aided Vietnam, all with the intent to dominate those lands." The premier paused. "Only Tibet remains within our control today, and our hold there is fragile, relying on force."

He recalled what Pau had said. "Are you saying that we should not then, or now, have national pride?"

"It seems all we have is pride. We are the longest-existing culture on this planet, yet look at us. We have little to show for our efforts, beyond a multitude of insurmountable problems. I'm afraid hosting the

Olympics had a similar effect as those maps once did. They are motivating the ambitious within the government to do foolish things." For the first time the voice bristled with anger, and the eyes flashed hot with rage. "We remain conscious of slights that occurred decades, even centuries, ago. Given any pretext we will avenge those, no matter how trivial. It is ludicrous, and that nonsense will be our downfall."

"Not all of us think that way," he said.

The premier nodded. "I know. Only old men. But there are many of us still, and there are young men ready to exploit our fears."

He knew exactly to whom that comment was directed.

"Mao lies there," the premier said, "for us to worship. A wax imitation of a failed leader. An illusion. Yet a billion and a half Chinese still adore him."

"I don't." He felt empowered to make the declaration.

"Don't. Ever."

He said nothing.

"Men like Karl Tang are a danger to us all," the premier said. "They will advocate the forcible reclaiming of Taiwan, then the entire South China Sea region. They will want Vietnam, Laos, Thailand, Cambodia, Myanmar, even Korea. Our lost greatness, found again."

For the first time the gravity of the coming battle began to take hold. He said, "And in the process they will destroy us. The world will not stand idle while all that happens."

"I have kept things in order," the premier said. "I knew I could not change anything, only hold what was there until my successor arrived. That man would be in a better position to exact change. Are you ready, Minister, to be that person?"

Asked the same question three days ago, he would have answered that he was. Now he wasn't so sure, and something in his eyes must have betrayed his doubt.

The older man nodded and said, "It's okay to be afraid. Fear keeps you humble, and humility makes you wise. That is what Karl Tang lacks. It is *his* weakness."

A few moments of silence passed between them. An inner voice cautioned him to be careful with his words, as another thought of Mao's came to mind.

The Hundred Flowers Campaign.

A time in the 1950s when criticism of the government had been encouraged, new solutions and ideas encouraged, and millions of letters poured in. Eventually, posters appeared on campuses, rallies were held, articles published, all advocating a shift toward democracy.

But it had been a political trap, a clever way to ferret out dissidents. More than half a million were imprisoned, tortured, or killed.

"You know of the eunuchs?" the premier asked, catching him unawares.

He nodded.

"Pau Wen and I both trained for the *Ba*. We engaged in the required two years of meditation and instruction, preparing ourselves for initiation. Both of us stripped naked and had our abdomens wrapped with bandages, our bodies bathed with hot pepper water. I held Pau while he was castrated, felt the tremble in his legs, saw the anguish on his face, watched as he accepted mutilation with honor." The voice had dropped to a mere whisper. "Yet when my time came and the *Tao* asked if I would regret what was about to happen, I said yes."

Ni stared in disbelief.

"I was afraid. When faced with the prospect of what was about to happen, something told me the knife was not my destiny."

"And that voice was right."

A tired look flooded the aged face. "Perhaps so. But know that men who can face the knife, and never utter a sound, possess a strength you and I cannot fathom."

He would not forget that.

"The official Party line, then and now, is that Mao was 70 percent right and 30 percent wrong. But we never identify which part of his thought is right or wrong." A chuckle seeped from the premier's thin lips. "What fools we are."

The old man motioned toward Mao's body.

"He supposedly lies upon a black stone from Tai Shan as a reminder of what Sima Qian wrote in *Shiji*. *One's life can be weightier than Mount Tai or lighter than a goose feather.* You must decide, Minister. Which will yours be?"

MALONE KEPT THE PLANE'S ALTITUDE AT AROUND 5,000 FEET. Never had he thought that he'd be leisurely cruising across Vietnamese airspace. Below stretched a panorama of jagged mountains and sloping hills, many striated by terraced rice farms, towering over lush green valleys shrouded in mist.

"We're approaching the border," Cassiopeia said to him. She'd been studying the chart Ivan had provided.

"The local officials in Yunnan province," Pau said, "have good relations with their neighbors. They front not only Vietnam, but also Laos and Myanmar. Beijing is a long way away, so their allegiance has always been more local."

"I hope that's still true," Malone said. "We're not carrying much in the way of armament."

"During Mao's purges, many fled to Yunnan. Its remoteness offered refuge. The terrain north of here, in China, is similar to what is below us now."

Ivan had told them to follow the Kunming–Hekou railway, a line the French built in the early part of the 20th century through Vietnam, into China, past the heavily populated cities of Gejiu and Kaiyuan.

"You work with the Russians often?" Pau asked him.

"Not usually."

"What is their interest here?"

"Like we're going to tell you," Cassiopeia said, turning around and facing Pau. "How about this? You tell us why you've come home and we'll tell you why the Russians are here."

"I'm returning to stop a revolution."

"More likely to start one," she said.

"Are you always so aggressive?"

"Are you always so deceitful?"

"You apparently have no knowledge of *guanxi*."

"Enlighten me."

"Throughout our history, to weather tough times, the Chinese have relied on friends and family. People who may be in a position to help. It

is called *zôu hòu mén*. 'Through the back door.' Of course, if a favor is offered and taken, the receiver is obligated to return it. This keeps the
guanxi in balance."

"And what keeps you from leading us straight into a disaster," she
asked.

"I am not the enemy. Karl Tang has that distinction."

"I see the border," Malone said.

Cassiopeia returned her attention out the windows.

The railway line snaked northward, crossing a highway that Ivan
had said now connected China and Vietnam. The roadway veered west,
the rail line north. A bridge spanned the Red River, clogged with cars
stopped at a checkpoint.

Malone dropped to just above 1,000 feet.

"Here we go."

FORTY-SIX

NI STORMED INTO THE OFFICES OF THE CENTRAL COMMISSION for Discipline Inspection, located purposefully away from the walled Zhongnanhai, Beijing's complex of palaces, pavilions, and lakes that served as headquarters for both the Party and the government. His visit with the premier had been troubling. Nothing made sense. Everything seemed inverted. He was torn with doubt, engulfed by a roiling cloud of unfamiliar emotions, and haunted by the premier's inquiry.

What would be the measure of his life?

Strength or weakness?

He'd called from the car and ordered his entire staff to assemble in the conference room. He required allies, not traitors, and it was time to find out where each one of them stood.

Fourteen people waited. Nine men, five women. He calmed the flurry of excitement with a raised hand and immediately excused the women. Then he said to the men, "Drop your trousers."

They all stared at him in disbelief.

He removed his gun and pointed it straight at them. "I won't say it again."

CASSIOPEIA STARED OUT THE WINDOW AT THE MOUNTAINOUS landscape. Sunshine warmed the thin air. They'd been flying inside

Chinese airspace for more than an hour with no problems. Glancing over, she was glad she was flying with Malone. Though Viktor Tomas had twice saved her life, she trusted Cotton.

Implicitly.

He'd come to Belgium when she needed him, and that meant something.

She'd allowed only a few men close. Keeping emotions to herself had always proven the best course. She'd read once that women with strong fathers gravitated to strong men, and Malone definitely reminded her of her father. He'd been a giant in business, a self-made billionaire who'd commanded the attention of Europe and Africa. A lot like Henrik Thorvaldsen, whom she'd admired more than she'd ever realized until he was gone. Death seemed to claim everyone she loved. The thought of her own demise, which the experiences in the museum had so vividly illustrated, remained fresh in her mind. Such a confusion of feelings. What a defining moment. Soon enough she'd be forty years old. She had no husband, no children, no one with whom to share herself. She lived alone in an ancient French manor, her life devoted to helping others.

And ignoring her own needs?

Maybe it was time to change all that.

She always looked forward to seeing Cotton, and regretted when they parted. Was she trying to find a replacement for her father, the one man in her life whom she'd never defied? No. That was too simple an explanation. Her mother would have said that men were like fields—they required careful cultivation and daily attention, all in the hope that one day they might prove productive. A somewhat cynical approach.

Not one that worked for her.

Here she was, flying across southern China, headed for who-knew-what. Was it worth it? If she found Lev Sokolov's son, then yes.

If not?

She didn't want to think about failure.

So she comforted her anxiety with thoughts of Cotton and that perhaps she may have actually found something for herself.

Something she wanted.

Finally.

NI WAS SATISFIED THAT NONE OF HIS CLOSE STAFF WERE TRAI-
tors. He recalled what Pau Wen had told him about modern pharma-
ceuticals and their masking effects on castration, so he'd pursued the
only investigative course that guaranteed results. He also ordered his
chief aide to conduct an immediate physical inspection of every male in
the building. While that was occurring, he reviewed what information
his staff had accumulated since yesterday.

There was absolutely no reference to any organization called the *Ba*
in any security files. Those records would have included prisoner inter-
rogations, witness statements, incident reports, news accounts, anything and everything that did not mandate a STATE SECRET stamp. The
archives contained millions of documents, many of which had been
digitalized, making a reasonably quick search possible. Historically, his
staff uncovered much of what Pau Wen had already told him about how
the *Ba* grew out of an ancient Legalist movement, supposedly disappearing around the 17th century.

Nothing indicated that the organization still existed.

He'd also ordered a vetting of Pau Wen, but no official record revealed any connections among Pau, the premier, and Karl Tang.

Yet these clearly existed, by their own admissions.

A tap on his office door disturbed his thoughts.

His chief aide entered. "Everyone has been examined. No eunuchs,
Minister."

"You think I'm insane, don't you?"

"I would never presume to judge you."

He liked this man, honorable and above reproach, which was why
he'd selected him as first assistant.

"I was unable to tell you before," his aide said, "while the others
were here. But we found something last night."

His attention piqued.

"An overseas call came to Minister Tang's satellite phone. I ordered
his lines monitored weeks ago. He utilizes several phones, with numbers that change weekly. It has been a challenge to stay ahead of him.

We don't tap every conversation, but we find enough." His aide handed him a flash drive. "A recording."

Ni inserted the drive into his computer and listened, immediately recognizing the voices of Tang and Pau. He heard the tension and conflict. Sensed the challenge these two men presented to the other. Tang's betrayal, then his pronouncement to Pau, *There is no legal way for you to re-enter China. No visa will be issued. On that, I have absolute control. The few brothers you have at your disposal there will be barred from returning, too.*

"Is this the proof we seek?" his aide said.

He shook his head. "Not enough."

But at least he knew the whole thing wasn't fiction.

FORTY-SEVEN

MALONE SPIED THE GREEN EXPANSE OF A HIGHLAND LAKE, ITS surface shining with ripples and dotted with junks.

Lake Dian.

Mountains bordered the west shore, the lush slopes sheathed in trees, the eastern side mostly plains of ocher-colored farmland. Smoke belched from chimneys in a fishing hamlet a few miles away.

He dropped the plane's altitude to 500 feet.

Cassiopeia released her harness and moved forward, gazing down through the forward windows. He'd noticed on the chart that the mountains to the west were called Xi Shan. Carved into the cliff faces he spotted paths and stairways linking a succession of temples, their towering pagodas, with curved tile roofs and painted eaves, reminding him of Tivoli and home.

"The undulating contours of the hills," Pau Wen said, "resemble a reclining woman with tresses of hair flowing to the water. So they are called Sleeping Beauty."

He noticed that the label seemed apt.

"The temples are from the Yuan, Ming, and Qing dynasties. There, where the chairlift stretches to the summit, in the 18th century a Daoist monk chipped a long corridor up the face of the mountain. Legend says the tip of his chisel broke as he neared the end. In despair, he threw himself into the lake. Fifty years later his followers reached the goal, which is now called Dragon Gate."

"Sounds like something for the tourists," Cassiopeia said.

"Actually, the tale is reasonably close to the truth."

Ivan had said that the lake stretched forty kilometers north to south, and Malone could believe that claim seeing nothing but water toward the horizon.

"Let's see what's down there before we land."

He eased the yoke forward and reduced airspeed.

The flight northward across Yunnan province had been quiet, the skies clear of traffic. He'd grown accustomed to the smooth journey but, suddenly, the Twin Bee's wings skipped air.

Engines sputtered, then quickly refired.

Projectiles pierced the hull and rocketed through the cabin.

Air rushed in through holes.

The right wing sheared further from more impacts and the ailerons went loose. The plane arched left as the starboard side failed to respond to commands.

"What was that?" Cassiopeia said.

The answer came as a jet roared passed overhead, its afterburners flaming in the late-morning sky.

"Cannon fire," he said.

The fighter's delta-winged triangle disappeared in the distance, but a vapor trail indicated a turn for another approach.

"That's a People's Liberation Army fighter," he said. "And it ain't here by accident. The Chinese knew we were coming."

He worked the rudder and used airspeed to regain some semblance of control. He'd been annoyed the entire flight by the lack of synchronization in the two engines. Pitch was a pilot's best warning, but the Twin Bee's engines screamed at each other like an arguing soprano and baritone.

"What can I do?" Cassiopeia asked.

"Tell me where that jet is."

"He's coming straight toward us, from behind," Pau calmly reported.

They were plowing through thick air, only a few hundred feet above the lake. He added altitude and rose to 1,000 feet. The Twin Bee was little match for modern avionics, cannons, and radar-guided missiles.

There was, though, one weapon they did possess.

"How far away?"

"Hard to say," she said. "Several miles."

He'd been around enough fighter pilots to know how they thought, no matter the nationality. Hell, he'd wanted to be one himself. This was easy prey, a hawk challenging a pigeon. The pilot would wait until he was close before firing.

He checked his airspeed.

A little under 110 kilometers.

He recalled what his instructor had taught him.

Nobody ever collided with the sky. Altitude is your friend.

"He'll be here in a few seconds," Cassiopeia said.

He hoped the Twin Bee could handle what he was about to do. The starboard control surfaces were damaged, but the port side and tail rudder seemed okay. Most important, the engines were working. He waited another two seconds, then slammed the throttle wide open and pulled back on the yoke. The amphibian rose in a steep climb, prying upward with a groan from her hull. Tracer rounds rocketed past as their altitude increased.

2,000 feet.

2,500.

3,000.

The fighter shot passed beneath them, its turbofans leaving a trail of black smoke. Fighters were not low-altitude machines. They worked best in the stratosphere, not near the ground where fuel and computers could be tapped to the max.

He topped off at 3,300 feet.

"My stomach is in my throat," Cassiopeia said.

"I had to do something he wouldn't expect."

"That certainly qualified."

He knew small planes were not her favorite mode of transportation, recalling a rough helicopter ride in Central Asia, when Viktor had been at the controls.

He focused through the windshield. The Annihilator loomed in the distance. He realized the fighter could easily shoot them down with air-to-air missiles. Another navy lesson flashed through his mind.

Learn from other people's mistakes.

"We're going in," he said.

He lowered speed and cranked the elevators. The outside air was capricious and inconsistent, which only aggravated the situation. He dropped the left wing and slipped into a slow bank. After a sharp turn he angled the nose and leveled off at 800 feet above the lake.

"You see the jet?" he asked.

Cassiopeia's head spun in every direction. "No. But that doesn't mean anything. He could still have us in his sights."

A fact he realized. He struggled to keep the wing level as the port side control surfaces ignored his commands.

"Apparently this was a trap," Pau Wen said.

"Brilliant observation."

He threw Cassiopeia a glance that she seemed to understand. *Viktor.* How else would they have known? China was a big place, yet here they were, waiting, over Lake Dian, exactly where Ivan had sent them.

Treetops grew in size as he glided toward the lake. Luckily, the nearest junk floated a mile or so away.

A rush of wind shoved them to the right.

He held the nose high.

He'd never landed on water and could already tell depth perception was going to be different. He would have to judge the distance correctly and make sure speed was perfect when the plane's bottom kissed the surface. The last thing he needed was to porpoise across the lake. He was also worried about stalling. Luckily, no crosswind blew, or at least none he could see on the treetops. He decided to make it easy and switched off the engines just as the last of the trees raced beneath and nothing but water loomed ahead.

Like he'd been told, *Gravity never loses.*

"I'm glad there's lots of room," she said.

He was, too. Plenty to glide to a stop. He eased down the yoke and pitched the nose up so the tail touched first. One thought flashed through his mind. The floats on the underside of each wing needed to stay on top of the water, as both could quickly become anchors.

The Twin Bee bounced twice, then hydroplaned. The rudder fishtailed and the plane came to a rest about two hundred yards from shore.

He popped open the door.

Cassiopeia did the same on her side.

The Twin Bee bobbed in the agitated water, its fuselage riddled with bullet holes. Malone studied the sky. The fighter was nowhere to be seen. Off to the south, a flash appeared. An instant later a vapor trail snaked a path across the morning sky.

He knew instantly what was happening.

Air-to-ground missile, its fire-and-forget active radar zeroing in on them.

"In the lake. Now. Go deep," he yelled.

He waited an instant to make sure that both Cassiopeia and Pau made it into the peaty-green water, then leaped in. He ignored the chill and powered himself toward the bottom, pawing with cupped hands.

Another disturbing thought swept through his brain. *Pollution.* Most likely this water was not safe.

A few seconds later an explosion rocked the surface as the Twin Bee was obliterated by the missile. He arched his body and kicked for the surface. His head found air and he opened his eyes to see nothing left of the amphibian except burning wreckage.

A second later Cassiopeia and Pau broke the surface.

"You okay?" he called out.

Both nodded.

"We need to get to shore."

He waded around the smoldering debris, toward them. He cocked his head toward the south. A black dot began to grow in size.

The Annihilator was returning.

"Float in the water, facedown. Play dead," he said, "and don't move until he's gone."

He quickly assumed the same position and hoped the trick worked. He'd wondered why the fighter had not simply shot them down. It would have been easy, especially in the beginning when its presence was unknown. But the idea had surely been to allow the lake to swallow the evidence.

He extended his arms and allowed his body to float, hoping the pilot did not ensure the kill with a strafe of cannon fire.

FORTY-EIGHT

LANZHOU

Tang left the laboratory, satisfied that the problem of Lev Sokolov had been resolved. He'd instructed the men he'd left to guard the facility that any attempt to escape should be met with deadly force. He now knew enough to know how to begin—with or without Sokolov. The Russian merely offered a more convenient way to confirm the discovery, not the only means.

And its implications were enormous.

China craved more than 300,000,000 tons of crude a year. Its industrial output—which meant its entire economy—was based on oil. Sixty % was currently imported from Africa, Latin America, and Russia, as a way not to be vulnerable to volatile Middle East politics and not be within America's sphere of influence. Why else, except to monopolize the Middle East oil supply, had America occupied Iraq? No reason he could conceive, and his foreign affairs experts said the same. Those same experts had repeatedly warned that the United States could easily wield Middle Eastern oil as a weapon. Just a minor disruption in supply could send China into a free fall, one that the government would be impotent to halt. He was tired of dealing with rogue nations rich in oil. Just a few weeks back, billions of yuan had been loaned to another African nation that would never repay—all to ensure that China was first on its oil export list. The present regime's foreign policy—a dizzying blend of appeasement, contradiction, dismissal, and defense—had long bartered away ballistic missiles, nuclear resources, and precious technology just to ensure that oil kept flowing inward.

That demeaned China, and exposed a weakness.

But all that could change if the thousands of wells that now dotted China could provide perpetual energy. He could not reveal the how, but he could exploit the what by keeping the oil flowing and eliminating the tankers that flooded into Chinese ports every day loaded with foreign crude. Results bred success, and success bred pride. Properly packaged and distributed, its effects could certainly bolster any political regime.

According to the fossil fuel theory, he knew China possessed a mere 2.1% of the world's oil reserves. The United States 2.7%. Russia 7%. The Middle East, 65%. *Nothing can be done about Arab dominance,* one of his vice ministers had recently warned. He disagreed. It all depended on what you knew.

His phone rang.

He stopped walking toward the waiting car and answered.

"The target is on the lake," Viktor Tomas said.

The idea had been to attack Pau Wen's plane with minimal attention. Radio traffic, monitored by countless governmental agencies, including officials in Yunnan province, would verify that an unidentified aircraft had been intercepted by an army fighter. Protocol required that the intruder be brought to the ground.

"Survivors?" he asked.

"Three. In the water. The fighter is making its final pass. He'll use cannons to make sure they will not be swimming to shore."

"You know what to do."

MALONE LAY PRONE, THE WATER SPLASHING IN AND OUT OF HIS ears making it difficult to hear. He was hoping three floating bodies would satisfy the pilot's curiosity. He risked only a slight angle of his head and determined that the fighter was still south, its afterburners growing in intensity.

Then a new sound invaded. From the east.

The steady thump of whirling blades biting through air.

He rolled over and shook the water from his face.

A helicopter roared in over the treetops. Bulkier than a swift-attack chopper, more an armed transport. The craft assumed a position over the lake, facing south. Cassiopeia and Pau both apparently sensed a change and started treading water, watching, too.

"Malone," a voice said through external speakers. "I'm contacting the jet and asking the pilot to retreat."

Viktor.

Malone treaded water and watched as the Annihilator continued its approach.

"He doesn't seem to want to listen," Viktor said.

Another few seconds passed, then flames exploded from the chopper's underwing as two air-to-air missiles erupted from their pods. Each followed a track for the fighter. Less than ten seconds later the jet disintegrated, its burning debris emerging from a dense cloud of black smoke and showering the distant shore with wreckage.

"We have to get out of this water," Malone called out.

They started swimming toward shore.

"Would you like a lift?" Viktor asked.

The chopper hovered over them.

Two cables with harnesses descended.

"You and Pau take them," he said. "I'll swim."

"A little foolish, isn't it?" Cassiopeia said, as she and Pau strapped themselves in.

"Not to me."

He watched as they were lifted from the lake and ferried toward shore, about two hundred yards away.

True, the lake's pollution worried him, but owing Viktor Tomas anything more seemed worse.

NI STARED AT THE DRAGON LAMP. WHILE HE'D MET WITH THE premier at Mao's tomb, he'd had it brought from the airport and deposited on his desk.

Karl Tang had gone to a lot of trouble to retrieve it. Why? He noticed etchings on its side and wondered what they meant. He should have some experts examine it. The buzzer from the phone on his desk irritated him. He'd told his staff that he did not want to be disturbed.

He stabbed the blinking button.

"The premier's office is on the line."

His anger vanished. "Connect me."

A few seconds later the same raspy whisper from Mao's tomb said, "Just a few minutes ago one of our J-10 fighters forced an unidentified amphibious aircraft onto Lake Dian. Then the fighter was shot down by one of our helicopters, piloted by a foreigner authorized to fly by Minister Tang."

He listened in shock.

"That helicopter was protecting three people who'd escaped into the lake." The premier paused. "One of those was Pau Wen."

He stood from his chair.

"It seems, Minister, Pau has come home. He has tried for many years to maneuver me into allowing him to return. What he told you is true. He and I have spoken many times since I assumed this post. We did, indeed, also speak of you. Those conversations were innocent. Two old men lamenting about lost opportunities. Pau has long wanted to return, but it is better he stay far away. Unfortunately, he seems to have found a way back without my consent."

A chill gripped him. "What is happening here?"

"An excellent question, one for you to discover. I truly do not know. But I would like to know why we lost both a man's life and a five-million-yuan aircraft."

As would he.

"I learned long ago that those who excel at defense bury themselves away below the deepest depths of the earth," the premier said. "Those who excel at offense move from above the greatest heights of Heaven. Pau Wen never acts from a defensive position. He stays on a constant offense."

He was jet-lagged and limp as a rag with fatigue. Riddles were no comfort. "What is it I am to do?"

"I know what Karl Tang is after, and I also know why Pau Wen has returned."

"Then involve internal security and the military? They can handle this situation."

"No, Minister. The last thing China can endure is an open civil war for political control. The chaos would be insurmountable. The world would take advantage of our turmoil. This must be a private affair. Between you and Tang. I will not involve anyone else, or allow you to do so."

"It seems Tang has involved the army."

"And I have taken measures to prevent that from happening again."

"So what am I to do?"

"You can start by listening. I have to tell you what happened, in 1977, just after Mao died."

CASSIOPEIA RELEASED THE HARNESS AND DROPPED THE REMAINing few feet to the ground. She was soaking wet, but thankfully the morning air carried warmth. Pau Wen dropped beside her. She was impressed with the older man's agility.

"You okay?" she asked.

"Quite fine." He smoothed out his soaked shirt and trousers.

They stood at the edge of a broad field that stretched eastward from the lake a kilometer or more. The chopper moved off a few hundred meters and touched down, spanking up a cloud of dust. She trotted back toward the shore, arriving as Malone emerged.

"There's no telling how many parasites and bacteria I now have inside me," he said, water cascading from him.

She smiled. "Can't be all that bad."

"Easy for you to say. You're not going have six toes and three arms in a few days."

Pau Wen stepped beside her. "Actually, this part of the lake is relatively clean. The northern portions are another matter."

"Where's your boyfriend?" Malone asked.

She didn't like his tone but understood the resentment. Viktor had known their destination because Ivan had known, which meant one or both had sold them out.

But that made no sense.

The Russians were intent on finding Sokolov. Why end the mission before it started?

She heard footsteps cracking across the dry earth behind them and turned to see Viktor, dressed in a green flight suit, walking their way.

Malone rushed past her and planted a fist in Viktor's face.

FORTY-NINE

MALONE WAS READY WHEN VIKTOR SPRANG TO HIS FEET. HE sidestepped the first lunge and landed another punch in Viktor's gut, which he immediately noted was hard as steel.

"You sold us out," he said. "Again."

Viktor lowered his fists. "Malone, are you that stupid? Karl Tang doesn't give a damn about you. It's *him* he wants dead." Viktor pointed at Pau. "All I did was step in and save your ass—which, I might add, may cost me mine."

"And you expect us to believe that?" Malone asked.

"Tang wants you dead," Viktor said to Pau. "In order to save them, I had to save you."

Pau faced Malone. "We need to head north. Tang has a long reach in this country."

"I can take you wherever you need to go," Viktor said.

"And why would we trust you?" Cassiopeia asked.

"I just blew a pilot out of the sky. That doesn't show you whose side I'm on?"

Malone caught the change of tone. Softer. Calmer. Reassuring. A voice seemingly just for her. But he wanted to know, "Karl Tang is going to let us roam free around China in a PLA helicopter? We can just do as we please?"

"If we hurry, we can be gone before he has time to react. My orders were to make sure the fighter strafed the lake with its cannons so no one swam to shore. I changed those. It'll take them a little while to regroup. One thing I've learned is that, unlike you or me, the Chinese are not improvisers. This was not an officially sanctioned action, so some local commander somewhere is right now trying to figure out what to do."

Malone ran a hand through his wet hair and tried to assess their options.

There weren't many.

He stared out on the lake and noticed that none of the junks approached either the debris in the water or the shore where they stood.

He turned and was about to ask Viktor another question when a fist slammed into his jaw. The blow stunned him, sent him to the ground, the bright midday blacking in and out.

"Don't. Hit. Me. Again," Viktor said, standing over him.

He contemplated retaliating, but opted not to. He was still gauging this foe, undecided, except that Viktor had just saved their lives and he apparently liked Cassiopeia. Both of which bothered him.

"Are you two through?" Cassiopeia asked.

"I am," Malone said, standing, his gaze locked on Viktor.

"I'm not the enemy," Viktor said.

He rubbed his jaw. "Since we have little choice, we're just going to have to take your word on that. Fly us north."

"Where?"

"Xi'an," Pau said. "To the tomb of Qin Shi."

NI STRAINED TO HEAR THE PREMIER'S SOFT VOICE THROUGH the phone.

"The time just before and after Mao died was chaotic. Politics shifted back and forth between Maoism and something utterly different. What that new direction was to be, no one knew. Mao himself tried to balance these conflicting views, but he was too old and weak to keep them in check."

Though young, Ni remembered the early 1970s, and knew that the Gang of Four, radical Maoists led by Mao's wife, had favored tactics such as class struggle, anti-intellectualism, egalitarianism, and xenophobia. Their opposition advocated economic growth, stability, education, and pragmatism.

"The balance tipped back and forth in the two years before Mao died. There were internal struggles, private battles, public purges, even some deaths. Eventually, Deng Xiaoping claimed power. But the struggle to arrive at that point was long and bitter. The scars ran deep. Pau Wen and I were there during every battle."

"On whose side?"

"That matters not. But the mistakes made then still haunt us. This is why the battle for control, between you and Tang, cannot be a public spectacle. I will not allow the same mistake to be made again."

The premier sounded like a Confucian.

"Deng Xiaoping was, in many ways, worse than Mao," the premier said. "To him, any reform was acceptable so long as it did not call the Party, the government, or Marxism into question. Improve the standard of living, regardless of the method—that was his philosophy, and look what happened. He allowed us to destroy our country."

He could not argue with that conclusion. The scars from unregulated and unrestrained development loomed everywhere. Nowhere had the nation been spared.

"We seem doomed," the premier said. "Once we were an isolated land, then the Portuguese came. Two hundred years later we were overrun with our own corruption. Western troops and gunboats controlled our ports, as we were but a colony of the Western powers. That atmosphere of defeat was perfect for the rise of a Mao, someone who told the people exactly what they wanted to hear. But communism has proved far worse than anything that came before. Mao isolated us again. Deng tried to change that, but went too fast, too far. We were not ready. That's when Pau Wen decided to act. He saw an opportunity and dispatched every brother of the *Ba* into the government or the military, charging them with but one duty—rise in stature and power. No one knew who would make the highest rise first, but Karl Tang has now emerged as that person."

"And he has others, not of the *Ba*, who will follow him."

"Many others. His arguments are persuasive, as were those of Mao and Deng. Many on the Central Committee, and in the National Assembly, will gladly support Tang in his Legalism."

His own advisers had warned of the same probability.

"History is a maiden, and you can dress her however you wish," the premier said. "Within ten years of Mao's death our government had been completely transformed, reorganized, thousands of new officials appointed, the past utterly eradicated. Pau Wen learned from that chaos. With careful skill, for the past three decades, he has directed the brothers of the *Ba*, including Karl Tang, on a singular course. I know that he left the country so he could more easily manage that plan."

Ni recalled the recorded phone conversation and told the premier, then said, "Clearly, Tang and Pau have parted ways."

"Careful, Minister. Eunuchs cannot be trusted."

His nerves were frayed to the breaking point. He waited for the premier to offer more, but there was only silence. Finally, the old man said, "Minister, I've just been told that a helicopter left Lake Dian with four people aboard. Three of them, Pau Wen included, swam from the lake."

"Intercept it."

"What would we learn from that?"

He knew the answer. Nothing.

"Thankfully," the premier said, "I believe I know where that helicopter is going."

He listened.

"Xi'an. You should head there immediately. But first, there is something else you must be told. Something not even Pau Wen knows to exist."

TANG WAITED AT THE AIRFIELD OUTSIDE LANZHOU. THE TERminal, a gray cement cubicle, with red velvet curtains adorning tall windows, cast the charm of an abandoned building. He could not leave until he knew exactly what had happened on Lake Dian. If everything went according to plan, Viktor Tomas would have all three passengers on board his helicopter. If that were so, Viktor would not make an oral report. Instead a code had been devised whereby a message could be sent without arousing suspicion.

He had placed much trust in this foreigner, but so far Viktor had performed admirably. He'd listened yesterday as past exploits with Cotton Malone and Cassiopeia Vitt had been explained, appreciating how that insight could be used to their advantage. He'd agreed with Viktor's assessment that to re-ingratiate himself with Malone and Vitt, to know precisely what the Russians and the Americans were after, something telling would have to occur.

Which was why he'd approved the downing of the fighter.

Now he could learn exactly what his enemies intended.

Once he assumed the premiership, in total command of the Party and the nation, enjoying the absolute backing of the Central Committee and the military, he would never be in doubt.

Until that happened, he was vulnerable.

So anything that minimized his risks was appreciated.

His phone alerted him to an incoming text message from his staff. He studied the screen. WEATHER ACCESSED FOR LINTONG COUNTY.

By monitoring the helicopter's data stream, it was possible to know what digital information was both sent and received from the onboard electronics. Viktor had said that if he failed to radio in, but instead requested weather conditions for a particular locale, then that was where they were headed.

Lintong lay in Shaanxi province, just east of Xi'an.

Where the tomb of Qin Shi and the terra-cotta army rested.

He answered the text to his staff with a concise order.

MAKE SURE THEIR PATH IS CLEAR. NO INTERFERENCE.

FIFTY

MALONE SAT IN THE HELICOPTER'S PASSENGER COMPARTMENT with Cassiopeia and Pau Wen, while Viktor flew alone in the cockpit. His clothes were wet from his dip in Lake Dian, but they were drying. They were flying northeast, a thousand kilometers across the heart of China, toward Shaanxi province and Xi'an. He remained skeptical as hell about trusting Viktor, so he motioned at Cassiopeia and Pau to remove their headsets.

He nestled close to them and said, "I want to have a talk without him listening." He kept his voice just below the din of the rotors.

"We're making progress, Cotton," Cassiopeia said, and he caught her irritation.

"I realize your goal is to find Sokolov's boy. But does either of you think all this is happening with no one knowing?"

"It clearly is not," Pau said. "But we are getting where we need to go. Once there, we can change the situation."

"And fighting with Viktor," Cassiopeia said, "is not going to make things easier."

"You've got a soft spot for him, don't you?"

"I have a soft spot for Lev Sokolov's son. I want to find that boy. To do that I need a sample of ancient oil to give Tang. To get that, we have to be in Xi'an."

"You don't really think that deal is still good, do you? Sokolov's apparently in deep trouble."

Her frustration was evident and he hated pressing, but it had to be said.

"Tang could already have Sokolov," he said. "He may have no use for you any longer."

"Then why are we still alive?" she asked.

He pointed at Pau. "Apparently, he's what interests Tang now. Viktor made that abundantly clear."

And there was what Ivan had not said. About Sokolov. The Russians wanted him back but, if left with no choice, dead was not out of the question.

He faced Pau. "What are *we* going to do once we're on the ground?"

"We will enter the tomb of Qin Shi, just as I once did. But we'll need flashlights."

He found an equipment bay where two lay and retrieved them.

"The tomb was not finished at the time of Qin's death," Pau said. "His son, the Second Emperor, completed it and buried his father. He then tricked the designers, and some of the builders, into going inside, trapping them underground. They died with their emperor."

"How do you know that?" Malone asked.

"I've seen their bones. They were there when I entered the tomb."

"But you're saying there was another way in and out," Cassiopeia said.

Pau explained that groundwater had been a challenge for the builders, as their excavations had been deep enough to tap the water table. So an elaborate underground drainage system had been created. Long channels bore through the earth, as much as 800 meters long, which prevented water from penetrating the chambers during construction. Once completed, most of the tunnels were refilled with tamped earth to form a dam.

A few, though, had been left open.

"I stumbled across one when I found Qin Shi's library. It bypasses all the traps that the builders set for robbers. Which was probably its purpose. They would have required a way to get inside to inspect the integrity, from time to time, without exposing themselves to danger."

"Why didn't they use it to get out once they were trapped inside?" Cassiopeia asked.

"The answer to that question will be obvious once you see the entrance."

"What about the mercury?" Malone asked, recalling their conversation yesterday at Pau's residence.

"I allowed the tomb to ventilate for several days before I entered. I also wore a respirator."

"And what about now?" Cassiopeia asked. "The tomb has been sealed for over twenty years."

"Preventive measures are in place."

Not entirely comforting, Malone thought, glancing toward the cockpit and his other problem. Outside the windshield, rain closed in on the sun as threatening clouds approached.

"He saved our lives back there," Cassiopeia said. "Yours included. He's our way to Tang."

"And what would have prevented Tang from already going into Qin's tomb and taking the oil sample himself? Viktor has known about this for two days."

"How would he get inside?" Pau said. "The tomb has never been excavated."

"You don't know what they've done," he made clear. "We don't even know if we're headed toward Xi'an."

"We are traveling in the right direction," Pau said.

"And what if someone's waiting for us when we land?"

"If that were the case," Pau said, "why not just allow the fighter to shoot us down?"

Good point.

"What's in the tomb?" Cassiopeia asked Pau.

"Not what you expect."

Malone said, "Care to elaborate?"

"I'll let you see for yourself, once we're inside."

FIFTY-ONE

NI STEPPED FROM THE CAR THAT HAD DRIVEN HIM EAST FROM Xi'an into Lintong County and the Museum of Qin Dynasty Terracotta Warriors and Horses. The premier had told him that the helicopter carrying Pau Wen would arrive within the next thirty minutes. He'd also told Ni something that he'd never known, something that only one person left alive knew.

The tomb of Qin Shi, China's First Emperor, had been opened.

Though the terra-cotta warriors had been dug from the ground and placed on display for the world to see, the tomb itself, a towering treed mound that dominated the otherwise flat, scrubby farmland, had supposedly never been violated. All agreed that the tomb represented one of the greatest archaeological opportunities on the planet. Qin Shi fundamentally changed the way his world was governed, solidifying Legalism, inventing a concept of government that unified China. He became the center of a nation and remained so even in death, taking with him not just a clay retinue, but a complete political system, one that reflected a supreme authority in both life and death. Those who came after him tried to diminish his influence by rewriting history. But entering the tomb, studying its contents, could well provide a way to correct every one of those edits.

Yet the communist government had always said no.

Officially, the reason was that technology and techniques did not, as yet, exist to properly preserve what lay beneath the mound. So it was deemed safer to leave the tomb sealed.

Ni had never, until a few hours ago, questioned that explanation. It was unimportant to his hunt for corruption. He'd only visited the museum once, a few years ago, when a series of thefts occurred in the restoration workshops—local laborers stealing pieces of the excavated warriors to sell on the black market. Now he was back, and the grounds swarmed with crowds, shifting and swaying like seaweed in a gentle current. Millions visited each year, and today—though a low-slung, oppressive gray sky yielded rain—seemed no exception. The car parks were full, an area specially reserved for buses packed tight. He knew a subway was currently under construction from Xi'an, a thirty-kilometer line that would ease traffic, but it was still a few years away from completion.

He'd told no one he was coming, commandeering a Central Committee helicopter that had flown him west. Karl Tang had left Lanzhou three hours ago, headed east, toward Xi'an, which meant his enemy should already be here. On the flight from Beijing he'd taken the time to read what his staff had amassed, studying a subject that he knew little about.

Eunuchs.

Their population had ranged from 3,000 to 100,000, depending on the era. To every Chinese, all naturally occurring forces came in cycles, reaching a peak with the *yang*, then receding with the *yín*. Maleness, strength, and virtue had always been associated with *yang*, while females, eunuchs, and evil were ruled by *yín*. He'd learned that there may have been a logical explanation for this dichotomy. All Chinese history was written by mandarins, the educated elite, who, as a class, despised palace eunuchs. Mandarins had to qualify for their position, after years of arduous study, by passing exams. Eunuchs acquired their influence without any qualifications. So it was understandable that what written records survived contained little good to say about eunuchs.

Not surprisingly, their mistreatment was common. Each time they encountered a member of the imperial family they were compelled to debase themselves as slaves. They realized early in life that they could never be venerated as scholars or statesmen. The inferiority complex generated from such treatment would breed resentment in anyone. They learned that their ability to survive, once their services were no longer needed, depended on how much wealth they could secretly amass. To acquire it meant to stay in close proximity to authority. So keeping themselves in good graces with their patrons, and keeping their patrons in power, became their primary interest.

There were, though, capable eunuchs who became valued advisers. Several achieved great stature. Tsai Lun, in the 2nd century, invented paper. Ssu-ma Chien became the father of Chinese history. Zheng He rose to be the greatest sailor China ever produced, building a 15th-century fleet that explored the world. Nguyen An, a veritable renaissance man, designed the Forbidden Palace. Feng Bao, during the 17th century, capably managed the affairs of the nation under Emperor Wanli. During that same time Chen Ju helped maintain a working inner court, while the outer court was torn asunder into warring factions. For his service, after his death, he was conferred the title *Pure and Loyal.*

From his reading, Ni realized that emperors simply came to believe that eunuchs were more reliable than government officials. Eunuchs were never taught lofty ideals or driven to consider the greater good over self. They simply came to represent the personal will of the emperor, while government officials presented the alternative political will of the established bureaucracy.

A classic clash of ideologies.

Which the eunuchs won.

Then lost.

Now they were back.

And their leader was here, in Xi'an, waiting.

TANG STUDIED THE CLOSED-CIRCUIT MONITORS. THE ENTIRE museum site was littered with hundreds of cameras that kept a constant watch on the three pits and their corresponding shelters, the exhibition hall, restaurants, information center, cinema, even the souvenir stalls.

He glanced at the wall clock and realized that a helicopter should be approaching soon. Nothing unusual. Government officials, dignitaries, even some of the country's new rich routinely flew to the site. The military likewise ferried personnel in and out. Tang had come in the same chopper that waited a kilometer away, just beyond the outer perimeter in a field designated as a landing spot.

Twenty-four separate screens filled the greenish wall before him within a dimly lit, air-conditioned building that sat two kilometers from the tomb mound. The building was part of an administrative complex where scientists, archaeologists, and bureaucrats were headquartered. He'd learned that faulty wiring had been blamed for the fire in Pit 3. A general unease permeated the air, since no one wanted to be tagged with responsibility. This was especially true of the administrator. The irritating fool had repeatedly offered his apologies about the *catastrophic loss to history*. Tang had decided to be more magnanimous than expected and assured the staff that he understood. Mishaps occurred. Conduct an investigation, then file a detailed report.

His gaze raked the television monitors.

An eager, active crowd—pushing, jostling—filled the screens. The rain had started an hour ago. He understood the value of tourist revenue, but the pandering required to secure those moneys irked him.

That, too, would change once he achieved power.

Images on the monitors changed every few seconds, numbers scrolling at the bottom indicating the time and location of each view. His eyes danced across the screens, absorbing the chaos, noticing uniformed guards that appeared from time to time, each in radio communication with the dispatcher to his right.

One display grabbed his attention.

"There," he ordered, pointing. "Number 45."

The monitor indicating camera 45 stopped scrolling.

"Where is that?"

"On the west side of the mound, near the tombs of the craftsmen."

The screen showed a man, dressed in a dark, short-sleeved shirt and dark trousers. He stood at the edge of a wet field, the forested base of the tomb mound in the background. He was facing the camera, rain soaking his body. Tall, slim, black-haired, and though Tang could not see such detail he knew the man possessed brown eyes, a broad nose, and distinctive features.

A murmur of alarm skittered across the room as the face was recognized.

"Minister Ni is on the premises," he heard one of the men say.

On screen, Ni turned and made a wild scramble across the wet soil, toward a cluster of stone and wooden houses with thatched roofs.

"What is that?" Tang asked.

"Restricted area. Orders from Beijing, Minister. Long ago. That area is off limits."

"No one enters there?"

The man shook his head. "Never. We monitor the fence, but do not go inside."

He understood the effect that an order from Beijing created. It was not questioned, only obeyed, until another directive from Beijing countermanded the first.

On the screen, as Ni hustled away, Tang noticed something protruding from the back pocket of his pants.

"Focus on what he is carrying," he immediately ordered.

The camera's focus zoomed as Ni continued to walk away, and the object became clear.

A flashlight.

He tapped one of the security men on the shoulder and motioned to his holstered weapon. "Give me your gun."

The man handed over the weapon.

He checked the magazine. Fully loaded.

"Take me to that area."

NI HAD PURPOSEFULLY STOPPED AND FACED THE CAMERA. IF Karl Tang was watching, which the premier had assured him would be the case, then he wanted him to know he was here.

Now to see if his enemy had taken the bait.

FIFTY-TWO

MALONE STARED DOWN THROUGH A WINDOW SMEARED BY RAIN at the tomb of Qin Shi. The green-forested mound rose like a boil from the flat brown landscape. He'd read about the site many times, a complex of underground vaults spread over twenty square miles, most of them unexplored. He'd even visited the terra-cotta warrior exhibition in London last year, but he'd never imagined that he might one day enter the tomb itself.

The helicopter approached from the south, swooping in over dun-colored hills at around a thousand feet. A steady downpour drenched the ground. More mountains rose to the west, the Wei River flowing to the north. About a mile away he caught a glimpse of the towering halls and other buildings that made up the museum site and a multitude of people with umbrellas, braving the rain.

"We'll land north," Viktor said through the headphones. "I'm told there's a spot reserved for helicopters there."

Malone preferred to carry a weapon and hoped that a locker he'd spotted earlier was accessible. When the latch opened he was instantly suspicious. Inside, four pistols were secured by clamps. He removed one and, remembering the last time he'd been inside a helicopter, with Viktor Tomas at the controls, he checked the magazine.

Fully loaded. Twenty rounds.

He removed a few of the bullets and examined them. No blanks.

He replaced the ammunition and handed Cassiopeia a weapon. He did not offer a gun to Pau Wen, nor did the older man ask.

He slid the semi-automatic pistol beneath his shirt. Cassiopeia did the same.

The rotors eased, and they gradually lost altitude.

TANG LEFT THE SECURITY BUILDING AND WAS HEADED FOR A waiting car when he spotted a military helicopter swooping in from the south. He wanted to go after Ni Yong, but he knew better.

"Keep the car ready," he ordered.

Then he headed back inside.

NI STOPPED AT THE RUSTED FENCE THAT ENCLOSED A CLUSTER of dilapidated buildings. The premier had told him that the cottage-like structures beyond had been hastily built in the 1980s. To the premier's knowledge, no one had been inside the enclosure for twenty years—and from the tall grass and vegetation that consumed everything, and gaping holes that dotted the thatched roofs, he could believe that claim. The buildings stood maybe a hundred meters from the base of the mound within the perimeter of an ancient wall that no longer existed.

He stared with a blend of fascination and wonder.

The premier had also advised him that Pau Wen was most likely headed inside the tomb of Qin Shi.

"How is that possible?" he'd asked.

"There are two ways inside. Pau Wen knows one. I know the other."

CASSIOPEIA JUMPED FROM THE HELICOPTER ONTO THE SOGGY ground, followed by Cotton and Pau. As the blades wound to a stop, Viktor emerged from the cabin and asked, "You find the guns, Malone?"

"And this time they actually have bullets."

"You're big on grudges, aren't you?"

No one had approached the chopper, and there was no vehicle in sight. They were probably a mile from the mound and half that distance to the museum complex. Another helicopter rested a hundred yards away.

"Friends of yours?" Malone asked

Viktor shrugged. "I have no idea."

"Security is a little lax," Malone said.

"And we're foreigners," Cassiopeia pointed out.

"But you came in a PLA chopper," Viktor said. "And that's what matters."

The rain fell in a steady pulse, resoaking Malone's still-damp clothes. But at least the air was warm.

Pau Wen pointed toward the museum. "We have to go. The exhibits will soon close for the day."

TANG STUDIED THE MONITOR, PLEASED THAT VIKTOR TOMAS had delivered Pau Wen, Cotton Malone, and Cassiopeia Vitt, exactly as promised. He was dividing his attention between the northern landing field and what Ni Yong was doing on the west side of the mound. His vantage point offered him the perfect perch, and he ordered the men working the cameras to not lose sight of either scene.

He'd assumed command of the museum security force knowing that no one would question his authority. Nor would anyone contact Beijing. The only person who could give him orders was the premier himself, and that was highly unlikely. The old man rarely concerned himself with politics any longer, and Tang had stopped paying attention to the premier's daily activities. They simply did not matter.

Ni Yong and Pau Wen.

They mattered.

And he now had both men directly within his sight.

His gaze switched back to the screen with Ni Yong. He watched as Ni scaled a rickety steel fence and dropped to the other side. He needed to head that way and see what was attracting his nemesis' attention. He'd been told there was nothing there, just a deserted storage area, yet that "nothing" was fenced, watched, and shielded by an order from the capital.

On the monitor he saw Pau and his three companions walk through the rain toward the Pit 3 hall. The same one where the imperial library chamber had been located. Where the watch had been found.

Interesting.

FIFTY-THREE

MALONE WAS AMAZED BY PIT 3. IT WAS THE SMALLEST OF THE three excavated sites, and a placard noted in English that this was the underground army's command center, complete with high-ranking officers, an imperial guard, and a chariot. Visitors filled a catwalk that encircled the excavations fifteen feet below. Weak sodium-vapor lights cast the surreal scene in a harsh, yellowish green glow. The air was moist and humid, the rain tapping on the ceiling high overhead in a constant drumbeat. A rich, earthy scent filled his nostrils. The lack of climate control was surprising considering that, surely, the whole idea of enclosing the pit would have been to keep moisture at bay.

Pau led them to the railing as a tour group moved farther along the walk. "This pit is unique in size and composition."

Malone assessed the layout. Many of the terra-cotta figures stood without their heads. On the paved floor below, shattered pieces of other figures lay in piles, like a puzzle poured from its box.

"Only 68 warriors were found here," Pau said. "Many thousands fill the other two pits. Here we found the underground army's imperial guards, its generals, the elite."

Malone studied the chariot, which sat at the center of the pit, at the base of a partially excavated ramp that led up to ground level.

"I was here in 1979 when this pit was first located," Pau said, "but it

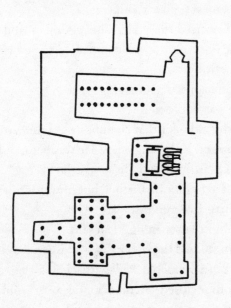

was not fully explored until the mid-1980s, at about the time I left China. So I have only seen photographs. Notice anything?"

Eight soldiers stood to the left of the center chariot, none to the right. All of the remaining soldiers filled two recesses on either side of the U-shaped pit.

"Why is there nobody on the right side of the chariot?" Malone asked.

"There's something else," Pau said.

"The chariot is cockeyed to the ramp," Cassiopeia said.

Malone saw that she was correct, making it impossible for the wheels to exit the pit without colliding with the ramp's wall. To negotiate the exit, the chariot would have to veer left.

"I noticed that from the images," Pau said. "For a people who were so careful with every aspect of design, that error could not have been unintentional."

"So the hole in the earthen wall, to the left of the chariot, is important?" Malone asked.

Pau nodded. "The designers sent a message that something important was located to the left. A few days ago, that chamber you see was rediscovered."

"Looks like a mess," Viktor said.

Malone, too, noticed the cables, shovels, rakes, and piles of dirt on either side of the opening, and what appeared to be a charred electrical box. "More like a fire."

"Accidents do happen," Pau said.

But Malone was not fooled.

"You knew the moment that chamber was found, didn't you?"

"More important, Karl Tang knew. He was here, and he set the fire. He intentionally destroyed Qin Shi's imperial library."

Malone wanted to inquire further, but now was not the time. "This place closes in forty-five minutes."

"We must enter that opening," Pau said.

Malone again studied the layout. Two additional ramps led down to the pit's floor. Both were blocked with chains that could easily be hopped. At least four closed-circuit cameras were visible, though there were probably more, the ones in sight sending a message that people were watching, the ones out of sight providing the best views. He counted six uniformed guards patrolling the catwalk and God knew how many plainclothes men scattered about. The crowd was quiet and orderly.

"We need a distraction," he whispered.

Cassiopeia nodded. "I was thinking the same thing."

"Be cautious," Pau said. "The security personnel here will react to anything rash."

"And if we're caught?" Viktor asked.

"Then we shall be arrested, and we can see if *you* are truly a friend or foe."

Malone liked that prospect regarding Viktor, though being detained in China sounded like a bad idea, especially given that they were here illegally and at least two of them were armed.

"I'll take care of the distraction," Viktor said.

"I thought you might," Malone said.

"I have a feeling you three don't want me along anyway."

No, Malone thought, he didn't.

"I'll be outside when you're through with whatever you plan on doing. I'll make some noise, but not enough to get arrested."

Viktor shuffled off, dissolving into the crowd, working his way to the other side of the catwalk.

"We need to avoid the ramps," Malone said. "Too obvious. Let's use that ladder." He gave a slight motion of his head to where a short length of chain blocked metal rungs. "Get down quickly and into that hole in the ground before the cameras regroup."

Pau and Cassiopeia nodded their assent.

Malone carried the two flashlights inside a pack slung over one shoulder, colored in the army's distinctive green with a red star. His gun remained nestled beneath his wet shirt.

A shout rose in the hall.

Malone saw Viktor flailing one arm in the air, and spewing out loud Chinese. It appeared he'd taken offense to something one of the visitors had either said or done.

Viktor shoved a man.

More words.

The crowd's attention zeroed in on the disturbance, as did security. All six uniforms rushed toward the rapidly escalating situation.

Malone waited for the cameras to angle toward the excitement, then whispered, "Go."

Cassiopeia hopped the short length of chain and climbed down.

Pau Wen followed.

Malone kept watch. No one seemed to pay them any attention. As Pau found the ground, he slid down the ladder behind him. Together they hugged the earthen wall and avoided the half-restored terra-cotta figures lining the way.

Cassiopeia entered the portal.

Before Pau disappeared inside, the older man grabbed one of the shovels. Apparently tools were needed, so Malone grabbed another and entered the dark space.

TANG WATCHED VIKTOR TOMAS ON ONE MONITOR AND PAU Wen and his two companions on the other. He'd inspected the library chamber thoroughly, prior to ordering its torching, and discovered that nothing of interest, besides the manuscripts, lay inside. Pau knew the manuscripts were gone, burned away—they'd discussed it on the phone—yet the first thing Pau had done on reentering China was head straight there.

Why?

"Order the building evacuated," he said. "Station a man at all exits and several on the catwalks. Keep this camera focused on that opening. If anyone emerges, have them immediately arrested. If they become a problem, shoot them."

He tightened his grip on the pistol.

"I'm headed there now. I want that building empty by the time I arrive, except for the foreigner who started the disturbance. Keep him inside."

MALONE SURVEYED THE TIGHT SPACE, MAYBE TEN FEET SQUARE, the floor and walls rough bricks, the ceiling stout timbers, one section long ago collapsed.

"I first came in through the break in the top," Pau said.

Three pedestal-like tables fashioned from stone stood empty, the floor littered with ash, the air thick with the smell of soot.

Something had definitely burned here.

"These tables were once covered with bamboo strips and silks, all with writings from the time of Qin Shi. His imperial library. Karl Tang ordered it destroyed two days ago."

"Why would he do such a thing?" Cassiopeia asked. "How could they be a threat to him?"

"Anything he cannot control is a threat to him."

Malone heard the din of noise from outside begin to recede. He stepped to the exit and peered upward. "People are leaving."

"I imagine Tang ordered that. Which means we have little time."

"For what?" he asked.

"To leave."

FIFTY-FOUR

NI WADED THROUGH A TANGLED MESS OF WET GRASS AND AP-
proached the second of the three low-slung structures. Rain continued
to fall. Vegetation had long ago consumed the outer walls, leafy vines
thick from ground to roof. Most of the windows remained intact, the
panes smeared with a layer of wet grime. He spotted beetles and mos-
quitoes smashed thick into torn screens.

He approached the wooden door. No lock prevented access, as he'd
been told, so he shoved it open. Rusted hinges fought back, then gave
way. The door jogged enough for him to slip inside.

He forced it closed once more.

Light from the filthy windows was filtered a gray-brown. Shadows
consumed the room, which measured perhaps five meters square, one
wall collapsed onto itself, exposing the weather and what lay behind the
building. Plows dotted the blackened earth floor, everything dusted
with a wet layer of rust and soil. A mass of clay pots and jars, piled in
pieces, rose against one wall. Cobwebs consumed the corners.

He eased himself through the break in the outer wall, back out into
the rain. For what he sought lay outside.

He heard the voice on the phone, from earlier.

"I employed spies to monitor what Pau Wen did at the mound site," the premier
said. *"He came to think that no one watched, and that may have been true of Mao and
Deng, but not of me. I watched closely."*

"And what did you learn?" Ni asked.

"Pau found a way into the tomb mound. Which surprised me. Qin's tomb was reported to contain large amounts of mercury. Yet he personally entered, staying inside for several hours one day, reappearing out of a hole in the earth near what would later become Pit 3. Strange occurrences likewise happened during the night for the next week, though no one officially reported anything."

He wanted to know more.

"Men and equipment working in the dark. Workers present who were not part of the site's labor force. One of the disadvantages of our form of government was that no one would have ever reported what they may have seen or heard. Pau was in charge and no one challenged him."

"Except you."

"I conducted a probe, but it was weeks later. We could not locate where Pau had disappeared into the ground. So much digging was occurring, the area ridden with deep gashes carved from the earth, it was impossible to know. But I did discover something else, years later. I was ordered back to the tomb mound by Beijing. This was after Pau had fled China. I was told to find a way inside the mound, and I did."

"Why has no one ever spoken of this?"

"There is a good reason for the secrecy."

He stared into the shadows that engulfed the dilapidated shanties. Trees blocked the sky allowing only thin fingers of light to poke through the canopy. Water, though, found a path and tapped the ground in a steady beat. The tomb mound started its rise less than fifty meters away. He was perhaps as close to the base as one could get. The fencing that had protected the front also ran behind the buildings, blocking any route upward.

He spotted the well exactly where the premier had said. A circular pile of masonry, two meters high, more wet vegetation clinging to its stones.

He hadn't walked around the buildings to the well because he wanted to slow down his adversary. This way, Tang would see him enter the building but not exit.

He stepped to the well and gazed inside. Less than a meter down, a rusted iron plate blocked the opening. Two makeshift handles had been welded to its surface. For all intents and purposes the plug was there to prevent anyone, or anything, from falling down the shaft.

But he knew better.

He gripped the handles, the wet rust staining his skin, making it difficult to keep a firm hold.

And lifted the plate away.

MALONE WAS PUZZLED. "WHERE ARE WE GOING?"

Pau knelt down and began to brush away a layer of dust and debris from the floor. "When I originally entered this chamber, the room was intact except that I noticed sunken areas in two places."

He understood. "Given these three stone tables, that meant there was solid ground everywhere—"

"Correct. I told you outside about the symbolism of the chariot and the ramp pointing left. The reason that is obvious to me now is because of what I found inside this room."

"It's getting quiet out there," Cassiopeia said.

Malone had noticed that, too. "Keep an eye out."

She assumed a position near the exit.

Pau completed his clearing and Malone spotted faintly etched symbols, one on each brick face.

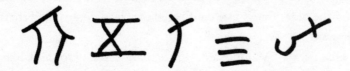

"What are they?" he asked.

"The one that looks like a house is the symbol for 6. The X with a line above and below is 5. The T-looking one is 7."

He noticed that the lines clumped together, which obviously was 4, appeared more often than the other numerals, except for the spoon with a line through its handle. "What's that?"

"9."

"There's a pattern," Pau said. "But I confess I was able to decipher it only because the floor itself had depressed."

Malone followed where Pau had pointed.

"The numbers 4 and 9 are important to the Chinese. 9 is pronounced *jiu,* which is the same for 'long' and 'forever.' 9 has always correlated to long life and good fortune. It came to be associated with emperors. 4, on the other hand, is pronounced *si,* which is the same as 'death.' 4 has always been regarded as unlucky."

He inventoried the symbols 4 and 9 and saw that there were two concentrations.

"When I entered the chamber, I saw that these bricks"—Pau pointed to a cluster of 9s—"were depressed. So was that cluster of 4s. I discovered that there were openings beneath the floor that led down to two separate passages."

"So you chose the lucky one," Malone said.

"It seemed the right selection."

Malone still held a shovel. He wedged the blade between two of the floor bricks with a 9 and pounded the sole of his shoe against the top edge. The ground was hard but gave way, and he angled the handle, forcing the brick upward.

"How we doing out there?" he asked Cassiopeia.

"Too quiet."

"Minister Tang is on the way," Pau said.

Malone stared down at Pau, who was helping free each brick. An idea of what to do came to him in an instant. Pau glanced up and the look on the older man's face confirmed that he'd determined their next move as well.

"That's scary," Malone said. "I'm actually starting to think like you."

Pau grinned. "I can't see where that is a bad thing."

TANG FOLLOWED A RED CARPET THAT FORMED A PATH UP A short set of stone risers into the brick-and-glass building that encased Pit 3. He'd been informed that the hall had been cleared and all exits were manned with guards. He'd brought two men with him, both brothers of the *Ba,* whom he'd ordered to be stationed nearby.

"No one leaves this building," he barked out as he stepped past three of the museum guards at the main doors.

Viktor Tomas waited inside.

"You did well," he said to Viktor.

"Delivered, as promised."

The excavated pit spread out before him. He approached the catwalk railing, pointed down, then turned to the two brothers, "Assume a position just outside that gash."

He watched as they hustled down a ladder, drew their weapons, and hugged the earthen wall on either side of the portal into Qin Shi's imperial library.

He handed Viktor his gun. "Finish the task. Now."

Viktor gripped the pistol and climbed down the ladder, approaching the two men, who stood ready to attack.

"Pau Wen," Tang called out. "The building is sealed."

No one replied.

"You are under arrest." His voice echoed through the interior, masked by the *rat-tat-tat* of rain off the metal roof.

Still no reply.

He motioned for Viktor to advance inside.

The two brothers moved with caution, glancing around the portal's edge, testing the situation, then rushed into the blackness, followed by Viktor.

He waited for the soft *pop* of sound-suppressed gunfire, but nothing came.

Viktor reappeared. "You should come down."

He did not like the quizzical tone in the man's voice.

He descended the ladder and entered the chamber. Just as he suspected, a charred smell of ash filled the musty air. Not a single silk or bamboo strip remained, only the three stone tables, the room not all that different from two days ago—except for two things.

In the floor, two sets of bricks had been removed, exposing openings about a meter square each, on opposite sides of the room.

He stared into them.

They dropped about two meters into the earth.

But which one had they taken?

FIFTY-FIVE

MALONE REALIZED THAT THEIR TRICK, IN EXPOSING BOTH OPEN-
ings, would only momentarily slow down any pursuers. But every second they could gain counted.

Another problem was more immediate.

He wasn't fond of tight, underground spaces, though he seemed to
find himself inside them more often than he wished. He knew Cassiopeia did not suffer from the same discomfort, so she led the way,
plunging through the coal-black darkness, the beam of her flashlight illuminating only a few feet ahead.

They walked without a sound, their entrance point now a hundred
yards behind them, negotiating sharp turns that had gone first left then
right. The floor, which carried a slight upward slope, was brick-paved,
similar to Pit 3, the walls and roof cut stone.

"This was part of the drainage that protected the tomb from
groundwater," Pau whispered. "The turns are meant to slow any water
that might accumulate, the rise making it difficult for the water to en-
croach. Behind these walls is poured bronze to add another layer of
protection. They were quite ingenious."

"And where does this lead?" Malone asked.

"Straight to the tomb, and the secret entrance used by the builders."

Malone recalled the distance from the museum to the tomb

mound—about half a mile, he'd estimated from the air. But that was in a straight line, which this tunnel wasn't.

His anxiety amplified.

Cassiopeia stopped and glanced back toward him. Her eyes asked if he was okay, and he motioned for them to head on.

They passed offshoots, dark doorways to the left and the right. Eight so far. He also noticed characters etched beside the portals, more Chinese numbers. Pau explained that the tunnels accommodated runoff, taking as much water as possible away from the tomb, allowing seepage back into the ground. Similar to a drain field for a septic tank, Malone thought.

"The numbers beside each portal, they're significant?" he asked.

"Critical," Pau said. "Take the wrong one and you may never get out of here."

TANG WAS NOT IN THE MOOD FOR TRICKS.

He stared at the holes in the floor and ordered, "Both of you stand guard. Don't leave this room unattended. If any foreigner emerges from those holes, shoot them."

They nodded their assent.

He motioned for Viktor to come with him.

Time to deal with Ni Yong.

NI SAW THAT HE WAS STANDING IN THE ENTRANCEWAY TO THE tomb of Qin Shi, exactly as the premier had described. Nearly twenty-five years ago, a select team of five individuals, headed by the deputy minister for internal affairs, who would later rise to become premier of the nation, had used ground-penetrating radar to find a way inside. Beijing had, by then, discovered the value of the terra-cotta warriors in promulgating a new world image of China. Adding the actual tomb of

Qin Shi to that repertoire could only enhance the effect. But after Mao's many failures, the Party gambled only on sure things.

So a secret exploration was ordered.

Luckily a tunnel had been discovered almost immediately, and they'd dug down, entering from above. When they finished, a well had been built over the entrance and capped with an iron plate, the entire area fenced and declared off limits.

His flashlight revealed a towering, arched passage, perhaps ten meters high. The floor was paved with veined stone. Archways appeared at regular intervals, holding the roof aloft. A cable lay against one wall, placed there by the first exploration team.

Follow it, had been his instruction.

If what he'd been told was right, no one had followed this path in more than thirty years. Before that, two millennia had passed between visits.

He walked for what he estimated as a hundred meters. The beam from his light revealed a stone gate, but two doors blocked the way.

He approached.

The glistening stone portal stood three meters high, dark green and black veins glistening in his light. Each door was carved from a single slab of marble, the surfaces littered with symbols and a bronze clamp. The right door was cocked open, which allowed a passage through the center.

He hesitated and shone his light left and right. Slits in the passage walls, high, near the roofline, indicated where crossbows had once been placed to fire on any interloper. The premier had told him that the reports of booby traps in some of the historical accounts had proven true, though 2,200 years of aging had rendered them useless. The doors themselves had been barred from the outside, and he spotted a heavy timber that had once rested inside the bronze clamps.

Every schoolchild was taught of Qin Shi. He was the embodiment of China, the founder of the longest-enduring political system on earth. A conqueror, unifier, centralizer, standardizer, builder—the first in a long line of 210 men and one woman to occupy the Dragon Throne.

And this was his tomb.

He negotiated the opening between the doors and stepped into more blackness on the other side. He'd been told to look to his right. His light found the cable on the floor, which had also passed through the open doors, ending at a metal box.

He bent down and examined the exterior. Still in good condition. He grasped a lever, prepared himself, and rotated it downward.

CASSIOPEIA LED THE WAY AS THEY TURNED ANOTHER CORNER and negotiated a third set of right angles. She realized that there would be another twist coming to swing them back on a line toward the tomb mound. She estimated they'd traveled maybe two hundred meters, so they should be getting close to whatever lay at the end.

She couldn't help but marvel at the engineering. Her own stone-masons, hired to reconstruct the castle that she'd been laboring to build for nearly a decade, had early on explained the difficulties. To build today exactly as they had in the 14th century, using 700-year-old tools and methods, was daunting. But the builders of this tunnel had not been nearly as fortunate. Their tools and technology didn't even approximate the sophistication of the 14th century. Yet they'd managed to accomplish the task, and their resounding success made her even more committed to finishing her own restoration.

"We are near the end," she heard Pau Wen say.

Surprisingly, the air was stale but not fetid. Apparently, ventilation had likewise been part of the builders' plan.

She knew that being enclosed underground was not Malone's idea of fun. But flying through the air, looping around in a plane or heli-copter, was not her favorite, either. Nothing about their situation was good. They were relying on a man who was utterly untrustworthy, but they had little choice. She had to admit that she was excited about the possibility of entering the tomb. Never had she imagined such an op-portunity would present itself. She felt better with the gun nestled at her waist and Cotton at her back, but remained apprehensive about what lay just beyond the beam of her flashlight.

They passed two more exits, both labeled with Chinese symbols. The passage right-angled ahead, just as she knew it would.

She stopped and turned.

Malone was a couple of meters behind her. She lowered her light, pointing the beam to the ground.

He did the same.

Then she noticed something.

"Cotton."

She motioned with her light, and he turned.

Pau Wen was gone.

"Why doesn't that surprise me?" Malone muttered.

"He must have slipped into one of the side passages along the way."

She found her gun, as did Malone.

"Lead the way," he said.

She approached the corner and carefully peered around. The tunnel extended another fifty meters, ending at what appeared to be a doorway. A thick slab of stone, cut into a near-perfect rectangle, filled the opening, one side cocked outward, as a door would be partially opened.

Light filled the space beyond, splashing back their way, into the darkened corridor.

"I didn't expect that," Malone whispered in her ear.

FIFTY-SIX

TANG SURVEYED THE INTERIOR OF THE TUMBLED-DOWN SHANTY into which Ni Yong had disappeared. Earlier, he'd watched on the closed-circuit monitor as Ni entered through the door, but now his nemesis was nowhere to be seen.

"He went out there," Viktor said, pointing to the collapsed rear wall.

Two other men were with him, more brothers of the *Ba,* eunuchs like himself and the two he'd left in Pit 3, all pledged by oath to do as he commanded. More of his forethought, which he silently applauded himself for having, especially given the way things were progressing.

The rain had eased, though the moist air reeked. His gaze locked on the wall, wattled and plastered, broken in a gash that exposed the bamboo beneath. He stepped across the damp floor, past rusted implements and broken pottery, and fled the building.

The others followed.

Outside was thick with shadows, the ashen sky blocked by a canopy of wet limbs and leaves. The first violets of the season bloomed beneath the trees. The fence that encircled the site stood fifty meters away, intact. Ni could have scaled it, but where would he have gone?

A well caught his eye and he approached.

Not unusual. The whole area was dotted with them. In fact, the digging of one in 1974 had led to the discovery of the terra-cotta army. But an iron plate plugged the opening.

Where had Ni gone?

He glanced around at the wet terrain, thick with trees, toward where the mound began its rise upward.

Ni had come here for a reason.

He'd learned that the fence had been erected in the early 1990s, on orders from Beijing, and that the area had remained off limits. Why? No one knew. Viktor had reported that Pau Wen had told Malone and Vitt that he knew a way into Qin Shi's tomb. Pau had then gone straight to the recently found imperial library and made good on his promise, locating two underground passages, one of which Vitt, Malone, and Pau had disappeared into.

"Minister," Viktor said.

His mind snapped back to the moment.

Viktor pointed inside the well. "See the scarp marks on the side. They're fresh. That plate was removed, then replaced."

The observation was correct. The yellowish white lichen had clearly been disturbed. He ordered the two brothers to lift the plate away and the top of a wooden ladder came into view.

They'd driven over in a museum security vehicle. "See if the car carries any flashlights," he ordered. One of the men ran off.

"Where does it go?" Viktor asked.

Tang knew. "Into the tomb. Where Ni Yong awaits."

MALONE APPROACHED THE BACKLIT DOORWAY, STAYING TO one side of the partially open portal while Cassiopeia stayed to the other. They'd switched off the flashlights and replaced them in their pockets. Both held their weapons.

He noticed L-shaped bronze clamps affixed to their side of the door, another to the left and right of the jamb. A thick cut of timber rested against the wall, standing upright. Easy to determine its use. Once it was dropped into the clamps, there would have been no way to open the door from the other side.

What had Pau read to them?

Concubines without sons were ordered to follow the emperor in death, and of the artisans and workers not one was allowed to emerge alive.

He peered around the edge into the lit space beyond.

The underground chamber stretched nearly the length of a football field. The rounded ceiling was thirty to forty feet high, held aloft by arches that stretched its width and columns that dotted the rectangular hall. Tripod lights had been placed every twenty feet or so on all four sides, casting upward a yellow-orange glow that illuminated what appeared to be a ceiling of crystals, pearls, and gems arranged as stars in a night sky. The floor was fashioned as a massive three-dimensional topographic map with rivers, lakes, oceans, mountains, valleys, temples, palaces, and towns.

"Holy crap," Cassiopeia muttered.

He agreed. Sima Qian's account seemed relatively accurate.

The constellations of the heavens were reproduced above and the regions of the earth below.

He noticed a glistening silvery hue from the representations of water. Mercury.

Using quicksilver, they made the hundred rivers of the land, the Yellow and Yangtse, and the wide sea, and machines kept the waters in motion.

He cringed, but recalled what Pau had said. *Preventive measures.* He hoped the SOB had at least told the truth about that.

No one was in sight. So who'd switched on the lights? Pau Wen?

He risked another look and determined they were inside the short wall of the rectangle, at the opposite end of what appeared to be the main entrance. All four walls were polished stone alive with carved animal heads and otherworldly images bursting from the lustrous surface. He spotted a tiger, a prone horse, a toad, a frog, a fish, and an ox. Color abounded. Yellow-glazed pillars and arches, vermillion walls, a purple-black ceiling.

At the center stood an elaborate plinth, wider at the bottom than the top, fashioned of what appeared to be jade. Two lights illuminated exquisite carvings that dotted its sides. Nothing lay atop. Bare, like the rest of the chamber. Stone pedestals adorned the four walls, spaced every twenty feet or so, about ten feet off the floor. He realized what they had once held.

Torches were made of oil to burn for a long time.

But not a single lamp could be seen.

Inside Qin's tomb are hundreds of lamps, all filled with oil. I even lit one.

Another of Pau Wen's lies.

He'd read enough about Chinese imperial tombs to know that they were designed as symbolic representations of an emperor's world. Not a monument, but an analogue of life through which the emperor eternally perpetuated his authority. Which meant the hall should be loaded with stuff.

He glanced over at Cassiopeia. Her eyes agreed on their next move.

He stepped from the darkened recess into the lit space. The floor represented the extreme southwestern fringes of Qin Shi's empire, showing what he knew to be mountain ranges carved of jade. A flat expanse to the north delineated desert, which stretched east toward the heart of the empire. Many meters away were more open plains, plateaus, blankets of trees, mountains, and valleys. Palaces, temples, villages, and towns, all fashioned of gemstone and bronze, sprouted everywhere, connected by what appeared to be a system of roads.

He noticed that the stone panel, which blocked the portal once closed, would have dissolved cleanly into the ornamented wall. An entrance capable of being seen and opened only from the outside. Coiled dragons, humanoid faces, and crested, long-tailed birds sprang from the adjacent walls.

He motioned toward the center with his gun and they threaded their way across the floor, careful to find smooth areas on which to step. He was still worried about the mercury, concerned about vapors, so he bent down close to one of the rivers and saw that the carved channel, maybe a foot wide and a few inches deep, flowed with mercury.

But there was something else, on top. Clear. Oily. He tapped the glistening surface with the tip of the gun and ripples spread. He examined the gun's end and risked a smell, catching a hint of petroleum.

Then he knew.

"Mineral oil," he whispered. "Pau coated the mercury with it to hold in the vapors."

He'd done the same once himself, in a basement floor drain trap, floating the oil on top of the water to slow evaporation, keeping sewer gases at bay. He was relieved to know that the air was not riddled with toxins, but still concerned about not only where Pau Wen had gone, but who else may be around.

They headed for the center plinth, which dominated a prominent platform. He'd been correct. The whole thing had been carved of jade and depicted a multitude of human, botanical, and animal images. The craftsmen had made excellent use of the stone's varying shades, and he couldn't resist caressing the translucent surface.

"It's incredible," Cassiopeia said. "I've never seen anything like it."

He knew the Chinese considered jade a gift from the gods, the key to everlasting life. It symbolized eternity, and was supposedly imbued with wondrous powers that could protect from evil and bring good luck. That was why Chinese emperors were buried inside funerary suits of jade, sewn together with gold threads and adorned with pearls.

"This was where the emperor lay," Cassiopeia whispered.

There was no other conclusion. For a culture that prized symbolism, this seemed the ultimate expression.

But the plinth was bare.

He noticed that the top was not smooth. Instead, images had been engraved from end to end, framed by a border of Chinese symbols.

"It's like the map in Pau Wen's house," Cassiopeia said.

He thought the same thing.

He studied the carving closely and saw that it was a compact representation of what the floor depicted—Qin Shi's empire. What had Pau said about the map hanging in his house? *It's a reproduction of something I once saw. With some changes.*

He found his iPhone and snapped a few images of the surrounding room and the map.

"He lay atop his realm," he whispered.

"But where is he?" she asked.

NI HAD BEEN SHOCKED WHEN THE LEVER HE TWISTED ACTI-vated lights. The premier had told him how power had been run underground to the site and tripods installed. The entire purpose of the incursion had been to ascertain whether the tomb could be used for further propaganda in conjunction with the terra-cotta warriors. But the complex was found empty, every artifact gone, including the emperor himself. Which explained why the government had not allowed any further archaeological exploration. Think of the embarrassment. The questions, none of which came with answers. So a well had been constructed over the makeshift entrance, the area fenced off, and access forbidden.

The premier had wondered if the bulbs would still operate. Most had, illuminating a series of three arched antechambers, and the main burial hall, in a phosphorous glow. He'd been told that the mercury was safe, sheathed by a layer of mineral oil that Pau Wen had applied during the first exploration.

He wondered if Karl Tang would find his way down. Surely he'd found the well, and the removal of the iron plate had left plenty of fresh marks. The sounds of footsteps, approaching from behind, deep in the tunnel from which he had just emerged, confirmed that someone was headed this way.

Then he heard something else.

Movement from within the main burial hall.

And saw shadows dancing across a wall.

Strange.

He stared through the remaining antechambers, which opened one into another, and watched the distant shadows. He was positioned to deal with Karl Tang, gun at the ready.

But he was also trapped.

Between the known and the unknown.

FIFTY-SEVEN

TANG HAD READ ABOUT IMPERIAL TOMBS, EVEN VISITED A COUple of notable excavations, but now he was walking inside one totally intact. Clearly, though, someone had been here before. A thick electrical cable lined the base of the tunnel wall and disappeared into the blackness ahead. Pau Wen? Was that why he'd traveled straight to Xi'an? But Pau had gone underground inside Pit 3, a long way from where Tang stood. No, Ni Yong had entered here. Which meant that his adversary knew things that he did not.

Viktor and the two brothers led the way down the passage, wide as an avenue, black as night. The care in the construction, the detail, the colors—they were all spectacular. Stamped decoration in light relief sheathed the walls. In the weak light of their flashlights he saw scenes of court life, the amusements of nobility, a royal procession, bears, eagles, and mythical beasts. Incense burners, shaped as mountains and fashioned of stone, dotted their path.

Fifty meters ahead a shaft of light revealed an entrance between two polished marble doors, both alive with more carvings. Stone lions flanked either side. Hybrid figures of horned bird-men—intended, he knew, to repel malevolent spirits—sprang from the walls on either side. Above the doorway were carved three symbols:

阿 房 宮

He knew their meaning. "Beside the capital." Which was fitting. He recalled what Sima Qian wrote of the First Emperor in *Shiji. Qin Shi made up his mind that the population of his empire had grown large while the royal palaces of his ancestors were still small.* So he built a massive new palace, south of the Wei River, adjacent to his capital. Nearly seven hundred meters long and more than a hundred meters wide, its galleries had been capable of holding 10,000 people.

He called it Afang, which reflected its location, "beside the capital."

He studied the doors and discovered that they hung with no hinges. Instead, a convex half sphere had been carved at the top and bottom, then fitted inside a concave opening in the ceiling and floor. He surmised that, most likely, the joints had once been greased with oil.

They stepped through the space where the doors parted, the crack about a meter wide, into a lit room that opened into another, then two more, all supported by wide arches and thick columns. This was a *yougong*—a secluded place.

Strangely, the rooms were empty.

He remembered more of what Sima Qian had written. *And there were marvelous tools and precious jewels and rare objects brought from afar.* The rooms and alcoves should be filled with silk fabrics, garments, ceramics, headdresses, crowns, belts, ornaments, bronze and tin funerary objects, lacquerware, wooden figurines—everything the emperor would have needed in his afterlife.

Yet there was nothing.

He noticed ornamented pedestals dotting the walls at regular intervals and realized that lamps—like the one he'd sought from Pau Wen, the ones Pau had promised Malone and Vitt existed—would have rested atop to light the emperor's way and nourish the spirits of the dead.

But there were no lamps.

Which meant no oil.

Nothing.

Only a blue-and-white urn, perhaps a meter wide and at least that tall in the center of the next chamber. He'd seen images of one before. An everlasting lamp, filled with oil, holding a wick afloat. He stepped close and peered inside, hoping that some of the ancient crude might remain, but the container stood dry.

Viktor advanced into the next chamber, the two brothers in tow.

Tang lingered, his mind alight with conflicting thoughts.

Qin Shi's tomb had clearly been explored—enough that electricity had been run and lighting installed. This could not have occurred during the last decade. His ministry would have known of any such effort. Obviously, though, Ni Yong knew about what had happened here.

"Ni Yong," he called out. "It is time to settle the matter between us."

MALONE FROZE AT THE SOUND OF A VOICE, THE WORDS RICOcheting through the silence like a gunshot. Cassiopeia reacted, too, and they both crouched to one side of the jade plinth, identifying that the voice had come from beyond the hall's main entrance.

Was the Mandarin being spoken to them?

If so, they had no way of understanding.

"That wasn't Pau Wen," Cassiopeia whispered.

He agreed. "And we don't have many options."

They were positioned in the center of a hall, the plinth their only cover. He risked a glance and noticed shadows in the next chamber, perhaps thirty yards away. Doubtful he and Cassiopeia could make it back to the break in the wall through which they'd entered without being spotted.

He saw worry in her eyes.

They were trapped.

TANG ADVANCED TO THE ENTRANCE OF THE BURIAL CHAMBER and called out again, "Ni Yong, there is nowhere for you to go."

From the open archway he studied the massive underground palace. The ceiling twinkled with thousands of lights, the floor a surreal three-dimensional map, sparkling with the shimmer of mercury from rivers, lakes, and seas. Now he understood why the government had resisted all requests to open the tomb. The site was bare. Except for a jade table, alive with carvings, in the center, where surely the First Emperor once lay.

The two brothers approached from behind.

"There are annex chambers," one of them said.

He'd seen the dark doorways, too. "And there is another way out of here." He pointed across the burial hall to a break in the marble wall on the far side, at least seventy or eighty meters away. "Where is Viktor?"

"Checking the annex rooms."

He pointed at the distant exit. "Let us see if Ni Yong went there."

NI SOUGHT REFUGE IN ONE OF SEVERAL ROOMS THAT OPENED off the three anterooms. No lights had been rigged here. He'd watched as Karl Tang and three other men marveled at what he'd already been stunned to see.

Though he was out of their immediate line of sight, there was simply no place to hide. The dim room he'd entered was bare except for a collection of murals. He'd heard Tang's declaration and knew that he'd have to shoot his way to safety.

This must be a private affair. Between you and Tang.

That's what the premier had told him. Was this what he meant?

I will not involve anyone else, or allow you to do so.

Unfortunately, Tang had not come alone. Could he take all four? It seemed to be the situation from Pau Wen's residence all over again, except this time he possessed no savior.

He hoped the burial chamber would capture Tang's attention long enough that he could slip out the way he'd entered. But before he could retrace his steps and make an escape, the doorway out was blocked by a man. Short, burly, fair-skinned, European, and holding a semi-automatic pistol.

Aimed his way.

The foreigner stood with his body backlit, spine straight, eyes locked ahead. Ni held his gun at his side, the barrel pointed to the floor.

He'd never lift it in time.

Two shots popped.

TANG STUDIED THE FLOOR AS HE CAREFULLY ADVANCED TOWARD the hall's center. He'd just crossed a narrow causeway that spanned what was surely the China Sea. In Qin Shi's time that would have been the empire's eastern boundary. The "sea," an area maybe twenty meters long by that many wide, shimmered with quicksilver. He was initially concerned about toxicity, but he noticed that a thin layer of mineral oil had been applied over the mercury.

Someone had thought ahead.

That was not an ancient innovation.

He knew that mineral oil only came about when petroleum was first distilled into gasoline—in the West's 19th century—a long time after Qin Shi. He'd also noticed the sodium-vapor lamps, their bulbs not of the size and shape currently in use. These were older. Larger. Warmer. He estimated their age at maybe twenty-plus years, and wondered about the last time they were lit.

The detail of the topographic floor map was amazing, the rising topography of the south and west illustrating mountains that gradually flattened into fertile plains. Forests were represented by trees carved from jade. More rivers of mercury snaked a path among temples, towns, and villages. He assumed the plinth in the center stood where the imperial capital had been located at the time of Qin Shi, not far from present-day Xi'an.

Two pops disturbed the silence.

Gunshots. Behind him.

From where Viktor had gone.

He stopped his advance, as did the two brothers.

Another pop sounded.

He turned and rushed back toward the shots.

MALONE WATCHED AS THE FIRST VICE PREMIER, KARL TANG, and two other men fled the burial chamber. He'd recognized the face from photos Stephanie had provided. Viktor had surely known that his boss would be nearby, which explained both the other helicopter and why he'd so generously offered to create a diversion.

"That was close," Cassiopeia said.

If the three men had found the table, avoiding them would have been impossible. He and Cassiopeia would have been exposed, and he'd already decided to kill the two minions and deal with Karl Tang separately.

"Who's shooting?" Cassiopeia asked.

"I don't know. I'm just glad they are."

FIFTY-EIGHT

NI HEARD THE TWO SHOTS AS THE MAN IN THE DOORWAY FIRED
at him. But the bullets zoomed over his head and pinged off the walls,
causing him to duck and shield his head. Clearly the man had readjusted his aim just prior to pulling the trigger, intentionally aiming
high.

He was not going to be so generous. He leveled his gun and
squeezed the trigger.

But the man was gone.

His bullet, like the two before, found only stone, ricocheting off the
walls, causing him now to drop to the floor.

He sprang to his feet, without using either hand for leverage, and
bolted for the exit. A quick peek around the doorway's edge and another bullet came his way, reeling him back against the wall. Why was
the man shooting at him, yet not wanting to hit him? And why was a
foreigner here with Tang?

He recalled what the premier told him. *The fighter did not crash. It was
shot down by a helicopter, piloted by a foreigner, authorized to fly by Minister Tang.*

Was this the man?

TANG FLED THE MAIN HALL AND REENTERED THE FIRST AN-
techamber. Viktor appeared from one of three darkened archways that
led out, his back leading the way, gun pointed behind him.

"I found Minister Ni," Viktor said.

Tang motioned for the two brothers to take positions left and right.
Both brandished their guns, while he held a semi-automatic.

"Is there any other way out?" Tang asked.

Viktor shook his head. "Only through here."

MALONE WATCHED THE UNFOLDING SCENE WITH INTEREST.

"What do you think is happening?" Cassiopeia asked.

She hadn't been privy to Stephanie's briefing, so he explained. "The
man there, in the center, giving orders, is Karl Tang."

He caught a glimpse of a fourth man now inside the antechamber.
Viktor. He should have known.

"You think it's Pau Wen they are after?" she asked.

"Could be. But he seemed to have anticipated this warm recep-
tion."

"That means somebody else is down here. Somebody Karl Tang
doesn't like."

"Which makes that person our ally."

"So let's help."

CASSIOPEIA GRIPPED THE GUN, READYING HERSELF. MALONE
slipped to one side of the plinth, she to the other. Luckily, the jade table
had been positioned diagonally, which offered them more protection.

Malone stood.

"Hey, assholes," he called out.

Tang, Viktor, and the two men whirled.

Malone sent a bullet their way, obviously not to hit anybody but to attract their attention. Which worked. All four retreated from view, two firing rounds as they disappeared from sight.

Both she and Malone hugged the plinth.

"I hope whoever we just helped appreciates it," she said.

NI HEARD SOMEONE CALL OUT, THEN HEARD THREE SHOTS fired. He advanced into a smaller, dimly lit space that opened between him and the brightly lit antechamber. He pressed his spine to the wall directly adjacent to the doorway and peered around the corner. Tang and two other men were standing as he was, against the wall for the entrance into the burial hall.

He did not see the foreigner and watched as one of the men swung around and shot through the archway into the burial chamber.

Then another did the same.

Something had commanded their attention, away from him.

He decided to take advantage of the situation.

He aimed and fired.

TANG WAS STARTLED BY THE SHOT FROM BEHIND.

One of the brothers cried out, then shrank to the floor.

The man writhed in pain.

Tang turned to see Ni Yong fleeing one of the darkened doorways, rushing into the next anteroom. He swung his gun around and fired, but Ni vanished through the archway, finding sanctuary on the other side.

Where was Viktor?

The wounded brother continued to moan in agony, exposed on all sides.

Only one thing to do.

Tang shot him in the head.

"Damn," Malone said. "Did you see that?"

"They shoot their own," she said.

"Which means they'll have little respect for us."

Ni wasted no time. As soon as he'd squeezed the trigger, he rushed for the exit, finding safety just before Tang could respond. He bolted into the next anteroom, keeping near a far wall, away from the vulnerable middle, fleeing toward the main doors. If he could make it into the passage leading back to the well, darkness would be his ally.

He slipped into the last antechamber.

He hugged the wall and stole a quick glance behind, catching a glimpse of Tang and the other man as they entered the room he'd just left.

One of them fired.

He ducked, then sent a response, using the moment to slip through the black crease between the partially opened main doors. Once on the other side of the entrance, he was safe from bullets. He could not waste a moment. In the blackness, beyond the lights, he'd be okay.

He turned to flee, but a man blocked his way.

The foreigner who'd shot at him earlier and intentionally missed.

"You don't know me," the man said, a gun in hand, pointed straight at him. "But I'm not your enemy."

The stranger stepped farther from the darkness into the light. Definitely European. Ni burned the face into his memory.

The man handed Ni his weapon, gripping it by its short barrel.

"Knock me silly with this gun, then get the hell out of here."

He did not have to be told twice. He accepted the gun and slammed its metal butt into the man's temple.

He then tossed the gun aside and fled into darkness.

TANG EMERGED FROM THE DOUBLE DOORS AND SPOTTED VIK-tor lying on the pavement, his gun a few meters away. His gaze raked the darkness ahead, but he heard and saw nothing.

Ni was gone.

Viktor was picking himself off the floor, rubbing his head. "I was waiting for him, but the bastard was quick. He slammed me in the head."

Tang had no time for excuses. With no way to safely pursue, he aimed into the blackness and laid down a spread of four shots, swinging his arm from right to left, one wall to the other.

Bullets pinged in the darkness.

Retorts banged off the walls, hurting his ears.

"He's gone," Viktor calmly said.

He lowered the gun. "We need to go back inside. Malone, Vitt, and Pau Wen are still there."

MALONE HEARD FOOTSTEPS, HEADING AWAY, AND SURMISED THAT the two men and Viktor had fled. He had no idea what lay on the other side of the archway for the burial hall's main entrance.

But now was the time to act.

Heading back to the secret panel through which they entered was too risky. Far too much real estate between here and there. So he motioned to Cassiopeia and together they abandoned the plinth, traversing the ninety feet to the entrance arch in just a few seconds. Luckily, the floor topography was mainly plains and ocean, over which extended a narrow walkway that allowed them to run a majority of the way.

The dead man lay still, blood pouring from his two wounds.

Malone risked a look inside the next chamber and spotted three men, Viktor and Tang among them, reentering at the opposite end, heading straight for them. Cassiopeia was watching, too, and together they decided a retreat was in order.

But first he fired a round that sent the three men scattering.

Cassiopeia led the way as they retraced their path to the center plinth. They made it there just as two more rounds came their way.

Apparently, their pursuers were not going to leave.

They hugged the far side of the plinth.

"You realize we have nowhere to go," Cassiopeia said.

"That thought has occurred to me."

FIFTY-NINE

NI STOOD. HE'D DOVE DOWN, LYING FLAT AS KARL TANG FIRED into the darkness, using one of the bulky incense burners for cover. He'd laid still as bullets cascaded off the walls, then watched as his three assailants disappeared back into the tomb. The man he'd knocked unconscious clearly worked for Tang, but he also apparently possessed a separate agenda.

But who'd called out, then fired from the burial chamber? Should he help them? What could he do, beyond place himself back in jeopardy.

Getting killed would solve nothing.

He had to leave.

MALONE CAUGHT THE SHADOWS REAPPEARING IN THE ANtechamber. He'd heard four rounds fired and wondered what was happening. But apparently one problem had either been solved or was no longer a concern. Instead—

"Our turn," he said.

He spotted heads peering around the archway, reconnoitering the burial chamber.

"Can we draw them out?" Cassiopeia whispered from the other side of the plinth.

"They're not sure we're still here. They see that hole in the wall behind us, too. We could be in there, as far as they know."

Unfortunately, their haven was a hundred feet away, the space in between wide open except for a few pillars, none of which would provide much cover.

His mind rifled through the possibilities.

Not many.

He studied the tripod of lights that illuminated the plinth. His gaze drifted down to a river of mercury flowing a few feet away—a representation, he surmised, of the Yellow River spanning the ancient empire from east to west. He recalled again what Pau Wen had read to them yesterday. *Using quicksilver, they made the hundred rivers of the land, the Yellow and Yangtze, and the wide sea, and machines kept the waters in motion.* Were the reservoirs connected? Regardless, what he had in mind should work.

"Get ready to move," he whispered.

"What are you going to do?"

"Create a problem."

TANG SPOTTED SHADOWS ON THE CENTER PLATFORM.

Someone was there. Two forms.

One on either side of the jade table that stood at a diagonal to the hall. His gaze raked the remainder of the chamber and confirmed that there was no other place to hide.

So where was the third person who should be here?

"Kill both of them," he ordered. Then, to Viktor, he made clear, "And this time I want them dead. We need no further distractions."

Viktor seemed to understand that things had not gone right and nodded. "We'll take care of them."

MALONE SAW THE BARRELS OF TWO GUNS, ONE POSITIONED AT either side of the archway.

Both fired.

Bullets popped off of jade.

Time to act.

He dropped back on his butt, lifted his right leg, and slammed the sole of his shoe into the tripod supporting the electric lamps. The spindly metal toppled, bulbs exploding in a shower of sparks and heat that ignited the mineral oil. He knew fire-breathers and special effects experts preferred mineral oil since it possessed both a high flash point and a low burning temperature. It didn't take much for it to ignite, nor did it last long once aflame.

Like magician's flash paper, it produced a spectacular effect.

Bright flames erupted across the burial hall as the burning oil atop the mercury in the lakes, rivers, and ocean consumed itself. A rush of air echoed off the walls, like a wave rushing to shore, generating quick heat and bright light.

Malone wasted no time, springing to his feet and joining Cassiopeia as they rushed the hundred feet back toward the break in the chamber wall. They avoided more rivers and lakes, but thankfully the western portion of Qin's empire was more desert and mountain.

The oil quickly exhausted itself, and the light faded. What remained was a dark cloud seeping up from the floor, and he knew what that deadly waft contained.

Mercury.

"Take a breath and hold it," he said.

TANG SAW THE TRIPOD CRASH TO THE FLOOR AND THEN FELT heat as the mineral oil ignited in a burst of blinding light. He shielded his eyes with a raised arm. The brother and Viktor did the same.

The unexpected flash left black spots winking in and out, but as his vision settled he saw through the rising clouds of gray-black fog two figures at the far side of the chamber running toward the break in the wall.

"We can't stay here," Viktor said.

Tang knew the smoke was toxic and its first wisps were only a few meters away, so he retreated from the archway.

Another *crack* resounded through the chamber and lights began to explode. He heard an electrical surge and something popped behind him in a shower of sparks.

The junction box into which the cable from outside fed power.

"They're shorting out," Viktor yelled.

Then the world went black.

CASSIOPEIA KEPT RUNNING, SENSING THAT THE ELECTRICAL current surging through the mercury had finally backtracked through the lines.

The last thing she saw before all the lights extinguished was the wall, about ten meters away.

She stopped short and heard Malone do the same.

"We have to go," he whispered.

She exhaled. "Find the wall. The exit was about twenty meters to the right."

"We might have a minute or so of good air this far over, but we need to hurry."

Darkness was absolute. She could not even see her hands. Carefully, she groped the air and found the wall with the tip of her gun. The flashlight was still in her pocket, but all that would provide was a perfect target for a spray of bullets through the fog.

"Go," Malone whispered. "Fast."

Beams of light erupted from the far side of the hall, the rays threading a path through the cloud, now maybe six feet above the floor and rising.

The beams found the wall and started searching left and right.

For them.

"THEY HAVE TO BE THERE," TANG SAID.

All three of them used their lights to scan the far side of the chamber for the two figures. The beams were weak, but strong enough.

"Find that opening," he ordered. "That's where they were headed."

The beams continued their dance. One of them located the break in the wall—and then, to its right, a figure.

Heading straight for it.

"There," he said. "Shoot."

"HIT THE GROUND," MALONE YELLED, KNOWING WHAT WAS coming.

The beam had located Cassiopeia just as she'd made it to safety. He decided not to give anyone a free shot.

He took aim across the room and fired at the center of the three lights.

TANG HEARD THE BULLET SLAM INTO THE BROTHER. THE MAN was thrown back by the impact, his light zigzagging in the darkness, his body thudding to the bricks.

Tang immediately retreated behind the archway, as did Viktor on the other side. The mercury cloud was advancing toward them, now only meters away.

They had to leave.

But first.

CASSIOPEIA SAW ONE LIGHT FALL AND TWO OTHERS DISAPPEAR, most likely seeking cover. She sprang to her feet, found the break in the wall with her hand, and slipped inside, a thick slab of stone between her and any more bullets.

Malone, though, was still out there.

"Are you in?" she heard him ask.

"I'm here. Your turn."

The lights were starting their search again, focused on the opening. But they were noticeably weaker from the fog, which she saw was thickening and advancing toward their end of the hall.

Another thirty seconds and it would be here.

The lights moved away and lowered.

Both locked on Malone.

"THERE HE IS," TANG SAID TO VIKTOR. "SHOOT HIM NOW."

Their guns banged.

MALONE SPOTTED THE DARK CLOUD, LESS THAN TEN FEET AWAY. He flattened himself to the floor just as guns fired from the other side of the hall.

He held his breath and the lights stayed just above him.

Standing, even crouching, would be fatal.

But he needed to go.

Now.

CASSIOPEIA AIMED AROUND THE STONE DOOR AND EMPTIED her magazine across the room, firing at the lights.

"Get your ass in here," she yelled to Malone.

MALONE REALIZED THAT IT WASN'T QUITE THAT EASY. THE beams had retreated from sight with Cassiopeia's barrage, which he assumed was the whole idea, but it also plunged the scene before him back into absolute darkness. He knew the opening was about eight feet to his right. Still, he had to feel his way across the wall, heading for the sound of her shots.

Repeated clicks indicated that her magazine was drained.

He found the opening, hopped inside, and exhaled.

"We need to get the hell out of here," he said.

TANG REALIZED THAT COTTON MALONE AND CASSIOPEIA VITT were gone, escaped into the far exit. The fog was nearly upon them, so there was no way to pursue them through the chamber.

He dropped back, as did Viktor.

"It doesn't matter," he said. "I have two brothers waiting for them when they emerge from the ground."

SIXTY

NI CLIMBED FROM THE WELL AND CHECKED HIS WATCH. NEARLY
six PM. He sucked a few lungfuls of warm, moist air. The rain had stopped.

He replaced the iron plate in the well.

Tang would surely be exiting soon, so he needed to leave. His adversary had come prepared, but so had he.

He found his cell phone and hit a speed-dial key. The number dialed and the connection was made. "I want you here, on site, in the next
fifteen minutes."

He'd brought twelve of his investigators with him, transporting them
in a separate helicopter that would have arrived about half an hour after
his. They'd been instructed to wait a few kilometers away until contacted.

"We're on the way."

"Meet me at the security center, at the administrative buildings,
east of the museum."

He ended the call and headed off.

MALONE LED THE WAY AS HE AND CASSIOPEIA SCAMPERED
through the tunnel, back toward where they'd entered. He knew that

there were four right angles to traverse, two remaining as they'd already once turned left, then right. He avoided all the doorways leading out, careful to retrace the path they'd used to enter. He'd be damn glad when sky once again loomed overhead.

He still held his gun, which contained a few rounds. Cassiopeia's was exhausted. They both toted flashlights.

"I appreciate what you did back there," he said.

"Least I could do."

"You realize Viktor was on the other side of one of those flashlights."

"We also know that neither one of us was shot."

He stopped. "You can't be serious. You actually think he helped?"

"Cotton, I don't know what to think. This whole thing seems one double cross after another. All I know is that a four-year-old boy is gone and I can't get anywhere close to finding him."

He saw the exasperation in her eyes, and awaited another verbal assault. Instead she drew close and kissed him.

Tender. Sweet. Not a question, more a statement.

"Viktor's not you," she said.

"You think I'm jealous?"

"I think you're human."

He was uncomfortable as hell. Feeling emotions was one thing, revealing them was quite another. "We need to get out of here."

She nodded. "Okay. Let's go."

They negotiated the final two turns. He spotted a splash of light in the tunnel ahead. The gash in the library floor. They stopped beneath the hole and glanced up three feet.

"I'll go first," she said.

Before he could object, she leaped up, secured a grip, and leveraged herself through the hole.

Halfway, she was yanked upward.

A man dropped through the opening and landed on his feet.

He wore the uniform of museum security and carried a gun, pointed straight at Malone.

"I believe they want you to come up," Cassiopeia said from above, "quick and quiet."

TANG STEPPED OUT OF THE CAR THAT HE AND VIKTOR HAD driven from the well site back to the security office. They had quickly found their way out of Qin Shi's subterranean world and fled the fenced enclosure. The two dead brothers had been left underground. There was little that could be done with their bodies, especially considering the site was now contaminated with mercury vapors.

Ni Yong was his immediate concern.

He'd had the perfect opportunity inside the tomb—privacy beyond measure—to end the problem.

But he'd blown the chance.

Or more accurately, Viktor had blown the chance.

He kept his displeasure to himself. An easy matter to deal with this foreigner when the time was right.

"Wait out here," he told Viktor.

He stormed back inside the air-conditioned security building. His clothes were filthy, his hair disheveled, his throat filled with the taste of musty air.

The men inside snapped to attention.

"In Pit 3, an hour ago, did an old man exit the enclosure?"

The supervisor barked out instructions and another man tapped a computer keyboard, apparently locating videotapes for the relevant time and place. He watched as one of the monitors came to life with Pit 3—the warriors standing silent guard, the chariot, the horses, the gash in the earthen wall. The view was an angled shot from what appeared to be an interior roof camera. He watched as an older man stepped from the black yaw leading into the library chamber, followed by the two brothers he'd left on guard. One held a gun and was directing Pau to a nearby ladder, where all three climbed to the catwalk. Another monitor switched feeds to show the exterior of the Pit 3 museum and the three men leaving the building.

He'd not seen Pau Wen in over twenty years, since just before Pau fled the country, but little had changed. Still the same long face, round eyes, and high forehead. The hair remained sparse, only now it was grayer. One of the brothers kept a gun pointed at his prisoner, and Tang watched as they slowly walked across the empty plaza.

"Where are they going?" he asked.

The supervisor nodded to the controller and the feed was switched to another camera.

"We followed them for a few minutes," the supervisor said. "Then captured this."

Tang saw that Pau and the brothers were now in the car park. People were still there, crowding onto tour buses and leaving in vehicles. He watched as Pau and the brothers approached a light-colored sedan. No one now held a weapon. Each of the brothers offered Pau a warm embrace, then all three left in the car.

He kept his face expressionless.

No one said a word.

"Two more individuals, a man and woman, should have emerged from the same underground room in Pit 3," he said.

The supervisor quickly nodded and snapped his fingers. Keyboard taps brought the correct images onto a monitor.

"When the two men you stationed left," the supervisor said, "I sent two of our men to keep watch."

At least someone had performed his job. "That was the correct thing to do."

The man bowed at the compliment and motioned for the video to be played. Tang watched as one of the museum security men emerged from the library chamber, followed by a man and woman, then another security guard with a gun drawn. Of course, if the two brothers had maintained their post Cotton Malone and Cassiopeia Vitt would be dead, and the problem they posed would be solved.

"Where are they now?" he asked.

"In custody."

"Take me to them."

He turned to leave.

The door swung open and Ni Yong barged inside, followed by ten armed men.

"In the name of the Central Commission for Discipline Inspection of the Communist Party of China, I am taking control of this facility."

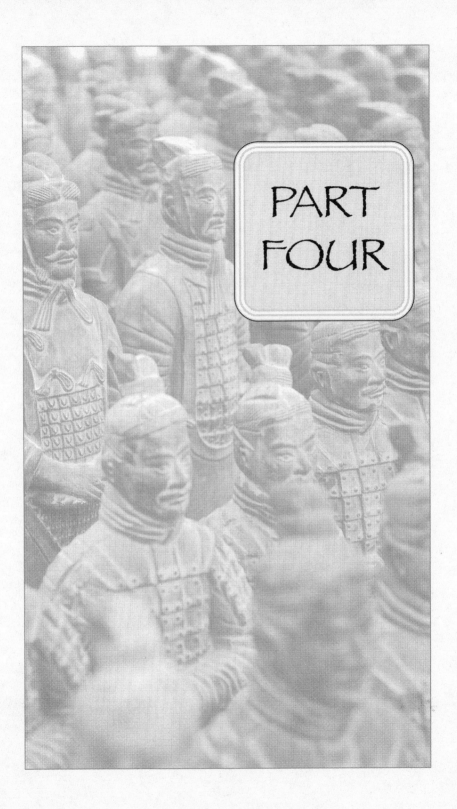

PART
FOUR

SIXTY-ONE

CASSIOPEIA SAT WITH HER LEGS PROPPED ON THE TABLE AND watched Cotton. He, too, was reclined in one of the metal chairs, his legs crossed, eyes closed. The room they'd been led to at gunpoint was windowless, bringing back memories of her cell in Belgium.

"Another fine mess we're in," he muttered.

"At least nobody will know you set one of the greatest archaeological finds of all time on fire."

He opened his eyes. "Nobody likes a smart-ass."

She smiled. "You think this room is wired?"

"I hope so. Hey, whoever is listening, I'm hungry. Bring us some food."

His eyes closed again. Interesting how he was the only man who actually made her feel uncomfortable—which, in a strange way, made her comfortable. There was nothing to prove with him, nor did he compete with her. He was just himself. And she liked that.

"Nice move with the lights," she said.

He shrugged. "I kept thinking about Tivoli. There's a fire-breather there that I've seen a few times. I was talking to him one day and he told me how he uses mineral oil for all his effects. Of course, he doesn't set fire to it atop mercury."

"That tomb is going to be toxic for a while."

"What does it matter? Nobody's going to know. Either Pau looted the tomb, or it was already looted when he went inside. Either way, the Chinese don't want anyone going in there. And lucky us, we've managed to get ourselves wedged between two political giants in a private civil war."

She knew him better than he'd like to admit and she could see that his mind was working. "What is it?"

He opened his eyes again and she caught the twinkle. "Who says there's anything?"

"I do."

"Why'd you kiss me?"

He was stalling, and she knew it. "I wanted to."

"That's not an answer."

"Sure it is."

Why she'd kissed him was a mystery to her as well, except that she'd simply wanted to. Hell, somebody had to make the first move. But now was not the time to jog across that emotional minefield. "Answer me. What does that photographic memory of yours see?"

"I wish eidetic meant photographic. That would be a lot easier. Instead, my crazy brain loves to remember every useless detail." He closed his eyes. "And that's the problem. I need some time to sort through them."

Ni stood toe-to-toe with Karl Tang. They were roughly the same height and he knew their ages were close, Tang a year or two older. He realized that this was a public place, brimming with eyes and ears, and how he and Tang performed would be the subject of much banter.

"You do not command me," Tang made clear.

"I'm here on direct order of the premier. You may call his office and verify, but I assure you that he has authorized this action. And he, Minister, *does* command you."

Tang's clothes were as filthy as his own, both of them wet, dirty, and angry.

"Am I the subject of an investigation?" Tang asked.

Ni wasn't going to fall into that trap. "I don't reveal that information, even to the first vice premier."

Tang seemed alone. Everyone else in the room wore museum uniforms. Ni had checked outside for the foreigner who'd saved his life in the tomb, but had failed to spot him anywhere. He'd wanted to question that man.

"You and I should speak," Tang said. "Privately."

He quickly considered the pros and cons and decided the advantages outweighed any pitfalls. His gaze locked on the superintendent, who motioned to a door on the far side, to the right of the video screens.

He and Tang retreated inside the windowless space and closed the door.

"You should be dead," Tang said to him, eyes on fire with hate.

"That's twice you've failed to kill me. You will not win this fight."

"I already have."

He did not like the confident tone. "I could have you arrested."

"For what? You have proof of nothing. And if you're counting on Pau Wen, good luck. He's as untrustworthy as they come."

"And if we removed your trousers, what would we find?"

"That I possess courage," Tang said.

"You're proud of what you are?"

"I'm proud of what I will do."

He knew his situation was perilous. No proof existed that Tang had done anything wrong, and revealing him to be a eunuch would accomplish nothing. To level a charge and not be able to prove it would only destroy his own credibility. His department flourished simply because it made good decisions. He knew that many in the government were waiting for a catastrophic failure, and an opportunity to end the autonomy that made his probes so successful.

"There's a pilot dead in Yunnan province," he said to Tang. "Shot down by a foreigner flying one of our helicopters. You authorized his flight."

"I did authorize the helicopter. To stop Pau Wen from illegally entering the country. But I never authorized the killing of a pilot. Do you have evidence to the contrary?"

"When I find that foreigner I will."

Who could well have been the same man in the tomb. The man who'd saved him. Tang obviously had no idea that his supposed ally was anything but.

Or did he?

He decided not to say anything about what had happened. If the man who'd helped him was indeed playing both sides, Ni might require his assistance again. If the whole thing had been a ruse, then silence was even better.

"This is you against me," Tang said. "The winner claims China."

"I know the stakes."

Tang's eyes burned with hate. "Know that you will not live to see me win."

His enemy opened the door and left, walking in silence past the others, out of the building.

Ni stepped back into the room and said, "I want to see everything Minister Tang saw and I want to know everything he was told."

MALONE VISUALIZED THE TOP OF THE JADE PLINTH CLEARLY IN his mind. A three-dimensional map of Qin Shi's empire, framed by a border of symbols. Both he and Cassiopeia had been reminded of the silk hanging inside Pau Wen's residence.

It's a reproduction of something I once saw. An ancient map of China.
With some things added.

He wished he still had his iPhone, but it had been confiscated, along with their weapons, when the guards searched them. Without it, he wasn't absolutely sure—but sure enough.

The door opened.

A man entered, perhaps mid- to late fifties, taut cheeks pitted with scars, dark hair piled thick shading ears splayed outward.

A grave determination filled his eyes.

"I am Minister Ni Yong."

SIXTY-TWO

TANG LEFT THE SECURITY BUILDING AND HEADED STRAIGHT for the car he and Viktor had commandeered. He'd told Viktor to wait outside, and apparently he'd been smart enough to conceal himself when Ni and his men arrived. Two of Ni's minions stood guard at the entrance to the building. He decided he should not be obvious in searching for Viktor, so he slid behind the wheel, started the engine, and drove away.

Movement in the backseat startled him.

Viktor's face appeared in the rearview mirror. "I was wondering when you'd come out."

"Minister Ni is looking for you."

"I'm sure he is."

He'd determined that Viktor's usefulness was at an end. If Ni managed to capture him, it would not take long for him to talk. Chinese interrogation procedures were quite effective. Unlike the West, there was no hesitation to employ torture.

But there was the problem of Pau Wen. Where had the old man gone?

His phone rang. He'd reactivated the unit as he'd left the security building. He wheeled the car to the side of the road and answered, placing the call on speaker.

"I have returned," Pau Wen said.

But he wanted to know, "You said that tomb contained lamps with oil. There was nothing there."

"It once contained many lamps, all filled with oil," Pau said. "But when I entered two decades ago, I removed all of the artifacts, including the lamps."

"Where are you?"

Pau laughed. "Why would I answer such a question?"

"You're inside China. I will find you."

"I'm sure you saw on the cameras that the two brothers stationed to guard the library chamber left with me. That should be proof enough that you do not enjoy the total support of the brotherhood."

"I have men enough to finish you."

"But whom can you really trust? Who else is likewise deceiving you?"

"I must have that oil sample. You know that."

"To get one of those lamps, you will have to deal with me."

"You assured me that I would have a sample. It is imperative to our plan."

"But it is not *our* plan any longer. You assumed control. It is now *your* plan. That was made clear the last time we spoke."

He knew what to say. "How can we resolve this impasse?"

"*Bao he dian,*" Pau said.

He realized Viktor understood Mandarin perfectly and knew the translation.

The Hall for the Preservation of Harmony.

"There," Pau said. "We will talk."

"And you can kill me?"

"If I wanted you dead, you already would be."

To prove the theory of abiotic oil, and free China from the bonds of imports, Sokolov had to be provided a verified sample of oil that had been extracted from the Gansu fields 2,200 years ago. Pau Wen was the only known source for that sample. Still—

"How will I know that the sample you provide is authentic?"

"I relocated everything from Qin Shi's tomb. That required great effort. It would be inconceivable for me to alter anything I went to so much trouble to save."

"Why did I never know this?"

"Because it was not necessary to tell you."

"I'm on the way," he declared.

"Then we shall speak again. There."

The connection ended, and he closed the phone.

"I assume we're both going?" Viktor asked.

The call had been troublesome on many layers, one of which told him that he still needed this foreigner.

At least for a while.

"That is correct."

NI STUDIED THE TWO STRANGERS. THEIR PASSPORTS IDENTI-fied them as Cotton Malone and Cassiopeia Vitt, which his staff had verified to be true. Spies didn't normally carry correct identification. They'd also been armed with two PLA sidearms, most likely secured from the helicopter that had flown them north from Lake Dian. A quick Internet vet had revealed Cassiopeia Vitt to be a wealthy woman, living in southern France, her father a self-made billionaire who left everything to his only child. Her name appeared in numerous news accounts from around the globe, most dealing with archaeological finds or some sort of threatened historical object that she'd either liberated or renovated.

Cotton Malone was a different story. A lawyer, navy commander, and former American agent working with the U.S. Justice Department. He'd retired two years ago and now owned a bookshop in Copenhagen, Denmark.

A cover?

Perhaps, but it seemed a bit obvious.

"I want to know about the pilot who flew you from Yunnan province," he said in English.

"That's easy," Malone said. "His name is Viktor Tomas and he's a pain in the ass. If you could arrest him that would be great."

"I'd love to do just that. He killed one of our pilots."

"Who was trying to kill us," Cassiopeia said.

Ni glared at her. "He was an officer in the PLA, following orders. *He* had no idea who you were."

"Viktor's around here somewhere," Malone said. "He works for Karl Tang."

He sensed animosity. "You don't care for this man."

"He's not on my Christmas card list."

"Why are you two here?" he asked.

"Sightseeing," Malone said. "It's a new tour being offered by the PLA. You get a ride in one of your choppers, attacked by a fighter, they throw in a sneak peek inside an ancient tomb."

Ni smiled at the humor. These two were no threat. At least not to him. "You were in the tomb, firing at Tang and his men?"

Malone eyed him. "Judging from your wet clothes and the grime that we all have all over us, you were there, too. 'Hey, assholes.' Remember that?"

"You gave me time to escape."

"That was the whole idea," Vitt made clear. "Though we didn't know who we were helping."

He decided to risk it. "This Viktor Tomas helped me escape."

Malone seemed surprised. "Lucky you. Seems you're on his Christmas card list."

"Is that a bad thing?"

"All depends on what side of the fence he's on today."

"Where is Pau Wen?" he asked.

"He's gone," Vitt said. "He disappeared in a tunnel on the way into the tomb. We have no idea where."

"You, of course," Malone said, "already knew that. He's left here, hasn't he?"

Ni noted that Malone possessed good instincts. But from a former agent, he would expect no less. "He drove away two hours ago."

"Seems you have a multitude of problems," Malone said.

"As do you."

The door opened.

"Minister, we need a word," one of his men said in Mandarin.

He wondered if Malone or Vitt understood.

Neither of them indicated one way or the other.

"I will return in a moment."

MALONE KNEW IT WAS COMING.

"There was no need to sell out Viktor," Cassiopeia said as the door closed.

"He was already sold out."

"You heard Ni. Viktor saved him."

"Which means the Russians want Ni to beat Tang for control of this corruptible place. No surprise there." He still did not mention Viktor's two other objectives—killing Tang and retrieving, or silencing if necessary, Sokolov.

"You finished sorting through that brain of yours?" she asked.

He ignored her and stood.

"What are you going to do?"

"Play a hunch."

He opened the door.

Two men reacted to his presence with hands that reached for holstered weapons. Ni Yong was speaking with the man who'd interrupted. He barked a command that Malone did not understand, but the men stood down.

"What is it?" Ni asked in English.

"I think I can help you."

SIXTY-THREE

TANG SETTLED INTO THE HELICOPTER AS IT LIFTED INTO THE evening sky. Viktor sat across from him.

The Hall for the Preservation of Harmony.

He'd not visited there in a long while.

"Brothers, this will be the last time we speak face-to-face," Pau Wen said.

Tang stood with a select group of fifty. Through open window frames he caught the scent of mountain air. A silk robe that he and the others wore provided little warmth from the afternoon chill, but he was not cold.

"We have planned well," Pau said to them.

The long hall was fronted by an elaborate lattice screen that shielded hundreds of pigeonholed shelves containing the ancient words. Each manuscript was nearly a meter long, comprising loose sheets of centuries-old silk and linen, wrapped in cloth and compressed between two carved boards. He'd personally repaired several of them as part of his training. Silver lamps dotted the walls, but there was no need for their light as a bright sun flooded through the upper two galleries. Outside, the moan of a conch shell, blown by another brother, indicated that three PM had arrived.

"Of all our number, you are the ones I believe have the best chance of ascending to positions of power and influence. One of you may even become premier, which will make our goal that much easier to achieve. I have ensured that all of you have an adequate start. Each of you is ready. So go forth. Tou liang huan zhu."

Replace the beams and pillars with rotten timber.

Tang understood the proverb perfectly.

Sabotage, destroy, or otherwise remove the key structures sustaining an opponent and substitute for them your own. Incapacitate your adversary, assume control from the inside.

"When the wheels are held up," Pau Wen said, "the chariot can't move. When the beams and pillars are withdrawn, the house will fall asunder."

Tang was proud to be part of what was about to begin.

"I will be leaving soon," Pau made clear. "That is necessary in order for our goal to succeed. But I shall monitor and command your progress from afar. Brother Tang will be my voice to you."

Had he heard right? Why not one of the older ones? He was not even thirty and he was new to the Ba. Yet he would be in charge?

"His youth is his asset," Pau said. "Our plan will take much time. Though there are many of you more experienced, time is not your ally."

He glanced around the hall and saw that none of the others betrayed the slightest reaction. The Ba was not a democracy. In fact, that concept was devoid from Legalist thought. The Hegemon made all decisions, without discussion or debate.

"And why is it you must leave?" one of the older men suddenly asked.

Pau Wen's face remained expressionless. "I could pose a distraction."

"Meaning that your enemies could interfere."

"You have long harbored reservations about our course," Pau said.

"That is false. My reservations are directed toward you."

Tang knew this man to be of nearly equal stature to Pau Wen. Favored in the capital, known to the Party. Respected. But Tang also realized what Pau was doing.

Lure the tiger from the mountains.

Rather than plunging into dangerous and unfamiliar territory to confront an adversary, it was far better to make him come out and fight you.

"You are setting us loose for an arduous battle," the adversary said. "One that you are not willing to fight with us. Some of us may succeed, many of us will not. You, though, cannot lose."

"What would you have me do?"

"At a minimum, stay here."

A smart stratagem, Tang thought. When an opponent possessed the edge, rather than resisting directly, deplete his resources, sap his strength. Cause a mistake. On a lesser man the ploy may have worked—

"But then you would not be able to undermine me," Pau said.

Gazes locked.

"I am aware of what you have been doing," Pau declared. "I know that once I leave, you will usurp all that I have planned. That is why you were not chosen as my emissary. That is why we are here, for all to know of your treachery."

The man stood his ground, his back as rigid as his attitude. "You will be our ruin."

Pau's arms were folded across his chest, each hand concealed within the robe's sleeves. Tang watched as only the older man's eyes glanced left, and the brother standing close to Pau's challenger advanced two steps, grabbed the man's head with both hands, and spun it right.

A crack broke the silence and the body sank to the marble.

None of the others reacted.

Pau Wen stood rigid.

"After writing The Art of War, *Sun Tzu was given an audience with the king of Wu. He wanted command of the king's army, but the king did not believe that anyone could be trained as a soldier, so the king presented Sun Tzu a challenge. Train the court concubines to fight and you may command my army. Sun Tzu accepted the challenge, appointing two of the women as officers and explaining the commands for marching. But when the drum signals were given, all the women burst out laughing. Sun Tzu knew that if orders are not clear, the general is at fault. So he repeated his explanation, but the officers and the women only laughed again. Sun Tzu also knew that when orders are clear but not followed, the officers are at fault. So he ordered the officers, the king's two favorite concubines, beheaded. After that, the remaining women followed orders perfectly and became well trained. The king, though disgusted and angry, gave Sun Tzu command of the army."*

All of them stood silent.

"Are my orders clear?" Pau asked the group.

They all nodded.

Tang recalled what had happened after the gathering. He and two others had taken the body outside, beyond the rocks, to the sacred place. There the limbs were cut away, the corpse hacked to pieces, rocks used to pound the flesh and bones into a pulp, which they mixed with barley flour and milk.

Then the vultures had been summoned.

He'd witnessed the *jhator* many times. The literal translation was "giving alms to the birds," the only practical way to dispose of human remains in a land too rocky to dig graves and too short of timber to cremate.

"It is a bad omen," Pau once said, "if the birds have to be coaxed to eat or even if a small portion of the offering remains after they fly away."

But on that day the birds had departed only after nothing remained to be eaten.

He wished he could deal with Ni Yong as easily as Pau Wen had dismissed his challenger. Ni's boldness was disturbing. Had the premier actually authorized Ni Yong to detain him? He decided to find out and ordered the helicopter pilot to connect him with Beijing. His chief assistant came on the line and he learned that the premier had left the capital a few hours ago.

"Where is he headed?"

"Xinjiang region. There is a ceremony in Kashgar commemorating the opening of a new water treatment facility."

Not something that would usually command the Party's premier and the country's president, so he voiced his concerns.

"I thought the same thing," his assistant said. "I inquired and was told that the governor is worried about more unrest in the region."

The far western reaches of China had always been a problem. Eight nations shared its border, the culture far more Muslim and Central Asian than Eastern. To dilute its nearly 90% population of non-Han Chinese, Mao had encouraged immigrations. Subsequent governments, the present one included, continued the policy. Of late, the violent protests against a perceived cultural invasion action had escalated.

"Is that all you could learn?"

"They began to question why I was so interested. I told them that you required a meeting."

An adequate ruse.

"Minister, I have just been informed of something else."

He did not like the change in tone.

"The laboratory in Lanzhou has been attacked. The men there are dead. Lev Sokolov was taken."

SIXTY-FOUR

NI STARED AT COTTON MALONE, WHO STOOD IN THE DOORWAY confident and sure. Daring, also, to fly into China unannounced. He'd requested more information on both Malone and Vitt, but nothing had yet been provided. Instead he'd just listened to a report about a mobile phone conversation intercepted a few minutes ago—Karl Tang speaking to Pau Wen.

"You assured me that I would have a sample. It is imperative to our plan."

"But it is not our plan any longer. You assumed control. It is now your plan."

"How was this obtained?" he'd asked.

"We are monitoring every phone number Minister Tang currently utilizes."

"Where is Tang?"

"He departed from here in a state helicopter. He has a plane waiting in Xi'an, and a flight pattern west to Kashgar has been filed."

He recalled the location Pau had mentioned in the call.

Bao he dian.

"What type of help can you provide?" Ni asked Malone.

"I know where Pau Wen has gone."

Actually, so did he. "And where would that be?"

"The Hall for the Preservation of Harmony."

MALONE STEPPED BACK INTO THE ROOM, FOLLOWED BY NI Yong. Clearly, he'd uttered the correct response to the question. Ni had immediately dismissed his aide and gestured for them to return inside. Cassiopeia was still comfortable in the chair, feet propped on the table, but he knew she'd heard him.

"What do you know of this hall?" Ni asked.

He sat. "First things first. We're not your problem."

"I don't know who you are."

"We're here," Cassiopeia said, "because of a four-year-old boy."

And she told Ni Yong the story of Lev Sokolov's son.

The man listened, seemingly with a genuine concern, then said, "It is a problem throughout China. Every day, hundreds of children disappear."

"And what do you do about it?" Malone asked.

Ni eyed him with irritation. "I do nothing. But I agree. Somebody should be doing something."

"We're not spies," Cassiopeia said.

"Maybe not. But you brought Pau Wen, and he is a threat to this country."

"That I believe," Malone said.

"How can you help me?" Ni asked.

"I need my iPhone."

Ni seemed to consider the request, then opened the door and said something in Chinese. A few moments later the phone was lying on the table.

Malone lifted the unit, tapped the screen, and found his photos. "I took this shot in Belgium, while we visited Pau Wen's residence. It's a silk map he had reproduced that he was mighty proud to show us."

A swipe with his finger and Malone slid another picture into view.

"This was taken inside the tomb, atop the plinth where Qin Shi would have lain."

Ni studied the new image. Malone waited for a comment, but the man said nothing. Instead Ni brought the screen closer, switching back and forth between the two pictures. Ni laid the phone down and found his own, hitting one of the SPEED DIAL buttons and waiting for the connection to complete. When it did, he barked out commands in Chinese and waited. He offered a few more words, then ended the call.

Malone tried to assess Ni Yong, recalling what he'd read on the flight from Belgium. From his own experience he knew the Chinese were difficult to read. They practiced, almost as an art form, a strategy of deception, keeping not only their opponents but also their allies on guard. This man, though, was no low-level operative. Instead, he was the head of the most feared institution in all China. He could literally topple anyone at any time. Stephanie had told him that the United States considered Ni a political moderate in a nation of fanatics. Far more preferable to Karl Tang as the new leader. The Russians seemed to have a similar belief since they'd apparently ordered Viktor Tomas to look after Ni. But Stephanie had also noted that the State Department feared Ni Yong was not tough enough to master China.

Another Gorbachev, she'd said.

Ni's phone chimed.

He tapped a button, waited a moment, then studied the screen. "When persons elevate to high office they bring things of value. These personal possessions are theirs alone. So to ensure that there is no misunderstanding as to origin, a photographic record is made by my department."

"So you take with you only what you came with," Malone said.

Ni nodded. "When you showed me that image it triggered a memory. In the presidential residence there's a private study used only by the premier. The current occupant decorated the room with items brought when he assumed office nine years ago. Rosewood furniture, vases, scrolls, inlaid wood screens. I have been inside that room several times."

Ni laid his phone down beside Malone's. Though its screen was smaller than the iPhone's, the image was nonetheless clear.

A silk map.

"This hangs on the wall there."

Malone and Cassiopeia leaned close.

"They're identical," she said.

Malone instantly realized the implications.

"I've admired that map," Ni said. "The premier told me the same thing, as Pau related to you. A reproduction that he had made from an ancient one he admired."

"Tang and Pau are both eunuchs," Malone said. "The *Ba*."

And what was unspoken hung in the air.

What of the premier?

"I asked," Ni said. "He says that he is no eunuch. He refused the operation."

"You believe him?" Vitt asked.

"I don't know what to believe anymore."

"There's something else," Malone said, motioning to the phones. "Notice the border surrounding the map in the premier's study."

"Chinese numbers," Ni said, pointing to the top left. "Three, four, six, eight, two, five, one, seven."

Malone gently balanced his finger over the character that appeared two up from the left-hand vertical side. "Nine. Up here. On the top row. Two over. Four."

He pointed to his phone and the image from Pau's residence. "They are identical. But check this." He flicked the screen with his finger and revealed the top of the plinth. "Different symbols in different places."

He watched as Ni assessed the fact. "These are not numbers. They are characters."

The thought seemed to occur to them all at once.

From an ancient one he once saw.

With changes.

"Pau has been in that tomb," Malone said.

"So has the premier," Ni added.

"Is that how those lights got there?" Malone asked.

Ni nodded.

Malone traced two lines in the air above the screen. One down from the four. Another over from the nine.

"It's a grid," he said, "created for their maps. Just like grids used on maps everywhere. They used four and nine. Lucky and unlucky. Pau showed me that in the library chamber. I'm betting that where those lines intersect is important."

He lifted his phone and enlarged the relevant portion of the map. The lines did indeed intersect at a defined point. What had Pau said? *A lonely locale in the western mountains.* Denoted by three characters.

阿房宫

"I know what those mean," Ni said. "Beside the capital."

"We can't see it on this tiny image on your phone," Malone said. "But if someone looks at the photo you have, I'm betting those same three symbols will be in the same location."

Ni placed another call, and it took only a few moments for the confirmation to be reported.

Dots were connecting in Malone's brain.

Ni's phone chimed again. He lifted the unit, tapped a button, and read.

Malone caught the consternation on the man's face. He and Cassiopeia listened as Ni explained about a telephone call his people had intercepted just a short while ago, between Tang and Pau.

"There's some sort of division occurring between them," Ni said. "Pau Wen enticed Tang, and now he wants me to come as well. A few years ago we opened a website to allow informants to report corruption electronically. Pau is aware of the site. He made mention of it to me. He sent a message through the site. *Inform Minister Ni that I await him in the Hall for the Preservation of Harmony. Much corruption can be located there. Tell Cassiopeia Vitt that what she seeks is there, too.*"

"The bastard knew all along where the boy is," she said.

Malone shook his head. "His information network must be top-notch. Pau knows we survived and that you have us."

"Spies," Ni said.

"We have to go there," Cassiopeia said.

"Karl Tang is headed west, as we speak," Ni quietly noted.

"She's right," Malone said. "We have to go."

Ni shook his head. "I can't allow it."

Cassiopeia didn't want to hear that. "Why not? I'm betting you know all about the *Ba*. You also seem to know quite a bit about Pau Wen. I don't know Karl Tang, but I've had enough experience with him the past few days to know he's dangerous. There's no telling how far this threat stretches. You've got Russia and America worried enough that they're working together to stop them. I know you have a problem with Viktor Tomas, and I'm not excusing what he did with that pilot, but he saved *your* ass. Now it appears the premier himself may be involved. You don't know us at all, Minister. But we're the most trustworthy allies you've got. This thing is about to end—" She pointed to the map still on Malone's phone screen. "—right there." She checked her watch. "It's nearly seven PM. We need to go."

Ni's expression softened. "There's something that has to happen first. I was informed of it outside, earlier."

Malone waited.

"We found Lev Sokolov. He's on his way here."

SIXTY-FIVE

TANG EXITED HIS JET AND STEPPED OUT INTO THE EARLY morning. The flight west across the Taklamakan Desert had been un-eventful, the air tranquil. He noticed that the clocks outside the airport were set two hours early, an unofficial defiance of the decree that all of China run on Beijing time. The present government had been tolerant of such slights. He would not be as generous. The riots and unrest that permeated the western portion of the nation would be quelled. Sepa-ratist leanings would be punished. If need be, he would raze every mosque and publicly execute every dissident to make the point that this land would remain part of China.

Viktor followed him off the plane. They'd spoken little on the flight, both of them sleeping a few hours, readying themselves for what lay ahead.

He needed to speak with his office, but had been unable to make contact.

A military chopper waited a hundred meters away, its blades al-ready whirling. The flight south, into the mountains, was only three hundred kilometers and should not take long.

He gestured and, together, he and Viktor trotted toward the heli-copter.

CASSIOPEIA HAD BEEN THRILLED TO SEE LEV SOKOLOV. THEY'D waited for him at the airfield in Xi'an. Her friend appeared tired and fragile, but otherwise in good spirits. As soon as Sokolov arrived, she, Malone, Sokolov, and Ni Yong boarded a Chinese turboprop, commandeered from Sichuan Airlines. With room for sixty and only four aboard, they'd been able to stretch out and sleep, even eat a little something, as the galley had been stocked before they left. Before crossing the Taklamakan wasteland, they'd stopped once for fuel.

During the flight they'd listened as Sokolov explained about his capture by Tang, the torture, then imprisonment in the lab. Earlier, Ni's men had stormed the facility, surprised the guards and freed him, killing two of Tang's associates. Sokolov's only concern seemed to be his son, and his spirits lifted when Cassiopeia told him that they may well know the boy's whereabouts.

"Why are you so important to Karl Tang?" Ni asked.

"I hate you Chinese," Sokolov spat out.

"He's here to help," she said. "Tang tried to kill him and me."

"I understand your resentment," Ni said. "But I did not have to bring you along, nor did I have to rescue you. I chose to do both, so I'm hoping that says something for my intentions."

Sokolov's face softened, his eyes cooled.

"I discover oil is infinite."

TANG LISTENED THROUGH THE EARPHONES AS HIS SUBORDI-nates reported what had happened in Xi'an after he departed, and what had happened at the laboratory in Lanzhou.

"Sokolov was flown south to Xi'an," his chief aide stated. "Minister Ni is on his way west, with two foreigners and Lev Sokolov."

"Do we know where?"

"No, sir. They filed no flight path."

"Locate the plane. Sichuan Airlines has transponders. I want to know where they land."

His aide acknowledged the order.

Time for some preventive measures.

"Connect me to the Pakistani defense ministry," he told his subordinate. "Now."

Viktor had been listening to the conversation through his own headset. While Tang waited for the call to be made, he said, "Ni has decided to utilize Malone and Vitt. Make them his allies."

Viktor nodded. "Smart play. But Malone is a problem. Ni doesn't understand what he's dealing with."

Tang didn't like any of this. He was being forced to take ever-bolder steps. So far he'd been able to operate within the confines of Party secrecy where no one questioned anything. But this was not Beijing.

He felt vulnerable.

"You want me to go handle Malone and Vitt?" Viktor asked.

"No. This time I'll do it myself."

Ni heard the words that Lev Sokolov had spoken. "Explain yourself."

"Oil is infinite. It comes from deep in earth and can be replenished. Its origins are abiotic. Biotic oil all consumed long ago."

"Is that why Tang wanted the lamp with the oil?" Cassiopeia asked.

The Russian nodded. "I need sample for comparison test that would prove theory. Some oil taken from ground long ago, at defined spot."

Ni's mind reeled. "Tang knows this?"

Sokolov nodded. "That why he took my child. Why"—the man gently touched his shirt above his abdomen—"he torture me."

"You have a way to prove that oil is infinite?" Malone asked.

"I do. It's my lifework. My friend Jin Zhao was killed for it."

Which explained why Karl Tang had been so interested in Zhao's execution. Ni told Malone and Vitt about Zhao's charges, trial, and death sentence, which Tang had personally overseen.

"He was good man," Sokolov said. "Slaughtered by you people."

"Not by me," Ni made clear.

"Your whole country rotten. Nothing about it good."

"If you feel that way, why immigrate?" Malone asked.

"I love my wife."

Ni wondered how many people the Chinese Communist Party had similarly alienated. Millions? No. Hundreds of millions. Not counting the tens of millions who had been butchered for no reason other than to sustain power. The past few days had opened his eyes, and he did not like what he was seeing.

"China's view of the world," Ni said, "has always been clouded by a belief of superiority. Unfortunately, our vulnerabilities are exaggerated by this conceit. Taiwan is an example. A small, insignificant island yet it has dominated our thoughts for decades. Our leaders have proclaimed that it must be reincorporated into China. Wars have been threatened, international tensions heightened—"

"And oil is your weakest point of all," Malone said. "China couldn't survive more than two weeks without foreign oil."

Ni nodded. "That is no secret. When Deng Xiaoping modernized us we became utterly dependent on oil, most of it foreign, which is why China was forced to engage the world. In order to produce the goods for sale, to accommodate a billion and a half people, we must have energy."

"Unless the oil coming out of the ground, inside China, is infinite," Cassiopeia said.

"China oil is abiotic," Sokolov said. "I test every well. It is consistent with theory."

Ni shook his head. "Knowing we are no longer dependent on imported energy would dramatically change our foreign and domestic policies."

Malone nodded. "And not for the good."

"Right now, we bargain for oil. Knowing he did not have to bargain, Tang would move to fulfill territorial dreams that China has harbored for centuries."

"Like Taiwan," Malone said.

Ni nodded. "Which could start a world war. America would not allow that to go unanswered."

"Is my son really where we go?" Sokolov asked.

Cassiopeia nodded. "We think so."

"But we're taking the word of an e-mail from Pau Wen, a pathological liar," Malone said.

Ni felt compelled to say to Sokolov, "We will find your son. Know that I will do all I can to locate him."

"And will you kill Karl Tang?" Sokolov asked.

A question he'd asked himself repeatedly, ever since fleeing Qin Shi's tomb. Tang clearly wanted *him* dead. That was why he'd been lured underground.

"You need to know," Cassiopeia said to Sokolov, "the Russians are involved."

Alarm filled the man's tired eyes.

She explained how they'd entered China with Russian help.

"They thought me dead," Sokolov said.

"Not necessarily," Malone said. "They want me back?"

Sokolov seemed to grasp the implications. So did Cassiopeia Vitt.

"Viktor's here to kill him, isn't he?" she asked Malone.

"Like I said. Having him back is good, but a lid on this is better."

SIXTY-SIX

TANG SAT SILENT DURING THE FLIGHT, THE HELICOPTER BUFFET-
ing across what he knew to be ever-thinning air into the western highlands. They were most likely following the Karakoram Highway, which
connected Kashgar with Pakistan through a mountain pass nearly five
thousand meters above sea level. This had once been the route used by
caravans traveling the Silk Road, patrolled only by bandits who took advantage of the impossible terrain to slaughter and plunder. Now it was a
forgotten corner of the republic, claimed by many, controlled by none.

He'd left the headphones on as a way not only to buffet the rotor's
drone, but also to avoid talking to Viktor Tomas. Luckily, the man had
closed his eyes and dozed off, his headset removed.

For a decade he'd intentionally avoided the Hall for the Preservation of Harmony. Only a few brothers still lived there, mainly to per-
petuate the illusion of a mountain monastery, a home to holy men who
wanted nothing more than to be left alone.

He told himself to be cautious.

Everything was happening for a reason.

"Minister," the pilot said in his headphones.

The word jarred him from his thoughts. "What is it?"

"A call from your office."

He heard a click, then, "Minister, we are fairly confident of Ni
Yong's destination. Yecheng."

Also known as Kargilik. He'd visited once, admiring for the state-run television cameras its 15th-century mosque and adobe-walled backstreets.

"There is a small airport south of town," his chief aide said. "The turboprop that Minister Ni commandeered can land there. It is the only available location on their route."

"Listen to me carefully. This must be done. I will hold you personally responsible if it fails."

Silence confirmed that his chief aide understood the gravity.

"Locate the municipal police commander in Yecheng. Wake him from his sleep. Tell him I want the occupants of that plane detained. One of them, a Russian, Lev Sokolov, along with Minister Ni, are to be isolated from the others and held until I send for him. Forward by computer or fax a photo of Sokolov so his identity will not be a question. Minister Ni, I assume, he will recognize."

"It will be done."

"One other item. I do not want Sokolov or Ni harmed. If they are, tell that policeman that he will pay a heavy price."

"And the other two?"

"I harbor no protective feelings for them. In fact, if they were to disappear that local commander might find himself rewarded."

MALONE SNAPPED HIS SEAT BELT INTO PLACE AS ROUGH AIR jostled the plane's descent.

"We're going to avoid Kashgar," Ni said. "I've been told that both Tang and the premier flew there. This plane can land much closer to our destination. There is a small airport, about an hour's drive away from our destination, in Yecheng."

Ni held a map of the region and explained how Afghanistan, Pakistan, and India, three volatile neighbors, had long claimed the mountains and valleys as their own. The Himalaya, Karakoum, Hindu Kush, and Pamir ranges all merged here, summits noted as high as twenty thousand feet. And though monasteries were common farther east into Tibet, they were relatively rare this far west.

"There is only one locale in the vicinity of what was noted on the silk maps," Ni said to them. "It's ancient, in the mountains, inhabited by reclusive monks. I'm told that it is a quiet place, and there have never been any reports of unusual activity."

"Why would there be?" Malone asked. "The last thing the *Ba* would want is to attract attention."

"Getting there could be a challenge. We will have to consult the locals."

"We'll need weapons," Cassiopeia said.

"I brought your guns and spare ammunition."

"Lot of trust," Malone said.

Ni seemed to catch the underlying message. "I placed a call before we left Xi'an, to a friend at the American embassy. He checked and said you are a man who can be trusted. He said, if you are here, it must be important."

"Ever heard of bullshit?"

Ni smiled. "No, Mr. Malone, I think both you and Ms. Vitt are far more ally than enemy."

For the past hour he'd talked with Ni Yong about China, Ni fielding his questions, delivering straight answers.

"I'm told you could be the next premier," he'd said.

"Is that what America wants?"

"I don't work for America."

Ni grinned. "You're a bookseller. That's what my friend at the embassy said. I, too, love books. Unfortunately, China does not feel the same. Did you know that not one book about what happened in Tiananmen Square is allowed in China. All websites and Web pages that even mention the words are filtered. It is as if that event never happened."

Malone saw the pain in Ni's eyes. "Were you there?"

Ni nodded. "I can still smell the odor, the stench of feces from a million people. Sanitation workers had tried to clear it in the months before, but they never managed to keep pace. When the people finally fled, only their waste remained. A horrible smell." Ni paused. "Made worse by death."

Malone had read about the massacre. Seen the video of the tank columns, trundling down the street, a young man in a white shirt and black pants, shopping bags in each hand, blocking their way. When the tanks swerved around him, he jumped in front. Would they run him over? Would soldiers shoot him? Their duel continued for several tense minutes until he was hustled away.

He'd told Ni what he recalled.

"I was there," Ni said. "I watched that duel. Many had already died. Many more were going to die. The whole time I kept thinking of the street where it was all occurring—Chang'an, Avenue of Eternal Peace. How ironic."

Malone agreed.

"It took two days to truck away the bodies," Ni said, his voice nearly a whisper. "What the West doesn't know is that the government would not allow the wounded to be treated by hospitals. They were turned away. How many died because of that cruelty, we will never know."

"Sounds like all that stuck with you."

"It changed me. Forever."

Malone could believe that. The pain he'd seen in Ni's eyes could not be faked. Perhaps this Chinese leader was different?

"Who has my boy?" Sokolov asked.

"Some extremely bad people," Ni said. "Eunuchs. I thought they no longer existed. And if you had told me this four days ago, I would have said it was impossible. Now I know how wrong I can be."

"Do we know anything more about the Hall for the Preservation of Harmony?" Cassiopeia asked.

"I'm told," Ni said, "that it's not open to the public. But that's not unusual. We have thousands of sites that are restricted. This region is disputed. We control the ground, while Pakistan and India fight over it. So long as the fight stays on the southern side of the mountains, which generally it does, we do not expend much on its defense."

Power began to decrease to the engines and they started to lose altitude. Outside was pitch-black.

"What about the premier?" Malone asked.

Ni sat in his seat, staring ahead, seemingly in thought.

The plane continued to descend.

"He landed in Kashgar several hours ago."

Malone heard the skepticism in his voice. "What is it?"

"I hate being lied to," Ni said. "Pau and the premier lied to me. I fear I'm being used, by both of them."

"Nothing wrong with that," Malone said. "So long as you know it."

"I still don't like it."

Malone had to say, "You realize Tang may know where we're headed. There's no reason for him not to." He pointed at Sokolov. "He'll want him back."

The Russian bristled at the prospect.

"There can't be that many landing strips in this area," Malone added. "Tang has surely checked."

"What do you have in mind?" Ni asked.

"A little deception of our own."

SIXTY-SEVEN

MALONE STARED BELOW AT YECHENG. THE TOWN SAT AT THE southern rim of the Taklamakan Desert, mountains just to its south. Ni had explained that it was home to about twenty thousand, blessed with a convergence of roads and rivers. Centuries ago, this was where caravans to India had started. Today it remained only as a market town, and a small airport had been constructed in the 1970s to accommodate commerce.

"Looks like the strip is a few miles from town," he said.

Not many lights burned, the town virtually blacked out. A lighted highway snaked a path across the flat terrain to a small tower, two oversized hangars, and a runway lit to the night. He wondered what awaited them on the ground, but a preview of what that might be could be seen from headlights speeding their way.

Two vehicles.

At this time of night?

"It appears that we have a welcoming committee," he said.

Cassiopeia was close to another of the cabin windows. "I saw them. Coming quick."

"Minister Tang is predictable," Ni said.

Sokolov remained silent, but the concern on his face could not be concealed.

"Stay calm," Malone said to the Russian. "You all know what to do."

NI'S BODY STIFFENED. THE LANDING HAD BEEN SMOOTH, AND they were now taxiing toward the tower. The tarmac was dimly lit, but the area around the two hangars and tower was brightly illuminated thanks to rooftop floodlights that cast an oily sheen across the black asphalt. The plane rolled to a stop, the engines still running.

Cassiopeia opened the rear door and hopped out.

Ni followed.

They walked about fifty meters, waiting for two vehicles to roar up to where they stood—one a Range Rover, the other a light-colored van, both bearing the insignia of the police. Ni had seen thousands of similar transports all across China, but never had he been the target of one.

He steadied himself.

Now he knew what the subjects of his investigations felt. Never quite sure what was going to happen, on edge, pondering what the other side may or may not know. He quickly concluded that it was definitely better being on the outside of the cage looking in.

The two vehicles screeched to a stop.

From the Range Rover a short, emaciated man with features far more Tibetan than Han Chinese emerged. He was dressed in an official green uniform and sucked deep drags from a cigarette. The driver stayed in the vehicle. No one exited the van.

Malone had explained what he had in mind and Ni had agreed—since, after all, there were few options.

"Minister Ni," the man said. "I am Liang of the provincial police. We have been instructed to detain you and everyone aboard this plane."

He stiffened his back. "Who instructed you?"

"Beijing."

"There are twenty million people in Beijing. Could you narrow that down?"

Liang seemed not to like the rebuke, but quickly recovered his composure and said, "Minister Tang's office. The orders were clear."

Cassiopeia lingered to his right, watching. They carried weapons, his concealed beneath a jacket, hers shielded by an exposed shirttail.

"Do you know who I am?" he asked the policeman in Mandarin.

"I am aware of your position." The last of the cigarette was flicked away.

"And you still want to detain me?"

"Is there a Russian aboard the plane? A man named Sokolov?"

Ni saw that Cassiopeia caught the name, so he said to her in English, "He wants to know if there is a man named Sokolov with us."

She shrugged and shook her head.

He faced Liang. "Not that we are aware of."

"I must search that plane. Instruct the pilot to switch off the engines."

"As you wish."

Ni turned, faced the cockpit, and waved his arms in a crossing fashion, sending a message.

Nothing happened.

He turned back. "Would you like me to have the two other men on the plane come off?"

"That would be excellent. Please."

He faced Cassiopeia and said, "Get them."

MALONE WATCHED WHAT WAS HAPPENING FROM A HUNDRED feet away. He'd correctly surmised that whoever Tang sent to greet them would expect four people so, when only two left the plane, at some point they would want to see two more.

And Cassiopeia was returning to get them.

NI WAITED AS CASSIOPEIA TROTTED TO THE OPEN CABIN DOOR and gestured.

Two men leaped down, and they all headed toward where he stood with the police chief.

Liang reached into his pocket and removed a folded sheet.

He was afraid of this.

Liang unfolded the page and Ni spotted a black-and-white photo, the face unmistakable.

Sokolov.

"Neither of these men is the Russian," Liang said. "The other man should be American. These men are Chinese."

MALONE COULD SEE THAT THINGS WERE NOT GOING WELL. After the wheels had touched ground and they were taxiing to the terminal, he and Sokolov had switched places with the pilots, who'd been unwilling to argue with orders from Ni Yong.

He saw Ni signal with his arms again, apparently wanting him to kill the engines. The police had not been fooled.

"What are you going to do?" Sokolov asked.

"Not what they expect."

CASSIOPEIA HEARD THE PLANE'S MOTORS REV, THE PROPELLERS spinning faster, the fuselage turning left and inching forward, toward them. The policeman spoke to Ni in an excited voice, and she did not require an interpreter to know what was being said.

The policeman pointed and Ni casually turned and watched as the plane kept coming, faster now.

Forty meters.

The two pilots panicked and ran toward the tower. The policeman let them go, clearly knowing they were not the men he sought.

The propellers' wash churned the dry air. It felt good. She'd been wearing the same clothes since yesterday, bathed in Chinese lake water, then dusted with the earth of a 2,200-year-old tomb.

The plane straightened its path.

Thirty meters.

Cotton was making an entrance.

Grand, as usual.

SIXTY-EIGHT

NI WAS SHOCKED BY MALONE'S MOVE. THE AMERICAN HAD told him that if the ruse didn't work he'd cover their backs, but he had not explained how. He knew little about Cotton Malone besides the bits his staff had located, which indicated he'd been a highly respected American agent, capable and intelligent.

The twin rotors of the plane were less that twenty meters away.

"Tell him to stop," Liang yelled over the roar. "Where is he going?"

He casually glanced at the policeman. "Apparently here."

Lights on the wings and tail strobed the night red and green. He wondered how far Malone intended to go, but he was determined to hold his ground and see if the plane or the policeman yielded first.

MALONE TIMED HIS APPROACH, WAITING FOR THE RIGHT MO-ment before turning the wheel, swinging the fuselage around, using the left wing and propeller as a weapon.

The policeman reacted, diving to the pavement, as did Ni and Cassiopeia.

All three disappeared beneath the undercarriage. The two pilots were long gone. The driver of the Range Rover rolled from the car just as the wing swung past, the propeller only a foot or so away.

Panic reigned, which was the whole idea.

Except for one problem.

As the driver emerged and lunged for the tarmac, Malone saw a gun in his hand.

CASSIOPEIA ROLLED, THE SMELL OF COOLING ASPHALT FILLING her nostrils, the propeller's roar deafening. She'd seen Ni and the policeman flatten themselves to the pavement, as well as the driver of the Range Rover, who'd emerged holding a pistol.

She found her weapon, straightened, and fired. Her bullet found the car door, which the driver was using for cover.

Unfortunately, she was exposed.

No place to hide.

NI HEARD THE SHOT AND SAW THAT HE AND CASSIOPEIA WERE vulnerable. No protection from sure retaliation. Except—

He unholstered his gun and jammed the barrel into Liang's neck, keeping him pinned to the pavement, one hand on Liang's spine, the other pressing the gun into the nape of the neck.

The plane was completing a full circle, the propellers now facing away, the tail swinging left as the nose came back around.

"Tell your man to stand down," Ni yelled, applying more pressure with the weapon.

The driver was taking aim, seemingly unsure of what to do. This situation had grown out of control, more so than the crew of this provincial police department routinely faced.

Orders were bawled out.

"Make it clear," Ni said.

Another command.

Cassiopeia lay on the asphalt, her gun aimed at the Range Rover. He caught her gaze for an instant and shook his head. She seemed to understand that he was trying to negotiate a way out.

"Tell him to toss away the weapon," Ni said.

Liang obeyed.

The driver seemed to not want a fight and complied, standing from the door, hands above his head.

MALONE COMPLETED THE ARC AND STRAIGHTENED THE PLANE'S nose, once again facing the two vehicles. He was pleased to see one of the policemen on the ground with Ni's gun to his neck and the other with his hands in the air, Cassiopeia rising to her feet. Apparently, his diversion had worked.

But an unease swept through him.

What about the van?

There had to be at least a driver inside, yet no reaction had been offered to the unfolding drama.

The van's rear doors swung open.

Four men leaped out, each carrying an assault rifle. They assumed positions on the ground, knees bent, guns aimed—two at the plane, one each at Ni and Cassiopeia.

"That's a problem," he muttered.

He'd taken a risk, gambling the locals could be either overwhelmed or outsmarted. Apparently, he'd underestimated them.

The propellers still spun and he could charge again, but that would be foolish.

They would simply obliterate the plane with bullets.

NI KEPT HIS GUN PRESSED AS THE REINFORCEMENTS ASSUMED A firing position.

"Let me up," Liang ordered, seeing that the situation had changed.

But Ni kept the weapon close.

"You cannot win this battle," Liang said.

No, he couldn't.

Unsure of how far Tang's orders stretched, and recalling what had happened in the tomb and the threats after, he withdrew his weapon and stood.

The plane's engines died.

Apparently Malone had realized the same thing.

They'd lost.

SIXTY-NINE

TANG LEFT THE HELICOPTER, HOPPING OUT INTO A DARK, GRASSY meadow adjacent to the town of Batang. He knew what surrounded him. Storied peaks, glittering glaciers, forests, and silty rivers fed by cascades that dropped hundreds of meters in perfect watery veils. He'd visited the hamlet many times as a young man, making the trek down from the highlands to retrieve rice, meat, chilies, cabbage, and potatoes—whatever the brotherhood required.

Dawn was not far away, but daylight came slowly in the highlands. He sucked in the crystalline air and rediscovered the strength he'd once acquired in this solitary land. This was a place without moderation—black nights, brilliant days—the air perilously thin, the sun hot, the shadows stabbing the earth like black ice.

A hundred meters away Batang slept. Maybe three thousand lived there, and not much had changed. Whitewashed buildings adorned with red ocher and flat roofs. A market town, busy with pilgrims, sheep, yaks, and traders. One of many that dotted the sporadic green carpets among the gray peaks, scattered like dice on the landscape. Cultural connections here ran far more to the south and west than east. Truly a world unto itself, which was why the *Ba* had long ago chosen this as its home.

He started to walk across the packed earth, Viktor at his side.

The helicopter lifted off into a salmon-colored sky. Rotors faded and the meadow lapsed into a deep silence.

Yecheng was a mere thirty-minute flight north.

Hopefully, there'd been success there and the chopper would return with Ni Yong and Lev Sokolov. He was dressed in his same filthy clothes. On the flight he'd forced himself to eat a few of the onboard rations. He was prepared. Ready for this day. One he'd been anticipating for two decades.

"What is going to happen?" Viktor asked.

"It doesn't concern you."

Viktor stopped. "Doesn't concern me? I killed a pilot for you. I delivered Malone, Vitt, and Ni Yong for you. I played out your game, exactly as you ordered. And this doesn't concern me?"

He, too, stopped, but did not turn around. Instead, he allowed his gaze to focus on the distant mountains, west, beyond Batang, and what he knew waited there. "Do not try my patience."

He did not need to face Viktor to know that a gun was trained on him. He'd allowed him to keep the weapon.

"You plan to shoot me?" he calmly asked.

"Could solve many problems, not the least of which is your ingratitude."

He kept his back to Viktor. "Is that what the Russians want you to do? Kill me? Would that please them?"

"You pay better."

"As you keep telling me." He decided to use diplomacy, at least until all of the threats were eliminated. "Know that I do need your assistance. I ask simply for patience. All will be clear in the coming hours."

"I should have gone to Yecheng."

Viktor had asked and he'd said no. "You were not needed there."

"Why am I here?"

"Because what I seek is here."

And he started walking.

MALONE SAT WITH CASSIOPEIA ON A FILTHY BRICK FLOOR. THEY were kept separately from Ni and Sokolov, all of them held at the landing field, inside the tiny terminal, locked in some sort of steel-walled storage room lit by a dusty yellow bulb.

"None of that went right," Cassiopeia said.

He shrugged. "Best I could do on short notice."

The fetid air carried the scent of a dumpster. He wondered what had been kept inside here recently.

"I doubt Sokolov is in danger," Malone said. "At least not for now. Tang went to a lot of trouble to get him back. Ni, though, is another matter. I think whatever is going to happen to him will not be good."

Cassiopeia sat with her arms wrapping bended knees. She looked tired. He definitely was, though they'd both slept some on the flight. They'd been sitting here for more than an hour without a sound from outside.

"What do we do now?" she asked.

"Play for a fumble."

She smiled. "You always so optimistic?"

"Beats the hell out of the alternative."

"You and I have some issues."

That he knew. "Later. Okay?"

She nodded. "I agree. Later."

But what went unspoken hung clear. *So long as there is a later.*

A new sound invaded their silence.

Helicopter rotors.

NI SAT IN THE LIT ROOM. ITS ONLY WINDOW WAS GUARDED ON the outside by one of the men with automatic rifles. Another surely stood on the other side of the closed door. He wondered what had happened to Malone and Vitt. Clearly, Tang wanted both him and Sokolov alive. Defeat clouded Sokolov's face, but not the panic he'd expected.

"Why hasn't anyone else ever considered what you discovered?" he asked the Russian in Mandarin. "Malone says the Russians have known of infinite oil for a long time."

"It's not that easy for them. How many samples of two-thousand-year-old oil exist on the planet? Samples verifiable, comparable with modern-day samples extracted from same field?" Sokolov paused, his gaze to the floor. "Only one place on the planet has that. Here, in China. No one else was capable of drilling for oil that long ago. Only the Chinese. The proof is here. Nowhere else." The voice stayed low, as if Sokolov was actually sorry he'd made the discovery.

"Your son will be okay."

"How you know that?"

"You're too valuable. Tang knows the boy is his only real bargaining power with you."

"At least until he learns what I know."

"Did you tell him?'

"Some. But not all."

He remembered the disgust the Russian voiced on the plane and felt compelled to say, "We are not all like Karl Tang."

Sokolov glanced up for the first time. "No. But you are all Chinese. That's bad enough."

TANG WALKED DOWN BATANG'S ONLY STREET, NOTICING THAT it remained a place of drab buildings and shadeless alleys, all swept by dust. Wooden carts dotted the edges, along with a couple of trucks parked at odd angles. Two prayer wheels creaked with each revolution and rang bells. A huge mastiff rocketed from one of the alleys and flipped on his back when he found the end of a rope tied to his collar. The dog stood and pounced again, seemingly determined to either stretch or break the restraint.

Tang faced the barking animal.

A gong hung suspended by beams and leather straps a few meters away. Soon it would announce the start of another day.

A small hotel, half ruined, with doors ajar and walls iced with grit and grim beckoned. That, too, had changed little.

The dog continued to bark.

"Wake the owner," he ordered Viktor.

He knew that venturing into the mountains without sunlight was foolish. The trails were fragile and subject to rockslides. Increasing daylight, and a diminishing haze, were already bringing the distant peaks into focus.

It would not be long.

NI WAS NOT AFRAID ANYMORE. THE INSIDE OF QIN SHI'S TOMB, underground, in a locale no one knew even existed, had offered Tang the perfect venue to kill him. But doing it here, with all of these witnesses, seemed out of the question. Not even the first vice premier could keep that secret. Instead, he realized they would be taken somewhere private, and the sound of rotors approaching signaled that his conclusion seemed correct.

Sokolov reacted to the sound, too.

"We are going to where your son is," he said.

"How do you know that?"

"Tang needs us both alive. Me for just a short while. You, much longer. So he will reunite you and the boy, as a way to placate."

"You are not afraid?"

"I'm more afraid of failing."

Sokolov seemed to understand. "What about Malone and Vitt?"

"I'm afraid their situation is much worse."

SEVENTY

MALONE LISTENED AS THE HELICOPTER ROTORS REVVED, THEN faded. The aircraft had stayed for only a few minutes, long enough, he assumed, to board Ni and Sokolov.

"Our turn," he said to Cassiopeia.

They both still sat on the floor.

"But we aren't going to be flown away," she said.

"We might. We'll just land a little differently."

They were foreigners, here illegally, spies that no one would claim or care about. One of those occupational hazards of his former job.

He didn't have to say it. She knew. They would take their chances at the first opportunity. Since they literally had nothing to lose.

The scrape of metal indicated that the steel door was being unlocked. Cassiopeia started to rise, but he placed a hand on her knee and shook his head. She stayed on the floor.

The door swung open and the police commander from earlier entered, carrying a pistol. He didn't look happy.

"Tough night?" Malone asked.

He wondered if the man understood. But this was not Beijing or eastern China where English was common. This was the middle of frigging nowhere. The man motioned for them to stand and leave. Outside the doorway, two more men waited with automatic rifles.

Malone studied them. Both young, unsure, and jittery. How many times had they been in this situation before? Not many, he guessed.

The commander motioned again.

He noticed that the steel door, which opened to the outside, contained no knob-operated latch, just a handle and a lock that engaged, once closed, in a steel catch, which required a key to release.

"I don't think these people understand English," he muttered to Cassiopeia.

The head man was impatient with their chatter but did not seem to know what they were saying. Malone smiled and said in a calm voice, never breaking his smile, "You smell like a pig."

The commander stared back with no reaction to the insult, offering only another gesture with the gun for them to leave.

He turned and said to her, "He knows no English. Ladies first. Be ready to move."

She stepped through the doorway.

He watched as the chief dropped back to give him room to leave, exactly what he thought the man might do. That way he could counter if they tried anything funny, the distance between them adding protection.

Except for one thing.

As Malone exited, he swung his right foot up and slammed the door shut, trapping the policeman inside. At the same time, his left elbow burrowed into the man nearest him, sending the guard careening back.

Cassiopeia pounced, attacking the man closest to her with a kick to his chest.

Both guards had been caught unawares.

Malone lunged forward and planted a fist into his man's face. The guard tried to retaliate while also keeping a grip on the rifle—bad idea—and Malone gave him no time to think. Three more right jabs and the man went down. He relieved him of the weapon, along with a pistol from a waist holster.

He turned to see Cassiopeia having a little difficulty.

"Hurry up," he said.

Two thrusts of the other man's fists missed as she dodged. The guard had already lost his weapon, which lay on the floor. Cassiopeia lashed out, but the blow just grazed her opponent's throat. She then spun and jumped, her right leg swinging in an arc that landed with full force in his chest. Another leg jab smashed him into the wall, and she finished with two thrusts to the throat, which sent the guard slinking to the floor.

"Took you long enough," he said.

"You could have helped."

"As if you needed it."

She stole the man's pistol from his holster and retrieved the rifle. The chief was no threat, locked away inside a steel room, banging on the door, screaming something in muffled Chinese.

"There were two more earlier," she said, "with rifles. Plus the two drivers."

He'd already done the math. "I suggest we move with caution."

He slipped close to one of the windows and glanced out, spotting the Range Rover parked fifty yards away. The van was nowhere in sight.

Which worried him.

"Let's hope the keys are in that Rover," he said.

They found the door and cautiously inched it open. Night still loomed thick and heavy, the landing field quiet.

"They were either taking us somewhere to kill us or were going to kill us here," he said. "Either way, they'd need that van."

He saw she was thinking the same thing.

"No sense waiting around."

She stepped out, her assault rifle leading the way.

He followed.

A hundred and fifty feet lay between them and the Rover. His gaze raked the darkness. Pools of light from the rooftop floods lit the way. They were halfway to their objective when the roar of an engine disturbed the silence and the van motored its way past one of the hangars, heading their way.

He saw an arm extend from the passenger side holding a pistol.

Cassiopeia did not hesitate, spraying the windshield with a barrage from the automatic rifle. The bullets caused the gun in the window to disappear and the van wheeled right, careening up on two wheels as it executed too sharp a turn, spinning out of control, sliding on its side, slamming into one of the hangars.

They raced to the Range Rover and hopped inside, Malone at the wheel. Keys hung from the ignition.

"Finally, something went right."

He gunned the engine and they fled the fenced enclosure.

"There is one thing," Cassiopeia said.

He'd been waiting.

"How do we get there? We certainly can't stop and ask directions."

"Not a problem."

He reached into his back pocket and produced a folded bundle. "I kept the map Ni used on the plane. Thought we might need it."

SEVENTY-ONE

TANG STOOD AT THE WINDOW AND SHADED HIS EYES FROM A bar of golden sun cresting over the eastern peaks. He nursed a cup of sweet black tea, scented with cardamom. He half expected to hear the romantic wail of a conch shell, its rising tone like a foghorn, echoing off the cliffs. A brother had once, each day at dawn, blown that siren from the monastery walls.

He glanced down at the street.

Batang was coming alive, a trickle of people slowly becoming a stream. Most wore wool gowns with red waistbands and saffron caps, ankle-length with high collars, which offered protection from a wind that leaned into the building and rattled the wooden walls. He knew the weather here was fickle, particularly this time of year. Though high in altitude, the late-spring air would be surprisingly warm, heated by UV rays that the thin atmosphere did little to negate.

Viktor was downstairs eating. Two hours ago he'd received word through his satellite phone that Ni and Sokolov had left Yecheng, in custody. He'd ordered the chopper to deliver his prisoners then come for him at seven thirty. He'd been pleased to hear that Malone and Vitt had been captured and, he assumed, were now dead.

All of the elements were finally dropping into place.

He breathed in the warm air, redolent with the smell of oily butter lamps. Outside the panes, the dull crystal ting of bells could be heard.

The door opened.

He turned and said to Viktor, "It's time for me to leave. The helicopter will return shortly."

On the bed lay equipment that Viktor had brought with him earlier. Some rope, a backpack, flashlight, knife, and fleece-lined jacket.

"The walk up to the hall is a little over an hour," Tang said. "The trail starts west of town and winds upward. The hall lies on the other side of the ridge, just past a suspension bridge. Buddhas carved into the rock, beyond the bridge, mark the way. It is not hard to find."

"What happened in Yecheng?"

"It's not important."

Viktor Tomas was apparently still concerned about Cassiopeia Vitt. Strange. To him, women were nothing but a distraction. Men like Viktor should feel the same way. Odd that he didn't.

Viktor gathered up his gear, slipping on a leather jacket.

"Take that trail," Tang said. "Make sure no one from here follows. Arrive at the hall unnoticed and enter with caution. I'm told there are few there, so you should be able to gain entrance easily. The main gates are left open."

"I'll cover your back," Viktor said. "But, Minister, you have a more immediate problem."

He didn't like the words or the tone. "Why do you say that?"

"Because Malone and Cassiopeia Vitt just drove into town."

CASSIOPEIA ADMIRED BATANG. WHITEWASHED ADOBE WALLS, red moon and sun designs above the doors, firewood and dung bricks piled on the roofs—all typical for the area. A mixture of Mongols, Chinese, Arabs, and Tibetans who, unlike the populations of their respective countries, had learned to live together. They'd just driven nearly two hours through a skeletal landscape, stripped to its rocky bones, across a rough road.

"My gut is still reeling from those rations," Malone said as they stepped from the Rover.

Along the way they'd found some food in the vehicle, rock-hard bars of cookie crumbs and milk powder mixed with what she thought was lard. Tasted like sweet cardboard. Her stomach was also upset from the bars and the jostling. Strange she'd get motion sick—one of those weaknesses she did not like to display or discuss—but firm ground felt good.

"Ni said the monastery is west of town," she said. "We're going to have to ask its location."

Guarded faces watched both her and Malone. Glancing up, she spotted two ravens tumbling over each other in the morning sky. The air had definitely thinned and to compensate she'd found herself breathing faster, but she told herself to stop, as that would solve nothing.

"Asking doesn't seem like a good idea," Malone said as he stood near the hood.

She agreed. "I don't think they get a lot of foreigners like us here."

TANG KEPT AWAY FROM THE GRIMY WINDOW, LOOSE IN ITS frame.

"Seems you were right about Malone," he said to Viktor. "He is a man to be respected."

"So is she."

He faced Viktor. "As you keep reminding me."

Frustratingly, his need of this foreigner seemed to never end. "I'm going to leave. Occupy those two until I am away from town."

"And what am I to do *after* I occupy them?"

"Make sure they head up into the mountains. Soldiers are there we can now use."

"And are those soldiers there for me, too?"

"Hardly. Since you know about them."

But he wondered if Viktor believed him. Hard to know anything about this guarded man. Always, something more seemed to percolate inside him. Like now. He'd come into the room knowing Malone and

Vitt were here, yet he'd held that information until *he* was ready to reveal it.

Thankfully, by nightfall he would be rid of this man.

Along with all the others.

MALONE HEARD THE SOUND AT THE SAME TIME AS CASSIOPEIA. The rhythmic thump of rotors. Low, steady, hypnotic, like a heartbeat.

"That's a chopper," he said.

"Coming closer."

He strained into the ever-brightening sky and saw the craft, swooping in from the north, miles away. The helicopter cleared the peaks, then headed for a meadow of edelweiss beyond the edge of town. A distinctive green color and red star emblazoned on its side made clear its owner.

The People's Liberation Army.

"It's for Tang," a new voice said.

Malone turned.

Viktor stood ten feet away.

TANG FLED THE HOTEL THROUGH A REAR DOOR. ITS PROPRIetor had been most accommodating, the few hundred yuan Viktor provided quelling any questions. He passed a carpentry shop, wood spinner, key maker, and tailor shop, following a rear alley that led straight to a meadow north of the town limits. Colorful edelweiss could be seen at the far end of the alley.

He heard the helicopter draw closer.

Malone and Vitt still being alive was a problem. They had been unknowns from the start, used for an advantage, but now they were drawing too close. And time was running out.

He found his phone and dialed his office, thankful for satellites unaffected by mountainous terrain. His chief aide answered immediately.

"Tell our friends in Islamabad that I want them to do as I asked."

"They are waiting to hear."

"Make sure they understand success is all that counts. Nothing less. Assure them I will not forget the favor."

"Still only one target?"

"No. Three. And I want them all eliminated."

SEVENTY-TWO

MALONE STUDIED VIKTOR. A COIL OF ROPE OVER ONE SHOULDER, backpack on the other, a thick jacket zipped in front. "Where are you headed? As if I have to ask."

"What are you doing here?"

Cassiopeia stepped forward. "Tang has Ni and Sokolov."

"He already knows that," Malone said. "You're a busy guy. First, you kidnapped Cassiopeia, tortured her, let her escape, then allowed us to fly into a Chinese ambush. After that, you disappear and allow us to nearly get killed two more times. Now you're here."

"You're still alive, aren't you? I saved your sorry hide in that tomb."

"No. You saved Ni. That's part of your mission."

"You have no idea about my mission."

Malone saw the chopper rising into the morning sky. "Tang's leaving?"

"I have to go," Viktor said.

"So do we," Cassiopeia said.

"The Russians want to make sure Ni Yong is the next premier of this godforsaken place," Malone said. "And they want Sokolov back."

"Get real, Malone. You think they're the only ones who want that? Why do you think Stephanie Nelle was in Copenhagen? I'm working for her. She knew I had Cassiopeia. She okayed it. She wanted you involved. I'm not the manipulator here, I'm just a pawn on the board. As are you two."

The realization struck him hard. Stephanie had played him. *Believe me, I hedged my bets. I'm not relying on Ivan 100 percent.*

Now he knew what she'd meant.

"I'm just doing my job," Viktor said. "Do yours, or get the hell out of the way."

Malone grabbed Viktor's arm. "You risked Cassiopeia's life for this game."

"No, actually Stephanie did that. But lucky for us you were around to save the day."

He shoved Viktor back.

The coiled rope dropped from his shoulder at the same time Viktor's other arm slipped free of the backpack.

But Viktor did not retaliate.

"You enjoy killing that pilot?" Malone asked. "Blew him out of the sky. Was that part of your mission, too?"

Viktor stayed silent.

"You're a murderer," Malone said. "You killed that pilot for no other reason than to suck us in. To prove to us you were on our side. Then, as soon as we get to the tomb, there you are, trying to kill us again. One of those flashlights searching through that fog was yours."

Anger flared in Viktor's eyes.

"Did you enjoy torturing Cassiopeia? Taunting me with what was happening. You pour the water yourself?"

Viktor catapulted himself into Malone, pounding them both onto the Range Rover's hood. The street around them cleared as they rolled down to hard earth. Malone freed himself of the grip and sprang to his feet, but Viktor was faster, already up, planting a kick to the stomach.

The breath left him.

He recovered and swung, catching Viktor in the chest with a sweeping jab. He struggled with the thin air, breathing in heavy gasps, the exertion taxing his lungs, the world spinning. The lack of oxygen, combined with Viktor's blow, stunned him more than he'd expected.

He caught hold of himself, focused, and advanced.

Viktor stood his ground, but Malone was ready, dodging one blow, then another, ramming his right fist into Viktor's gut. He followed with two more blows. Like slugging stone, but he did not relent. An uppercut to the jaw and Viktor teetered on weak knees, then fell. He waited to see if Viktor would stand, but he remained down.

He sucked deep breaths. Damn this altitude. He turned and started back toward where Cassiopeia stood.

He never saw what hit him, but it was solid and delivered square across his spine. Pain doubled him over, his knees buckling. Another blow to his shoulders drove him forward, and he hit the pavement, then rolled, Viktor on top, grabbing two handfuls of his jacket, yanking him up.

"STOP," CASSIOPEIA YELLED.

She'd watched as Viktor had grabbed a shovel propped beside one of the shop doors and blindsided a retreating Malone. Then he'd followed the blow with another. Now he straddled a clearly woozy Cotton, ready to slam the back of his head into the pavement.

"Let him go," she said, staring hard into Viktor's angry eyes.

His breaths came quick and hard.

"Let him go," she said again, her voice lower.

"I told you next time it would be different," Viktor muttered as he released his hold and climbed off.

The spectators drifted off. Fight over. No police were in sight. She doubted this town employed any. Viktor moved toward his backpack, reshouldered it, then looped his left arm through the rope coil.

Cotton was reaching for his spine, still on the ground.

"Tang has ordered an attack on you," Viktor said. "From the Pakistanis. The border is up there on the route to the monastery. There are soldiers, waiting."

"You realize that he's probably ordered that attack for you, too," she said.

"The thought occurred to me. That's why I'm going up first. I'd prefer that neither one of you follow, but you're not going to listen to me, are you?"

"You're going to need some help."

"Malone was right. I risked your life too many times."

"And you also saved it."

"I'm not doing it again."

"Risking? Or saving?"

"Neither one, and since I know you won't stay here, the trail west of town leads to a suspension bridge. Beyond are some carvings that point the way to the hall. Wait an hour. That should give me time to do something. Maybe I can lead them off." Viktor pointed at Cotton. "He's not going to be ready to go till then anyway."

He started to leave.

She grabbed his arm and felt him shudder. "What are you going to do?"

"Why do you care?"

"Why wouldn't I?"

He gestured with his head toward Cotton.

"Why didn't you just tell me in Belgium that you were working for Stephanie?"

"It's not my way."

"Torturing me is?"

"Don't think I enjoyed that. I had no choice."

She saw the pain in his eyes and wanted to know, "Are you loyal to anything?"

"Myself."

But she wasn't fooled. "There's more to you than you want anyone to know."

He gestured again. "A lot like him."

Then she realized. "You wanted a fight here, didn't you?"

"I had to delay your departure. Tell him I regret the cheap shot, but it seemed the only way to slow you down."

"Are you here to kill Tang?"

"There are a lot of people who would be pleased with that. I had the chance, just a short while ago, to shoot him down."

"Why didn't you?"

"Too soon. I need to know what's up there in those mountains. Ni is up there. I have to get him out."

"What are you going to do with Sokolov?"

He did not answer her.

"You going to kill him?"

More silence.

"Tell me," she said, her voice rising.

"You're just going to have to trust me."

"I do."

"Then we'll be fine."

And he left.

SEVENTY-THREE

N I ADMIRED HIS PRISON. THE BEDCHAMBER WAS SPECTACULAR. Marble columns sprouted upward toward a coffered ceiling, bas-relief dragons twisting from bottom to top. Frescoes on the walls depicted an emperor's journey, one wall showing him leaving his palace, the procession unfolding through the mountains along two more, and ending on the fourth at a cluster of buildings streaked with purple, gray, and shades of ocher, rising from the shoulder of the mountain.

Here. This exact place.

As depicted by the artist, and as Ni had seen flying in on the helicopter, glaciers brooding above a barren valley.

He and Sokolov had been flown straight from Yecheng. They'd been treated well, escorted from a landing pad outside the walls by two younger men adorned in woolen robes, their hair wound on top, secured with red tassels, red woven sashes wrapping their waists.

A butter lamp the size of a washbasin and fashioned of beaten copper burned in one corner, scenting the room. Windows hung open, cool air seeping inside, mellowing the flame's hypnotic influence. Occasionally, the distant bellow of a yak could be heard. He realized there was no danger of him escaping since the windows opened into a courtyard within the outer walls.

Sokolov sat in one of several lacquered chairs, the furniture exquisite in both detail and design. Expensive rugs cushioned the marble floor. Apparently, the *Ba* believed in living comfortably.

The door opened.

He turned to see Pau Wen.

"I was told that you had returned to China," Ni said to the older man.

Pau wore a golden-yellow robe, an interesting choice in color since Ni knew it symbolized the throne. Two more younger men stood behind Pau, each carrying a loaded crossbow, held ready.

"Minister Tang is on his way," Pau said.

"For me?" Sokolov asked.

Pau nodded. "Your revolutionary discovery is vital to what he has planned."

"How do you know of my discovery?"

"Because Karl Tang is a brother of the *Ba*."

He recalled the phone conversation and the split between Pau and Tang. "You lie well."

Pau seemed to absorb the insult. "I have been of the brotherhood nearly my entire adult life. I was subject to the knife at age twenty-eight. I rose to Hegemon by age forty. Never doubt, though, that I love China. Its culture. Its heritage. I have done all I can to preserve it."

"You are a eunuch, as deceitful as all of them who came before you."

"But there were many of us who did great things, who performed our duties with skill and honor. In fact, Minister, history shows that there were far more of those than of the other."

"And which one are you?" Ni asked.

"I am no monster," Pau said. "I have willingly returned home."

He was not impressed. "And why is that?"

"To see who will lead China."

"That seems already decided."

"Your cynicism is self-defeating. I tried to warn you of that in Belgium."

"Where's my son?" Sokolov asked. "I was told he was here."

Pau motioned and the two brothers standing behind him parted. Another brother strode forward holding the hand of a small boy, perhaps four or five, the same hair and face as Sokolov. The boy spotted his father and rushed forward. They embraced and Sokolov began to rattle off words in Russian, both of them sobbing.

"You see," Pau said. "He is fine. He has been here all along, well cared for."

Sokolov was not listening, smothering the boy with kisses. Ni, unmarried, could only imagine the agony the father had endured.

"I have gone to a great deal of trouble to lure everyone here," Pau said.

That he did believe. "And what will that decide?"

"The fate of China, as has happened many times through the centuries. That's what has made our culture so special. It is what set us apart from all others. No emperor ever ruled solely because of his bloodline. Instead it was the emperor's responsibility to set a moral example for both his government and his people. If he grew corrupt, or incompetent, rebellion has always been regarded as a legitimate recourse. Any peasant who could gather an army could found a new dynasty. And that happened many times. If prosperity came from his rule, then he was deemed to have gained the 'mandate of Heaven.' His male heirs were expected to succeed him, but they, too, could be overthrown if judged unfit. The mandate of Heaven not only must be maintained, but must be earned."

"And the Communist Party earned theirs'?"

"Hardly. They manufactured it. But that illusion has become all too obvious. They forgot both their Legalist roots and Confucian morals. The people long ago judged them unfit to rule."

"And you now have raised the army to overthrow them?"

"Not me, Minister."

Out the window he heard a helicopter approaching.

"That is Tang," Pau said. "Finally, he arrives."

MALONE SAT PROPPED AGAINST THE RANGE ROVER'S TIRE, RUB-bing his back. He recalled clearly what had happened last year in Central Asia, when he and Viktor had first squared off, and what Stephanie had said.

Viktor, if you ever get tired of freelancing and want a job, let me know.

Apparently, Viktor had taken the offer to heart.

He resented what Stephanie had not told him, but liked the fact that Ivan certainly didn't know Viktor was working every side.

Served the smug SOB right.

The street had returned to normal, the locals resuming their routines.

"That hurt," he muttered. "How long has he been gone?"

Cassiopeia knelt beside him. "Nearly an hour."

Malone's head had cleared from the dizziness, and though his spine was sore he was otherwise okay.

He stood in a half crouch.

"He said to wait an hour before we followed."

He glared at her. "He say anything else?"

"He was sorry for the cheap shot."

He glared at her.

"And for us to trust him."

"Yeah, right."

"I think he's trying to help."

"Cassiopeia, I don't know what the man is trying to do. We know the Russians want Sokolov back, but you have to realize that, if necessary, they'll kill him to keep him from the Chinese, or the Americans."

"If Stephanie is yanking Viktor's chain, she wouldn't want Sokolov dead."

"Don't sell her short. She wants him alive, but she doesn't want the Chinese to have him, either."

"You realize that Stephanie probably knew I was being tortured," she said. "Viktor was hers."

"No, she didn't. She told me she only knew Viktor nabbed you after he made contact with me. I told her about the torture."

He saw the frustration in her eyes. He felt it, too.

She told him about the Pakistanis whom Tang had involved, waiting for them in the highlands.

He forced himself to his feet. "I'll take my chances." He glanced around. "We need to find the route up."

"Not a problem."

"Let me guess. Viktor told you that, too."

SEVENTY-FOUR

TANG ENTERED THE MAIN COURTYARD. EVERGREENS PLANTED during the Ming dynasty rose from breaks in the pavement. Colossal gates, which to him had always seemed to require giants to move, hung open, their doors carved with neolithic images that spoke of adventure and ruggedness. The flagstones beneath his feet had been laid centuries before, many engraved with poems, which gave the glazed structure at the courtyard's center its name—*Huan yong ting*, Pavilion Encircled by Songs. Water flowed in a carefully mapped course along a man-made stream, spanned by several rounded wooden bridges.

Above each of the multistoried buildings enclosing the space, an upturned eave reached out. At the corners, slender wooden pillars polished with layers of red paint and lacquer shone like glass. For centuries brothers had resided here, divided by a hierarchy defined by age and status. A place once innocent of electricity, far more suitable for birds than people, it had been transformed by the *Ba* into a sanctuary.

The helicopter was gone.

Only his footsteps, the trickle of the water, and a metallic din of chimes disturbed the serenity.

Two brothers waited at the end of the courtyard, up a terraced stairway, each dressed in a wool gown with a red waistband. Their hair was shaved short in front but plaited in back. Olive-black eyes barely blinked. He strode straight toward a veranda supported by more pillars painted blood red and decorated in silver and gold. He climbed three-quarters of the way up, stopping at the base of the third terrace. Behind the brothers opened double doors, flanked on either side by two massive elephant tusks.

Pau Wen stepped from the portal.

Finally, they were face-to-face. After so many years.

Pau descended the steps.

Tang waited, then bowed. "Everything went according to your plan."

"You have done well. The end is now in sight."

He enjoyed the feeling of pride. He handed Pau the watch from the imperial library chamber. "I thought you would like this back."

Pau accepted the gift with a bow. "My thanks."

"Where is Ni Yong?"

"Waiting. Inside."

"Then let us finish this and begin a new day for China."

"IT'S AWFUL QUIET UP HERE," MALONE SAID.

Their trek, so far, had been uneventful.

An ocean of jagged, snowy summits engulfed them. What had he once read? A land of black wolves and blue poppies—ibex and snow leopards. *Where fairies congregated,* he recalled another observer noting. Possibly even the inspiration behind James Hilton's *Shangri-la.*

No sign of Viktor yet, or of soldiers.

Little sound besides the scuffle of their feet on the rocky trail.

In the distance rose hardscrabble hills, washed with green and streaked in red. Herds of livestock and nomad tents flying yellow flags dotted the slopes. Down in one of the gorges he spied the decaying carcass of a donkey that had slipped to its death.

He caught movement out of the corner of his eye, ahead and above them.

He kept walking, as if unaware, and whispered to her, "Did you—"

"I saw it," she muttered.

Four men.

The trail ahead led into a stretch of poplars. Cassiopeia led the way.

"Get ready to move," he breathed, his hand reaching for the gun beneath his jacket.

He heard the crack of a weapon, then a bullet zipped by.

TANG ENTERED THE ROOM AND STARED AT NI YONG. PAU WEN had already removed Sokolov and the boy. Hopefully, a father-and-son reunion would calm the Russian and ensure his cooperation.

"Our battle is over," he said to Ni.

"And how will my death be explained?"

"A tragic helicopter crash. You were in Xinjiang province investigating more corruption. Isn't that what you do?"

"My staff knows where I was going and why."

"Your staff will either cooperate or be silenced."

"And what of the police in Yecheng? The two pilots on the plane I commandeered in Xi'an? They know things."

He shrugged. "All easily eliminated. Did you think me so stupid? I knew you were monitoring my satellite calls. We used that as a way to send messages. Did you enjoy the debate between Pau and myself?"

Ni shrugged. "Hardly a dramatic feat for two such accomplished liars."

"I was kept informed of everything you did. That is how I knew you were headed for Belgium."

"And the attempt on my life there?"

"That was real. I was hoping to end the problem. But you apparently were able to avoid the men I sent."

"Actually, Pau Wen saved my life."

Had he heard correctly? Pau? Viktor had been unable to learn what had happened at Pau's residence since he'd been in Antwerp, dealing with Cassiopeia Vitt. None of the men he'd sent had ever reported back, and Pau had, characteristically, offered nothing. He would have to speak with the master about the matter. For now he made clear, "The Hegemon is not afraid to shed blood. If he intervened, then there was good reason."

"Spoken like a true Legalist. Congratulations, Minister, on your victory. History will note you as the man who finally destroyed China."

MALONE DOVE TO ROCKY GROUND AND SOUGHT WHAT COVER the sparse poplars offered. Cassiopeia did the same and they belly-crawled across sharp gravel, finding a boulder large enough to provide them both protection.

More shots came their way.

"This is getting serious," Cassiopeia said.

"You think?"

"They're not Chinese," she said. "I caught a glimpse. Definitely Pakistanis. They seem to know where we're headed."

"That thought occurred to me, too." So he had to add, "I told you he was trouble."

She ignored him.

"We have to go that way." He pointed behind them. "And those soldiers are close enough to do some damage."

"We have to trust he'll handle it," she finally said.

"That was your call, not mine. You go first. I'll cover."

He gripped the Chinese double-action pistol.

Cassiopeia prepared herself, too.

Then she scampered off toward a stand of junipers.

NI GLARED AT KARL TANG.

Though Tang had tried hard to conceal it, he'd caught the surprise when he'd explained that Pau Wen had been the one to stop the gunmen. Perhaps there had been more to their debate than staged drama?

"We have led you like a bear on a leash," Tang said. "You listened in on our calls, and we fed you exactly the information we wanted you to know. You traveled to Belgium, then to Xi'an, and finally here, all at our invitation."

"Does that *we* include the premier?"

"He is of no importance. An old man who will soon be dead."

That prospect saddened him. He'd come to admire the premier, a moderate who'd done much to temper communist fanaticism. Not a hint of scandal had ever touched him.

"Pau Wen is our master," Tang said. "The brothers, myself included, have all pledged our allegiance. We thought a perceived war between Pau and me would lull you into a false sense of security. I do have to say that this was to have played out differently. You were to die in Belgium."

"And Pau never mentioned that he killed all four men?"

Tang's face was like stone. "Whatever he did was correct."

"Surely Cassiopeia Vitt and Cotton Malone were not part of your plan."

He shrugged. "The master required the use of her and Malone to return to China."

A distant crack echoed out the windows.

Then more.

"Gunfire," Tang said. "For your allies."

"Vitt and Malone?" He kept his tone casual, though he was deeply concerned.

"They escaped Yecheng, but now they will die here, in the mountains, like you."

SEVENTY-FIVE

CASSIOPEIA WAITED FOR COTTON TO REACH HER. HE'D COVERED her retreat with some well-placed shots.

He arrived and they both raced forward, using more trees as protection. Sharp bursts of rifle fire accompanied them, and bullets pinged around them. Their cover vanished as the trail twisted out of the trees. To her right she saw more sheer canyons lined with shadows. They paralleled the trail's loose edge, careful with each step. A brilliant sun blazed on the far side of the gorge, dulled only by black mountain slate. Thirty meters below, water the color of road dust rushed and tumbled, tossing foamy spray high into air. They clambered up a steep embankment, past scree slopes of collapsed moraines.

She spotted the bridge Viktor had mentioned.

Ropes ran from crossbeams anchored into stone piles on either side of the gorge. The piles weren't much, just rocks, one atop the other, brushwood in between acting as mortar. A footwalk of boards held aloft by hemp stretched thirty meters across the river.

Intermittent gunfire echoed in the distance.

She glanced back.

No soldiers.

More shots chattered.

"Maybe he's leading them away," she said.

No comment, though she could see he was skeptical. He stuffed his gun into a pocket.

She did the same, then stepped onto the bridge.

NI HEARD MORE FARAWAY SHOTS.

"You will have a grand state funeral," Tang said. "It will be quite the spectacle. You are, after all, a respected man."

"Then what will you do?"

"Assume control of the government. The premier is not long for this world, so it is logical that he would gradually pass control to his first deputy. That is when we will start our return to glory."

"And unlimited oil will help that journey?"

Tang smiled. "I see Sokolov told you. Good. You need to know what you missed. And yes, the prospect of no longer having to prostitute ourselves to Russia, the Middle East, and Africa—to fear what America might do—just to ensure that our factories continue to produce, is worth the effort."

"So going after that lamp in Belgium was all part of the grand display you and Pau devised?"

"Make no mistake, the lamp was important. But it also served as the perfect bait to lure you there. And you were supposed to die."

"Instead, four other men died."

Tang shrugged. "As you said, Pau killed them."

"But you ordered the murder of the pilot."

Tang said nothing.

"You have no conception of what troubles China."

"But I do. This nation needs a firm hand."

He shook his head. "You are a lunatic."

His fate seemed sealed.

And more gunfire from the mountains signaled that Malone and Vitt were likewise in deep trouble.

CASSIOPEIA FELT THE BOARDS BENEATH HER FEET VIBRATE from the rush of water. Malone had gone across first, saying that if the bridge held him it would surely hold her. The extra weight had also broken the rhythm, reducing the nerve-racking sway. They were now suspended in open air, halfway across, with zero cover, moving from shadows to sunlight. She spotted a trail on the far side, leading across loose gravel into more trees. A figure, maybe five meters high, carved in the rock face beyond the trail—a Buddhist image—told her they were in the right place.

"This bridge has seen better days," she said as Malone turned back toward her.

"I hope it has at least one more left."

She gripped the twisted ropes that held the span aloft, forming a makeshift railing. No sign of any pursuers. But a new sound rose over the rushing water. Deep bass tones. Far off, but growing louder.

She caught the first glimpse of a shadow on a rock wall, maybe two kilometers away, where the gorge they were crossing met another running perpendicular. The distant shadow grew, then was replaced with the distinct shape of a helicopter.

And it wasn't a transport. An attack aircraft, equipped with cannons and missiles.

"That's not here to help," she said.

Then she knew. The soldiers had herded them to this spot.

The pilot started firing.

TANG HEARD THE RAPID BURST OF CANNON FIRE AND KNEW what was happening. The Pakistanis had used one of their Cobras. He'd told them that an aerial intrusion into the mountains would not, at least this time, be viewed unfavorably. On the contrary, he wanted the task done right and thought the bridge might offer the perfect venue.

He could only hope that Viktor had teamed with Malone and Vitt, and all three were crossing.

If not, the soldiers could finish the job.

"I will be the next premier of this nation," he said to Ni. "China will retake its superior place in the world. We will also retake Taiwan, the southern lands, Mongolia, even Korea. We shall be whole again."

"That kind of stupidity is what has brought us to where we are now."

"And you are the brilliant leader who can save us? You could not even see that you were being manipulated. You are fatally naïve."

"And the world will simply sit by and allow you to do as you please?"

"That's the interesting part. You see, knowing that oil is infinite comes with a great advantage. Keep that information close, use it wisely, and we can orchestrate the collapse of more than one foreign power. The world fights over oil as children fight over sweets. They battle one another both physically and economically to satisfy their needs. All we have to do is direct the fight." He shook his head. "The armies of the world will not be a problem for China. You see, Minister, a single piece of knowledge can be more powerful than a hundred nuclear weapons."

He motioned for the door.

"Now, before you leave this world, the master thought you might like to see something. Actually, he thinks we both will find it of interest, since it is something I have not seen, either."

"Then by all means. Let's see what the Hegemon wants to show us."

CASSIOPEIA DOVE BELLY-FIRST TO THE BRIDGE BOARDS, STARing past her feet at Cotton as a steady procession of cannon fire came their way. The helicopter roared toward them, its blades slicing through the limpid air. Rounds found the bridge, ripping wood and rope with a savage fury.

Anger filled her eyes and she found her gun, came to her knees, and fired at the copter's canopy. But the damn thing was surely armorplated and moving with the speed of a hummingbird.

"Get the hell down," he yelled.

Another burst of cannon fire annihilated the bridge between them. One moment the wood-and-rope construction existed, the next it was gone in a cloud of debris. She realized the entire span was about to collapse.

He sprang to his feet.

No way he could get to her, so he wisely tried to negotiate the final six meters on his side of the divide, clinging to the ropes as the bridge dropped away beneath their feet.

The helicopter zoomed past, toward the opposite end of the gorge.

She grasped the ropes, too, and as the bridge separated, each half swinging toward different sides of the gorge, she clung tight and flew through the air.

Her body slammed into rock, rebounded, then settled.

She held on tight and risked a look to the other side. Slowly, Cotton was pulling himself upward, negotiating the remaining few meters to the top.

Rushing water and the thump of chopper blades filled her ears.

Another look across the gorge and Cotton had found the top, standing now, staring at her. She clung with both hands to the other half of the bridge as it dangled against the tawny face of the gorge. Clattering scree prevented any foothold.

The helicopter executed a tight turn within the gorge, arching upward, and began another run their way.

"Can you climb?" he screamed over the noise.

She shook her head.

"Do it," he yelled.

She craned her neck his way. "Get out of here."

"Not without you."

The Cobra was little more than a kilometer away. Its cannon would start firing any second.

"Climb," he screamed.

She pulled herself up, but the next handful of hemp she grabbed gave way.

She plunged downward.

Into the rushing river.

SEVENTY-SIX

NI FOLLOWED TANG THROUGH THE COMPLEX OF BUILDINGS. Galleries of red and yellow connected the various wings. Ornate pillars, their golden decoration uneffaced by time, held the high ceilings aloft. Incense burners and braziers warmed the halls. Finally, they entered a cavernous three-storied chamber.

"This is the Hall for the Preservation of Harmony," Tang said. "The most sacred site for the *Ba*."

It was different from the other buildings, even more elaborate, with alternating red and yellow galleries up three levels. A forest of pillars spanned its perimeter on three sides, with graceful arches in between. An arsenal of swords, knives, lances, bows, and shields decorated the ground level along the edges, and half a dozen copper braziers blazed with glowing charcoals.

Sunlight seeped from windows in the upper galleries. At the far end, on a raised terrace, the wall, reaching up thirty meters, comprised hundreds of diagonal bins brimming with scrolls. Silver lamps dotted the remaining three walls between the levels, but remained unlit. Light came from electric lanterns dangling from the ceiling.

"Inside those shelves is the accumulation of our knowledge, written on silk, preserved for the Hegemon to consult," Tang said. "Not translations or secondhand accounts. The actual words."

"Apparently, the *Ba* is well financed," he said.

"Though we are ancient in origin, we are recent in reincarnation. The eunuchs from the time of the last emperor, in the early part of the 20th century, ensured that we were properly endowed. Mao tried to appease them, but many brought their wealth here."

"Mao hated eunuchs."

"That he did. But they hated him more."

"It's a shame I won't live to see you fail."

"I don't plan to fail."

"No fanatic ever does."

Tang stepped close. "You lost the battle, Minister. That's what history will record. Just as the Gang of Four lost their battle. Several of them died from the effort, as well."

Behind Tang, on the far side, a section of the towering wall hung open, the panel cleverly concealed among the shelves.

Pau Wen emerged from the doorway that the panel revealed.

"Ministers," Pau called out. "Please, come."

Ni saw that Tang did not appreciate the interruption, so he decided to twist the knife. "Your master calls."

Tang glared at him. "That is precisely what is wrong with China. It has forgotten fear and respect. I plan to reacquaint the nation with both."

"You may find it difficult, keeping a billion and a half people afraid."

"It has been done before. It can be done again."

"Qin Shi? Our glorious First Emperor? He barely ruled twelve years, and his empire disintegrated at his death." He paused. "Thanks to a scheming eunuch."

Tang seemed unfazed. "I will not make the same mistakes."

They walked in silence across the long hall, perhaps fifty meters in length and half that wide. Short steps led up to a raised floor.

"I was unaware that there existed a door in the wall," Tang said.

Ni caught the irritation in the words.

"Only the Hegemon and a select few brothers know of this chamber," Pau said. "You were not one of those. But I thought now a good time to show you both the *Ba*'s most precious possession."

MALONE STARED DOWN AT THE WATER, SPEWING BETWEEN ROCKS as it bounded down from the mountains.

He waited for her to surface.

But she never did.

He focused on the roaring gush, which surely carried in its formidable current silt and more rock along with a swish of foam. He wanted to leap after her, but realized that was impossible.

He would not survive the fall, either.

He watched, disbelieving.

After all they'd been through the past three days.

She was gone.

On the opposite side of the gorge movement caught his eye. Viktor emerged from the rocks and approached the cliff edge.

Malone's anger boiled to rage. "You sorry bastard," he yelled. "You set us up. You killed her."

Viktor did not reply. Instead he was hauling up the remnants of the bridge, tying the rope he'd brought to its tattered end.

"Go," Viktor yelled. "Get up there. I'll go after her."

Like hell, he thought.

He found his gun.

Viktor tossed the bridge back over the edge. The rope found the water, its end dipped into the churning river. His enemy stared across, as if to say, *Are you going to shoot me or let met try to find her?*

The helicopter was swooping around for another pass.

Malone leveled the gun.

Cannon fire roared through the gorge. A deadly hail of heavy-caliber rounds pinged off stone just yards away, approaching in an ever-widening storm.

He dove for cover as the chopper zipped past.

"Get up there," Viktor yelled. "Ni and Sokolov need you."

And Viktor started climbing down.

What he wouldn't give for some rope of his own. He wanted to kill Viktor Tomas, but the bastard was right.

Ni Yong and Sokolov.

Find them.

TANG ENTERED THE WINDOWLESS CHAMBER, ITS SPACE DIVIDED into four rooms. Pau Wen had stepped inside first, followed by Ni Yong. Two brothers waited outside, each carrying a crossbow.

Soft lights illuminated rose-red walls, the ceiling a deep blue and dotted with golden stars. The center chamber was dominated by a bronze plinth upon which lay a jade burial suit.

He was stunned by the sight, and now understood why the First Emperor's tomb had been bare.

"I rescued Qin Shi," Pau said. "Unfortunately, the jade altar upon which he lay was too large to transport. It obviously had been constructed within the mound. But this I could retrieve." Pau pointed to the artifact. "The head and face masks, jacket, sleeves, gloves, pants, and foot coverings were tailored for the occupant. Which meant Qin Shi was no more than a hundred seventy-five centimeters tall and quite thin. So different from the image of a towering, portly man history has created." Pau hesitated, as if to allow his words to sink in. "Two thousand and seven pieces of jade, sewn together with golden thread."

"You counted them?" Ni asked.

"This is the most important archaeological find in all Chinese history. The body of our First Emperor, encased in jade. It deserves careful study. We estimate about a kilogram of golden thread was utilized to bind the stone. This suit would have taken artisans about a decade to produce."

Tang wanted to know, "You plundered the entire site?"

"Every object. Here it all rests, in safety, inside a makeshift *dixia gong-dian*. Not quite a traditional underground palace, but sufficient."

The remaining three chambers brimmed with funerary objects. Bronze sculptures, copper vessels, lacquered wood, and bamboo ware. Objects of gold, silver, and jade. Musical instruments, pottery, and porcelain. Swords, spearheads, and arrows.

"Two thousand one hundred and sixty-five items," Pau said. "Even the bones of the builders and the concubines. I made a complete photographic record of the tomb. The exact location of everything is precisely documented."

"How gracious of you," Ni said. "I'm sure historians will one day appreciate your diligence."

"Does sarcasm make you feel superior?"

"What am I supposed to be? Impressed? You are a liar and a thief, just like I said the first time we met. Along with being a murderer."

"Do you realize what Mao would have done with this?" Pau asked, motioning to the jade suit. "And the incompetents who ruled after him. None of it would have survived."

"The terra-cotta warriors have," Ni said.

"True. But for how long? The site is deteriorating by the day. And what is being done? Nothing. The communists care nothing for our past."

"And you do?"

"Minister, my methods may have been unconventional, but the results are clear."

Ni stepped close to the plinth.

Tang kept back, himself drawn to the surreal image—like a robot lying there, stiff, unbending. But he was growing impatient. He wanted to know why Pau had killed the four men in Belgium and allowed Ni to survive. Why had the master lied to him about the oil lamps in Qin Shi's tomb?

"Did you open the suit?" Ni asked.

Pau shook his head. "That did not seem right. Qin deserves our respect, even in death."

"How many hundreds of thousands died so he could rule?" Ni asked.

"That was necessary in his time," Pau said.

"And it still is," Tang felt compelled to add.

"No," Ni said. "Fear and oppression are no longer viable mechanisms. Surely, you can see that we have progressed beyond that. Two-thirds of the world practices democracy, yet we cannot embrace even a few of its qualities?"

"Not while I am in charge," Tang declared.

Ni shook his head. "You will find, as our communist forefathers learned, that force is only a short-term solution. For a government to survive, it must have the willing support of the people." Ni's face tightened. "Has either of you ever visited the petition office in Beijing?"

"Never," Tang said.

"Every day hundreds of people from all over the country are there, waiting in line, to register complaints. Nearly all of them have been victimized. Their son was beaten by a local official. Their land was taken by a developer, with the local government's help. Their child was stolen."

Ni hesitated, and Tang knew he was allowing that charge to hang in the air.

"They are angry at local officials and are convinced that if only someone in the capital hears their case, then their wrongs will be addressed. You and I know they are sadly mistaken. Nothing will ever be done. But those people understand basic democracy. They want the ability to address their government directly. How long do you think we can continue to ignore them?"

Tang knew the answer.

"Forever."

SEVENTY-SEVEN

CASSIOPEIA HIT THE WATER HARD AND WAS SWEPT FORWARD with a rush from an overwhelming current, her body tossed about as if in a tornado. The water was cold, but that was the least of her problems. Breathing was her main concern and she managed to thrust her way to the surface, grabbing a quick breath through the foam before the water assaulted her again.

She had to stop moving forward. Eventually she would be propelled into rocks, breaking a bone, smashing her skull, if not killing her. Her ears were filled with a deep rumble and the swirl of a trillion bubbles. She'd yet to touch bottom.

She snagged another breath and caught sight of what lay ahead.

Boulders. Big ones. Their soaked profiles protruding from the surge.

She'd have to risk it.

In a wild scramble, she pawed at the water and tried to steer her course. Her body was tossed with no regard, the water oblivious to everything but gravity. A cloud of brown foam boiled against her face. She kept her arms extended, leading the way, feeling until her hands slammed into something hard.

But she did not bounce off.

Instead, she held tight.

Her head emerged.

Water thundered past her shoulders, but at least she wasn't moving.

She sucked several deep breaths, shook the blur from her eyes, and finally realized she was freezing.

MALONE FOLLOWED A TRAIL LINED WITH CHORTEN AND PRAYER walls. A sudden breeze brought the chilling breath of nearby glaciers. He trembled from both the brisk air and a nearly overwhelming intensity, fists closed tight, eyes moist with emotion.

How many more friends did he have to lose?

Gray rabbits scurried across the path, then dove into crevices. He could still hear the water tumbling behind him. The helicopter was gone. Viktor was presumably at the bottom of the gorge, doing whatever he thought he could do.

Damn that son of a bitch.

He hadn't felt such rage since Gary was taken last year. He'd killed his son's abductor without the slightest remorse.

And he'd do the same to Viktor.

Right now he had to focus. Protecting Sokolov was the key. Helping Ni Yong, imperative. Obviously, Stephanie had considered both of those objectives important. Why else would she have used both him and Cassiopeia, and enlisted Viktor's help. He'd wondered in Copenhagen why Stephanie had not been overly concerned about Cassiopeia's predicament. And how she knew so much about abiotic and biotic oil.

Now he knew.

She had Viktor on the scene, supposedly looking after her.

But had he been?

Stephanie, too, would have to face a few consequences when this was over.

He spotted a stone altar lit by two lamps and approached with caution. The trail ahead veered right and a sheer wall blocked what lay past the turn. Light splintered off the towering gray rock in shimmers and sparkles. He lived in fear of emotions, denying their existence, burying them under an avalanche of responsibilities. Yet in truth, he was utterly dependent upon them—a fact he'd never realized until far too late.

He'd miss Cassiopeia Vitt more than he ever imagined.

He'd loved her—yes, he had—but could never bring himself to utter the words.

Why the hell not?

A gong sounded in the distance.

Deep tones faded, and a great, empty, reverberating silence engulfed him.

NI WAS DETERMINED THAT HE WAS NOT GOING TO SHOW WEAKNESS. He would face these fanatics down to the end.

"The Soviets maintained," he said, "that they could force the people to serve them. Even you, Pau, in Belgium pointed out that mistake."

"The Soviets did indeed make many errors. We must avoid those."

"But I will not allow China to lose its way," Tang declared. "The West tries every day to promote its values and ideologies here, believing that we can be destabilized by some sort of *marketing campaign*. By *democracy*."

"You have no idea the dangers we face," Ni said. "We are not the China of Qin Shi's day."

"We are still Chinese," Tang said. "Toppling our government, whether from outside or within, will be far more difficult than it was in the Soviet Union."

Ni watched both Tang and Pau Wen. Men so deceitful were no different from the despots who'd come before them. China did indeed seem doomed to repeat one mistake after another.

He stepped away from the plinth and stared into the three other chambers, not as large as their underground counterparts in Xi'an, but roomy, each filled with grave goods.

Pau approached. "A few of the bronze vessels are filled with liquid. I broke the seal on one and savored an ambrosial aroma. The liquid inside tested for alcohol, sugar, fat—a buttered rum, from over two thousand years ago."

Any other time he'd be impressed, but at the moment he was trying to determine how to avoid dying in a helicopter crash.

"Those bronze lamps," Tang said. "There. Are they the same?"

Ni had already noticed them. Arranged around the walls on pedestals, on shelves, and on the floor. A dragon's head on a tiger's body, with the wings of a phoenix. Maybe a hundred of them. Just like the one he'd retrieved at the museum.

"They are the same as the one in Antwerp," Pau said. "Each is filled with oil extracted from the ground in Gansu over two millennia ago. I kept one, as a keepsake, and took it with me to Belgium."

"I need that oil sample," Tang said.

"I'm afraid the emperor's tomb is no longer pristine," Ni said.

Malone and Vitt had told him what happened after he fled. About the fire and the smoke. He told Pau.

"Hopefully," Pau said, "the damage was minimal. The mineral oil I left to shield the mercury would have caused no real damage. The mercury, though, is another matter. Its vapors will take time to flush away."

"It matters not," Tang said.

"Unlike you," Ni said to Pau, "he seems to care little for the past."

"A fault he will remedy. We shall discuss the matter."

"There are many things we need to discuss," Tang made clear. "Things you seem to have neglected to mention."

Pau faced Tang. "Like why I killed the men you sent to my home?"

"That's one."

"We will talk. But know that I explain myself to no one."

Tang clearly did not appreciate the rebuke.

"This more of the show?" Ni asked. "You two fighting."

"No, Minister," Pau said. "This disagreement is real."

CASSIOPEIA'S GRIP WAS WEAKENING, THE FREEZING CURRENT lancing her joints with pain. For the third time in two days death seemed close. She doubted she would survive the ride downstream and, surely, at some point there'd be a waterfall to the valleys below. A cloud of brown foam engulfed her face and she shut her eyes to the onslaught.

Something firm gripped her right arm, from above, yanking her grip free from the rock.

She opened her eyes to see Viktor staring down at her. He was balancing atop a boulder, right hand locked on her arm. She reached out with her left hand and her body spun as she was lifted from the water.

He'd saved her life.

Again.

"Thought you weren't going to do that anymore," she said, catching her breath.

"It was either that or be shot by Malone."

A chill swept through her, one she could not control. Viktor knelt close, both of them atop the rocks, and removed his jacket. He wrapped its thick fleece around her chest and held her close.

She did not resist.

She couldn't.

The chills came uncontrollably.

Her teeth chattered and she fought to calm her nerves.

Viktor continued to hold her tight. "I tried to divert the soldiers until you and Malone were beyond the bridge, but I didn't know about the chopper. It came quick, apparently knowing you'd have to negotiate the bridge. Tang planned well."

"Where's Cotton?" she managed to ask, hoping the cannon fire had not found him.

"I told him to go. That was after he decided not to shoot me. The chopper wanted to take me out, too, but couldn't get a shot down here. So it left."

She stared up into his eyes and saw both concern and anger. "How'd you find me?"

"When I saw you hanging on, that bought me enough time. I actually expected to find a few broken bones."

"You and me both."

She was steadying herself, the shakes fading. Glancing back she saw the risk he'd taken, step by step, fumbling across the exposed boulders. One slip and he'd have been swept away.

"Thank you, Viktor."

"I couldn't let you drown."

She freed herself of his embrace and stood, but kept the jacket close. Water poured from her clothes. Her hands were blue from the cold. Direct sunlight could not, at this early hour, find its way down the perpendicular walls that towered above her. But she knew there was warmth, higher up. "We have to get to that hall."

He pointed to the far bank. "There's a trail that leads back up. Malone should be at the monastery by now."

"You and he can make your peace, when this is over."

"I doubt that will happen."

"He can be reasonable."

"Not when it comes to you," he said.

"And what about you?"

He pointed out the safest path across the rocks to the bank. "It's a good twenty minutes to the top. We need to hurry."

She grabbed his arm. "I asked you a question."

"Malone was right back in town," he said. "I murdered that pilot for no reason other than to gain your trust." He paused. "Like Malone says all the time, I'm a random asset. Another term for *nobody*. What about me, you asked? Who the hell cares."

"Stephanie does. She sent you to get Sokolov."

"And Ivan sent me to kill Tang. Yet here I am, saving your life. Again."

She didn't know what to say, so she released her grip.

And he leaped to the next rock.

SEVENTY-EIGHT

MALONE APPROACHED THE MONASTERY WITH CAUTION. HE'D rounded the bend in the trail and immediately studied the great pile of crenellated walls, all a purplish red, that formed a solid rampart, its parapets broken only by a single gate.

He stopped at the entrance, tiled in a golden yellow. Above the massive red-lacquered doors hung a tablet with symbols.

He'd seen it on both the silk map at Pau Wen's residence and on the map the Chinese premier displayed.

Afang.

The name of Qin Shi's palace. And also the symbol of the Hall for the Preservation of Harmony.

The gates were open, seemingly inviting him inside, so he stepped onto a six-person-wide, stone-paved avenue. Three more elaborate gates gave way to a courtyard surrounded by multistoried buildings and colonnaded porches. Ornamental trees, shrubs, flowers, and the trickle of water through a man-made stream created a feeling of peace.

But he realized this place was anything but untroubled.

A figure of a deity with multiple arms and several faces rose before him. At the far end, up three narrow terraces, past a veranda, a set of doors hung open, guarded by ivory tusks, the space beyond well lit.

He still hadn't seen anyone.

He kept the gun at his side, finger on the trigger, fighting violent heartbeats and a faint feeling from the thin air.

Then he heard a sound.

Laughter.

A child.

Speaking in Russian.

He scanned the courtyard and identified the source. To his right, one floor up, through an open window.

Sokolov and his son?

He had to find out.

CASSIOPEIA CLIMBED THE TRAIL, ZIGZAGGING UPWARD, TOWARD where she and Cotton would have arrived if their river crossing had not been interrupted. Trees provided handholds, their gnarly roots gripping the earth with rigid tentacles.

The exertion restored her body. Viktor led the way but occasionally glanced back, keeping watch on her. He'd held her tight on the river. Too tight. She'd sensed his emotions, knew that he cared, but like herself and Cotton, he kept far more inside than he ever allowed out. The murder of that Chinese pilot seemed to bother him. Unusual. Men like Viktor rarely analyzed their actions or expressed regret. A job was a job, ethics be damned. At least that was the way Viktor had always treated things. She believed him on Sokolov. Stephanie would want the Russian alive. Ivan, though, was another matter. He would want Sokolov silent.

Her wet clothes, stained brown from the silty water, hung heavy, dust from the trail clinging to her as if magnetized. She'd lost her gun in the fall and noticed that Viktor carried only a knife, so they were headed into God-knew-what unarmed.

They found the top of the trail and passed rock carvings and an altar. Around a bend they spotted the purplish mass of the monastery, perched high, overlooking a natural amphitheater of cliffs and valleys.

And heard a gong.

NI EASED HIMSELF CLOSE TO A DISPLAY OF BRONZE SWORDS. THE slim-faceted blades shone in the incandescent lights, their edges and tips sharp.

Do something.

Even if it's wrong.

Pau turned toward Tang, and Ni used the moment to grip one of the weapons, instantly wrapping his arm around Pau, bringing the blade to the older man's throat, flat edge to the skin—for the moment.

"This will easily slit your throat," he said in Pau's ear.

Tang reacted to the threat by summoning the men outside. Two brothers rushed in and leveled their crossbows.

"Tell them to lay down the bows and leave," Ni commanded Pau. "It won't take much to cause you to bleed to death."

Pau stood still.

"Tell them," he said again, and to emphasize the point he twisted the sword ninety degrees, bringing the sharp edge to the skin.

"Do as he says," Pau commanded.

Both brothers laid down their weapons and retreated.

MALONE ENTERED ONE OF THE BUILDINGS THAT LINED THE courtyard and ascended a staircase one level. At the top, he inched his way down a wide corridor to an intersection. Carefully, he peered around the corner and spotted a younger man in a woolen robe standing guard outside a closed door. He estimated that the room would face the courtyard at the location of the open window.

Twenty feet lay between himself and the apparently unarmed guard. He decided a direct approach was best, so he tucked the gun into his back pocket and readied himself.

One.

Two.

He rushed around the corner and charged. Just as he'd assumed, the sudden sight of someone caused a momentary delay in reaction, enough for Malone to coldcock the guard with a fist, slamming the back of the man's head into the stone wall.

The man collapsed to the floor.

Malone checked to be sure. No weapon. Interesting. Perhaps they weren't thought necessary behind the impressive fortifications that encased this complex.

He found his own gun, checked behind him—all quiet—and slowly opened the door.

TANG WONDERED WHAT NI HOPED TO GAIN. THERE WAS NO-where to go. "You cannot escape."

"But I can kill your master."

"I do not fear death," Pau said.

"Neither do I. Not anymore. In fact, I would rather be dead than live in a China ruled by you two."

He silently congratulated himself on his forethought. All he had to do was coax Ni back out into the hall.

There, he could end this problem.

MALONE SAW THE LOOK OF RELIEF ON LEV SOKOLOV'S FACE, SAW the boy curled in his lap.

"Malone," Sokolov muttered. "I wondered what happened to you."

He crossed the empty bedchamber and stole a quick look out the window. The courtyard remained quiet. "How many men are in this place?"

"Not many," Sokolov said. "I have seen only a few. Tang is here, though."

"Where's Ni?"

"They separated us about one half hour ago."

The boy stared at him with hard eyes.

"Is he okay?" he asked Sokolov.

"He seems fine."

"We have to go, but he must remain quiet."

Sokolov whispered to the boy, and several nods confirmed that the lad understood. Malone motioned and they left the room, with him leading the way down to ground level.

Heading toward the gate out required a crossing of the open courtyard.

He studied the upper galleries. Seeing no one, he gestured and they hustled forward. They passed through a lower gallery, negotiated one of the arched wooden bridges over the man-made stream, and sought a momentary refuge in a gallery on the courtyard's opposite side.

So far, so good.

NI REALIZED THAT THE LONGER HE LINGERED WITHIN THIS confined space, the greater the risk. He had no idea how many brothers were waiting outside. More than he could handle, that was certain. But he was determined to act.

"Move out of here," he told Tang.

His adversary drifted toward the door.

"Careful, Minister," Pau whispered. "He seems to want you out there."

"Shut up."

Yet Pau was right. He'd seen the same thing in Tang's eyes. But he could not stay here. What had the premier said to him? *One's life can be weightier than Mount Tai or lighter than a goose feather. Which will yours be?*

"Move," he ordered Pau.

Slowly, they inched their way out into the hall. His gaze raked the galleries, searching for threats, while simultaneously watching the three men only a few meters away.

So many places to hide.

And he was totally exposed, on a raised platform, an old man the only thing standing between him and death.

"There is nowhere to go," Tang calmly said.

"Tell anyone in those galleries to show themselves," he said to Tang.

To emphasize the point he pressed the blade into Pau's throat, and the old man flinched. Good. About time he experienced fear.

"Tell them yourself," Tang said.

"Show yourselves," he called out. "Now. Your master's life depends on it."

MALONE HEARD A SHOUT.

As did Sokolov, who cradled the boy in his arms, keeping his face buried in his shoulder, holding tight.

"That sounded like Ni," he whispered.

"Something about showing themselves or their master will die," Sokolov interpreted.

He allowed a soft exhale to escape his lips while he considered his options. He spotted an open doorway a few feet away. He grasped Sokolov's arm and led him into the building. Another long corridor lined with doors spread out before them. He crept to one of the doors and slowly released its latch. Inside was a small windowless chamber, perhaps eight feet square, filled with oversized pottery, perhaps for the courtyard.

Wait in here, he mouthed to Sokolov.

The Russian nodded, seemingly saying, *You're right, we can't leave him.*

"I'll be back, hide behind some of this stuff."

"Where's Cassiopeia?"

He couldn't tell him what happened. Not now. "Just stay quiet. You'll be fine."

He closed the door, fled the building, and headed straight for the open doorway at the far end of the courtyard, where voices could still be heard.

TANG WAS ENJOYING THE MOMENT.

Ni Yong was trapped.

Only nine brothers manned the monastery. Two were here, one more watched over Lev Sokolov. The remaining six were scattered throughout the complex, awaiting his command.

MALONE ENTERED.

Beyond the open portal, he found a vestibule, and then an assembly hall, majestic in dignity, topped by a roof of more gleaming yellow tiles. The glow from six braziers, arranged three to a side, splashed the colorful walls with a fiery brilliance. Displays of armor and weaponry lined the perimeter. At the opposite end he saw five men.

Pau, Tang, Ni, and two others.

Ni held a sword to Pau's throat.

They stood before shelving of diagonal bins, stuffed with rolled manuscripts. Thousands of them, rising fifty feet. He kept to the shadows, confident that nothing had betrayed his presence. He noticed that lesser rooms and pavilions formed a closed perimeter around the ground floor, screening out the world. Light streamed in from the upper colonnades, which apparently were lined with windows.

Outside, a gong rang again.

He used the armor and weaponry for cover. His gaze raked the upper two stories of galleries. He thought he caught movement, but wasn't sure.

He had to help Ni.

One of the braziers burned a few feet away, just outside the gallery where he was hiding. He advanced and shielded his body with the huge copper vessel, its heat intense, glancing left and behind to see if any danger existed.

Nothing.

"Minister Ni," he called out. "It's Cotton Malone. I have you covered with a gun."

N<small>I</small> COULD NOT BELIEVE HIS GOOD FORTUNE AND CALLED OUT, "It is good to hear your voice."

He saw Malone emerge from behind one of the braziers, gun pointed his way.

"Now I can slit your throat and be done with it," he whispered in Pau's ear. "Your lies are over."

"Have you found the courage to take a life?"

"Yours would not be a problem for me."

"Choose wisely, Minister. Much is at stake."

The blade rested tight to the skin, an easy matter with one swipe to sever the old man's throat. He stared at Karl Tang, wishing it was him, not Pau, who faced the sword.

That decision would be an easy one.

And he noticed something in Tang's eyes.

"He wants you to do it," Pau whispered.

SEVENTY-NINE

CASSIOPEIA AND VIKTOR ENTERED THE MONASTERY AND FOUND a central courtyard. Everything was quiet except for voices rising from an open set of double doors at the far end. With caution, they advanced in that direction, staying within the colonnades. Once there, Viktor pressed himself to the building's wall and carefully peered past the doorway.

"Malone is in there," he whispered.

Together they crept in, staying within a vestibule that led into what appeared to be a grand hall. Cotton stood about halfway toward a raised portion at the opposite end, facing Tang and two brothers, along with Pau Wen. Ni Yong stood behind the older man, holding a sword to Pau's neck.

They hid behind a thick pillar and watched.

Tang was talking to Cotton, but what was happening above grabbed Cassiopeia's attention. A man in the first-floor gallery, tucked within one of the arches, held a crossbow. The angle made it impossible for Cotton to see the danger directly above him.

"He doesn't know," Viktor whispered.

"Let's tell him."

He shook his head. "We need to keep the element of surprise. You take that guy out. I don't see anyone else up there."

She could not argue with the plan.

He motioned behind them, to the left. "That way. Cover our backs."

"What are you going to do?"

He did not answer her, but she didn't like what she saw in his eyes.

"Don't be foolish," she said.

"No more than I have already been? Tang will be off guard when he sees me. Let's use that."

She wished they had a gun. "Give me your knife."

He surrendered the blade. "It won't be any good to me."

"Cotton probably thinks I'm dead."

He nodded. "I'm counting on that."

MALONE BREATHED IN THE WARM AIR, HEAVY WITH THE SMELL of charcoal. He kept himself fifty feet from where the others stood. The upper galleries were a problem, which was why he hugged the right edge of the hall, from where he could clearly see the left galleries and anyone above him would have to show themselves in order to obtain a clear shot. Ni also could keep a watch.

"I managed to avoid the welcoming committee you sent," he said to Tang, trying to steal a glimpse above.

"And what of Ms. Vitt?"

"Dead. On your orders." He made no effort to disguise his bitterness. He also realized Tang surely wanted to know something else, so he said, "Your man Viktor may still be alive, though."

Tang said nothing.

"Where's Sokolov?" Malone asked, buying more time.

"He's here," Ni said. "With his son."

"And will he get a sample of oil? One that can prove it's infinite?"

"I see you, too, know what is at stake," Pau said.

"You wanted me to see that map in your house, didn't you?"

"If you had not noticed, I would have made sure you did."

"Were you the one who set Qin Shi's tomb on fire?" Tang asked.

"That was me. Kept you from killing us."

"And allowed Minister Ni to slip away," Tang said.

"That's not—"

CASSIOPEIA HUSTLED TOWARD THE STAIRS AND CLIMBED THE marble risers to the first-floor gallery. She crouched, keeping herself beneath the balustrade that protected the gallery from the hall beyond, and eased herself to the corner. A quick look confirmed that one man stood about a third of the way down, dressed in a woolen robe, holding a crossbow, his back to her.

Quietly, she shed Viktor's fleece jacket.

She listened, hearing Cotton's voice.

Then Tang's.

And allowed Minister Ni to slip away.

That's not—

"Malone."

Viktor's voice.

Knife in hand, she crept forward.

TANG SAW VIKTOR APPEAR, SEEMINGLY FROM NOWHERE. He wondered how long he'd been inside the hall. The man should actually be dead, along with Malone and Vitt.

Was anyone else here?

NI SAW THE FOREIGNER, THE SAME MAN WHO'D SAVED HIS LIFE inside Qin Shi's tomb.

Was he friend or foe?

At the instant he decided foe, and was about to cry out an alarm, the man shouted Malone's name.

MALONE WHIRLED.

Viktor was rushing toward him, then leaping forward, tackling him to the floor.

Malone lost his grip on the gun, but grabbed Viktor by the throat, raining down blows with his right fist, yelling, "Where is she?"

Viktor broke free, a mad glaze coating his eyes. "She's far downstream. Gone."

Malone lunged and slugged away in earnest, enjoying the thud of his fist hitting bone.

Viktor retreated.

Lots of room existed for them to maneuver among the arches, the weaponry, and the braziers. He thought one of the swords might come in handy. Viktor seemed to read his mind, his gaze darting to lances displayed beside armor and shields. Viktor rushed forward, grabbing the bamboo hilt of a lance, brandishing its tip, keeping Malone at bay.

His breath came racked and shallow and his light-headedness returned.

His insides boiled like lava.

This man had been nothing but trouble on every occasion. Now Cassiopeia was dead, thanks to him.

"Aren't you a tough guy with a spear?" he taunted.

Viktor tossed him the weapon, then grabbed another.

CASSIOPEIA HEARD THE FIGHT. SHE NEEDED TO POSITION HERself to help. That meant taking out the man she was creeping toward, whose attention was on the melee. She passed wall mirrors and a pair of cabinets displaying bronze, jade, and porcelain treasures. The morning sun filtered in through mussel-shell panes dotting the gallery's length. She held the knife, but another option formed in her brain. To her right, displayed in a wall niche, were a dozen or so figurines. Human bodies with animal heads, arms folded across their chests. Maybe thirty centimeters high. She stepped close, stuffed the knife in her pocket, and grabbed one.

A dog-faced piece, heavy, with a thick rounded base.

Perfect.

She headed straight for her target.

One swing to the base of the neck and the man crumpled to the marble. As he fell, she relieved him of the crossbow. He'd have a headache later, but that was better than being dead.

She glanced down.

Viktor and Cotton faced each other in the center of the hall, each holding a lance. Ni still had the sword to Pau's neck. No one seemed to have noticed what had happened one floor up. She stared across at the remainder of the first-floor arches and spotted no one.

She was alone, armed, ready.

TANG HAD INSTRUCTED ONE BROTHER TO POSITION HIMSELF in the upper first-floor gallery, crossbow ready. He should be stationed to his left, about halfway down toward the main entrance. Two other brothers waited to his right, within the ground-floor gallery, out of Ni's sight.

As the fight continued in the center of the hall, he casually glanced right and caught sight of the two brothers.

A gentle shake of his head signaled, *Not yet.*

But soon.

MALONE KEPT HIS EYES LOCKED ON VIKTOR.

Pupils that smoldered like black embers stared back, and an ugly scowl twisted the face.

"Do you know how many times I could have let you die?" Viktor asked.

He wasn't listening. Memories washed over him in sickening waves. All he could see was Cassiopeia being waterboarded, her body dropping into the river, Viktor taunting him on the video, appearing on the rocks, to blame for it all.

He lunged.

Viktor countered, deflecting the jab, sliding his lance across Malone's, angling downward, then twisting back.

Malone held tight and deflected the maneuver.

Viktor's brow was covered in sweat. Malone, too, was warm from the fires burning less than thirty feet away. He decided the braziers might present an opportunity, so he cowered back, dueling with Viktor, drawing his opponent closer. Each hearth stood on three-legged iron stands, elevated about four feet off the floor.

Just unstable enough for his purposes.

Viktor kept coming, following Malone's lead.

NI PRESSED THE EDGE OF THE BLADE INTO PAU'S NECK. THE OLD man was not resisting, but the two brothers, though unarmed, worried Ni.

He kept his attention on them.

"You can both learn something from their courage," Pau said.

Tang seemed to resent the jab. "I didn't know that I lacked courage."

"Did I tell you to kill Jin Zhao?" Pau asked. "He was a brilliant geochemist. A husband and grandfather. Harmless. Yet you arrested and beat him into a coma. Then you had him falsely convicted and shot while he lay unconscious in his hospital bed. Does that exhibit courage?"

Tang's shock at the rebuke was obvious.

"When you trapped rats on Sokolov's stomach and watched his agony, was that courage? When you destroyed Qin Shi's library, how much courage did that require?"

"I have done nothing but faithfully serve you," Tang declared.

"Did I tell you to burn that museum to the ground in Antwerp? One of our brothers died in that fire."

Tang said nothing.

"And you, Minister Ni," Pau said. "How much courage is required to slit an old man's neck?"

"Not much, so it should be an easy matter for me."

"You sell yourself short," Pau said. "In my home you faced the challenge of those killers. It is similar to what we are watching here, as two men confront each other. Both came here totally unaware of what awaited them. Yet they came. That is courage."

CASSIOPEIA COULD SEE THAT COTTON WAS DRAWING VIKTOR toward the brazier. She debated whether to intervene, but she commanded only one arrow. The robed man unconscious on the floor beside her carried no more.

Revealing her presence now would be counterproductive.

She had one shot, so it had to count.

MALONE KNEW HE WAS CLOSE TO THE HEAT. HE COULD HEAR snapping coals behind him as he fended off another thrust from Viktor's lance.

He needed a moment, so he swept his spear around in a wide arc, which forced Viktor to grab the shaft with two hands, countering, blocking the blow. In the moment when Viktor readjusted his grip and prepared a strike of his own, Malone slammed his right foot into the iron stand, toppling the copper vessel.

Hot coals spilled across the floor, hissing and smoking.

Viktor cowered back, caught off guard.

Malone used the tip of his spear to pluck one of the coals from the floor.

He slung it toward Viktor, who sidestepped the white-hot projectile.

Malone speared another hot coal and this time slung the ember toward where the other men stood.

NI WATCHED AS MALONE TOSSED ONE OF THE COALS THEIR way. The smoking chunk flew over Tang's head and disappeared into the shelves behind him. Silks within one of the bins vaporized from the heat, the manuscripts literally disappearing before his eyes.

EIGHTY

MALONE TOSSED THE SPEAR ASIDE, FACED VIKTOR, AND ALLOWED his black mood to envelop him. "We finish this now."

Viktor did not hesitate. He lost his weapon, too. "I've been wanting to do this for a long time."

They sprang into each other, both landing punches. Viktor's caught Malone near the left temple and the room exploded in a whirl of lights.

He lashed out with his leg, catapulting Viktor, buying the moment he needed to plant a right jab into Viktor's jaw.

A vicious kick to his lower leg twisted Malone sideways.

He absorbed a couple of blows, drawing Viktor closer. Before a third punch could be landed, he popped Viktor's throat, then slammed a solid right into the rib cage.

The thin air sliced his lungs like razor blades.

He advanced on Viktor, who was coming back upright, one hand across his gut, his face contorted in rage.

"I'm going to kill you, Malone."

CASSIOPEIA HEARD VIKTOR'S DECLARATION. EVERY NERVE IN his body seemed taut. He'd plunged into the hall intent on a confrontation. Cotton seemed likewise wired tight.

She was careful to stay behind the pillar, out of sight.

A sharp cry from below drew her attention.

MALONE HEARD A YELL AS VIKTOR'S SHOULDER SLAMMED INTO his chest. Momentum drove them both off their feet. Together they pounded into the hard floor and slid.

Something popped in his own shoulder.

Searing pain shot through his brain and heat surged at the back of his head. He smelled the pungent scent of burning hair.

His own.

Viktor was on top, hands to Malone's throat.

TANG WAS SHOCKED BY PAU WEN'S VERBAL ATTACK. NEVER HAD the master spoken to him like that, outside of their scripted conversations, performed for Ni's benefit.

He wondered if this were another—Pau doing what he did best, improvising. He decided to play along. "I was unaware that you thought me such a coward."

"There are many things you are unaware of."

"Like the imperial library you found decades ago? Or the fact that you looted Qin Shi's tomb and brought everything here?"

"All done before you rose to any position of prominence. I, on the other hand, was Hegemon."

"Why did you flee the pit in Xi'an, with the brothers, leaving Malone and Vitt alive? They should have died there." That he truly did want to know.

"With all the attention that would have generated? Not even you, the first vice premier, could have explained that."

"If you think me so incompetent, why are we doing this?"

"Tell him, Minister," Pau said to Ni. "Why are *we* doing this?"

NI WAS NOT FOOLED BY PAU'S REBUKE OF TANG, BUT HE DE-
cided to answer the inquiry with a question of his own. "How many
people are you willing to kill for power?"

"As many as necessary," Tang said.

"Then the answer to your question is clear," he said in Pau's ear.
"You are doing this so that a great many people may die."

A SUDDEN RUSH OF PAIN TO THE TOP OF HIS SKULL ENERGIZED
Malone. He swung his right arm up and wrapped Viktor's neck in a vise
grip, rolling, reversing the situation.

Viktor landed atop the coals, which crunched beneath his jacket.

They rolled again, this time away from the heat. But Malone had a
problem. His left shoulder hurt badly, and the pain robbed his right arm
of strength.

And Viktor pounced.

CASSIOPEIA SAW COTTON REACH FOR HIS LEFT SHOULDER JUST
as Viktor swung a fist upward, clipping his jaw, toppling him backward.
Viktor seized the moment and found the gun that had slid away at the
beginning of the brawl.

She had to do something.

So she reached for the knife in her pocket and tossed it over the rail,
angling for the coals near Cotton.

MALONE HEARD SOMETHING LAND IN THE EMBERS.

His eyes darted right and he spotted a knife at the same moment Viktor found the gun.

His shoulder was probably dislocated. Every movement sent electric agony to his brain. His right hand gripped his left arm, trying to hold the joint in place even as he reached for the blade—warm to the touch—flipping the tip between his fingers, ready to toss.

Viktor's eyes were two hard flints.

Icy sweat beaded on both of their brows.

Viktor aimed the gun.

TANG CRIED OUT IN MANDARIN, "NOW."

And the two brothers in the shadows raced forward, leveling their crossbows at Ni.

"Your show of courage is over," Tang said. He caught a look of satisfaction in Pau's eyes and said, "I thought ahead."

"You apparently think little of your master," Ni replied.

"On the contrary. I regard him highly. Enough that if you kill him, we shall kill you."

"You believe him?" Ni asked Pau. "Or will he kill us both?"

"Lower the blade," Pau quietly said to Ni.

NI COULD SEE THAT HIS OPTIONS WERE GONE. HE COULD KILL Pau Wen and die right now, or he could lower the weapon and take his chances.

Tang, not Pau, was who deserved to die.

He withdrew the blade and tossed it to the floor.

CASSIOPEIA AIMED HER BOW DOWNWARD, READYING HERSELF. She was unsure of what was happening, other than the fact that Cotton was hurt, Viktor was pissed, Ni was in trouble, and she was in a position to do something.

"Don't do it," she shouted.

MALONE HEARD CASSIOPEIA'S VOICE.

His head spun toward its source and he saw a crossbow projecting from the shadows of the first-floor gallery, near one of the pillars, aimed at Viktor.

"Drop the gun," she yelled. "Now."

Malone stared at Viktor, who did not move, the weapon held tight with both hands, eyes sighting an aim straight at Malone's chest.

"Shoot me and she shoots you," he said to Viktor.

He doubted he could flick the blade before the gun fired.

"That's my knife," Viktor quietly said. "I gave it to her."

"And she gave it to me."

Which spoke volumes.

Viktor's eyes closed, then opened. Malone caught a flicker of understanding, the gaze telegraphing a different intention from the aimed weapon. Then he knew. What Stephanie had said.

Actually, we'd like Tang dead.

"You take care of her, Malone," Viktor said.

Then he swung around and adjusted his aim.

Straight at Karl Tang.

Tang grew impatient of Viktor's face-off with Malone.

What was he waiting for?

He grabbed the crossbow from the brother beside him and yelled, "Shoot him now, or I'll shoot you."

Viktor whirled.

Every fear he'd ever harbored for this foreigner now bubbled to the surface as the gun barrel focused on him.

He fired the crossbow.

An instant later the arrow slammed into Viktor Tomas.

The other brother, sensing danger, had likewise readjusted his aim. A second arrow pierced Viktor's chest, the shaft sinking deep. Viktor choked, blood spewing from his mouth. The gun fell from his grip. A hand came to the throat.

His knees dissolved into jelly.

Then he collapsed.

Cassiopeia winced as Viktor's body was pierced in quick succession by two high-speed arrows. Only a few seconds passed before he teetered, tried to find his balance, then collapsed to the floor with a grunt.

She stepped from the shadows to the balustrade, aimed her bow at Karl Tang, and fired.

Ni realized that Cassiopeia Vitt was in the upper gallery and apparently armed. The two brothers had shot their arrows. The foreigner was down. Malone held a knife, but he was a long way away.

She was their only chance.

Vitt came into view, a crossbow in her hand, and she fired.

Tang, though, had anticipated the move, diving to his right.

The arrow found the floor and careened away.

MALONE COULD SEE THAT CASSIOPEIA'S SHOT HAD MISSED. HE held the knife, but little good it could do.

The gun.

Which lay near Viktor.

He had to get it.

TANG CAME TO HIS FEET AND DARTED TOWARD THE SWORD NI Yong had discarded. He gripped the hilt and commanded the two brothers to seize Ni.

He'd show Pau Wen who possessed courage.

He cocked his arm and advanced toward Ni.

NI TRIED TO FREE HIMSELF BUT THE TWO BROTHERS WERE strong. Pau Wen had drifted away, closer to the shelves, watching.

His gaze darted out into the hall.

Malone was searching for something.

Tang was less than three meters away, the arm holding the sword ready to thrust the blade into his gut.

MALONE FOUND THE GUN.

The pain in his shoulder was excruciating. He'd doubted he would have been able even to toss the knife. His right hand lifted the weapon, finger on the trigger. He wondered if there were more brothers in the hall, preparing at this moment to skewer him, too.

No matter.

He had no choice.

He aimed the gun and fired.

TANG HEARD A RETORT, THEN FELT SOMETHING POUND INTO his right side. Strange, the feeling. Nothing at first, then unimaginable pain, as if a surge of energy had passed through him, scorching his insides.

He stopped his advance and staggered to the right.

He stared out into the hall and saw Cotton Malone aiming a gun straight at him.

Another bang, and a bullet pierced his chest.

A third shot.

Then he saw nothing at all.

EIGHTY-ONE

CASSIOPEIA HAD BEEN SHOCKED BY VIKTOR'S DEATH. TANG'S, though, pleased her. His head exploded with Cotton's final volley, propelling him off his feet, to the floor.

"None of you move," Malone called out, the gun still aimed. "Minister Ni, get that sword."

Ni obeyed.

"This matter is now over," Pau Wen calmly called out.

NI STOOD WITH THE SWORD IN HAND.

He stared at Pau Wen and said, "Explain yourself."

"You and I spoke in Belgium. You believed I lied to you there. I did not. Everything I said was the truth. China must change. What that change is to be was the question. A return to strict Legalism? Autocracy? Or something gentler? Confucianism? Democracy? I confess that, in the beginning, twenty years ago, I thought a return to Legalism the answer. But I no longer know that to be certain. What I do know is that both the decline and the glory of a state can arise from a single source."

"Those are Confucius' words," Ni said.

"That they are. He was a wise man."

"Strange talk from a Legalist."

Pau shook his head. "I am no such thing."

MALONE LISTENED TO THE EXCHANGE BETWEEN NI AND PAU, but kept his gun ready, his eyes searching the hall.

"Decades ago," Pau said. "I removed all of the Confucian texts from Qin Shi's buried library. Those words had to survive. It would have been criminal to destroy them. Now they are ready for your use, however you see fit. Those ethics may be precisely what China needs to help counter both corruption and the growing inequality in our society." Pau hesitated. "Minister, the *Ba* has not been a party to this battle between you and Tang. We influenced nothing, we took no side."

"Tang was one of yours."

Pau nodded. "That he was. But that does not mean I wanted him to succeed. The battle had to occur, without interference, and it has. You have now prevailed. From this day forward, the *Ba* pledges its allegiance to you."

"Why would I believe a word of that?" Ni asked.

Malone wanted to know the answer, too.

"Tang's discovery of infinite oil changed everything. The power of that discovery became too much for him. His ambition took hold. I came to fear that he would be no better than those who came before him."

"Yet you allowed my life to be threatened. You allowed all of us to be captured by Tang."

"And brought here, Minister. I made sure that happened."

Ni did not seemed impressed. "You are a murderer."

"Four men died in Belgium. But was that not self-defense?"

"Not the one you tortured, then shot in the head."

"Where's Sokolov?" Cassiopeia called out from above.

"He is safe," Pau said.

Malone decided to keep quiet about the actual location. He wasn't necessarily buying Pau as an ally. Instead, he kept his gun aimed and asked, "How will Tang's death be explained?"

"He will suffer a car crash, here in the mountains," Pau answered. "He had come to clear his head, refresh his spirit."

"And the bullet holes?"

"Tragically, the car caught fire, the body burned to a cinder."

Ni stood silent a moment, holding the sword.

Malone kept the gun trained, but Pau never moved. "It's your call, Minister," Malone said to Ni. "What do we do?"

"I believe him," Ni said.

"Why?" Cassiopeia called out.

"Lower your weapons," Ni ordered.

Malone wondered about the strategy but realized they were stuck in a mountain stronghold with an indeterminate number of men surrounding them and little in the way of weapons besides a sword and a few rounds in his gun. He decided to trust Ni's judgment and lowered the gun.

He glanced up, asking Cassiopeia, "You okay?" Thank God she was alive.

"I'm okay. How about you?"

"Shoulder took a hit."

"You both risked your lives coming here," Ni said to them.

"And Viktor gave his," she said.

Pau faced Ni. "You asked me in Belgium why I care. I told you then the explanation would take too much time. I also told you that my only interest was what would be best for China. I was speaking the truth."

Ni remained silent.

"The *Ba*," Pau said, "was created to ensure a strong political system that guaranteed a collective safety. In the early dynasties, force and violence worked best to accomplish both goals. But over time, those have become less effective. Today, as you know, they are counterproductive. The *Ba* is about the preservation of China, not the preservation of itself. What is best for the nation is what we support. The battle between you and Tang was inevitable. No one could stop it from occurring. But we could be there when it ended."

"Why not just tell me?" Ni asked Pau, anger in his voice. "Why not just help?"

"I did," Pau said. "I told you things you never knew existed. When you came to Belgium, and I saw how little you knew, I realized my task was to drive you forward. You had to face the coming challenge, but to do that you had to know its extent. Be honest, Minister. You knew nothing of what I told you."

Ni's silence served as his answer.

"Do not fault me for choosing to *show* rather than *tell* you the problem," Pau said. "The appearance of Vitt and Malone helped me to do that. If I had not opened your eyes, Tang would have bettered you. You and I both know that."

"You lied to me, and murdered a man in cold blood."

"I saved your life."

"Are all of the brothers in agreement with what you are saying?" Cassiopeia asked.

Pau nodded. "They have sworn their allegiance and will do what is best for China. Minister Ni has emerged as the stronger. The *Ba* respects strength."

"What am I to do?" Ni asked.

"Make your move for power. Tang is gone. Achieve elevation to first vice premier, then have responsibilities gradually transferred to you. The premier respects and trusts you. I know that for a fact. The *Ba* will support your policies, whatever they may be. We realize the government will evolve, become a reflection of its new leader, as it has many times before, and we are prepared for that change."

"The government *will* change," Ni declared. "We shall have a new constitution."

"And we can help obtain approval for that," Pau said.

"What about infinite oil?" Malone asked.

Pau turned and motioned. One of the brothers disappeared into the open wall panel.

"An unexpected by-product of this battle," Pau said. "To his credit, Tang realized how that discovery could be wielded, if held close."

The brother reemerged holding an object, which Malone recognized.

A dragon lamp.

Like the one in Belgium.

Pau presented it to Ni. "This is yours. A sample of oil from the fields in Gansu, extracted from the earth 2,200 years ago, stored in the tomb of the First Emperor. Hopefully, this will prove Lev Sokolov's theory."

Ni accepted the lamp.

"Minister," Pau said. "You realize that I could have simply given the lamp, with the oil, to Tang. Or given him one of the many that are here. I did not do that. Instead I kept it from him."

"You used it as bait to lure me to Belgium. To kill me."

Pau nodded. "That was Tang's objective, not mine. Which is why I saved your life there. I also allowed Miss Vitt to take the lamp. She did us both a favor. It bought time."

Malone didn't necessarily agree with the favor part, but saw the logic. Pau could have simply given Tang what he wanted.

"The world will be told of the discovery," Ni made clear.

Pau nodded. "And China will receive some credit. China has forgotten its greatness. We once led the world in imagination, and we can again."

Pau bowed.

Malone watched as Ni considered the offer.

Finally, Ni returned the gesture.

He stared at Viktor, blood oozing from the fatal wounds, sightless eyes staring at the ceiling, arrows sunk deep in the chest. He bent down and gently closed both lids. He'd read this man wrong.

He glanced up at Cassiopeia.

Tears streaked down her face.

EIGHTY-TWO

MALONE SIPPED BLACK TEA AND ALLOWED THE PAIN IN HIS shoulder to ease. A makeshift sling had been fashioned to hold the joint in place. He'd need to see a doctor once they left this stronghold.

Three hours had passed since Viktor had died. He'd spent half an hour inside the makeshift tomb of Qin Shi, admiring a jade burial suit, along with stunning funerary objects.

Ni Yong sat with him on the terrace. Beyond the low wall, an afternoon sun tinted the mountains in shades of red, black, and yellow. The air remained mild, a gentle breeze flapping some nearby prayer flags. He'd kept a close watch on a marble sundial that stood a few feet away. It sat on a circular base, supported by four square pillars.

"Every temple in China," Ni said, "has a sundial. It is a reminder that virtue should shine at all times, like the sun at high noon. Good advice that we long chose to ignore."

"Do you believe what Pau Wen said to you?"

"Not a single word."

"I was hoping you weren't that foolish."

"There is a story that we are all taught in military training," Ni said. "A great warrior named Chao led 40,000 troops to besiege a town defended by a tiny force that was commanded by an opponent named Zhang. After forty days the town's residents were trading their children for food. But Zhang refused to surrender and even beheaded the officers who advocated that course. Eventually, Zhang's forces ran out of arrows, so he ordered the residents to make a thousand life-sized straw figures, clothed in black. Then, one night, he lowered the figures down over the city walls on ropes. Chao's forces loosed tens of thousands of arrows at what they at first thought were escaping enemies. The arrows stuck in the straw figures, which were hauled back inside. Zhang's forces went from a total lack of ammunition to a plentitude."

"Smart guy."

"There's more," Ni said. "Later that same night Zhang sent 500 of his bravest men down the ropes. Chao's side thought they were the straw men again and paid no attention. Zhang's men stormed Chao's camp and chopped off the heads of the sleeping enemy. Chao's forces were thrown into disorder and retreated."

He caught the point.

Ni said, "Zhang transformed a passive position into a potent one. I remembered that lesson when talking with Pau Wen. We were out of ammunition, so I lowered a decoy and drew Pau's fire, reloading our weapon. He is anxious to be on the winning side, so I used his anticipation."

He could not argue with that strategy.

"But I will eventually 'shut the door to catch a thief.'"

He smiled, knowing what that maxim meant. "Encircle the enemy. Close off all escape routes."

Ni nodded. "We were taught that, too. But there are five things to remember while doing that. First, to close the door you must have an absolute superior concentration of forces. Second, there has to be a door to shut. Third, you cannot wait passively for the thief to enter. He has to be lured. Fourth, the door has to be shut at the proper time so the thief is truly shut inside. And fifth, all other outlets of escape must be closed, too."

He realized what Ni had done. "So you rocked Pau to sleep."

"As he tried to do to me in Belgium."

"That whole thing of denying Tang an oil sample. He was plying every angle, trying everything he could. He didn't give a damn about you."

Ni nodded. "He is a liar and a cheat. I have simply used his own weapons against him. But what choice did I have? We are on his turf. This is an uncertain place. He offered to be my ally, so I accepted. But I assure you, when the time is right I shall close all the doors."

"What about all that 'not using violence' stuff?"

"Men like Pau Wen are why China is failing. They are a cancer on our society. It is time they receive exactly what they so easily like to give. Legalism is nothing more than opportunism. It relies on force and terror to generate respect. I will give them what they already understand, what they have long proclaimed to be the only way to govern. That seems only right."

Malone agreed.

"If I have to drop the pants of every man in government and the military, I will purge China of all eunuchs."

He heard the change in Ni—a confidence that had not been there before—and asked, "You've thought about this a long time, haven't you?"

"I've watched while stupid, selfish, petty men destroy our country. They are, to a man, corrupt. That will stop. I'll use the *Ba* to my advantage, until the time is right to eliminate them."

He hoped this man could actually do what he proposed. But he was curious, and Washington would want to know. "Is democracy in your plan?"

"That word has many negative connotations here. It has, for so long, been used to generate hate. But the people *will* have a say in the new government. We will be accountable from the top down." Ni smiled. "Democracy actually owes much to Confucius."

"You seem ready."

Ni nodded. "I spoke to the premier a little while ago. He will have me elevated to the second post. He is glad Tang is gone, and will support my purge of the *Ba,* when the time is right. Pau has greatly overestimated his worth in today's China. His day is over."

"This is not my thing," Malone said. "I couldn't play all of these games."

Ni grinned. "It is China, Malone. Our way. Unfortunately, deception is organic to our way of governing. I would like to change that, too, but that will take a little longer."

"You do know Viktor Tomas worked for the Russians and the Americans?"

"I am not surprised. But with their agent dead, neither one of those foreign powers will learn anything." Ni paused. "Beyond what you and Ms. Vitt report."

He caught the word *agent,* as applied to Viktor.

Damn right he was an agent.

"What about Sokolov?" he asked.

Cassiopeia was with the Russian and his son, making sure they were okay.

"He will be returned to Lanzhou and his laboratory, with the oil sample. He says he will cooperate with me. Of course, the lingering threat from the Russians plays to our advantage. He understands they want him dead. He and his son are returning to Kashgar with me. His wife is anxious to see the child. I am having her flown west as we speak. I will do all I can to protect them, and gain his trust."

"Keep a close watch on him."

"We shall. But when I tell the world of his discovery, I doubt the danger will be there any longer."

"You're really going to do that?"

Ni nodded. "It is the only course. That realization should change the world, to everyone's advantage."

"And place China in a different light in everyone's eyes."

"We can only hope."

Which should satisfy Washington. Ivan? Too damn bad.

"What about Pau Wen and those four murders?"

"They will not be forgotten."

He was glad to hear that. "Why did you trust us in Xi'an?"

Ni shrugged. "Something told me that you and Ms. Vitt were people I could rely on."

Malone thought of Henrik Thorvaldsen and wished his old friend had died thinking the same thing.

"I'm leaving for Kashgar shortly to meet the premier," Ni said. "He and I are returning to Beijing together. I'll make sure a helicopter returns for you and Ms. Vitt."

Ni stood and extended a hand. "I thank you. I owe you my life."

Malone shook his hand and waved off the gratitude. "Just do what you said you were going to do." But there was one other thing he wanted to know. "If I had not come along, would you have slit Pau's throat?"

Ni did not immediately answer, as if seriously considering the inquiry. Finally, he said, "I'm not sure. Thank goodness we didn't have to find out."

He smiled.

"Take care, Mr. Malone."

"You, too."

Ni disappeared through an open doorway, heading back inside. He understood why he and Cassiopeia weren't leaving with him.

Time to fade into the background.

As all agents do.

Malone had read about a sky burial. Dicing a corpse into pieces, beating it to a paste with flour, tea, and milk, then allowing carrion to feast on the mixture represented a return to fire, water, earth, and wind, the basic elements of man. A great honor.

He and Cassiopeia stood and watched the ancient ceremony. A couple of hours ago Viktor's body had been brought outside the walls, to a nearby valley, and prepared.

"Our brothers are trained in the *jhator*," Pau said. "It is a ritual we have performed many times."

"Are you really going to help Ni Yong?" Malone asked.

"Legalism? Confucianism? Communism? Democracy? An emperor? Or an elected president? Our problem for the past sixty years is that no single concept or philosophy has dominated. Instead we have languished in an uncertain middle, bits of each vying for control. Chinese fear chaos. We despise uncertainty. We have many times accepted the wrong system in the name of certainty." Pau hesitated a moment. "At a minimum, Tang and Ni offered a clear choice. Now it has been made. So the *Ba* shall be Ni's ally."

"Where I was raised," Malone said, "there's a saying. *Don't go through your asshole to get to your appetite.* Maybe the Chinese can learn from that."

Pau smiled. "Is that wisdom from one of your great American philosophers?"

"A group of them, yes. They're called rednecks."

"What's to prevent someone else from simply taking Tang's place?" Cassiopeia asked. "Surely he has followers ready to take up the cause."

"No doubt," Pau said. "But this is not America or Europe. Those followers have no access to media, nor to the Party hierarchy. Those privileges have to be earned, over many years of loyal service. Politics here is a personal journey, one that takes an excruciatingly long time. Tang's own rise required nearly twenty years." Pau shook his head. "No. Minister Ni is now the only one poised for ultimate power."

Which Ni well knew, Malone thought. He was disappointed that he would not be around when Pau Wen received a dose of his own medicine.

"You sound confident," Cassiopeia said.

"Fate has intervened on China's behalf."

"You don't really believe that?" he asked. "Fate? You determined most of this."

Pau smiled. "How else could all of our involvement be explained? Isn't it odd that we were each in the precise location, at the precise time, to precisely affect the outcome? If that is not fate, then what is?"

Ni's assessment of Pau seemed correct. He did overestimate his worth. And you didn't have to be a genius to understand the ramifications of that mistake. But that wasn't Malone's problem. His job was done.

Half a dozen brothers encircled Viktor's prepared remains, chanting, incense wafting from copper vessels.

Overhead the vultures had arrived.

"Can we go?" Cassiopeia asked.

They left before the birds arrived and walked back toward the monastery across rocks and cobbles littered with ribbons of pale green grass. Neither one of them turned to see what happened.

"I was wrong about Viktor," he quietly said.

"That was an easy mistake to make. He was tough to read."

"Not in the end."

"He took himself out with Tang, counting on me to land the kill shot," she said.

He'd thought the same thing.

"I heard what he said as he turned," she said.

You take care of her.

He stopped.

So did she.

He said, "We've played a lot of games."

"Too many."

"What do we do now?"

Her eyes were pools of water. "Strange. You and I having this conversation while Viktor is dead."

"He made his choice."

She shook her head. "I'm not so sure I didn't make it for him. When I tossed that knife down. That's what really gets me. He played many parts to many different audiences. You have to wonder, were those final words just more of the act?"

Malone knew the answer. He'd seen something she could not have witnessed. At the moment of his death, Viktor Tomas finally conveyed the truth.

You take care of her.

Yes, indeed.

She stared at him, seemingly summoning the courage to reveal something. He sympathized with her. His thoughts were likewise muddled. When he'd believed she was dead, a future without her had seemed unimaginable.

"No more games," she said.

He nodded.

He cupped her hand in his.

"Cotton—"

He silenced her lips with two fingers. "Me, too."

And he kissed her.

WRITER'S NOTE

This book took Elizabeth and me to Copenhagen and Antwerp but, unfortunately, not to China. That excursion would have taken far more time than was available. A book a year demands a tight schedule. So, with Antarctica from *The Charlemagne Pursuit,* China remains at the top of our must-see list.

I did, though, have the characters visit as much of the country as possible. Chongqing, Gansu province, Xi'an, Kashgar, Yecheng, Beijing, Lanzhou, Yunnan province, and the western highlands are all accurately depicted. The statistics relative to China in chapter 2 are accurate, as is all of the other vital information noted about the country throughout the story. It is truly a place of superlatives. The town of Batang and the Hall for the Preservation of Harmony are fictitious. Dian Chi (chapter 47) is real, though its pollution is far worse than I allowed (chapter 48).

Time now to separate more fact from fiction.

The Central Commission for Discipline Inspection of the Chinese Communist Party exists and functions as described (chapter 4).

All of the ancient scientific discoveries, innovations, and inventions attributable to the Chinese, detailed in chapters 4 and 7, are factual. Once, China was the technological leader of the world. That dominance changed around the 14th century when a variety of factors—among them the lack of a workable alphabet, the influences of Confucianism and Daoism, and the propensity of each succeeding dynasty to eradicate all traces of the ones that came before it—resulted in not only ideological stagnation but also cultural amnesia. The story noted in chapter 7, about Jesuit missionaries displaying a clock the Chinese did not know they themselves had invented 1,000 years before, is real. A British academic, Joseph Needham, during the 20th century, made it his lifework to document China's lost technological and scientific past. The research and publications that he began continue today through the Needham Research Institute.

Tivoli Gardens, in Copenhagen, is a wonderful place to visit. All that is described in chapter 3 exists, including the Chinese pagoda. The Café Norden (chapter 13) anchors Højbro Plads in Copenhagen and continues to serve some delicious tomato bisque.

Sadly, child stealing plagues China (chapters 8 and 9). More than 70,000 children do, in fact, disappear there each year, the vast majority young boys, sold to families desperate for a son. Including this incredible reality in the story is my way of drawing attention to the problem. There's an excellent documentary, *China's Stolen Children,* that you can watch if you want to learn more.

The debate between Confucianism and Legalism has raged for 3,000 years (chapter 10). One of these two competing philosophies has defined every ruling dynasty, including that of the communists. It is also true that none of Kong Fu-Zi's original texts have survived. All that remains are later interpretations of his originals. The failures of Mao (chapter 49); the rise and fall of so many corrupt imperial dynasties (chapter 12); the Hundred Flowers Campaign (chapter 45); and the disastrous Cultural Revolution are all reported accurately. Likewise, violent divisions within China's political structure are common, as are destructive internal civil wars. The battle between the Gang of Four and Deng Xiaoping did occur in the late 1970s (chapter 12). Three of the four in the defeated gang lost their lives. Here, I simply created another war for political control between two new contenders.

Centuries ago, the *Ba* flourished. The history of hegemony, the *Ba,* and Legalism are indeed accurately related (chapter 24). Hegemony (chapter 45) is a concept uniquely Chinese, one that has long defined its national conscience in ways the West has difficulty comprehending. And as Karl Tang realizes in chapter 24, totalitarianism is a Chinese innovation.

Antwerp is a wonderful European city with a distinctive Old World feel (chapter 18). I've long wanted to include it in one of my stories. The Drie Van Egmond Museum (chapters 25, 27–31), though, is my creation. Since I knew I was going to destroy the building, I thought something fictitious would be a better choice. Interestingly, though, I modeled it after an actual Antwerp museum—which burned while this book was being written.

Lev Sokolov and Cassiopeia Vitt have a history, which is hinted to starting with chapter 36. If you'd like to know the full story of how these two met, and why Cassiopeia owes him, there is a short story, "The Balkan Escape," which can be downloaded as an e-book original. Check it out.

Eunuchs (chapter 7) are an important part of Chinese history. Nowhere else on the planet did they exert so much political influence. Definitely, there were good (chapter 51) and bad personalities. Their history as told throughout the story is accurate, as is the process of their emasculation (chapters 7 and 33). Associating eunuchs with the *Ba* is my invention, though most certainly they would have played some role in that movement.

Two tortures are utilized: the first with scalding chili powder (chapter 23), the second with rats (chapter 39). Both were created by the Chinese. The *Records of the Historian,* or *Shiji* (chapter 38), remains a vital source of ancient Chinese history. The passages cited throughout the story are faithfully quoted. China's censoring of the Internet happens every day (chapter 43). An *intranet*, solely for use within the country, is currently being created.

Quotations from Chairman Mao, or *The Little Red Book* (chapter 43), is the most printed book in history with some 7,000,000,000 copies. Once, every Chinese carried one. Not anymore.

The sky burial, described in chapters 63 and 82, is a part of death in both Tibet and the western Chinese highlands. The dragon lamp (chapter 4) is real, though found in another Chinese imperial tomb, adapted here to Qin Shi.

Halong Bay, in northern Vietnam (chapter 41), is a stunning locale that I could not resist including. Mao's tomb (chapters 42 and 43) also fascinates me. The stories of the Chairman's corpse, the botched embalming, a wax effigy, and the possibility that the body itself is gone are all real. And though it's much more recent history, what happened in Tiananmen Square, and what happened there in June 1989 (chapter 43) remains a mystery. To this day, no one knows how many people died. Many parents did indeed venture to the site, after the tanks withdrew, looking for their children (chapter 43). And as related in chapter 66, all books and websites that even mention the incident are censored in China.

The terra-cotta warrior museum (chapter 6), near Xi'an, forms an important backdrop for the story. When the traveling warrior exhibit visited the High Museum in Atlanta, Georgia, I visited twice. I was so enthralled that I purchased a replica, which now stands in my den. I tried to incorporate as much of the Xi'an museum as possible, focusing on the massive Pit 1 (chapter 6) and the intriguing Pit 3 (chapter 53). Of course the imperial library chamber (chapter 10) is my addition. The concept of the chariot facing left and the lack of any warriors displayed on the left side of Pit 3 (chapter 53) is not mine. That came from *The Terracotta Warriors: The Secret Codes of the Emperor's Army* by Maurice Cotterell.

Qin Shi's tomb mound, which rises near the underground army site, is accurately portrayed (chapter 38). The drainage tunnels, dug more than 2,220 years ago, remain in the ground (chapter 55). The description of the tomb interior, quoted in chapter 38, is the only written account that exists. My vision of the interior (chapters 55–57) is imagined, but I tried to stay accurate to not only *Shiji* but also other known imperial tombs. To this day the Chinese government will not allow any excavation of Qin Shi's final resting place. The description of Qin Shi in chapter 38 is based on the most popular representation, but it was fashioned centuries after his death. In reality, no one has a clue what the man looked like.

Incredibly, the Chinese did in fact drill for oil 2,500 years ago in the manner described in chapter 21, becoming the only people at the time capable of achieving such a feat. They found not only crude but also natural gas, and learned to use both in their daily lives. China's current dependency on oil (chapter 17) is a reality, as is its policy of foreign appeasement to obtain massive quantities. Its lack of reserves is a strategic weakness, as is the fact that a simple naval blockade of two straits, far from the country, could bring the Chinese to their knees (chapter 17).

The debate between biotic and abiotic oil is real, and continues to this day. Does oil come from decaying organisms or is it naturally produced by the earth? One source is finite, the other infinite. The Russians, at Stalin's prodding, pioneered the abiotic theory in the 1950s and continue to find oil, utilizing the concept, in places where fossil fuels could never exist (chapters 15 and 17). Likewise, as Stephanie Nelle points out in chapter 15, wells in the Gulf of Mexico are depleting at an astoundingly slow rate, one that has confounded American experts. Diamondoids, or adamantanes (chapter 44), were first isolated from Czech petroleum in 1933, then from U.S. samples in the late 1950s. Of late, these amazing compounds have shown promising applications in nanotechnology. I adapted them as proof of abiotic oil since diamondoids can form only under extreme heat and pressure, the kind experienced deep within the earth, far away from where any fossil fuels may lay.

And what of this long-standing myth of finite oil?

"Fossil fuel" is nothing more than a theory, created in 1757 by a Russian scientist named Mikhail Lomonosov. In proceedings before the Imperial Academy of Sciences, Lomonosov wrote, *Rock oil originates as tiny bodies of animals buried in the sediments which, under the influence of increased temperature and pressure, acting during an unimaginably long period of time, transform into rock oil.*

Many scientists question this claim, but, over time, we have simply come to believe that oil originates solely from organic compounds.

In 1956 the senior petroleum exploration geologist for the USSR said, *The overwhelming preponderance of geological evidence compels the conclusion that crude oil and natural petroleum gas have no intrinsic connection with biological matter originating near the surface of the Earth. They are primordial materials which have been erupted from great depths.*

But few people listened to those words.

Raymond Learsy, in his 2005 book *Over a Barrel,* wrote, *Nothing lasts: not fame, fortune, beauty, love, power, youth, or life itself. Scarcity rules. Accordingly, scarcity—or more accurately, the perception of scarcity—spells opportunity for manipulators.* The best example of this is OPEC, which continues to extract obscene profits from a scarcity of its own creation.

Learsy, though, leaves no doubt.

He, and many others, the Russians included, are absolutely convinced.

Oil is not scarce. We only fear that it is.

ABOUT THE TYPE

This book was set in Requiem, a typeface designed by the Hoefler Type Foundry. It is a typeface inspired by inscriptional capitals in Ludovico Vicentino degli Arrighi's 1523 writing manual. *Il modo de temperare le penne.* An original lowercase, a set of figures, and an italic in the "chancery" style that Arrighi helped popularize were created to make this adaptation of a classical design into a complete font family.